DAYMARE

About fifty armed Nakan warriors—their bodies gray with ash and banded with fresh blood—were entering the bush. Sounds of their chant reached Reydak in chilling waves.

Reydak squeezed off half a magazine into the killzone, waited for the cultists to drop. He heard the report of Highway's automatic shotgun, the stammer of the Russian's AKM.

Reydak slammed another magazine into the rifle and laid down a sweeping arc across the naked runners. He followed the tracer rounds home, watching them strike, seeing blood spurt and bits of flesh explode from painted bodies. And yet . . . *and yet!*

The Nakan didn't even break stride.

Highway yelled, "They're not going down, blokes! The buggers are bloody *immune!*"

Ukulele's warriors let loose their spears and raised their arms above their heads to show wrist razors and finger knives . . .

By James Luceno
Published by Ballantine Books:

RIO PASION
RAINCHASER
A FEARFUL SYMMETRY

A
FEARFUL
SYMMETRY

James Luceno

A Del Rey Book
BALLANTINE BOOKS · NEW YORK

For Carmen and Carlos,
ten years after.
And in memory of my parents,
Syl and Skeeter.

A Del Rey Book
Published by Ballantine Books
Copyright © 1989 by James Luceno

Library of Congress Catalog Card Number: 89-91739

ISBN 0-345-35957-7

Manufactured in the United States of America

First Edition: December 1989

Cover Art by Alan Daniels

I suspect that, after all, we're useful—that among contesting claimants adjustment has occurred, or that something now has a legal right to us, by force, or by having paid out analogues of beads for us to former, more primitive owners of us—all others warned off—that all this has been known, perhaps for ages, to certain ones upon this earth, a cult or order, members of which function like bellwethers to the rest of us, or as superior slaves or overseers, directing us in accordance with instructions received from Somewhere else—in our mysterious usefulness . . . But I accept that, in the past, before proprietorship was established, inhabitants of a host of other worlds have dropped here, for all I know—been pulled here, been pushed; have come singly, have come in enormous numbers; have visited occasionally, have visited periodically for hunting, trading, replenishing harems, mining; have been unable to stay here, have established colonies here, have been lost here; far-advanced peoples, or things, and primitive peoples or whatever they were: white ones, black ones, yellows ones—

—Charles Fort,
The Book of the Damned

Sometimes I've believed in as many as six impossible things before breakfast.

—Lewis Carroll
White Queen

Prologue

Just October and winter was already in the air, a chill wind through bare trees, leafless since midsummer. A summer of wrathful sunsets and blue moons; stillborn under clouds of volcanic ash delivered from the other side of the world.

An angry gust rattled the windowpanes at Tedman Brady's back and he turned shivering to the sound, the mansion's would-be inviolate chambers breached. Bulletproof glass tinted the landscape an unearthly shade; the manicured lawn appeared green and vibrant, a vernal lie.

Catherine, he whispered to the wind, missing her more than he could bear.

From his desk Brady contemplated the view: the tended grounds, the dying roses and naked trees, the obelisk basking in a broad fan of oblique sunlight, too blinding to regard and shimmering in the cool air of that recolored world like some instrument of awesome power. And Brady felt himself go out of body for a moment, set dangerously adrift . . .

This was more and more the case since Shangri-la, the night they had come for him in the lodge. No easy access now to the expansive states he had cultivated for half a lifetime, employed as a refuge when the world was too much with him. It was as if his captors had stripped him of that defense, too, the way the wind was working the trees.

Were they the same ones who had taken her from him? he asked himself. And did they know his every thought then? Long fingers searching the nape of his neck for telltale signs of their sinister accomplishments.

But of course there was nothing to find. Any more than there was verifiable internal evidence of their cruel midnight visit. Dr. Masters had examined him, probed and scanned him head to toe and found nothing, no cause for concern. So Brady had simply stopped talking to any of them about it, his aides and advisors; they were cause-and-effect ridden in any case, proof-and-detail-oriented. Demanding appropriate responses above all, clear-cut solutions he scarcely believed in. And yet the half-recalled images of that night were with him still: a profound commingling of fear and elation, of light and sound, locomotion and paralysis, an oscillating babel of tongues he did not need to hear to understand. All somehow veiled from conscious recall.

What was that presence lingering at the periphery of his vision even now? Some dark shadowing of his faith perhaps. He had reread the mystics—Eckhart, Ruysbroek, Loyola, and St. John—but discovered no answers there. And he had consulted with Jesuit friends who had gone on to complete what for him had been only an exercise. And finally he had spoken with Miso-roshi, and the roshi had suggested Gabriel Ouro.

Ghostly laughter in the office brought Tedman around, pale eyes searching the room in vain. He watched an amber cursor pulse insistently at the top of a display screen on his desk and leaned over to regard the monitor, hoping to see some message of clarification or instruction enter itself. Instead, the wind howled at his back and the laughter of his insubstantial visitors modulated to a piercing shriek and dispersed.

The president stiffened, massaging his forehead with a palsied hand. He had hoped to avoid outside influence, but he understood the need for that now, and promised himself that Ouro could help negotiate the crossing, that he would prove an ally in these desperate straits.

Certainly their intrusions could not be allowed to go unchecked; and Brady thanked God he was so positioned to stop them.

Part One

BETWEEN UNICORN
AND
UNIFIED FIELD

CIA'in't got you pinned, they send out MIBs
And FBI'deal if you were really VIPs
AF's Bluebook's bullshit, no Grudge no UCTs
LGM ET UFO, BVM CE3.

—from Hot Cross Nuns'
"XT Lover"

1 The Eigenstates of America

The stage, Eli decided, was set for disaster.

The speaker was addressing his audience from dead center, but it was Gabriel Ouro who had their attention, seated off to one side, dark hands folded calmly in his lap. The Brazilian woman, Dolores Sueño, sat at his right hand, a rack of matte-black amps step-pyramided behind them. Others were onstage, as well, somber faces bathed in rainbow light from theatrical spots—the Whole Earth Movement's sales force, as Eli Brady had come to think of them. Spiritual guides, some would have argued, walking point through the tangled foreland of the New Age.

It had been billed as a Wholist's Convergence, twenty-four hours of Endtime prognostication and ecstatic dance, purposely staged in one of the nation's most polluted zones. *Live Jive*, Philbert Base had muttered to Eli earlier that day. It was evening now, time for sermonizing after a mostly percussive jam. Brady, Base, and their small retinue of Wise-Eyed agents had an unobstructed view of the arena from a secure booth in the dome's uppermost tier.

"Do you believe?" the speaker asked the crowd. A frail woman in cherry-red tights stood just behind him, signing for tv cameras with a ballerina's grace. "Are you *Experienced*?"

Shouts of affirmation answered him, the colored beams of thousands of solar-assisted bioluminescent batons dancing crazily across the dome's geodesics. Globes and stalactites of synthetic crystal returned the light with interest. And, as always, WEM's ambiance directors had orchestrated a crowd-pleasing holographic accompaniment.

Dropping into Newark's drizzle and industrial outpourings that afternoon, Eli thought the dome resembled a glistening egg, half-buried in its circumferential womb of tinted concrete, plastics, and concentric bands of parked vehicles; a brilliant egg about to crack and birth who knew what mutation or monstrosity. People had been streaming in for days across continents and oceans, swelling the egg, feeding off the energy of nearby New York and northern New Jersey's conurban sprawl.

Robert Potus had insisted on their using a civilian bird. No Marine Two this trip—Eli's concession to the Secret Service chief. The visit had built-in risk factors, high-flap potential. *We can't simply announce your presence, Mr. Secretary*, Potus had cautioned. Stressed, as they all were, the privileged of Eli's abbreviated bigot list. Potus thrived on precautionary measures, so he had tasked three times the usual number of agents to advance the stop, talked Eli and Base into donning ridiculous disguises. Half a dozen agents were in the corridor outside the booth, others stationed by the door or keeping watch at elevator banks and emergency exits, mingling with the arena's private security force at the entry scanner aisles, in touch with one another through throat mikes, lapel pins, earrings, and conduction implants. Eli could feel their shifting, doctored eyes on him now, while Base's sardonic laugh deteriorated into a coughing fit. The speaker had just said something about the elemental building blocks of life having arrived from the stars. *Been gifted from the stars*, his actual words.

"Instant karma," the former petroman managed, clearing his throat. "That and two bucks'll get you a coffee."

Eli stepped back from the observation window to regard the booth's flatscreen monitor. Cameras were panning the crowd for reaction shots, the speaker's androgynous face a satellite square in the lower left corner. The stage's ballistic shield had been removed for the occasion; a gesture of trust, Eli thought, much like Ted's ordering Citadel filled in as a demonstration of his faith in the defensive shield.

". . . and in thanks we have done irrevocable damage to our world. Succeeded, not without some effort, in all but obliterating a planetary immune system that has protected us for millions of years." The speaker threw his arms wide in a questioning gesture, the blousy sleeves of his shirt falling back along slender forearms. "Is it any wonder that the planet is in rebellion now— our seas coughing up the trash we've dumped, our mountains scouring the skies with their airborne ash, our very neighborhoods belching radioactive gases? Need we ask ourselves why our children have to be kept out of the rain, or why our coasts have become the graveyards for our oceans' mutilated dead?

"We have tried to torture and ravage the planet into submission, and now we're paying the price. But we're the ones threatened with extinction. Not the creatures of the deep, the forests or savannas, but *humankind*. Each and every one of us!"

Eli recognized Gabriel Ouro's touch there; those were his words, and the crowd knew it.

"And our leaders would have us believe this so-called error-tolerant defensive shield can protect us from harm. Premier Korzliev has surely told the Russian peoples as much. But what have these shields accomplished except to throw the rest of the world into chaos? What have they done but make us wonder whether we're all being monitored in our homes, or whether it won't be long before one or two of us are removed—*surgically* removed, as the Pentagon would say."

Base winced. Eli swung to him briefly, then turned to watch the monitor while cameras labored to catch the self-satisfied gleam in the speaker's azure eyes.

"The shields *contain* as much as they *protect*." His voice was lowered now, conspiratorial.

Base shook his head in a mournful way. "These are the kids of the same people that put Ted in office, Eli. How the hell did we lose them? Where did we go wrong?"

Eli smiled sadly. We've forgotten how to speak to them, he thought. We don't understand each other. But there was no need to remind Base of that. They both knew the shield was to blame for a lot of it; distorting priorities as it had, subverting ecological promises.

"We don't know for certain that the government is watching us," the speaker said, "but I will tell you what *is* monitoring us." He motioned behind him to the lineup on the stage. "We have seen the Blue Star . . . And I know that hundreds of thousands of you out there have seen it. Those of you who know it isn't mass hysteria, or just some 'Piscean nebulosity.' The *seers* among you, the *Experienced* among you.

"And you don't need me to stand up here and tell you why this star has appeared in the heavens now, or why it's headed for the heart of our home system." He directed his attention to the lead camera. "But for those of you who choose to remain in the dark—through fear, ignorance, or an unwillingness to believe—I will say that the Blue Star's purpose is clear: It seeks *corrective* communion with Earth. These movements of the planet's plates and crust, these earthpangs, are not the cries of a planetary body in labor but in *pain*. Like a dying plant sending out a high-pitched call for destructive insects, Earth is crying out for termination. And lest we fall as the New World fell to the Old, as the Aztec city of Tenochtitlán fell to Cortes and his mercenary army, humankind must be *readied* for the encounter!''

The crowd fell silent while the speaker's forefinger jabbed at the air.

''But this need not be Armageddon or the Apocalypse if we are suitably prepared to receive the Star's influx of energies. If we can prepare ourselves for the *transformation* its approach ushers in. If we're ready to begin doing right by the world.''

Cameras found youthful faces and shoulders—tattooed whites and people of color, a planetary cross-section of Wholist delegates and representatives—as the speaker moved to the edge of the stage and reached out to his audience.

''Isolated by smart weapons, hunter-killers, and shields, our local space littered with comsats and mirrors and orbital arrays, Earth shouts to the stars: *I defy you to come!* But freed from this martial stance and united under a *psychic* umbrella of our own devising, we can guide home the miracle we need and prevail!''

From the shadows, a dozen ecologically correct fifty-year-old rock-and-rollers keyed a deep, resounding chord and brought the crowd to its feet.

Applause rumbled the booth's speakers. ''Turn that damned thing off for a minute,'' Base shouted to one of the Secret Service agents. ''Can't hear yourself goddamned think . . .''

Eli glanced out the observation window as he perched himself on the padded arm of the couch. Chants continued to filter up from the arena, a sea of transformed faces. The speaker was introducing one of his cohorts—a buxom woman in a flowing operatic gown, striding confidently toward centerstage. The ultrasuede drank in the perspiration that beaded his palms. Base was staring at him when he looked up.

''We're actually going to permit Ted to meet with these lunatics? You're his brother, man, talk some sense into him.''

''As far as Ted's concerned they're still his constituency,'' Eli said, hoping his harsh tone would bring the chief of staff around. Base was one of the president's top advisors, but what friendship existed between them was restricted to a highly defined area of influence. ''I don't have to remind you why we're here.''

Base frowned and passed a hand through a regrown crop of silver curls. ''Don't let this whole-grain bullshit fool you, Eli.

They call themselves enlightened and they talk about wanting a better world, but they're as fixated on power as the next bunch. Absorption into the whole, loss of self . . . If you want my opinion, it's got a skin-crawling master-race ring to it, and this Blue Star thing's already giving us the requisite haves and have-nots. They're going to be talking racial hygiene next, offering better lives from the turrets of T-54s."

"I read the same editorial, Phil," Eli said tiredly.

Base waved a bejeweled hand. "Look, I appreciate the fact you want to help Ted work through this . . . *vision*, or whatever the hell it was. Christ, you think I want to see him go off the deep end? But we all worked hard to put your brother where he is and I'll be damned if I'll participate in any play that ends with a fumble—and I don't care what Masters or any of his shrink team says."

"We'll meet with Ouro's people, determine the best approach, make the necessary arrangements." This was old ground, and it bothered Eli to have to cover it again. "After that, it's in Ted's hands. All we can do is monitor the situation."

"From the sidelines, Eli," Base started to say when one of the detail agents interrupted.

"Excuse me, Mr. Secretary, but Ouro's getting ready to speak." Eli nodded and the agent switched on the speakers.

Eli stood up to track the shaman through the booth's binocular scope. Ouro was brown-skinned, slight, more youthful-looking than his years—if one could believe the gossip, the biographical information bandied about by the media. His jet-black hair was shoulder-length, framing a tattooed face that had come to be synonymous with impenetrable jungles and lost tribes. He wore loose-fitting *capoeira* garb, the martial arts look that had followed him up from Brazil.

Eli swiveled the scope left and Dolores Sueño's face focused in the field. She could have passed for Ouro's twin, a mute Batuque priestess given to shamanic drumming and trance. Her soft features had graced the pages of *New Look* when Ouro's own had appeared on the cover of *Trendsetter*.

"I want to talk about timesickness," the shaman began, this man who had been called *the last guardian of the dreamtime*.

Eli returned to him, boosting the scope's magnification in search of nuance or unspoken message, some weakness he could exploit, some justification for rejecting Ted's appeal. *I intend to meet with him one way or another*, the president had said only the day before. Hands flat on the Oval Office desk, leaning forward to drive the words home. *Let Potus and O'Denvy run their security checks on him. Meet with him yourself, Eli, you'll see there's nothing to fear.*

The shaman's accented English whispered from the stage, his tone sure, self-effacing, and properly prophetic. But Eli sensed that Ouro wasn't fully comfortable with the fame America had thrust upon him, that there was an uncertainty about him.

He was like Ted in that.

Though it wasn't especially warm in the booth, a trickle of sweat coursed down along Eli's ribs under a WEM T-shirt and satin jacket. The audience was rapt, silent beyond belief, and he imagined for a moment that the Wholists had somehow succeeded in launching the dome into deep-space rendezvous with their Blue Star.

He tucked his hands in his armpits and threw Philbert Base a bloodless look. The president's chief of staff snorted and began to gnaw at his lower lip.

Eli decided he had good reason to sweat.

Now that events had conspired to make his brother a believer. Now that the president of the United States considered himself one of the Experienced.

2 Spheres of Influence

The president's rich baritone voice filled the room, wafting from speakers that flanked a three-by-four high-definition wall-screen. The audience was a select one, the secretary of state's hand-picked ad hoc interagency committee—a bigot list that had been expanded to include CIA director Milo Colton; Enoch Keyes of the Special Intelligence Group; national security advisor Niles Obstat; domestic affairs advisor Jose Darpa. Those already privy to Eli Brady's meet with Gabriel Ouro were also present: White House physician Loren Masters; Secret Service chief Robert Potus; Patrick O'Denvy of the FBI; and Professor Herman Sachs, founder of the Bureau's Cult Activities Division. The men were lounging on issue furniture, sipping at drinks or designer seltzers. Most of them were quick to identify the speech as one the president had recently delivered in Dallas.

The face onscreen was both media-appropriate and expressive, handsome enough to market. Where some read lines of character others saw furrows brought about by the strain of high office. Recent streaks of silver were either premature or distinguished. The lips were thin; the eyes pale gray, deep-set and unreadable. Eli, brown-eyed and far sturdier in frame—with more of Alison's blood perhaps—always considered himself the more generic of the two.

". . . And we must bear in mind," the chief executive was saying, "that it is our obligation—our *covenant*—to check their . . . dark . . . advance. With God as our wit—"

"Pause," Eli instructed the machine for the second time. Turning to Herman Sachs, he added: "Take us back over it and run it through once more."

Milo Colton's size thirteen loafer tapped into the sudden silence. The director of the CIA set his drink aside and wedged his thumbs into the beltless waistband of wool trousers. "Mr. Secretary, I'm willing to concede it was more than a pregnant pause if it will speed us toward establishing the purpose of this meeting." Colton kept it light as was his habit with Brady, drawing on a friendship that had been forged in Annapolis years back.

The president's cantankerous chief of staff flashed Colton a displeased look from the conference table, where he was extracting files from a leather carrycase. "Admiral," Base said, "I'm beginning to think you've been overrated. You think we'd call a huddle for a 'pregnant pause'? It's the references, man. Pay attention to the words."

The DCI tried to appear chastised. It was obvious where things were headed: Eli and Phil Base were looking for possible links between the president's Camp David nightmare and the god campaign he'd been on for the past month. Colton smiled into his drink; nothing compared to watching amateurs at work.

Sachs stabbed the remote, reverse-scanning the disc and allowing it to advance once again to the trouble spot the secretary of state had indicated.

". . . with God as our witness—"

Eli's voice was uneven when he finally spoke. He was thankful, however, that he'd taken Phil's advice and held the meeting in the Executive Office Building rather than at Langley. Hearing himself, he could well imagine the Agency's stress-analyzers registering red-shifted leaps on every other word.

"Several weeks ago," he began, "the president had an episode . . . an encounter, that is—"

"Mr. Secretary," Loren Masters cut him off. "Before we suggest any labels for this thing, suppose we let Agent Kubark tell us what he saw." The physician drew once at his pipe, then used it to motion to the Secret Service agent seated by the door.

Kubark, going on twenty-five, was far and away the youngest man in the room, a steroid-laden six-footer with a casual but deadly grace. With deliberate belligerence, he allowed his doctored eyes a moment to roam the room, cataloging and processing bits of body language, deciding just where and to whom he should direct his remarks. They had all of course been doctored one way or another—smoothed, tucked, chelated, and suctioned—but Kubark fancied his enhancements a notch above the cosmetic, and he used the artificiality of his face to make it clear to everyone present that he wanted no part of conspiracy. The Service didn't debrief to outsiders, especially when the data was sensitive and concerned The Man's private life. He had said as much to the chief.

"Go ahead, Randy," Robert Potus said, noting his agent's consternation.

Kubark checked an impulse to rise and cursed under his breath. "Just before three A.M. on Labor Day I was positioned outside the terrace slider of the lodge—"

"This is the Aspen at Shangri-la?" Colton asked, using the president's preferred name for the wooded, Catoctin range retreat at Camp David. Brady was fond of leaving his personal stamp on things, a trait the nation worked around.

"Yes, sir. I heard the Monk, uh, the president call out—a kind of nightmare groan. I waited for a prompt. When the president screamed again, the shift chief gave me the go-to and I went in. I found the president sitting on the edge of his bed. He'd called on the ceiling lights. His whole body was shaking. Uncontrollably. I asked the president if he was all right, and he asked me if I'd seen them."

Colton said, "Seen *them*?"

"*Them*, sir. Those were the president's words. He asked me how they got in without my seeing them. Agent Fusilli came through the hallway door, and the president repeated his question. Neither of us had registered movement, and we informed the president of this. After a few minutes he ordered us to leave and he went back to sleep. We communicated our conversation to the detail chief, who ordered a sweep run of the area. The sweep revealed nothing unusual."

Masters smiled tolerantly, catching himself in the act of exhaling an invisible smoke ring. He looked at his pipe with distaste; there was just no getting used to the smokeless blends. He had been part of the Brady family for two generations, as physician and friend, and had been something of an uncle to both Ted and Eli when Jed died. "Agent Kubark, you've been one of the president's in-close agents for how long now—two years?"

"Twenty-three months, eighteen days, sir."

"And you've been twice decorated by the Treasury Department, isn't that right? A Medal of Valor, and . . . what was it?"

"The Exceptional Service Award, sir."

Masters showed the room a smile. "And you say that you'd stationed yourself outside the sliding door to the terrace. Is that your normal routine?"

Kubark shook his head. "I'm normally the inside man, sir, but Fusilli had a flu that night and I—"

"Were you asleep when the president called out?"

"Sir?" the agent asked, alarmed.

Masters made a dismissive motion with his pipe hand. "Don't get me wrong, son, I'm just wondering if you were napping on your feet or anything."

Kubark tightened his lips. "I was fully awake, sir."

Philbert Base coughed. "Didn't you indicate in your sitrep that you were surprised to find the sliding door open when you rushed the room?"

"Yes, sir."

"You further stated you didn't recall hearing the president get up to open it."

"That's true, sir, but—"

"And the president himself claims that he did not at any time that night get up to open the door."

Kubark worked the muscles of his square jaw.

"Well?" Base demanded. "It's obvious *somebody* opened the door. And yet you maintain you weren't napping on duty."

"I don't like where this is headed," Robert Potus interrupted, his loose face flushed. "This agent isn't on trial."

"Calm down, Bob," Base told him. "I'm only trying to establish something. Doors at Shangri-la don't open of their own volition—not yet at any rate. Now it's quite possible the president simply doesn't *remember* getting up that night. But we can't rule out the possibility that Agent Kubark drifted off for the minute or so it took for that to occur unnoticed."

Kubark glared at him, but said nothing.

"My people don't nap on the job," Potus barked. "Randy, take off your glasses."

Kubark lowered his head and began to twist out of his wraparound Wise-Eyes, but Eli stopped him. The last thing he wanted to hear was a rundown of the man's bio-upgrades. "We're not questioning the report, Bob," he assured Potus. "We're simply trying to learn what exactly went on that night."

"Am I missing something?" Colton asked, glancing about with elaborate concern. "I mean, is there supposed to be some connection between the president's god-stroking in Dallas and this mysterious sliding door?"

Eli and Base traded looks.

Weakly Eli said, "The president insists that something happened to him that night. He claims that he was . . . *visited* by someone, something . . ."

"In the argot of the cults it's called a close encounter," Sachs offered. "An actual physical confrontation with nonhuman beings."

Here was that silence again, Eli thought, recalling the rapt Wholists in the Newark Dome. "The president's memory of the episode is incomplete—which I'm told is SOP in experiences of this sort. He described it to me as a 'vision.' As Agent Kubark has stated, the Service detail didn't find anything out of the ordinary, so I asked Professor Sachs to run a check on UFO sightings in the area."

"I made some discreet inquiries," Sachs explained, repositioning the glasses that gave him an owllike look. "The saucer-watch group that monitors that entire area—the Blue Ridge Aerial-Phenomenon Center—reported no sightings on Labor Day weekend."

"That's surprising," Colton said, straight-faced. "No shortage of power lines out there, plenty of limestone deposits to attract them."

The chief of staff stood up and paced to the center of the room. "Two days after this incident the president suggested we rethink our position in the Horn. *His* position, actually. And when the press questioned his decision to commit, he told them— if any of you recall—that he had just come by some 'revelatory information.' Well, I can tell you, friends and neighbors, that everyone from the lowest UPI scavenger in the Press Club to the Joint Chiefs wanted to know where the hell this new information had come from. As a matter of interest, Mr. Obstat, some of us assumed it came from NSA."

Niles Obstat's dark brown face remained impassive.

"After the Horn came the god talk, along with a couple of choice double-edged statements." Base returned to his chair to snatch a sheet from an unlabeled manila file. "Let me refresh your memories. On September fifteenth, the president made reference to 'hostile planetary agencies.' Premier Korzliev and the entire goddamned Islamic Front thought he was referring to their actions in the Horn. Then, at September twentieth's press conference, the president practically admitted to having second thoughts about the shield's effectiveness to 'no-notice penetration.' "

"Hell," Milo Colton muttered, "don't tell me you're looking for a connection between this 'no-notice' midnight episode and the president's policy shift?"

"We're considering it," Eli said quietly.

Jose Darpa, Ted's string-tied advisor on domestic affairs, looked at Eli in disbelief. "Ridicoolous," he said, in a voice that brought

Desi Arnaz to mind. "Tose quoes don mean a ting. An if you take da time to check da polls, jour gonna find record-low resistance ratios to da idea of UFO visitations." Darpa made it a word: *oofo*. "One outta tree people has seen dem, and God knows how many more have been taken for rides, esamined, or even fucked by XTs. Iss a modern 'urosis, like a religious esperience, *verdad*? So let Ted avis fling. Laz spring it was zen, now iss *oofos*."

"It's become fashionable to be adbucted," Obstat muttered.

"But that's exactly the point," Base said gruffly. "It *is* a new religious experience. Why the hell else would I be feeling like somebody's got their fingers up my butt?"

Sexual proclivities being what they were among the members of the committee, the chief of staff's discomfort did not find universal sympathy.

Loren Masters attended to his pipe. "The president has been experiencing flashbacks since the episode," he said after a moment. "He refuses to admit this, but I'm certain his sleep habits have changed. He seems to have little or no appetite at times, and I'm not talking about weekend fasting. He's spending more time in meditation. Last week I finally got him on the diagnostic table. His pulse was rapid, blood pressure elevated, pupils dilated." The physician stopped to consider his words, then added, "These references to 'hostile agencies' and no-notice assaults . . . They have a delusional sound to them. Almost . . ."

Colton leaned forward in his chair, hanging on the physician's words. "Almost what, Doctor—paranoid? These are paranoid times, Loren."

"Not when those delusions involve telepathic messages," Masters argued.

"And is that the case?"

"It may be," Base answered. "And Dallas isn't the only example we can point to."

The DCI turned to Eli. "I'm still not clear on the purpose of this meeting, Mr. Secretary. If Dr. Masters' team doesn't want to handle things, I could provide the president with a list of the psychiatrists the Agency numbers among its officers. We have three Freudians, two Jungians, a—"

"The president isn't interested in psychiatric counseling," Eli said, trying to sound emphatic about it. "You're here because Phil and I want you appraised of the fact that the president has decided to seek help outside the community. In fact, he's already asked us to function in his behalf by scheduling a meeting with . . . Gabriel Ouro."

Eli paused briefly to let it sink in. Niles Obstat exhaled a slight whistling sound. Colton and the SIG director, Enoch Keyes, were regarding one another blankly. "We met with Ouro in New York on Tuesday night," Eli went on. "Professor Sachs, if you'd care to—"

"Save it, Professor," Obstat said. "I think we're all acquainted with Ouro's reputation. But may I be permitted to inquire who the hell suggested the Shaman of Self-help?"

"The roshi," Base said, spitting the words out. "That little Jap bastard told him Ouro could help him recall the details of this goddamned encounter."

"At least Miso-roshi is security-cleared," Obstat said.

"I don't see any reason to overreact," Masters cautioned. "Gabriel Ouro's success with this sort of thing is well documented. I certainly don't buy any of this Blue Star idiocy he's selling, but Ted's encounter coincides closely enough with the anniversary of Catherine's death to suggest a strong underlying psychic component. People in crisis turn to bartenders, whores, and personal trainers. And, frankly, I believe Ouro might be more effective than any outside ear or psychoimmunologist we could bring in."

"His powers have been laboratory-tested," Sachs volunteered.

"And we do have a clearance on Ouro," the Bureau chief said, perhaps too boastfully. "He has a full understanding of the need for security precautions, and has agreed to go on the box to corroborate our background on him."

Base scoffed. "He'll dazzle those goddamn detectors of yours without batting an eye. Besides, I've read the Bureau's file on Ouro, Pat, and it sounds to me like you've been cribbing from *Trendsetter*. Just how do you run a security check on a man without a past? The fact is, Ouro isn't a doctor, alienist, or priest, but a goddamned drug-taking Indian headshrinker who's garnered a following based on his purported ability to pick brains. My grandson has an action figure of the guy, for Christ's sake." He paused a moment to quiet Eli's objection before it could be raised. "Eli, you know I'm as fond of your brother as any person in this room, and I know that Ted's a team player and he'll come through for us in the end, but I told you once: I won't run the risk of turning a treatable problem into one hell of a grand delusion. Let alone a monumental threat to national security."

"I thought it was Company business to find plots where none

exist," Colton said soberly. "The president already has friends
in high places—his seminarian coterie, and 'that little Jap bastard,' as you so quaintly characterize the Soto zen master. So
Gabriel Ouro's name is entered in the Blue Book. The worst I
can see coming of this is a political cartoon."

"The worst that can come of this," the chief of staff rejoined,
"is that the president will damage his credibility beyond repair,
at a time when our Soviet and Islamic counterparts would like
nothing more than to confront a crippled presidency at the summit table." Base extracted a second sheet from the unlabeled
file. "I want to read you something that bears directly on my
concerns—something your dossier doesn't touch on, Pat."

Base's fingers traced down the printout sheet.

"Here it is," he said, looking up. "This passage relates to
the . . . 'deflection of power' and 'the *imposition of vision*.' This
is Ouro talking: 'Although the Human Beings no longer had to
concern themselves with territorial enemies, there were occasions nonetheless when *the throwing of vision* was employed.
The method is more accurately described as a throwing of *power*,
and the resultant vision—usually meant to confuse an opponent
or compel him to perform in some fashion—takes its shape from
activated elements within the victim's mind: fears or unpurged
negative memories, the psychological baggage from previous
lives over which all but the most unflinching warriors have no
control.' "

"Primitive magic," Masters said. "Remnants of infantile
beliefs in the omnipotence of thought."

Base slapped the sheet. "Primitive magic my ass, Doctor.
He talks right here about his ability to throw visions. How the
hell do we know that group of high-fiber fanatics didn't *throw*
this vision to begin with? And if you won't subscribe to that,
then how do we know Ouro isn't going to *compel* the president
to act a certain way now? Worse things could happen to that cult
than to have the president join hands and dance around the May-
pole with them. And what about these rumors surfacing about
Ouro's past?"

A red-faced Masters said, "I don't see their relevance."

"You don't see their relevance . . . People are calling him a
literary fakir and it doesn't concern you. Would you feel the
same if you learned that that supposed Amazonian upbringing
of his really took place in some KGB training camp in South
Irkutsk? I don't trust anyone in that damned church."

Sachs said, "Strictly speaking, it isn't a church. It's basically an alternative healing movement. UFOs constitute only a small part of it.''

Base curled his lip. "Let them find a cure for cancer or the cough that won't go away if they're such healers. And did they or did they not recently apply for church status, Professor?"

Sachs swallowed hard. "Only because of the botanical concoction Ouro imbibes—"

"The *hallucinogen*, you mean." Base looked around. "Their goddamned communal sacrament.''

"It's the sixties all over again," Obstat said.

Base eyed him from across the room. "Coming back to haunt us, Obstat. Your kids are doing what you did to your parents.''

"It's simply that the plant hasn't received FDA approval yet."

"Sleeping prophets and happy mediums," Base snarled. "Just an alternative healing movement . . . You tell that to all those Blue Star seers out there. Next thing you know they'll be scratching symbols in the sidewalks." He shook his head. "This isn't just equinox egg-balancing, gentlemen. I am not prepared to let this administration go down in history as the Constantine presidency.''

Niles Obstat and Jose Darpa swapped quizzical looks.

"Constantine, gentlemen, one of the last of the Roman emperors. One day he had a vision of a cross in the sky, and the next thing anyone knew he had the Empire converted to Christianity and condemned to a slow death. Now instead of crosses it's UFOs. Haven't we heard enough from these 'American Century' theorists without giving them something else to chew on?"

"Regardless," Sachs retaliated, "Cult Activities is satisfied that the Whole Earth Movement does not employ mind-control tactics. It's not as if we're dealing with the New Tao here, Mr. Base. There are no chambers, no virtual rigs, no bipolar magnetic futons, no brainwipe cases wandering the barrios in neuroelectronic dazes. People generally seem to be drawn to the movement *after* they've seen this alleged Blue Star, not vice versa.''

"What are your sources?" Milo Colton asked the FBI chief.

"HUMINT," O'Denvy told him. "We've been somewhat less successful with electronic surveillance. They appear to have their own internal security force.''

"And you don't find that suspicious?" Base said.

O'Denvy shrugged. "They're no different from any other corporation or multinational. Even the Vatican employs an intelligence network.''

"So we're right back to *church* again."

"All right," Eli Brady broke in, standing to confront them. "I think we've all had a chance to voice our personal feelings about this. I realize that the Horn Crisis has already put everyone on overtime, but what I'd like to propose is the formation of a special committee to assess the Bureau's preliminary findings and to monitor all subsequent developments. The president and Gabriel Ouro will meet, that much is certain. In the meantime, we can begin to look for ways to discredit the movement, or at the very least put an end to the concerns any of us are entertaining about manipulation."

Eli turned to the CIA and SIG directors. "Mr. Colton, Mr. Keyes, I want you to set up a pooling operation. Find an operative who can penetrate the movement and get us some core data on these people."

"Mr. Secretary," O'Denvy said cautiously. "I feel the Bureau should be permitted to pursue this case unassisted, especially if there's a suggestion of foreign involvement here." The FBI chief was well aware of Brady and Colton's naval bond, but there were territorial protocols to maintain. "Our counterintel—"

"I'm aware of this," Eli said, while Colton was shooting O'Denvy a stone-faced look behind his back. "But it's my understanding that Special Intelligence has agents who are better equipped to handle a penetration of this sort. Am I right, Mr. Keyes?"

The SIG director nodded.

"I expect Mr. Colton to set up appropriate liaison between his people and the Bureau," Eli continued, "and position his players for downfield blocking in the event of a fumble. For the time being we'll put this on a need-to-know basis: Everyone here, with the exception of Agent Kubark, will have eyes-only access to all incoming mail. I'm giving you command authority to lay this thing open, Mr. Colton, but our window's a narrow one. The Jakarta talks are slated for the end of November, and I want to have a hold on this situation by then."

As the meeting was breaking up, Jose Darpa said, "I tought tis *oofo* business was finish d'jears ago."

" *'In Hoc Signo Vinces,'* " Base told him, pushing folders into his briefcase. "The words Constantine claimed to see on that airborne cross of his. 'By this sign you will conquer.' "

3 The President's World-Line

"But what were your impressions of him?" the president asked eagerly from behind the Oval Office's wide, antique desk. "Eli? Phil?" When they hesitated, Brady offered them a knowing smile and struck a mindreader's pose. "Now don't tell me . . ."

The two men forced a short laugh, trying for comfort on the ladder-backed chairs. Each piece of office furniture demanded a kind of yogic posturing—a physical statement of the inner sanctum's suffering-together the president favored, the spirit of spartan sacrifice. The entire thrust of his administration had been aimed at excising fat from the government, redressing the excesses of the past, toning and firming, cutting back on padding, whether that referred to the size of one's staff or a quality of the decor. A lean but not necessarily mean America. Brady's advisors often wondered in private when he would get around to moving pews into the White House chambers.

"You have to understand, Ted, this isn't just tai chi on the South Lawn." Base risked showing him a hard look. "Frankly, this Whole Earth church—"

"Movement," the president corrected him.

"Movement, then. They've cut you loose. They claim you've broken your promises to clean up the environment. They're zealots, Ted, and they're preaching apocalypse. If word leaks out—"

"That's why I'm leaving the security matters in your hands," the president said. "Listen to me, both of you: I'm not unaware of the risks, and I trust you made this abundantly clear to Ouro. If it'll put you more at ease, think of him as an ambassador. Maybe it isn't too late to patch up differences." Brady watched Base for a reaction. "If that doesn't wash, Phil, you can think of him as my choice of doctor." He turned to his brother. "O'Denvy tells me you got him to sign a security oath."

The secretary of state nodded, thinking: If only Ouro were a doctor.

"Then what's there to worry about?"

Eli knew that Ted prided himself on having a healthy detachment from in-depth gossip, but Ouro was too controversial a figure to sit down and break bread with. Ted just wasn't reading this one right. Not that it was the first time. From the start there had been Tedman Brady the president and Tedman Brady the private seeker, and somehow Ted has always managed to carry the contradictions lightly. Like the house and the staff, they came with the job. But they were part of the persona rather than the man, a mask to display at the public games. And telegenic Ted, America's "Silicon President," was not above manipulating the media with his well-practiced unreadableness, the smile called frugal, the thoughtful gaze and near-Eastern poise. He had long ago confided his personal beliefs to Eli: that God had created matter so that spirit might have a vehicle to utilize in returning to the Source. So, too, the individual soul had been given a body to carry forth the self-assertive mission.

"Our sessions will be a strictly private matter," the president was saying. "I have no intension of discussing policies of state with him, and I think you know me well enough to accept my word on this. If you require more assurance, I'm sure Loren will be glad to furnish you with a complete evaluation of my physical and mental well-being."

A poor coverup, Eli thought. "That won't be necessary, Mr. President," he said flatly, eliciting an enigmatic grin from his brother.

"Thank you, *Mr.* Secretary."

Eli returned the look, hollowed by misgiving.

With equal measures of admiration and envy, people had called their father "the prince of darkness." Because wherever Jed had sent his surveyors they were certain to strike ore—so consistently that Jed's competitors had spread tales of subterranean contacts, diabolical contracts. But the explanation for his remarkable success was not as Faustian as some had imagined; Jed Brady was an ore-diviner. The talent has come prepackaged in genes handed down from their grandfather, Elijah—pioneer, prospector, and mountain prophet. Three times wed but never divorced: He had bartered his Cheyenne bride for three pack mules, his Spanish wife had fled to Mexico with a man half her age, and he had survived Nancy Sears, the only daughter of a displaced Chicago tycoon who had moved his family to Albuquerque for health reasons. Elijah had founded *Brady Ore—Mining Concerns*. And while consolidating Elijah's vast holdings, son Jed had carved out a small Arizona–New Mexico empire for himself, at one point employing nearly one-quarter of the labor force of those states in his various enterprises. Jed had sold off huge tracts of desert waste to the federal government prior to World War Two, and afterward donated land freely, hoping scientists would develop the H-Bomb on what was once his property. *Anything to contain those Reds*, Jed would tell anyone who listened. He had raised two sons, seeing to it that they absorbed as much of the American ethic as he was humanly able to impart, and died tough as the sixteen-penny nails that secured the lid of his handbuilt pine casket.

Eli, who didn't see an ocean until he was fifteen, went on to Annapolis, a submarine command, and eventually the State Department. Tedman's first stop (after one year at the University of New Mexico), was the Holy Trinity Novitiate, a Catholic seminary at Aguas Calientes in the Sandia range above Santa Fe. Jed had encouraged his two sons to make friends with solitude, and each in his own way had.

Critics and psychohistorians would later state that Brady's flirtation with seminary life was an act of rebellion directed against his father, bolstering their claims with quotes from Tedman's early speeches, diatribes against "a generation who had raped the land, polluted the gene pool, and attacked the noosphere of the planet with wanton disregard." Other scholars fond of this sort of thing viewed Brady's seminary period as an acceptable postadolescent ascetic response. But the truth was that Brady had been *called*. An introvert, an intellectual from birth, a compulsive diarist from the age of eight years on who dreamed of becoming a priest, a doctor, an influence in the world, and who had entered the political arena only as a last resort, Tedman had no taste for the transitory. The challenges he sought were not faced on the sports or battlefield, but in that interior zone where disciplined soul and spirit did battle with nonordinary reality. Brady stopped short of taking final vows, but the disciplines of self-denial he absorbed would remain an integral part of the man who won his way from city councilman to president in seventeen short years.

Brady had thrown himself into politics with the same fervor that had enabled him to adhere to the harshness of monastic life, the five A.M. awakenings, the hours of silent meditation and physical labor, the three-day fasts and ascetic regime. He gave all of his energy over to the various campaigns, yet always managed to maintain the separation between private and public lives that was to become his trademark. He was not so much the dark horse as the political horse of a different color.

When Brady had first appeared on the presidential scene, he seemed to be the antithesis of all that had corrupted the System, someone who thought of politics as more than the art of the use of power. He was honest, accessible, well informed—a man who could speak eloquently about reuniting with Nature and restoring the health of the planet through "intelligent apperception of the needs of the planetary body." Why, Tedman Brady even claimed to have seen a UFO and was not afraid to admit it. His nonpartisan forward-looking vision bridged party lines, and as the public began to catch up with him, the references to esoteric concerns—"creative evolution," "the limits of growth," and "organism Earth"—met with applause rather than ridicule. Indeed, if there was anything that had kept him from ascending sooner to the secular see it was an unvoiced fear among the voters that the presidency was just another stop in Tedman Brady's personal odyssey; that it was not above the man to abandon politics without notice and place himself in satorical self-exile on some remote Sandian peak.

It was never entirely clear to his friends and supporters just what greatness Brady was saving himself for, but they saw it as their near-sacred obligation to help engineer his success—even when that had sometimes involved machinations Brady himself would never have approved.

The defensive shield was already well underway when Brady took office, but it had fallen upon him to complete and deploy the few remaining pieces of the system's laser, mirror, and satellite architecture. Carefully controlled computer-technology leaks had allowed the Soviet Union to ready a similar system at the same time, yet the results were anything but expected. Where the twin shields were to have paved the way for a joint effort to clean up the atmosphere with sky-seeding rail guns and ozone blimps, they had proved an economic nightmare and driven a wedge into more than a decade of hard-earned détente. Suspicions arising out of concern for the shields' offensive potential fostered a Byzantine system of checks and counterchecks and gave birth to a slew of projects aimed at reestablishing parity and a balance of power. The European Alliance, meanwhile, along with most of the emerging nations of the nonaligned world, cried foul and accused Washington and Moscow of conspiring to create what amounted to a global police force. Brady, however, had remained loyal to his campaign promise to see the system through to operational status, and in his inauguration address referred to it not as a shield—which denoted something to hide behind—but as a "celestial ring," America's commitment to the ideal of lasting peace. That same day he had ordered the White House bomb shelter, the Citadel, filled in.

For a time—for much of the first two years—Brady, in the hope of rescuing America from debt and unchecked foreign investment, had succeeded in quieting the nation by using a minor recession to stimulate a period of therapeutic isolationism. And he had continued to do a passable job managing the present, even while the first lady lay dying of cancer. But Brady could do little about incursions from the past, things once thought buried that were suddenly resurfacing.

Then out of left field came the Crisis in the Horn, presenting Brady with the most severe test he had faced since Catherine's death. But God's will be done: Brady had heeded the warnings implicit in his Labor Day vision and acted on the side of right.

And with the Crisis behind him, it had seemed his intent to give God His due through public acknowledgment of His hand in the affair. Wasn't it after all God's absence from the public domain that lay at the root of the world's problems?

The Dallas speech Eli had screened for the committee was but one of those acknowledgments, and the editorial swipes it stirred had come fast and furious.

GOD MAKES A COMEBACK, the *Post* wrote, THANKS HIS NEW AGENT, BRADY. And from the *Times:* BRADY CREATES GOD IN HIS OWN IMAGE.

Neo-Feminists took issue with the use of *his*; but most people no longer knew what to think . . .

"If I could just be clear about all that went on that night," the president told the state secretary and chief of staff. "At times I'm so close to remembering . . ."

Ted's hands were pressed to his temples, shaking fingers splayed across his forehead. When Eli could stand no more of it, he rose from the chair and laid a calming hand on his brother's shoulder, wondering which was more dangerous: the known or the unrevealed?

"It'll be behind us soon," he said, trying to sound comforting. But as Gabriel Ouro and the Blue Star came to mind, Eli thought: If it hasn't gained on us already.

4 Special Intelligence

Milo Colton was screening the disk the Bureau chief had sent over when Enoch Keyes knocked and carded himself through the hardwood office door. There were few at the Agency's expanded and revamped Langley, Virginia, complex who enjoyed such privileges.

"Take a load off, Rusty," the DCI said, gesturing to an easy chair by the window.

Keyes settled in, centering a briefcase between his feet and glancing out the window; Mt. Kalau's ash-shroud had brought an early winter to the Potomac Valley. "I see you added a Chagall to the lobby."

Colton shrugged and swiveled in his chair, a VDR remote in hand. "Art is an investment. They gave us the funds, we're making them work for us."

Keyes nodded, smiling thinly. The Special Intelligence Group's own headquarters was a windowless brick building in College Park, midway between the District and Fort Meade.

Colton nodded to the screen. "Have you seen this?"

"This morning," Keyes said, as Colton thumbed the remote.

"Complacent, we try to turn our backs to the atrocities our inaction has spawned," Gabriel Ouro returned to saying. The disk was a pay-tv recording of his recent appearance at the Newark Dome. "We hide ourselves away in fortified places under defensive umbrellas. But no one, I tell you, is doing *the thinking for Earth*. And as a result we find ourselves at the mercy of things loosed from other worlds and other epochs against which these shields are powerless. It is a *psychic* shield we require. Not one born of particles torn from their just centers, but fabricated from the collective will of the Experienced . . ."

The Agency's penetrations inside the FBI and the Secret Service had kept Colton fully informed of Secretary Brady's tryst with Gabriel Ouro, so the revelations at the committee meeting had come as no surprise.

" 'Psychic net,' " Colton said contemptuously. "Sounds more like zen sports than latter-day talk. Maybe this Blue Star's their volleyball, what d'ya think?"

Keyes smirked. "An interesting notion. We should slip it into the Bureau's datanet."

Colton applauded the idea. Both men knew that Phil Base's accusation had been right on the money: The FBI *had* padded Ouro's dossier with data gleaned from the glossy pages of *Trend-setter*. In Patrick O'Denvy's defense, it was true that Cult Activities had managed to scrape together a chronobio of sorts; but on the whole the Bureau had relied on those same sources that fed the public's appetite for star gossip and bits of the bizarre. Investigative journalists were sometimes the Bureau's unwitting agents, and often—when the Bureau wished to press a point—their useful idiots, as well.

"What do you have on him, Rusty?" Colton asked, switching off the digital player and laying aside the remote.

Keyes lifted his chin and exhaled a calculated sigh. Colton thought he could hear the man's 175-IQ bytes accessing and processing.

Keyes was close to eighty, a small, nattily attired man with a trace of red left in his wispy hair—one result of a strict regimen of age suppressants. He had resided among the intelligence community for longer than almost anyone around, clear back to the Agency's early days, working in the field for the OPC and the CIG while bureaucrats sought the letter-perfect combination. Keyes was a survivor of numerous massacres, the reigning monarch of the Old Boy Network, a man whose ascension was less a reflection of ambition than an instinctive ability to keep his head down when the long knives came out. He had a knack for keeping himself and ultimately the Special Intelligence Group clear of the falls it seemed his duty to assume. Tedman Brady was Keyes' tenth president, and although this latest caper posed some unique problems, Keyes had been faced with greater challenges.

Outsiders still liked to think of SIG as an offshoot of the Agency's Technical Service's Division when in fact it was the closest thing the intelligence community had to a psychic research and development department.

"Born Jorge Culho, in Manaus, Brazil, 1943," Keyes had

begun. "The father was Joachim Sufenz Culho, a cabinetmaker, died in 1956. As for the mother, RID's best guess is one Embla Munnin, a dancer of mixed German and Portuguese ancestry, whose stage name, interestingly enough, was Gabriella Lauro. She apparently abandoned the infant to Culho early on and fled South America. Died in Bangkok, June 1950."

"Promising," Colton commented, thinking: And undoubtedly correct. He recalled that the chief of SIG's Records Integration Division insisted on employing double Virgos only. "So our celebrated shaman is not an Indian after all."

"Not pure blood. Brazilian records show that a Gabriel Sufenz was enrolled in São Paolo University from 1960 to '65, receiving a degree and graduating with honors in both linguistics and anthropology. His papers on Native American languages generated considerable enthusiasm among the faculty."

Colton raised an eyebrow.

"Then we draw a twenty-year blank."

"Out wandering in the wilderness, I suppose."

"Presumably. Although there's no reason to doubt he spent at least part of that time living among an Amazonian tribe. He had to learn the shamanic techniques somewhere."

"And get himself tattooed."

Keyes adjusted the knot in his silk tie. "He surfaces in Bahía in 1985 as Gabriel Ouro. A healer, a kind of exorcist/priest in one of the coast's spirit-possession cults. There were rumors of miracles. Ouro curing the sick, ridding people of demons, conversing with the dead. His fame spread among the poor."

" 'South America's Culture Hero,' " Colton said, quoting *Time*.

"Messiah's more like it. West Coast Africans began paying attention to him. It was Christianity, psychism, shamanism all wrapped up in one neat package with genuine cures to boot. New Agers were returning from Brazil with incredible tales. This is what aroused the interest of Wiles ParaResearch. They sent a team down there and somehow enticed him to come to the States."

Colton knew the rest of it, but listened along anyway. Ouro was soon presiding over weekend Aquarian workshops sponsored by psychic counterforce groups. At a world congress of the Twantisuyu Confederation—a worldwide league of indigenous healers—Ouro had been named "the Long-Awaited Brother." But it wasn't until years later, when Ouro threw in with the Whole Earth Movement and announced the arrival of the Blue Star, that his popularity had taken a quantum leap.

Before Ouro, WEM was a loosely organized conglomerate of New Age spokespeople promoting various paths to self-fulfillment, all of whom had merged their individual power bases with the Movement's across-the-board human-potential appeal. But after Ouro, WEM was the place to be; the Blue Star a new dividing line between the seers and blind. Overnight WEM had big money behind it, and Ouro became the darling of the upscale and trendy, of Hollywood, New York, and Tokyo. Cultural commentators had dismissed the group as a Ghost Dance movement, a crazed cargo cult filled with science-fiction fans waiting for a mother ship to arrive and carry them off. Still, with an estimated five million followers in America alone, WEM had become a powerful spiritual and political force.

"What about it, Rusty," Colton asked, "have you seen this Blue Star?"

Keyes took a moment to respond, doffing his glasses and holding them up to the window light. "Beth and I were in Georgetown Tuesday night on our way to dinner. There was a crowd gathered on M Street, a dozen hands in the air. Group of Hare Krishnas dancing on the corner didn't even bother to look up."

Colton nodded. "I've seen this picture. Happened to me at the club. Young woman, couldn't have been more than nineteen, swearing to everyone she was seeing it. Pointing it out through holes in the ozone. None of us could find it."

"It's apparently headed straight for us. Pioneer 10 picked the thing up. Launched in seventy-two and that little devil just keeps making trouble for everyone."

"Those people over at LBA and Hubble haven't helped any. What are they calling it?"

" 'A Piscean nebulosity'—blue-shifted, which suggests negative velocity, an *approach*. They were looking for remnants of supernova explosions. It's no wonder Ouro's playing to sold-out venues."

"Does he work with loaves of bread or fish?"

"It'd be fluke-fish sushi if anything," Keyes said. "Black beans, soba noodles, and star anise."

Colton's loafered foot began to tap arhythmically. "So what happens—my house is haunted, my daughter thinks the family dog is sending her messages, I've got a statue of a black jockey bleeding on my front lawn . . . Or one night I walk outside, look up, and see this Star? How do I enroll myself in the Movement?''

"You go into one of the Centers or one of their field offices. You call 1-800-WHOLIST, or you mail in one of the cards they've spread around. You use your modem if you have one.''

"Field offices . . . Who do they think they are, some spook network?''

"They set up an appointment for you to meet with a Listener—black-mind types, people who have been through the course.''

"This takes place at a Center?''

"At a Haven,'' Keyes said. "There's a screening period. To sort the chaff from the grain. We're fairly certain they're looking for legitimate events—episodes of telepathy, stigmata, possession, extraterrestrial abduction. Blue Star seers, at the very least.''

Colton stroked his chin. "Sounds like it would be easy enough to lie your way in once someone's pointed out the Star. What's kept O'Denvy's people out?''

Keyes shrugged his frail shoulders. "The Listeners are discriminating.''

The chaff, he explained, were sent off to the Centers—a strictly North American epiphenomenon—wherein Wholists learned paths to personal power essential to psychic health in the aftermath of Earth's encounter with the Blue Star. Badges of rank were awarded for each level attained; completion of the course entitled one "Experienced,'' and apparently a seer, as well.

"The agent O'Denvy tasked for penetration resigned from the Bureau at level five. She hasn't been heard from since.''

"Does Eli know?''

Keyes shook his head. "And this is where the hallucinogen comes in. WEM wants to make it the prize in the Cracker Jacks— although they may be forced to go the church route here to have that happen. The South American and African chapters aren't under any such restraints, but the FDA isn't exactly eager to legitimize another narcotic right now.''

"Something new?'' Colton asked with heightened interest.

"Not at all. It's *yage*, the juice of a rain-forest creeper. Powerful but not unlike LSD in effect. We've been working with it on and off since sixty-six.''

"Okay,'' the DCI said after a moment. "But what about the ones that show talent—the grain?''

Keyes grinned, showing expensive implants. "This is where things get interesting. There seems to be an inner circle, with ties to Amol Woolley and Kiri Haguchi of the Lakehaven Institute for Advanced Research."

Colton had heard as much; Woolley was the Nobel laureate astrophysicist Ouro had reportedly cured of a degenerative disease some years back. Contributions, along with funds taken in at the Centers, had allowed the Movement to back its own paraphysical research projects, consolidating the efforts of many smaller organizations and employing the skills of Fifth Force scientists who had allied themselves to Ouro's nebulous designs.

Keyes snapped open his briefcase and passed over a thin sheaf of National Recon opticals. "Several years ago WEM purchased a Caribbean island," he continued. "It's called Inaccessible on the few charts that show it. A pyramidal facility has been under construction for the past three years. We assumed it was just the latest Center going up, but now we're not so sure. It's too tightly wrapped. We put pressure on some of WEM's hardware suppliers and assembled a parts list. Woolley and Haguchi seem to be building themselves some sort of particle installation."

"An accelerator?"

"Not likely, given the pyramid shape."

"Well, maybe they're just trying to corner the market on reusable razor blades," Colton suggested. "And this inner circle you mentioned . . ."

Keyes named names, and the DCI recognized several of them: Susan Vide, Hiawatha Fountain, Leigh Burmandy.

"Didn't you try to recruit these people?"

"It's worse than that," Keyes confessed. "In fact, I think SIG may have inadvertently brought this inner circle into being. The nine members we've identified are the same ones we gathered at Advanced Weapons-Experimental eight years ago. The goal then was to locate individuals with mind-control abilities who could run enemy agents without danger of compromise. But we were also interested to learn if any of the nine could remote-view cloaked installations, communicate telepathically with submarines, scramble the thoughts of world leaders, throw nuclear switches, if necessary."

"I remember," the DCI said, mulling it over. He was the Agency's DDO then. "We've been ordered to penetrate, investigate, collate . . . But it might behoove us to insure that we don't alienate."

"My thoughts exactly. WEM's tax statements show some

discrepancies. I could put in a few words with Rissler over at Internal Revenue.''

"Save that for last resorts." Colton cleared his throat meaningfully. "Do you have an operative for me?"

Keyes said, "Lexus, Nexus," as one might intone abracadabra, and produced a green-banded folder. Colton opened the dossier and spent a moment perusing the contents.

"Karel Reydak," he said uncertainly. "Good, strong family ties, I see."

"John Reydak's son," Keyes told him, narrow-eyed.

"I know John. Ran into him at the Pentagon last month."

Keyes steepled his fingers, pensive.

The DCI regarded him for a long moment and glanced at the dossier again. "Two years at Sense Augmentation, advisor on PP ops, Ground-truth specialist, firsthand experience with saucer cults . . . he's certainly qualified. So what's wrong with him, Rusty? You've got that look."

Keyes leaned forward in the chair. "You've heard of Pavel Reydak?"

"Pavel Reydak . . . I'm not sure."

"John's older brother. Made a name for himself with a daring escape from Czechoslovakia in the early fifties. Company man before your time. Used to be known as 'Mr. ESP.' "

"You knew him?"

Keyes sniffed. "Quite well."

"And?"

"Karel inherited his uncle's talents, along, I'm afraid, with his paranoid tendencies, as well. I have some reservations about him, but he remains my first choice. Suppose we leave it at that."

Colton pursed his lips. "Have it your way, Rusty. So where is Colonel Reydak now?" he asked, bringing things back on track.

"Uganda. This Nakañ thing."

Colton recalled a photo in the Sunday *Times* of naked black warriors displaying bullet wounds that didn't bleed.

"Bring your officer home," he said. "Let's see if we can't put the Brady bunch back together again."

5 Desperate Straits and the Irie Ites

Years of rampant poaching, civil war, locusts, and drought had so reduced the region's wildlife population that the sight of four elephants suddenly emerging from the tall grass at the edge of the muddy pool made the Ground-truth team sit up and take notice. The only pachyderms Reydak had seen in his three months in East Africa were members of a cloned herd in Hemingway Park outside of Nairobi; so the rogues constituted a first of sorts, and he shot them from close range, getting it all down on cassette for posterity's sake, hardened fingers curled around the minicam's plastic pistolgrip, ears attuned to sounds the directional mikes wouldn't be able to pick up. The shots would have gone out live, but uplink had been lost the day before.

Beyond the watering hole and towering ant-infested bush rose the perpetually veiled Mountains of the Moon, the precipitous eastern face of Rainmaker, the "celestial castle" said to stand at the center of the world.

Dusk had already eased its way over the six-member team's small encampment. A splinter group from a UN peacekeeping contingent deployed to curb acts of terrorism, they had moved fifteen miles that day without incident.

Reydak returned to camp when the elephants moved off, downing a meal of plastic-pouched nutrients and blister-packed supplements, while mist swirled about and evanesced. Ian Highway was well into one of the monologues that came gratis with his services as guide.

"I'm not saying that I sympathize with these Nakañ buggers, but Anyoto Leopardmen they're not. An Anyoto had to spit into the mouth of a black chicken and eat a close relative just to prove himself worthy of membership. Ukulele's baptizing 'em in urine, passing out 'protective water,' and sending them out to kill.''

Protective water was dehydrated milk laced with *chat*, a local variety of backyard stimulant.

Highway laughed and poked absently at the fire. He was fluent in Swahili and Kingwana and could get by reasonably well in the local Bantu dialects. But his fondness for reminiscing about drinking days with media idols in the New Stanley bar put Reydak off. Barrel-chested, walrus-moustachioed, Highway liked to have it understood that he was the sole non-African member of the Lega Bwame secret society.

"So Ukulele's promising to make festishes out of the scrota of outsiders, to clothe his people in the flayed skin of Americans, Russians, and Chinese . . . If it wasn't for this human meat business, he'd pose no threat. You might say he's fed up with outsiders. Fear tactics are what you UN people are responding to."

The Great White Commentator, Reydak thought, eyeing the guide. Under the crackling of the fire, he could hear the faint hum of the ultrasonic antiintrusion devices he had placed along the perimeter. They had nothing to do with Ukulele; rodents and hyenas had been spreading some virulent shit around. Reydak gave the movement indicator screens a glance to confirm what his ears were picking up.

The country—a narrow mountainous interface between Zaire and Uganda—was for the moment known as Batora. It was bordered on the north by Lake Albert, on the south by Lake Edward; and while Ruwenzori provided an effective western barrier, Batora's embattled eastern frontier was somewhat less distinct, stretching in some places deep into Banyankole territory, almost to the fringe of Lake Victoria. At one time it had all belonged to Uganda, but for several years now the nation had been up for grabs. East and west, right and left, had pushed and pulled and succeeded only in fracturing the nation into some dozen principalities, territories, and microstates. Missionaries and militant chieftains had made a strong comeback.

"Fear tactics," Highway repeated. "But face facts, which of our governments hasn't preyed on superstition at one time or another? You blokes did it in Cuba, didn't you?" he directed to Reydak. "Tried to convince Havana that a Second Coming was at hand and Castro had to go?"

Reydak could think of even more recent examples. Psyops had them gouging out eyes to leave on the backs of the dead in

Peru. *Malo Ojo*, the evil eye. But the Senderos had a few tricks of their own, thanks to tactical support from Jivaro headhunters who'd maybe invented the game. You'd come across some poor grunt who'd been shrunken down to midget size—"leather men," they'd called them, boneless and stuffed, with hair down to their ass—or you might find someone's head stitched up inside somebody else's carcass . . . Sensory enhancement didn't help with any of that, especially for the poor fuckers who'd walked point with their olfactory upgrades. Remote-gagging was the order of the day; vomiting put everyone on alert. That's when Reydak had first begun to hate the Augment Center; curse the implants he'd agreed to wear. Ukulele's warriors wielded war-clubs fashioned from human femurs, but Highway was off-base: It wasn't the butchery that had brought the team in but the attendant paranormal stirrings.

"UFOs, vampires, animal mutilation," the guide carried on. "Now you blokes know how these defensive shields of yours make the rest of the world feel."

Reydak and the Russian, Yronskiy, exchanged brief looks; the night sky held bits and pieces of reflected light each could point to and call his own.

The paranormal situation wasn't unique to Batora; and it was a rash of similar outbreaks that had prompted the beleaguered UN to establish a special committee under the auspices of the Peaceful Uses of Outer Space Commission to study and evaluate claims of UFO sightings, alien visitations or harassment, corporeal mutilation, and climatic or geomagnetic manipulation. Ground-truth observers like Reydak, Yronskiy, and the rest were often sent into high-contact zones to investigate surges of said activity.

Forty-six, Reydak stood just over six feet tall and had the wary, wiry look of a combat-ready soldier or career paranoid. His hair was brown, wavy and thick, and although he tanned easily to a deep enduring golden brown that belied his Czech roots, his face—strong jaw and high cheekbones—was almost archetypally Slavic. Peacekeeping was a novel assignment.

Early on he had demonstrated a natural talent for seeing things in the sky; looking up while saucers, cigars, and globes were executing impossible aerial maneuvers. But it was SIG that had fine-tuned Reydak's abilities as an adjunct to his paramilitary training. He had yet to see one close up, one that he could believe in; but the consensus was that *something* was out there, undetectable by any of the shield's radar arrays, and often ap-

pearing in the airspace of nations on the verge of civil unrest—
especially those of imminent Marxist persuasion. Reydak had
run ops in Ethiopia, Afghanistan, Nicaragua, and Peru looking
for them, even while helping to spread the terror when it suited
the Agency's purpose. National Recon, preserving a forty-five-
year-old tradition, wanted to blame the Russians, but still
couldn't explain why the Soviet Union itself was so frequently
visited by those same enigmatic lights. And it was this discrep-
ancy that had led the KGB chiefs to theories of their own, and
accounted for the presence of Colonel Feliks Yronskiy on the
Ground-truth Team.

Highway was still lecturing. "I remember when the Little
Sisters first came to the Ituri Forest. Straightaway they begin
handing out candy and cigarettes, so the Bambuti can end up as
Christians with tooth decay and lung cancer. That right?" he
shouted to one of two shadowy figures seated at the edge of the
firelight.

"That right, *mangese*"came the quick reply.

Reydak recognized Masisi's raspy voice, breath and words
inhaled. The pygmy and his Rastaman companion were sharing
Captain Africa comics and tokes of resinous black ganga Masisi
had thumb-tamped into the ceramic bowl of a calabash water-
pipe. Ras McDonald, as the Jamaican called himself, was a
dreadlocked Niyabingi who had recently served Ethiopia in the
Horn War. For the past month Masisi had been reinstructing
him in the aboriginal ways.

People were calling it the Horn War even though little of the
action had taken place on land. Waterways had been at stake;
not oceans, but gulfs and inlets, hotly contested straits and nar-
rows.

"These blokes like Ukulele or Albert Einstein Ojoki don't
take well to rapid changes. You can strip them of their gods and
teach them to read, but at the first sign of drought or failed crops,
every 'reformed' witch doctor is spilling out cans of CARE
alphabet soup looking to divine the cause."

Reydak caught Eusi Uzuri's grin and returned it. The team's
radio operator, she was born in Malindi, Kenya, of a Galla
mother and an Arab father—a union that had blessed her with
an almost Egyptian, Nilotic beauty. Reydak had acquired a special fondness for her tiger-striped jumpsuit with its strategically
located Velcro closures. Their second night on patrol, he'd had
the privilege of tearing those closures open during a close encounter of the sweetest sort. A memory of Miss Universe thighs,

of nipples like chocolate kisses . . . On Eusi's left wrist was the ultrasonic repellent bracelet Reydak had picked up from the Nairobi chief of station.

"Candy and cigarettes." Yronskiy smirked. "Wonderfully capitalistic. It's no wonder these wretched black asses are miserable."

He was a powerfully built man with closely cropped hair, firelight touching the planes and angles of his large features, his face a mask of highlights and dark hollows. Reydak had crossed paths with him once before in Ecuador, and knew him to be one very squared-away trooper—a *Vysotnik*, the Soviet analog of a Green Beret. Like Highway, Yronskiy was outfitted in an open bush jacket and shorts. Pinned to a lapel was the *mushonga* he had taken from a terr in Zimbabwe—a hammer-and-sickle-inscribed ivory power amulet, supposedly effective against the forces of the nation it depicted. But Yronskiy—paragon of Sword-and-Shield thaumaturgy, with an Order of the Red Star and two Orders of the Red Banner—felt he had successfully reversed the spell by blowing away the charm's former bearer. Even now the Russian was cradling his AKM assault rifle as if it were some sort of prosthesis.

"Karel is the only happy capitalist," the Russian said, slapping Reydak on the shoulder with his free hand. "But that's because of his Slavic blood. When are you going to return to the monastery, little brother, eh?"

Prague's ancient Monastery of the Knights of the Cross now housed the STB, the Czech State Secret Police.

Reydak said, "I know we've got to stop meeting like this, Uncle. But you've heard about relatives turning over in their graves . . ."

Yronskiy's smile straightened some. "Your fearless uncle Pavel, yes . . . But all the better—a hero's homecoming."

Hearing this, Eusi moved over to link her arm through Reydak's and engage the Russian in a mock tug-of-war. "We won't let him go without a fight."

Masisi's startled cry of *bwana!* interrupted the jostling. The pygmy was up on his feet, pointing to the western sky, where a band of silver light split the night. Several centimeters in length and moving parallel to horizon, the light was moving at odd angles to the ground, as if speedwriting in the sky. Reydak tried to train the camera lens on the thing, while Yronskiy glanced at his chronometer and began to monitor readings on the team's tracking equipment. Eusi was already on the Motorola calling in coordinates.

"Well, I'll be a grub-eating son of a bitch!" Highway muttered.

The light-circle swept silently toward them, then vanished with a rapid right-angled ascent to the midheaven that seemed to take it to the stars.

Reydak lowered the camera. "Anything?"

The Russian shook his head. "Not a flutter."

"Masaka's dispatching a spotter," Eusi said.

"They won't tag anything," Reydak said.

Highway was wide-eyed, looking back and forth between the two men. "What the hell was that, Yank?"

Reydak snorted. "Swamp gas, ball lightning, a meteor, an ultralite . . . take your pick."

"It is the eyes of Ngoogoungounmbar," Masisi uttered in a quavering voice. Reydak turned to find the Bambuti cowering behind his tall Jamaican friend. "The eyes of Ngoogoungounmbar—the dragon's scouts."

Masisi had recounted the tale to Reydak the previous week: how the first pygmy—a thief who had stolen a pawpaw fruit—had been responsible for God's departure from the world and a resultant tilt in the world's axis of orientation. The serpent Ngoogoungounmbar ruled now, the swallowing dragon who would ultimately engulf the planet.

"You see, it comes from the dragon's lair," Masisi added, pointing again. "The blue light, there."

Reydak's grin collapsed. He moved to Masisi's side and squatted down to sight along the Bambuti's small black hand. Seeing nothing, he turned to Yronskiy and the others. "Anybody else see it?"

Heads shook. The Rasta said, "I be seein it by and by, mon. Wit de dancer's help."

Reydak looked at him with narrowed eyes. "A few more days with that smoke and you're gonna to be seeing anything he wants you to see."

Masisi smiled impishly, revealing a gap in his teeth where two lower incisors had been extracted to facilitate entry of the *tete*'s bamboo mouthpiece.

"The dragon lair is there without smoke."

"And the Bambuti are to blame for throwing the world out of whack," Reydak said.

Ras McDonald made a disapproving sound. "Keep you upright when dat dancer speak," he cautioned Reydak. "He talkin bout de *axis*, mon. Dis is deep reasoning. You got to keep you safe when Babylon fall."

Reydak recalled that Babylon was the white world, Satan and the Pope in conspiracy. Ras had already told him how his body was denatured; how he lacked spiritual diagnosis and high-tension wires.

"Seen?" Ras asked. "Black man been payin de price of dat ab'riginal transgression. But Rasta an da dancers redress dat wrong wit right-living. We seen Jah, we seen Ras Tafari, Haile Selassi I, da instrument an power of da Trinity."

Ras turned to the Bambuti. "Life everlivin, dancer. Black man gonna 'herit da Earth."

Masisi tittered, embarrassed by the Rasta's praise.

"Babble on, Ras," Reydak said with a certain finality. "And if we cross paths with any of Ukulele's followers, I'll just plant a kiss on their foreheads, congratulate them, and wish them better luck than we had with it."

The team broke camp before sunrise and headed north into the lush forests that adorned the hills above the Bankonjo River, lobelia and thick highland grasses giving way to mimosa, acacia, and stands of bamboo. They crossed at the Lulutanga Bridge and made for Fort Portal, where they were expected to rendez-vous with a UN A-team moving south from Lake Albert.

A crossroads linked by an all-weather highway to Kampala in the east and Sudanic settlements in and around the Ituri Forest north and west, Fort Portal was a once-prosperous town, now deserted save for a small garrison of blue-helmet UN forces. Those few residents who hadn't fled when the border war erupted had been frightened off by Ukulele's inspired mayhem.

Reydak knew that something was wrong long before the team neared town. The air reeked of rot and blood; and the nearer they drew to the place the more his visions of death intensified. They were a klick outside Fort Portal when they began to find the bodies. The garrison had been butchered—literally hacked to pieces—the stores ransacked, and all lines of communication cut. Highway thought he recognized the body of the A-team's local guide, an old African hand named Carter, but the corpse was headless, so he couldn't be sure.

Eusi raised headquarters at Masaka to report the massacre and arrange for extraction. It was deemed best that they stash most of the gear they'd humped in, recross the Bakanjo, and strike south for the small settlement at Nasese, less than a day's journey south along the river. Whomever or whatever had descended on Fort Portal had either caught the garrison unawares or severely outnumbered it. Reydak thought both explanations unlikely. Ukulele's Nakañs had overrun missionary posts, but Fort Portal would have taken a highly coordinated effort and more weapons than the cultists were believed to possess. And what really disturbed him was the absence of gunshot wounds in the bodies.

He took the point and kept the team moving at a good clip, sheer dread propelling him along. He didn't like using the road, but bushwacking to Nasese would have added another day to the trip and all of them were itching to leave. It was as if he could see the cultists in his mind's eye—remotely from above, running in unison like some multilegged creature, bone warclubs and long spears balanced on their shoulders—hear their guttural cry.

Then he realized that he was in fact seeing them: lined up like Hollywood Indians along a cleared ridge west of the road. Sunlight glinting off dozens of spear tips.

Masisi was down on one knee, his torso twisted over, one ear pressed to the ground. He sprang to his feet a moment later and motioned everyone to follow him into the thickets bordering the red slash of road.

It was easy going for a kilometer or so, because the land had a gentle downhill slope and the ground cover was sparse. But they were soon face to face with a heavily forested ridge that stood between them and the Bakonjo drainage. The team dispersed and began to scramble upward, Highway and the Russian using their short-bladed machetes to cut a rough switchback ascent. As they neared the summit, the road came into view behind them. The Nakañ had picked up their trail. About fifty armed warriors—naked save for penis sheaths, their bodies gray with ash and banded in what Reydak knew was fresh blood—were leaving the road and entering the bush. Sounds of the chant reached him in chilling waves.

Mai Ukulele! Mai Ukulele! Mai Ukulele!—the milk of Ukulele! Instinctively Reydak released all but his web gear and weaponry.

Once over the ridge they would have the Nakañ at their back and the river gorge in front of them; so instead they opted to hold the high ground, spreading themselves just short of the crest, finding cover and forming a tight semicircle into which the cultists rushed like rabid animals.

Reydak set his rifle on burst, propped himself up, and squeezed off half a magazine, pouring rounds into the killzone and waiting for the cultists to drop. He heard the dull *clack* of Eusi's weapon close by; farther off the report of Highway's automatic shotgun, the stammer of the Russian's AKM.

The Nakañ didn't even break stride.

Reydak thumbed the selector to full-auto and emptied the magazine. His mouth fell open in astonishment as the Nakañ continued their charge.

He heard Highway yell, "They're not going down, blokes! The buggers are bloody *immune!*"

But Reydak refused to accept it. After slamming another magazine into the rifle, he laid down a sweeping arc across the naked runners. *Drop, you motherfuckers*, he sneered through bared teeth, following the tracer rounds home, watching them strike, seeing blood spurt and bits of flesh explode from painted bodies. And yet . . . *and yet*!

It was all the horrors he'd help deploy paying him a return visit.

Ukulele's warriors let loose their spears and raised their arms above their heads to show wrist razors and finger knives. Highway took a solid hit midsection and went down, half a dozen zombies piling on top of him, ravenous for fresh meat. Reydak turned to Eusi's blood-curdling scream in time to see her fall under a like wave of frenzied flesh. He knew now what had befallen the Fort Portal garrison.

Reydak and Yronskiy broke from cover at the same moment and made a mad dash for the river gorge, trying desperately to close Masisi's fleet-footed lead. The pygmy was leaping and skittering effortlessly through the tangle of vines and clawing undergrowth, defying all natural laws of motion. Ras McDonald was nowhere in sight.

Reydak thought: Life everliving, Rastaman.

Still the cultists pursued them; but Reydak could hear the river's swift and inviting flow, and the sound was enough to bring on renewed hope for escape. Masisi was screaming something about transgression when a spear impacted a tree limb just centimeters from his head. The dancer shrieked like a wounded rock rabbit and disappeared into the foliage. Yronskiy and Reydak were running side by side, out of breath and assisting one another across logs and fractures in land thick with vegetation. Exhaustion hit them both and they sank to the ground together, fiddling with their weapons as if they hadn't a care in the world.

The Russian inserted a fresh banana clip into his rifle and turned a crazed grin to the American officer.

"Looks like neither of us will live to bury the other, comrade."

Some perverted sense of solace flushed the fear through Reydak, but the chanting soon drew him back to reality. The two men raised themselves and trained their automatics on the Nakañ as they came tearing through the grass and bush. Two spears caught the Russian in the chest, throwing him back against a resilient curtain of vines, which supported him like a net while the zombies had their way with him.

Reydak emptied his rifle against them, then reached for his Mamba sidearm and unloaded it into four ghouls who were stalking him like hyenas. Rounds found limbs and torsos, foreheads brailled with raised rows of cicatrization scars. All to no effect.

Vines were holding him fast now and he had nowhere to turn.

The cultists took deliberate aim, releasing their spears like competitors going for the grand prize.

And Reydak miraculously managed to dodge the volley. His eyes were opening in a kind of blank but amazed stare when he realized that his squirming had achieved a second effect, as well: The living net was weakening.

But before he knew what to think or whom to thank, he was falling—clear through the curtain, through space and time for all he knew, the Bakonjo below him like a wet dream.

6 Strange Attractors

Tedman Brady sat zazen at Shangri-la, awaiting the arrival of the shaman and the Soto zen master. The president was no closer to unraveling the details of the encounter than he had been six weeks before, but paralyzing flashbacks were becoming something of a daily occurrence—presidential work in the wake of the Horn Crisis notwithstanding.

Brady himself had supervised the renovation of the Aspen Lodge shortly after Catherine's death. The simple decor of the study—the flat white walls, tatami, and Japanese inks—carried on a look he had imparted to similar rooms at the Santa Fe ranch, the Georgia retreat, and the White House. The notion was that each room should overlook a different aspect of planetary splendor: mountain peaks under vast skies; golden beach washed by ocean waves; the earthly glory of monuments humanmade. But there was little splendor to be found in choked skies and polluted shores, and marble obelisks become terrifying to behold.

Cold Halloween light poured in through the bulletproof glass of the window wall. Outside, below a split-level redwood deck, stretched an expanse of wildflowers, zen-positioned rocks, and raked sand Shangri-la's marine sentries called "the Sandbox."

Shortly Brady's meditations were disrupted by a soft rapping on the oak door.

"They've arrived, sir," Agent Kubark announced. "Secretary Brady is accompanying them."

The president rose dextrously from his cross-legged posture on the mat. He considered assuming a regal position behind the desk, but passed on the idea of manipulating the meet. As the roshi, Ouro, and his female companion were shown in, the president caught sight of the chagrined look on his brother's face at finding him on his feet. Eli's consternation seemed to increase when Tedman stepped forward with his right hand extended.

"Mr. President, Gabriel Ouro," the roshi said while the two men were shaking hands. "And Dolores Sueño."

"I'm very happy to meet you," Brady said, taking the woman's dark and lovely hand. She signed a greeting, which the president returned with a charmed smile.

The roshi's youthful face lit up as he grinned. Brady always felt that one had to look deep into the man's glycerin-clear eyes— ever-ascending, as if on the verge of rolling up and out of view, or turning inward to fix upon their unmatched mate—to find the stillness and wisdom that guided him. The president and the zen master had been friends for a decade, meeting sometimes as often as once a week when their individual schedules permitted it. Brady had found a kindred soul in the quiet Japanese; he respected and envied the master's choice to live permanently in the realm of the spirit. And if pressed for a response, Miso-roshi, too, might have confessed to a certain envy; for Brady was a man of great secular power who had managed to make progress in both worlds—except lately, when baffling visions had begun to crowd the president's thoughts. Visions, for the roshi, were just expansive dreams, and Western man—mystical or otherwise—tended to treat them with undue reverence.

Brady noted that Gabriel Ouro radiated the same sense of implied asceticism—despite his obvious attachment to Dolores Sueño—a preoccupation with issues most people hadn't the time for.

"Our meeting presents some difficulties," Brady said when Eli, Sueño, and the roshi had excused themselves from the room.

Ouro inclined his head slightly to the right, as if monitoring another conversation just out of earshot. Brady took in the man's shoulder-length hair, dark eyes, and cat's whiskers tattoos. He wore a small leather amulet bag or medicine pouch around his neck, and a crystal peeked from beneath his shirt—in stark contrast to the red Visitor's badge clipped to the breast pocket of his white cotton jacket.

The president waved a hand dismissively. "It's nothing that can't be handled."

"Secrecy has its place," Ouro said.

"Yes, there is that. The members of my staff can't seem to agree. You fall somewhere between psychiatrist and security risk."

Ouro's expression became serious. "Tell them they have

nothing to fear from me. I leave the politics of this world in your hands. I care only about its mistreatment.''

Miso-roshi was fond of making the same claim, Brady thought.

Ouro lowered himself to a cross-legged posture on the tatami, supporting himself on his fists for a moment, before he smiled up at the president. ''May I smoke?'' he asked.

Brady nodded uncertainly as the shaman, tongue between his lips, took a large hand-rolled cigar from the inner pocket of his jacket. The roshi and other holy men Brady numbered as close friends came to mind. There seemed to be a kind of folly they were all attuned to, something they alone could share in, laugh and wink at. Brady read real power in Ouro, and decided to abandon caution, confident of being accepted.

''I've had a vision,'' he began, placing himself opposite Ouro on the mats. ''An encounter. But it's unclear—some of it, at any rate. I remember a buzzing sound, brilliant light, a group of small, dark-eyed beings. Voices and a ship of some sort. I was led to a place, shown something . . .''

Ouro puffed at the cigar and toyed with the amulet pouch at his neck. ''What were you shown?''

Brady shut his eyes and hugged himself. The cigar smoke was wafting through the room, encircling him. ''I'm awake all night. I haven't told anyone. Sometimes I can go three or four days without sleep, but I feel no fatigue. Except for the details of the vision my recall has never been so acute. It's as if I've been given second sight.'' He looked at Ouro. ''They think I should see a doctor or a shrink with a security clearance. They'd like nothing better than to find some physical abberation.''

''We are not unthinking stuff,'' Ouro said. ''To believe such is to deny our place in world.''

''Exactly,'' Brady said enthusiastically. ''But you understand why I can't discuss this with just anyone. Why I can't let this become public knowledge. 'The President's ET.' They'd crucify me.''

''It's not a public concern, is it?''

Brady thought for a moment. ''The vision seemed to be a warning and a premonition—two separate things. I need your help in controlling the aftereffects. Like it or not, there is political work to be done in the world. We're not far apart in our wishes for this planet, you and I. But priorities exist, and the shield has been one of them.''

''I can travel with you,'' Ouro said after a moment of reflection. "And perhaps I can address the demons of your landscape and learn what they want. Expect nothing more of me."

Brady began to relax. Ouro was a doctor, he now realized, projecting kindness, caring, empathy . . . And wasn't that what healing was all about? Abruptly, then, Ouro leaned forward and tapped Brady on the forehead with an index finger. The president's first reaction was to draw back, but Ouro's touch deactivated something, and he felt himself begin to drift.

"Return to that night," he could hear the shaman say, as if far removed from the lodge . . .

The shaman regarded the president peripherally, switching to a half-kneeling posture with his hands palm-down atop his thighs—a shapechanger's pose. Although hours of zazen had mitigated the vision's stranglehold, Brady's aura was all but imprisoned by mist, an infectious despair that had touched even the roshi with its evil intent. The aura's few unsullied areas were banded by heavy gray lines, leaden and weeping.

As the president's mind surrendered its memories of the encounter, Ouro began to take in the room's power. And once he had become conversant with it, he returned himself to his own power spot: a clearing in the forest the Human Beings' shaman had given him. *This place is yours*, N'ntara had told him long ago, *yours to recall*.

Ouro's palms began to drink in the coolness of an earthen floor, the warmth in a shaft of sunlight piercing the thatch. A trapezoid of golden light on the ground in front of him, the jungle beyond the doorway breathing odors and perfumed aromas into the hut. His view encompassed objects hanging from rough-hewn rafters: an open-weave basket stuffed with hourglass gourds; vines and plants, herbal helpers and allies left to dry slowly in the shade. The smoke from smoldering coals stung his nostrils, and the spirits of the vision vine forced sweat from the back of his neck and hands, his forehead and naked chest. The whispering tone within him was a chant that sang itself forth, assuming control of his tongue and facial muscles. And glimpses of the Real World were revealed—strobelike variations in his visual field, the outer world drained of essence, relinquishing its life to color an inner landscape of dreamtones and windbrushed shapes.

The shaman was tenuous now, detached and weightless.

In the lodge with Tedman Brady on that September night, with faint rustling sounds surrounding the bed, a chirping of high-pitched voices in the dark, a leak from the ceiling, drops falling to Brady's tongue. They had infiltrated the grounds some-how, slipped past dogs and devices and countless men on watch; a transparent door eased aside, a brilliant flash of temporal dis-turbance illuminating the room.

Brady was awake, paralyzed with fear, unable to call out, unable to move, locked in the grip of a power impossible to resist. As a group of squat, limpid-eyed, bipedal things in blue suits maneuvered him from the room and out across lawns and on into the woods. The light had blinded him momentarily, but through his vision's haze he could discern an aircraft of unclear design, a swirling sphere of frightful colors, humming a deaf-ening sound that coiled like thunder in his chest.

In some confining nightmare chamber now, gray-faced fig-ures with almond-shaped eyes approached and retreated, a few with sympathetic intent, while angry others positioned them-selves at intervals around him, readying instrumentality of an unearthly sort. Thoughts were exchanged: silent threats, calm-ing phrases, words to both ease and cajole. Mechanical tentacles extruded from myriad incomprehensible devices found his ori-fices and penetrated him—embarrassed and humiliated him with their unspeakable purpose.

Then a golden-robed figure appeared suddenly through a breach at the edge of Brady's vision. He wanted desperately to register his protests to it—this dream running wild in the night—afraid not of the figure, but of that breach. If only he could have held back for a moment, given himself time to think. The figure was telling him to open his eyes, to pay attention to what he was being shown.

But, enslaved to the demands of the aliens' instrumentality, he could not see.

If your faith is strong enough to contain them, the figure said, *then open your eyes*.

And again he tried, while they continued their assault upon him, slipping a hair-thin needle into the base of his skull.

Draw on the power of your faith, the angelic figure intoned, arms opened wide, heart aflame.

So Brady had prayed. And in piercing through his fear, their plan was revealed to him: their fleet of interstellar ships, their murderous weapons . . . Visions assaulted him, visions of black suns and blood moons from another man's apocalyptic night-mare. Falling figs and heaven's departure—as a scroll when it is rolled together.

They must be contained, the radiant figure warned him one final time.

And Brady was instantly transported back inside the lodge, back to the lonesome bed he and Catherine had once so lovingly shared. Agent Kubark standing over him with a concerned look, doctored black eyes peering down at him . . .

"I asked, did you see them!" the president told Ouro in a loud and panicked voice. "How could they have gotten past you!"

Brady's aura had become violently agitated—the cocoon's gray bands constricting, squeezing the life out of him. Ouro leaned forward, clasping his hands over the president's mouth to prevent any exit of life's light.

Brady's lotus collapsed suddenly, as if his skeleton had dissolved.

The roshi, Sueño, Agent Kubark, and Eli Brady rushed into the room just as Ouro was lifting the president's ashen face.

Eli saw his brother's eyes snap open. A piercing scream issued from Tedman's slack mouth:

"They must be contained! They must be contained!"

7 Thought-Experiment

Dr. Amol Woolley accepted the color-enhanced prints and thanked the monkey, receiving in return a gummy grin and side-show bow.

"Come 'ere, you little trickster," Ruby Dos said, laughing.

Obediently the capuchin snapped to, executed a neat back flip, and hurried around to Ruby's side of the laboratory work station, where it perched itself on the contoured back of her drive-chair and hid its eyes in feigned embarassment.

Ruby laughed again. "He 'sists on being a character. I think it's all the vids we watch." The monkey flicked out its tail to tickle the back of her neck. "An imp you are! Behave yourself, or mind me, no Chevy Chase for you."

Woolley couldn't help but smile. Ruby's file indicated that she and the glial-enhanced capuchin had been together for close to three years, since the train accident that had taken the life of Ruby's husband of twenty years and left her paraplegic. The monkey had been donated by CHMPS—Capuchin Help-Mates for the Physically Special.

The sound of machines busy at their tasks hummed into the silence: the dry clack of keyboard keys, the *om*-drone of buried turbines.

Woolley thought Ruby Dos remarkable; vibrant, dynamic, possessed of that same quiet power he detected in all those the Listeners sent to Lakehaven—LIAR, as the place was affectionately known, the Lakehaven Institute Accelerator Ring. The California complex had been built in the mid-eighties to facilitate the search for supersymmetries, strings, and top quarks, but the advent of heavy-ion–hurling superconductor cyclotrons had rendered the ring archaic if not obsolete, and the Whole Earth Movement had managed to pick it up for a song. Thanks to

Percival Flage, that was, Flage and his inscrutable ways with mega-finance transactions.

"Between you and me, Doctor," Ruby was saying, the monkey peering over the top of her head, "I don't know what I'd do without him."

Watching her, Woolley recalled his own years of confinement to a similar chair, limbs and vocal cords paralyzed, his very mind besieged by darkling forces. He credited Gabriel Ouro with the recovery—for the healing if not the cure.

Ruby directed a tattooed hand to the photos her helpmate had returned to Woolley. "They look like doodles—the kind of thing I do when I'm on the phone." The tattoo was a jungle cat, its spotted coat rippling as Ruby's hand flexed. She wore a Sixth Level crystal brooch on the collar of her blouse, one short of Experienced.

The physicist's perpetually pink face wrinkled up in delight. God's doodles, he was tempted to tell her, but what he said was: "Think of them as Godzilla's doodles."

"Godzilla?"

"I should explain: Godzilla is Dr. Haguchi's name for Lakehaven's accelerator ring." Woolley picked up one of the photos. "You see, these are actually photographs of subatomic events that occur inside bubble chambers like the one here at LIAR."

Behind Ruby's back, the monkey showed a perplexed look.

Woolley cleared a laugh from his throat. "A bubble chamber is essentially a vessel filled with a heavy, transparent liquid, maintained under pressure at a temperature close to its boiling point. We refer to this as a superheated state."

"Like Florida," Ruby said, trying to keep a straight face. "Or Puerto Rico."

"You're fighting me, Ruby."

"Sorry," she said sheepishly.

Woolley took a sideways glance at Ruby's onscreen evaluation file. The Listener at the Santa Monica Haven had commented on her joking nature. Her psi scores, however, were in the highest percentile. She had become seer a year ago, after a Class IV Abduction Encounter compelled her to seek out the Movement's assistance. WEM's healers had helped her find the steps and songs of power necessary to reverse some of the paralysis.

Woolley put the photo aside. "Now, as protons accelerated in the ring enter the bubble chamber, they collide with the atoms that make up the tons of liquid in Godzilla's belly and create numerous types of charged subatomic particles. Many of these are extremely short-lived—let's say about one-millionth of a second—''

"Give or take a nano."

"—but they transfer their energy as they move through the liquid," Woolley pressed on, "and the liquid begins to boil only in that region where the particles travel. Bubbles form, creating a short track capable of scattering light, and electromagnets positioned around the chamber swerve the particles to provide us information concerning charge, momentum, and so on. The lines, these Godzilla doodles, are simply stereophotographs of various interactions and collision tracks."

"Well, isn't that *spatial*," Ruby said, affecting a comical southern accent. The monkey had its paws pressed to its ears. She turned Woolley a frown. "The Listener and I talked about my close encounter—about the warnings my late husband gave me. These creatures have nefarious plans in store for us, Doctor. Aren't you interested in hearing any of that?"

"I'm very interested," Woolley said in earnest. "But these tests are equally important." He reached across the table and took a gentle hold of Ruby's soft hands. "What we're hoping to do here is discover some evidence that mind and matter interact at subatomic levels. We're searching for the underlying physical principles that govern these interactions—perhaps the very ones responsible for the self-healing your close encounter promoted. One day we might be able to do the same for others less fortunate."

"People who refuse to see the Star," Ruby mused. "You know, Dr. Woolley, it still amazes me that my friends and family can't see it—even when I point it out to them."

"You were called to power," Woolley said, using WEM's phrase. "But don't worry too much about your friends. It won't be long now." He thought back to a time a year or so ago when friends at the Radio Astronomy Observatory had labeled the Star an Einstein Ring—a focusing distortion resulting from gravitational lensing, distant radio waves warped by the pull of some invisible galaxy. But that had changed now. The earlier Pioneer 10 transmissions had given Ouro and the Movement's inner nine hope, but recent detection by the Large Baseline Array had provided Woolley with the verification he sought—proof of the Concentricity's ability *to exteriorize an event* . . .

Ruby directed a look at Woolley's withered left hand. "I know you were ill once, Dr. Woolley, that you healed yourself."

"I make no secret of it."

"So why question the workings of these things? Why not simply accept a miracle for what it is?"

Woolley's bushy white eyebrows twitched. "Some can do just that, Ruby," he confessed. "But there are those of us who need to know what makes the miracle work. Who need to calculate it in numbers, or watch it occur the way a god would. We need the big picture and the small one before we can be sure. We need to be able to repeat the event."

Ruby shook her head disapprovingly. "But what do all these doodles have to do with it? First there's Dr. Haguchi's with his 'random-event generator,' now you and this bubble-chamber business . . . I'll tell you, it doesn't seem very *scientific* to me. More like magic."

"Perhaps it is," Woolley told her. "We admit our procedures aren't in strict keeping with scientific methodology. But then we're not out to *prove* the existence of psi. You and I and Dr. Haguchi *know* it exists. And we don't have to worry about having our funds cut by people who aren't satisfied with our results. *All* results are positive to us, Ruby. Do you understand?"

Ruby's lips tightened. "I suppose."

"Besides, this test is more important than the ones Dr. Haguchi ran," Woolley emphasized, back in voice now. He held her gaze. "What we'd like you to do is bring yourself into a state of receptivity—use whatever method you prefer—and indicate on the screen the form you intuit the interactions will follow in today's collision experiments."

Ruby studied the matte-black tabletop screen, tracing her fingers around its inlaid edge. The capuchin scampered down to have a closer look, appraising its reflection in the thick glass.

"This mean I'm going to have to wear another one of those neural thingamagigs—the headband?"

"We'd prefer that you would. The headband gives us a look at what's going through your mind when you're putting your talents to work."

"Messed my hair up last time," Ruby said sullenly. "I only just had it done Wednesday."

"Ruby, it's important."

She blew out her breath and regarded the screen. "So do you mean you want me to pick one from of those photos—whichever one I think fits?"

Woolley shook his head. "No. I want you to use the lightpen to draw whatever interactions you intuit."

"But there must be an infinite variety!"

He smiled. "No one said it was going to be easy."

Ruby adopted an uncertain expression. "The one I think will occur?"

"No," Woolley said again, "the one you *want* to occur."

He leaned back from the table and ran a hand through his shock of gray hair, while Ruby and the monkey conferred. Three of Haguchi's biotechs entered to assist her into the fiber-optic rigs that would bring her on-line.

In the ring that surrounded LIAR's central cluster of buildings, protons whipped to near light speed raced toward spacetime encounters.

Conceived in liberty and dedicated to the proposition that all beings were created equal in Buddha nature, President Brady sat sunrise zazen in the Lincoln Sitting Room of the White House. But unlike upright Abraham in his memorial's marble throne, Brady sat in full lotus—left foot on his right thigh, right on his left, chakras aligned, hands forming the cosmic mudra. He was dressed in the loose-fitting trousers and black cotton jacket he had worn years earlier at the Holy Trinity Novitiate in Aquas Calientes, the ones Catherine had called his "god pajamas."

How I yearn for you, he thought. He had a fleeting glimpse of her as she was before the doctors at Bethesda had gone to work on her, hooking her up to machines, injecting her full of lethal chemicals, irradiating her—

But this was all wrong: This was remembering, when it was emptiness he sought.

The president sat facing the tall windows that overlooked the Ellipse, Constitution Avenue, and the Washington Monument, dimpled panes of eighteenth-century glass vibrating audibly in November's wind. In sympathy with his thoughts. The Shangri-la sessions with Gabriel Ouro had left him with a koan to unravel, and in true zen fashion he was working at the knot by not-trying. Nothing special. But the puzzle was an extraordinary one: The sound of one hand slapping the face one wore before one's parents were born.

When, the koan asked, *was a UFO both devil and angel?*

Brady showed the security cams a cross-eyed look, studying himself studying himself in the room's wallscreen monitor. For a soundtrack, the Service detail tucked away in their west wing command post would have the controlled rhythms of his yogic breathing.

Establishing the correlation between unidentified flying objects and otherworldly spirits was somewhat less problematic than the question posed by the koan itself. When UFOs had first appeared in the mid-fifties as dismantled vacuum cleaners and pie tins sent to Earth from oddly named planets, Air Force Intel (hoping to forestall mass hysteria even while investigating the possibility that the crafts were manned not by little green men but Reds) had responded with a now-classic bit of disinformation: UFOs, if not outright hallucinations, were either swamp gas or sundogs. The debunking attempts, however, had only served to further the cause, and cultists were soon pointing to fresh evidence culled from ancient and unassailable texts, to flaming wheels, heavenly orbs, and chariots of the gods. Rather quickly then, a new dimension was added to the UFO experience—the encounter—and the sophisticated theories needed to fit this new phenomenon came not from frightened bureaucrats but from theologians and psychologists: Close encounters, so the explanations went, were *visions*, the exteriorization of psychoidal stuff—semiotic, archetypal projections from humankind's collective unconscious—activated especially during periods of stress, social upheaval, future shock. Investigators, seizing on what they read as a positive trend, began to attribute an angelic quality to encounters—those visions of light-filled globes and robed guardians with cabalistic-sounding names— and yesterday's extraterrestrial had suddenly become today's archangel.

In the late seventies, however, the angels threw Earth a curve, and almost overnight the visitors began to reveal their dark side. In place of visionary enlightenment came reports of abductions, dispassionate examination, and in some cases forced impregnation. Widespread accounts of animal mutilation appeared at about the same time, and even more disconcerting was the fact that cases of so-called high-strangeness were rarely accessible to conscious recall; contactees, *percipients*, were apparently being brainwashed by the once-angels become treacherous aliens, and could retrieve the details of their horrible experiences only through carefully structured hypnotic sessions. How many people, then, investigators began to ask, had already been unknowingly, unwittingly contacted?

Brady had never seen the stats, but he was certain he was one of them. He even had the scar to prove it: a small inexplicable crescent on his abdomen—something multiple-contactees had in common, and a sure sign that he had been tampered with long before the incident at the Aspen Lodge, perhaps as far back as childhood.

Gabriel Ouro had brought most of the ghastly details of the encounter to the surface, like a neurosurgeon triggering the release of stored memories with precisely placed cerebral probes. And while it was undeniable that the shaman had taken some of the sting out of the encounter's aftereffects, Brady was unhappy with Ouro's assessment, for he made no distinction between visions, close encounters, and psychic episodes. To him they were all aspects of a more all-encompassing experience the Whole Earth Movement had christened the *chimera*—personal or collective "calls to power," transpsychic harbingers that signaled periods of intense inner growth, for individuals or entire cultures. A process both demanding and perilous but ultimately of incalculable reward. But whereas the members of Ouro's Amazonian tribe all shared in one mythic reality, humankind in the modern world lacked integration; hence the diverse forms the *chimera* could assume.

Brady just couldn't buy it. Ouro, after all, hadn't lived the experience, only *relived* it through his mind. And Tedman Brady knew a premonition when he experienced one. The vision was *His* warning—Christ's warning—that hostile forces were plotting Earth's destruction.

Ouro had tried to convince him that Christ's appearance was the result of a commingling of personal and collective mythic elements. But through the years Brady's efforts at establishing one-to-one contact with the godhead had been far too arduous and heartfelt to fall to such a facile explanation. And yet, how to properly interpret it: Was Christ on Earth's side—Earth's personal guardian and ally—or was He just on the side of Tedman Brady? Whichever, the revelations had at the very least laid to rest his continuing doubts concerning the Horn Crisis. His commitment of America's men and women to the front had been fully justified. Brought to the brink of nuclear exchange, the world had learned an important lesson. Now, Brady thought, to convince everyone that life under the Bomb, under sword or shield, had simply been a rehearsal for a confrontation with an even more terrible evil. The Horn Crisis had provided the fear that brought unification; now that unification would have to be tempered to assure victory.

Not all of the road ahead was clear, and he still knew moments of dark contemplation—horrific visions of black futures he would somehow have a hand in fashioning—but his faith had been restored. Though it seemed sometimes as if the polar twins of goodness and evil were vying for his personal attention, beckoning him down one path or another . . .

The president took a deep cleansing breath, rubbed his hands vigorously, and cupped them over his eyes. He had chosen the Sitting Room in the hope that Lincoln's lingering presence might assist him in curtailing the angelic/demonic alternations that had overshadowed all his recent zazen sessions. But the anxiety remained, even throughout the nine bows meant to rid him of dualistic ideas. He had paid his respect, but had not been able to enter Big Mind or solve the koan, not yet become one with the Buddha-Christ.

The White House was uncommonly active that morning as he made his way to the Cabinet Room for a presidential checklist briefing, agents Kubark and Fusilli in tow. Twice the usual number of Marines, military social aides, and Secret Service personnel were hustling about, and already the press secretary and protocol director were pushing memos at him. Lance Underwood, the House's gay decorator, had a pressing question about window treatments for the upstairs study; he was thrilled by the changes Brady had already made and sought out every opportunity to rid the mansion of its brooding period pieces. Elsewhere, Alison Brady, "First Mother" Alison, was supervising the setup of a luncheon she was hosting for a hermaphroditic alliance opposed to new guidelines placed on surrogate parenting. Autumn's incandescent skies and chilled air had enlivened everyone to the point of frenzy.

The same seemed true of his advisors at the overnight developments briefing, who were jockeying for post position like a gang of anxious trotters. The room was filled with the smell if not the smoke of Premier cigarettes. Philbert Base was questioning foreign affairs advisor Duke Cottel's evaluation of the stance the Soviets and Islamic Front would assume at the summit. Colton, the DCI, and Obstat of the NSA had to be reading from different fact sheets. Silvia Glitch, the newly appointed secretary of science, was trying to introduce a position paper concerning military use of the proposed orbital solar collectors. And in the midst of it all, arms crossed in a gesture of defense and defiance, sat five-star General Conus McVee, chairman of the Joint Chiefs.

Noticeably absent from the discussion—conspicuous in their

absence—were the Shangri-la revelations. The president's hidden agenda.

Brady pushed the *PICKLE* sheet aside and phased out of the in-progress discussions to isolate McVee from the background din—a relatively easy task given that McVee stood nearly seven feet tall. Of course, it took someone McVee's size to bear up under the weight of the medals and battle ribbons that adorned his uniform. The man's head alone obscured two of the room's trio of side-by-side monitors. The scowl hadn't been there five years before when Brady had first met him, but had become something of a permanent fixture since the Peruvian debacle that ushered out the previous administration. After a long moment, the general seemed to sense the intensity of Brady's scrutiny, and gave all appearances of awakening from some conquering-hero daydream.

"Sir?" he said loudly, meeting the president's eyes, as everyone looked up from their display screens and discussion broke off midsentence around the mahogany table.

Brady congratulated himself on being sharp this morning, in telepathic rapport, a result of making some of the vision's power his own. "I asked what our contingencies were for outer space assaults?"

Out of the corner of his eye he caught the recording secretary's puzzled expression. She had one hand pressed to her headset, presumably checking her onscreen notes with playback from the recording devices.

"Mr. President," Eli said, hesitantly coming to his feet. "I'm sorry, but . . . I don't think we heard you the first time." Colton, Base, Niles Obstat, and Jose Darpa wore equally concerned looks. Only McVee's ears had pricked up.

"What are our contingencies for outer space assaults?" the president repeated, allowing a note of impatience to creep in.

Eli's eyes swept the table. "Mr. Obstat, perhaps you'd care to—"

"That's actually National Recon's concern, Mr. Secretary," the NSA director was quick to say.

Milo Colton threw Obstat an angry look. "As I'm, uh, sure the president is aware, our Boost Surveillance System monitors everything in orbit and down below. In the event of a launch, or even a release simulation, Wimex or the EWS—"

Brady held up his hands. "I don't want to hear all that alphabet soup, Mr. Colton. Don't any of us speak the same language anymore? I'm talking about attacks from *outside* our surveillance field.''

"Outside, sir," the DCI said uneasily. "I'm not sure I follow you . . . Perhaps the president is referring to NORAD's Space Control Center or the Shield Monitoring Facility?"

"Well, I follow the president." General McVee's voice boomed out. "You mean, sir, an attack from outside our planetary perimeter. From the Soviets' La Grange platform, for example."

Philbert Base shot to his feet. "I'm certain that's not what the president had in mind, General." An implied *please* was evident in his tone.

"That's precisely what I had in mind, Phil. And will all of you quit referring to me in the third person. We've been over this more times than I can count." Brady nodded to McVee. "Now what about it, General? Do our satellites have the capability to look both ways?"

"No, Mr. President, they don't," Silvia Glitch said when McVee hesitated. "There is, however, sir, NASA's orbital scope and the large array planned for—"

"You mean to tell me that your black yonderboys in the shield surveillance stations can only look *down*, General?"

McVee tugged at the sleeves of his jacket, as if attempting to cover his hands. "With your permission, sir, I've been pressing the Defense Science Board—"

"May I ask what prompts the president's, uh, your concern, Mr. President?" the chief of staff asked. "If there's some indication . . ."

Brady fixed Base with a silencing stare and returned his attention to McVee. "General, didn't one of my predecessors commission a study on scenarios for possible responses to extraterrestrial attack?"

"Yes, sir, I believe you're right. We called it WANT-ADZE—Warfare Alternatives and Negotiations, Advanced Deployment Zones. Had some help from the people at SETI. Dealt with extraterrestrial sneak attacks and problems that might arise if the creatures weren't conversant with earth tongues."

Silvia Glitch tried unsuccessfully to check a laugh. "I'm sorry, Mr. President, it's just that, well, verbal communication could prove the least of our worries in a confrontation of this sort. Ignorance of Terran languages might only be the beginning of it. Perhaps these extraterrestrial biological entities wouldn't even utilize language the way we understand it."

"You're suggesting the EBEs might be telepathic?" the president asked.

"That's possible, sir. Of course—"

"Then all our codes, our entire system of encryption would be worthless."

"Yes, sir, but—"

Brady waved a hand to silence her. "I suggest we dust off this WANT-ADZE study, people. Just because we've managed to launch a ring of satellites and relay mirrors around this planet doesn't necessarily guarantee our safety from eccentric assaults. Particularly from these advanced deployment zones." The president looked to Niles Obstat, Milo Colton, and McVee. "Put your heads together on this one, and assume the worst: The enemy can read our minds; their strategic forces are superior to our own; and their attack will be launched from out of the blue—perhaps we won't even be able to see them until the last moment."

"You are talking about *outer* space, Mr. President?" Eli said quietly.

Brady closed the folders piled in front of him on the table. His staff—while confused—followed suit, recognizing the signal for adjournment.

"That's correct, Eli," the president said at last. "Outer space."

8 The Center of the Cyclone

With Tedman Brady recalled to Washington and matters of state, Ouro had little recourse but to return to the Annapolis Haven and await the inevitable crisis that would summon him back to Shangri-la. Fearing the worst, the shaman had canceled all upcoming personal appearances and requested WEM's inner circle of Listeners—the Concentricity—to rendezvous with him at the mansion on the bay.

Until then there was painting work to complete in the upstairs den, the shaman and his dark mistress signing while they worked, frustrating the efforts of the FBI surveillance team parked beyond the tall hedges that bordered the Haven's sweeping front lawn.

Ouro observed the motion of the clouds as he fine-sanded the window mullions; observed the shadows oaks and elms cast on the lawn. He noted the way the red enamel adhered to the fluted trim, the curl and overlaps of brush marks left by his strokes. All the elements that comprised the world, all things and forces and states of being, were interrelated. Each object and action contained an intrinsic knowledge of the whole; and this knowledge was there to read and apply to seemingly unrelated situations.

He had cautioned the president not to make too much of the temporary exorcism their brief sessions had effected, but Brady had refused to listen. Nor was he ready to accept the notion of the *chimera*. This wasn't unusual—people were slow to change and accept responsibility for their lives—but beneath the president's reluctance, Ouro had discovered a more troubling complication: Brady, like Miso-roshi, was passive in his quest for wholeness. Though he professed to seek ecstasy, in truth he sought escape, a way to resign from the world. It was a curious contradiction to encounter in a man of power, but present none-theless. And while there were methods for opening a fledgling's eyes to the Real World, even these would prove ineffectual as long as Brady continued to focus on the particulars of his vision and refused to embrace it as a call to power. Ouro had once confronted the same reluctance in himself, but the Human Beings had successfully altered his vision. The Concentricity had sustained him since.

The nine who made up WEM's inner circle were a power ring long before Wiles ParaResearch had financed Ouro's first visit to the States. Each had been called to power—by XTs, demons, and spirits, in sensory dep tanks and Goodwill collection boxes, at Ouija boards and solstice ceremonies in circles of standing stones—and each had glimpsed Earth's destruction and been transformed.

Endtime was their term for the final days; and although there were dozens of other names for it—Judgment Day, Two Minutes to Midnight, the Night of the Beasts—catastrophe was the common theme: Earth turned upside down. The notion of the *chimera* experience was theirs, as well—the Concentricity's unified field theory of the inexplicable, their attempt to gather all spiritual ills and transpsychic events under one roof and lay the blame to premillennial panic.

The nine had been drawn to reports of Ouro's miracle-working, but it was his jungle-bred planet-centered approach that earned him their allegiance. Premillennial *chimeras* were the Endtime nightmares of a tortured world, he had told them. And no one at the time cared whether his powers had been birthed in the heart of the Amazonian rain forest or in the basement lab of some third-world university. Ouro was the culture hero the movement needed: charismatic but genuine, powerful but accessible—an American original.

He had introduced the idea of the Blue Star shortly after the brujos, curanderos, and sabias of the Twantisuyu Confederation had crowned him the "Long-Awaited Brother." Simply preaching about Endtime wasn't enough, Ouro argued, when the goal was not merely to survive catastrophe but to *prevent* one from taking place. And what that required was a symbol upon which the movement could forge the psychic shield it proposed to deploy—the introduction of a wrathful, mythic element into the prevailing belief system that would entice followers to align themselves with the cause. If UFOs were nothing more than unconscious projections, think, he had challenged them, what could be done with a *conscious* projection like the Blue Star.

The Star was already known among the Hopi, who called it Saquasohuh, but WEM adopted it as its own. Ends justifying the means, the Concentricity got things started by fixing their gaze on a piece of sky off in the direction of the constellation Pisces, and the movement had taken over from there, the Centers turning out seers who were more than willing to admit a transforming presence to the celestial paradigm. No matter that it was mass hysteria in the beginning; the nine never doubted that people would begin to *see* the thing eventually—that once the *idea* of star took hold there really would be something to point to, a grand illusion they could all share. But even they hadn't figured on the star's making a personal appearance; when it revealed itself the nine were forced to reevaluate their position: Something *was* in fact on its way.

Thus convinced that a number of historical, zodiacal, and occult cycles were culminating as the end of the twentieth century approached, the Concentricity took it upon itself to function as Earth's intelligence network to the Whole Earth Movement's planetary government and constituency, ferreting out instances of evil design and manipulation in any number of paranormal theaters. Their in-depth interviews with the world's future-shocked were simply a means to gather information about the planet's unseen, perhaps otherworldly opponents: to appraise their strength, decrypt their coded transmissions, turn their agents, and funnel power and research money to enclaves of resistance fighters.

And if Ouro was already their uncontested leader when Pioneer 10 radioed home the first of its Blue Star transmissions, he was their messiah afterward.

Dr. Amol Woolley and his team of Era III renegades at LIAR believed the Concentricity had somehow *created* the Star, actually brought it into being; while others in the movement suspected that Ouro's precognitive abilities had enabled him to predict its Endtime arrival. In either case the Star's emergence suggested the possibility that WEM, given enough collective power, could *rethink the world*. It was only a question of continued enrollment, a unification of planetary consciousness before time ran out.

And here was Ouro bringing word of the president's close encounter . . .

* * *

The shaman, Sueño, and the nine convened in a secure, windowless room on the second floor of the Annapolis Haven's east wing. Listening devices planted on the grounds and inside the house by the FBI had been easily detected by the Haven's security personnel, but Ouro had given instructions for them to be left in place. He had no intentions of breaching national security, and wanted nothing more than to give Brady's people ample reason to trust him. A proviso in the security contract—initialed by Eli Brady—stated that while certain topics had to be considered off-limits for outside discussion, Ouro was free to consult with his "advisors" if it was deemed essential to the president's health and psychological well-being. The east wing free-talk zone was a denied area even to the movement's own internal security teams.

The house itself was an eighteenth-century Georgian mansion, with pedimented windows, corner quoins, and a roof balustrade that overlooked the Severn River. It had been donated to the movement some years back by Terrine Contra, chairperson for the nation's largest wishnet organization, cofounder of the Concentricity, and one of the movement's most gifted Listeners. From Lemuria by way of Lodi, New Jersey, Contra was channel and amanuensis for a discorporate entity named OObe, a self-described Akashic chronicler, who, through Contra, had dictated the spiritual history of the planet as recorded in the *Volumes of Light*, I–XXII.

"But this is incredible," Terrine Contra was saying. "With the president behind us we'll have all the help we need!" She was a large woman, with bright, expressive eyes and abundant energy. For dress, she favored robelike garments, and was seldom seen without an entourage of followers. Contra had spoken at the recent Newark Dome Convergence. "An alliance with Brady could prepare the way for all of us."

Some at the round table concurred—Susan Vide, Hiawatha Fountain, Leigh Burmandy—but Ouro shook his head. "He is like a river swollen by unexpected rains. We must wait for the waters to subside."

Terri hated when he spoke in parables. "But he's the walk-in we've dreamed of," she pressed. "We have to find some way to leak the news to the press. I could call my friends at the *Post*. Or we could sick Flage on this."

Amber Swift disagreed. "We need a willing operative, not some sleeper awakened by the other side. President Brady's progressed chart shows nothing but opposition and quincunx."

Known in some circles as Ama, she was tall, dark, and shapely, an astrologer to the wealthy and well placed.

"Nonsense," Contra said. "We've failed time and time again to recruit politicians. Washington remains the most unsuccessful of our theater operations, and now you'd throw away the opportunity." Her eyes sought Ouro's. "We've all agreed to do whatever it takes to reverse the tide, haven't we? How much time do we have before the planet rolls over and dies—fifty years, twenty years?"

No one answered.

"Besides, we're going to go broke if we don't increase our membership. The Centers just aren't taking in enough, and Dr. Woolley is being positively spendthrift on Inaccessible. Soon there won't be even enough money to found a new chapter let alone a Center, and I'm getting nothing but complaints from Experienced members who are waiting for the go-ahead to open workshops. One word of endorsement from the president and our worries are over. Not to mention what his recruitment will mean to all of us in the long run."

"He's unwilling to accept the *chimera*," Ouro explained, pulling his long hair into a hand-held ponytail. "He prolongs the event in an attempt to have it suit his purpose. I couldn't reach deep enough to pry it loose from his grip."

Dolores Sueño watched Sue Vide's hands sign a translation, then laid a hand on Ouro's paint-speckled own.

"What about the encounter?" Ray Mayana asked. "Can we learn anything from it?" UFOlogist, former member of the MJ-12 Organization, and talk-show personality, Mayana had written a series of nonfiction fictions based on his single contactee experience. He, too, had addressed the multitudes in Newark.

"An abduction," Ouro said. "Blue suits, gray skins, an angelic being . . . Earth imperiled but forewarned."

Mayana nodded sagely. "Another cameo appearance by Christ. More and more of this lately."

"Another reason to push for recruitment," Contra said. "We don't know that the transformation won't entail physical confrontation of some sort. The president could be the redundancy our shield requires."

"All these editorials about the president's references to god," Melva Chizedek offered, a flaxen-haired child nursing at her breast. "So there's something to them after all."

"The *chimera* has gripped him since early September," Ouro

told the blond former priest, now wicca-worker and crystal-dripper. "Before the crisis in East Africa."

"I've always suspected that Brady was a player," Florence States said from the opposite end of the table. "He just doesn't know it yet." She was the oldest of the nine, and the one most closely attuned to Ouro's shamanic techniques of ecstasy. A psychic surgeon, her search for the miraculous had taken her around the world. "Has he mentioned the Star?"

Ouro folded his arms. "He's not yet a seer. The vision and the events of this past month conspire within him like a dark, impenetrable cloud." He sensed Contra's question and spoke to it. "Of course I could intervene—like a doctor treating symptoms. But Brady has grown dangerously uncentered since his wife's death, and the healing is his alone to perform. If I can't lead him to accept the truth, he'll fall prey to the *chimera*'s demands."

"And do what?" Leigh Burmandy wanted to know.

"Disease is inevitable. Death, if the *chimera* demands it."

"My god." Florence States gasped. "There must be something we can do to help him?"

"Not unless he asks for our help. It will be only a matter of weeks, days perhaps, until the vision reasserts itself. In the meantime we can keep this to ourselves and demonstrate to Brady's advisors that we mean no harm."

"You're right," Contra said, sighing to concede the point. "Although I can't say I enjoy having their sick-think vans parked out front."

Amber uttered a short laugh. "It's not the first time they've been there, Terri."

OObe's channel frowned. "Just the same . . . And I know I sound cold-blooded, but I think we should at least figure out what we're going to charge. Perhaps we can cut some sort of deal with the FDA, or secure tax-exempt status with the IRS." She turned to Ouro. "Do you expect Brady's people to notify you if he suffers a follow-up episode?"

Ouro's familiars probed the imminent. "They will notify me. But I won't need to hear from them to know it."

Eli and Philbert Base had gone directly to Loren Masters after the overnight developments briefing; but the White House physician wasn't nearly as put off by Ted's decision to exhume WANT-ADZE as the president's brother and chief of staff were. In fact, Masters had tried to assure them the proposal might even have a therapeutic effect, especially if Boost Surveillance's recon sats and the planet's own earthbound scopes and dishes could prove to Ted there was nothing out there to fear. Masters not only backed the idea, but planned to encourage it.

Later that same day, the three men were gathered round autumn's first fire in the Oval Sitting Room. Alison Brady—known to the Service detail as ''Mother Superior''—was reclining on one of the House's few remaining overstuffed couches, her edematous legs elevated on embroidered cushions. The president had slipped off to the Lincoln Room to fit in a few minutes of meditation before a scheduled cabinet meeting.

''It's not enough these hermaphroditic alliance people have the best of both worlds,'' Alison was saying, ''they want the right to surrogate children besides. Now I ask you, boys, is this country fucked or what?''

''Please, Mom,'' Eli said from the fire. The medication Mallory prescribed for the edema never failed to leave her more feisty than usual.

''Oh, sorry to offend you, Eli. I guess you never used cuss words at Annapolis, huh? Or in one of your little underwater boats.'' She laughed, winced, and cast a serious look in Mallory's direction. ''So what's going on with my second, Loren? Another religious crisis, or is it one of those midlife things?''

''Mom, just cut it out, will you?''

''Must be religious,'' Alison said. ''I mean, somehow I just can't see Teddy worrying about prowess or anything. God knows he barely uses what nature gave him. Why, the things Catherine used to tell me—''

''That's enough!'' Eli said, brandishing a poker.

Alison eyeballed the iron and snorted. ''What, 's everybody been taken over by aliens? It's that damn witchdoctor's what it is. Must be costing us a pretty penny in black-bag funds to keep this one under wraps.'' She turned to the chief of staff. ''What about it, Phil, you okay with Teddy's headshrinker?''

Base ran a hand over his mouth. ''I don't know what Ted's going through, Alison, but I'm sure he'll work it out in his own way.''

Alison looked down her nose at him. ''Always the politician, Phil. And is that your medical opinion, as well, Loren? That Teddy'll work things out in his own way? Yesterday he asked me if I could remember how he got some stupid little scar on his belly. He near to orgasmed when I told him I couldn't.''

Eli and Base looked at Masters. "What's this all about?" Eli said.

The physician made an offhand gesture. "Nothing to worry about."

Alison glowered at him. "Loren."

Masters tried to calculate how much time remained before the trank she'd downed with her lemon grass tea would take hold. He knew defending Ted was going to result in Alison's accusing him of malpractice; at the same time, expressing his real feelings would only give her cause to berate him for not showing a stronger hand. He'd taken the former course with Eli and Phil earlier on, soft-pedaling some of his growing concern, but Alison wasn't as easy to fool.

"It's all in the encounter literature. In cases of high-strangeness, people tend to blame aliens for every strange scar, every unrecalled event, every missing moment in their lives."

"So this Indian's going to tell Teddy how he hurt himself?"

"Ouro's a specialist in treating right-hemisphere deviations," Masters said, hoping to dazzle her. "The right is the seat of nonverbal perception, and the whole right-lobe experience is of such archaic origin, of such bizarre design, that the mechanisms of translation overload. As a consequence, the left simply cannot find words to express what the right has experienced." Masters risked a glance at Alison and was relieved to find an attentive look.

"It's at this point that compensation comes into play," he went on. "The brain attempts to eliminate the threat, or at least render the experience palatable by reaching into the mind for something upon which to hinge the unknown quantity. In this way psychological makeup determines whether one sees UFOs, saints, virgins, or devils. Ted's always been a believer in extra-terrestrial life, and he's also predisposed to apocalyptic thinking. As for Ouro, Ted's choice couldn't have been more sound. It takes someone with nonordinary abilities to get into all this right-lobe confusion and straighten things out . . ."

Alison's eyes were closed. Masters had begun to draw a breath, when she yawned, stretched, and inclined her head to regard him through half-drawn lids.

"Doctor," she slurred, "that is far and away the biggest load of bullshit I've heard you drop in one place. You're all sounding like Wholist converts. Dammit, Eli, you used to nail that little peckerhead's ass to the hacienda wall when he stepped out of line. Can't you shake some sense into him?"

Eli had moved to the bar. "Until someone can show me that Ted's acting irresponsibly, I don't intend to do anything more than keep lines of communication open. If Ted says he met an alien, then he did. Maybe he even spent the weekend on Jupiter. But that has no bearing unless there's just cause—'a hiatus from normalcy,' am I right?"

Philbert Base muttered agreement.

Eli turned to Alison. "Christ, Dad would have applauded the strength Ted showed during the Horn Crisis."

"Eli," Alison said slowly, "your father used to say that people who claimed to have religion were as dangerous as commies. They'd push the button in God's name and say the world would be better for it."

Eli laughed bitterly. "Right. He wanted a man with a *rational* mind to push the button."

"Okay, so Jed was the biggest peckerhead of the lot. But I'm telling you, Eli, your baby brother is *not* acting responsibly. I'm worried, son, and I don't care what any of you say." Alison's voice broke. "That little peckerhead's going to put us in a war to end all."

9 Left-Handed Thinking

The problem was in the measuring, Amol Woolley told himself as he studied Ruby Dos' test results—enhanced schematics full of curlicues and Aries glyphs, impressionistic renderings of seagulls in flight. The evidence was there, on screen and stored away in databanks, only LIAR's detection systems couldn't *see* it. Woolley let his breath whistle out. All the more reason to force Percival Flage's hand on Inaccessible; it was imperative the island facility be completed if the test results were ever to yield up their secrets.

The astrophysicist's eyes were fixed on the laptop's screen while he sampled a bowl of Quark Soup in Lakehaven's rooftop commissary—the soup de jour (in several flavors) from a kitchen staff forever concocting "GUT-wrenching uncertainties" for the menu: Heisenburgers, Aunty Proton's Midnight Surprise, Meson Pie à la mode or with QUIPped cream. A couple of Kiri Haguchi's biotechs dressed in virtual helmets and sensor-studded gloves were huddled in a corner arguing with LIAR's neural net over some issue concerning the morning's particle lottery. Lakehaven's resident genomist himself was certainly off somewhere toying with his Toyota Power Pod.

Woolley realized that he was too preoccupied to eat and pushed the tray aside. He pulled the computer toward him, positioning the portable's photovoltaic grid in a tablecloth square of California sunshine. Several of Ruby's precognitive hunches fell within the parameters dictated by LIAR's neural network, but none of her "manifest diagrams"—as Haguchi liked to call them—revealed the presence of force-carrying particles that may have shaped the collision event. Mindons, psicons, fourth-generation lepto-quark hybrids . . . Woolley was ready to call them whatever they answered to. But time after time the tests failed to summon them from their twilight zones of quantum concealment. The same had been true when Woolley put the nine to the test—a group of like minds: Subatomic events had sometimes obeyed the Concentricity's dictates, but the physical evidence of their intrusion, their *shaping*, remained elusive.

The search had commenced in earnest when Ouro's Blue Star had appeared in Pisces. Even if the event was simply a case of prescience, Woolley told himself then, it confirmed that Ouro had somehow drawn knowledge from the future, that he had access to or was himself a kind of superluminal receiving device. But Woolley was more inclined to believe that Ouro had precipitated the event; that the shaman was functioning on some level of self-organizing reality, on an *information* level of the universe where matter and energy surrendered the upper hand to consciousness itself. Woolley had to ask himself whether the subatomic particles he'd spent a lifetime researching hadn't in some similar fashion been *thought* into being by the consensus reality of the paradigm.

Creation myths recorded in Ouro's writings about the Human Beings—the tribe he had either been born into or adopted by— were remarkably similar to the theories of contemporary astrophysics. The universe was said to have been a vast knot that the Infinite Creator had untied, allowing the finite to unwind. It contained pouches and hollows where alternate realities could take shape. And like all things in nature, it knew phases of expansion and contraction, and was bound to retangle itself at the end of each world age. But the Infinite Creator had allowed humankind's massmind to determine the face of the world, just as an individual's thoughts at the moment of death were believed to organize the structure of the afterlife.

The thinking was decidedly retro—a return to the human-centered beliefs most thought science had laid to rest with Copernicus—but what were quantum theory and uncertainty if not science's response to the millennium? The eigenstates of a consensus or probabilistic reality, a meaning-sensitive universe in which consciousness was the software, a plastic deity that was not omniscient but grew with time or perhaps played roulette with the world . . . Woolley had himself been a contributor to the emerging paradigm. And deep down he believed that life evolved in punctuated bursts, and that humankind's observations actually did shape what were perceived as physical laws; but the mechanic in him demanded more in the way of proof than a mere catalog of the mind-boggling odds and coincidences normally evinced to shore up theories of life's miraculous origins. Woolley was after *observable* proof—proof of mind's interactions with matter in the microcosm. Proof analagous to the Blue Star's confirmation by the Large Baseline Array. He was willing to accept that he might never discern a pattern to it all, that in the end Chaos would rule, but he yearned to see the mindstuff dance of those virtual psicons before he died.

And what it came down to was measuring devices and observer systems. Ouro, the nine, and a few of the movement's more gifted recruits like Ruby Dos were capable of interfacing with the quantum. But what was Woolley to ask the Concentricity to do with Godzilla: fill its bubble chamber with some new-flavored quark, line up mesons for inspection, rustle up some of that plasma? LIAR had been built to detect the inclinations and propensities in matter, not mind. And that was where Inaccessible came in.

Woolley switched off the laptop and smiled in spite of himself. Here he was chasing figments of imagination when most of his contemporaries were at work on railguns, eximer, and X-ray lasers.

He slid the computer aside with his good hand to make room for the vid-phone and entered Flage's vanity number. The power broker's prerecorded response ran a moment later: a short loop put together by the F/X wizards at Cosmic Amusements, Inc., featuring a smiling Flage emerging unscathed from a nuclear blast cloud with the cheery greeting: "I'm back . . ."

Woolley announced himself and waited for Flage's deceptively youthful and fashionably pale face to appear onscreen. "How are you, Percy?" he asked when it did, centering himself for the phone's camera lens.

"Ultra, Doc," Flage said, pinning a smile on it. "How could I otherwise?"

"I'm glad to hear it, Percy," Woolley said.

WEM's rarely silent partner had just finished serving six months of house arrest for a computer felony; and while he hadn't actually been found guilty of introducing the virus into a competitor's system, there had been enough circumstantial evidence to convict him on a lesser charge. Not that a half-year stretch in Flage's LA home was much in the way of a deterrent or a punishment, Woolley thought. The house once belonged to a magazine publisher who had turned it into a rest stop for models and starlets, many of whom had stayed on as furniture when the place changed hands. There were indoor swimming pools and game rooms, a basketball court, brain spa, and a gallery of radioactive-fingerprinted art. Flage had conducted most of his business from the house even before the sentencing. Still, the confinement had sentenced him to miss out on film premieres and restaurant openings, sports events and galas, awards ceremonies and impromptu excursions to the Seychelles or the Maldives.

Flage was by one of the pools, now, sporting shades in the tinted light from sun-tubes that lined the room's redwood ceiling, a gaggle of perfect bodies splashing about in the aquamarine hourglass behind him. His shirt read: *As long as we're making money* . . .

"So what's on the menu, Doc?"

"Inaccessible," Woolley said, adhering to Flage's dictim of coming directly to the point.

The Hollywood smile faltered some. "Doc, Doc," Flage said. "Inaccessible, Inaccessible, that's all you're entering lately."

"It's important, Percy. We'd like it operational by the first of the year."

"By the first? Of this year? Jesus, Doc, give me a chance to punch help here. I mean, this isn't off-the-shelf stock you people are ordering. These fiber-optic rigs, the gallium arsenide collectors, the yttrium composites . . . gold-plated mylar alone goes one hundred large *per* sheet, Doc—*per sheet*. Besides, the crew's already working Zulu time, and I'm paying off left and right just to confirm backgrounds and keep doctored spooks off the island. I've got my hands full down there."

"And you're doing an excellent job. But we need to intensify our efforts. Use your influence."

"Use my influence," he muttered. "That's valid, Doc, really it is. You think I've been sitting on my butt just 'cause they've had me locked up in here? I'm enabled, Doc, you can buy it. But as for my influence . . . Influence works best in ingot form." Flage rubbed his fingers together. *"Verdad?"*

"I'll see that whatever you need is transferred," Woolley said, "if you can give me some assurances."

The smile returned and then some. "What d'ya take me for—recombinant? It's not there, Doc, the well's dried up. You're taking in a little at the live shows, and some of the Centers are turning a profit, but you can't carry this thing on promises."

Woolley's mouth tightened. "Just help us along on this one, Percy. You'll be paid."

Flage showed his palms. "Hey, who am I always here for?" He leaned offscreen for a moment and returned with a tall, frosted drink in hand. "You know what I've been asking for, Doc, and it's not a major prompt, all things considered. Just a few predictions on the market, the Super Bowl, whatever, and I'll keep you people floating for as long as you need. You tell Gabe that: a few choice tips for Percy and I'm yours to keep."

"I promise I'll see what I can do," Woolley said quietly.

"Then we're nominal, 'cause that's all I ask. Now, do you have the updates on those parts lists ready?"

Woolley pulled the laptop toward him. "Is your modem on-line?"

"Click, bang, what a hang," Flage sang, doing input off-screen. "Scrambled and set to receive."

Woolley jacked the computer into the phone and coded the order list. By New Year's Day, he said to himself, finding some irony in the thought.

"Sit down, cowboy," Enoch Keyes said to Reydak after the two men had exchanged salutes and a back-patting *abrazo*. "It's good to have you back."

"Good to be back," Reydak told him, in jacket and tie for the occasion. He pulled a chair up to the director's desk and laid the alloy cane across his knees. *Good to be anywhere*, he thought.

Keyes eyed the cane as he settled himself across the desk. "So how are you feeling?"

"It'll be awhile before I two-step."

The plunge through the vines had delivered him relatively unharmed into the Bankonjo River, save for a wound in his right thigh where one of the Nakañ's spears had grazed him. The current delivered him to a small settlement north of the bridge, and some Bantu-speaking tribesmen there helped get him to the regional headquarters at Masaka. The COS in Nairobi, already apprised of the Fort Portal massacre, had given him up for dead; so the Operational Immediate orders that recalled Reydak to Washington had to be fished from a closed file. The Nakañ had cut the heads from the bodies of Highway, Eusi, and the Russian, and put them on display in front of the Mambasa police barracks. There was no word on Masisi or Ras McDonald.

He had been flown to the States in a Company high-flying hypersonic air-breather and spent three days in Walter Reed, where his leg wound was attended to while the Africa Division chief debriefed him.

Sitting in the SIG director's office now, Reydak realized that his six-month tour, scarcely two weeks behind him, already seemed like a half-remembered dream. He had tried to keep from thinking too much about the gruesome deaths of his Ground-truth teammates, letting culture shock deal with some of it, the soporific effects of television the rest. But, bottom line, it took two nights with Waxie to clear out the lingering horrors. His part-time user-friendly lover and investment counselor, she was a lingerie mannequin and exotic dancer who worked the topless bars on Ninth Street and gave peerless input.

Keyes was appraising him. ''I've seen your afteraction report . . .''

Reydak let the inference hang. ''I entered it like I saw it, sir. We must've put five hundred rounds into them.''

''I'm not doubting you, Karel. I read the follow-ups on the Fort Portal attack.'' Keyes returned to a conversational tone. ''Look on the bright side: You're the only one in Washington with a tan. We haven't seen the sun in five months.''

''Yeah, I'm the luckiest guy in the world.''

''And the spear wound makes you another first. The list just keeps right on growing, doesn't it?''

Reydak responded with a shrug.

Keyes gestured to the file a SIG runner had delivered to Reydak on his final day in Walter Reed. Designated O/RING, the dossier had an EXDIS legend and index sheet. ''Comments?''

Reydak glanced at the room's security camera.

''Off the record,'' Keyes said, one hand under the desk. ''We're in real time.''

''Only that I figure it's got to be the liberals who are calling the president's behavior 'erratic'—close encounter or not. The Pentagon's been urging a show of force for months.''

''Sure,'' Keyes said. ''The generals are elated. They even thought we'd doctored him to bring him around.''

''Without the Oversight Committee's permission? Not a chance.''

Keyes flashed a grin. ''But what about the encounter, Karel?''

''It scans like standard stuff, but that doesn't mean Ouro or some of this inner circle couldn't have *thrown* the thing. Granted, Brady'd be a choice catch, but maybe that's as far as it goes. They don't want his mind, just his support. Ouro.'' Reydak sniggered, shaking his head. He had first learned of the shaman five years before in Peru, where he had a huge following among the Quechua-speaking highlanders. ''Sure, why the hell not? The president'll get himself tattooed and dance for the House. One more war and we'll all be living in the stone age anyway.''

Keyes tugged at the knot in his tie. "Phil Base doesn't agree; he's convinced WEM is calling the shots. Hard to say where Eli Brady stands, except squarely behind his brother. But it's this inner circle we're interested in," he added, stroking his smooth chin. "We've been trying to recruit several of those people for quite some time now. Of course, Colton had to be circumspect about what we knew, especially with O'Denvy."

"Then you do have an operative in place?"

"Had." Keyes paused. "That's where you come in."

Reydak was left to consider this, while Keyes directed a few words into the intercom. A moment later a tall, gland-tailored pro entered the office, face, hair, and suit, all very up to the minute. Keyes introduced him as Dr. Franklin Cage, head of the Advanced Weapons—Experimental Division.

"From the people who brought you doctored eyes," Reydak said, accepting Cage's fish-belly hand. He knew AWED as Dirty Tricks.

"An honor, Colonel, an honor," Cage said, pumping his hand. The honorific was light; but if Reydak was below the zone, he was within the limit. "I'm a great advocate of your uncle Pavel's work. No doubt you derived your singular talents from him."

"I wouldn't know," Reydak replied. "The man died when I was just a kid."

"A brilliant mind, absolutely brilliant."

"Dr. Cage is a gland-man, Colonel—"

"Exoendocrinologist," Cage amended stiffly.

Keyes smiled lightly. "Exoendocrinologist. His team thinks they've perfected a way to get you by WEM's Listeners."

"Glandular implant," Cage began on an excited note. "Nothing complicated, we go in through your no—"

"Christ," Reydak said, whirling on Keyes, "you're talking about more *doctoring*!"

Cage made a calming gesture. "Just a temporary implant, Colonel. After all, if you're going to be fluttered by telepaths, we have to equip you with something that at least *feels* real. A vision—easily accessed by the triggering of a hypnotically introjected code. We can accomplish this by means of an organic microprocessor switch."

Reydak glowered at Cage, about to respond when Keyes waved him silent.

"We can manufacture a close encounter for you. The implant and a bit of compensatory behavior modification will concretize it for both conscious and unconscious modes. Buzzing sounds, a craftlike device that fades from sight, brilliant lights, electromagnetic distortions of local space, alien voices, temporal anomolies. The contactee experiences an immediate sense of intellectual abdication, usually as a result of early patterns of inferiority or ritual abandonment. Racial or technological impotence in the face of the vision, changes in sleep, cessation of dreams, a newfound sense of mission . . . We can give you all of these.''

Reydak assumed that Cage was not briefed on the president's UFO, so he put down an impulse to size up Tedman Brady's behavior against the doctor's stereotype. "I'm the luckiest guy in the world," he said to Cage. One look at Enoch Keyes told him it wouldn't do much good to cry foul again.

"We'll have to mask the tan, of course," Cage said, studying Reydak with his eyes. "It's not only suspect but highly unfashionable. Laser-comb the hair, a bit of cosmetic surgery to mask the scars—we could tighten the chin while we're at it . . . The majority of the Listeners are women, so we might want to consider utilizing a pheromone-laced cologne or aftershave. If we knew which of them would be interviewing you, we could have the computer work up an approach profile—''

"That'll be all for now, Dr. Cage," Keyes interrupted. "You'll get your turn when I'm through with him."

Cage exited with a short bow.

"Just who am I working for," Reydak asked, "SIG, AWED, Ground-truth, the Family . . . ?''

"You're terminated, Colonel," Keyes told him flatly. "Karel Reydak's in cold storage for a time."

"And, uh, why was I let go, I forget."

"Stress, nightmares, modern illness. But you could re-up at a later date. In the meantime, Records Integration will provide you with a new identity, an apartment, backstopped phone number, and the rest. Surveillance International is recruiting agents. Jim Wave will brief you in New York."

Reydak felt suddenly fatigued.

"But listen to me, Karel, this has to be handled sterile. Flap potential is about as close to macro as it gets. And right now the success of your penetration depends on Cage, is that understood?''

Reydak simply nodded. It wasn't, he supposed, the best time to tell Keyes about the faint blue light that had begun to cloud the periphery of his night vision since the Batoran highlands.

10 Overtaken by Events

"Get over to the House as quickly as possible," Ted had told him. No explanation, save to say that it couldn't wait; Ted's face derezzing on the screen, eerie white noise on the truncated line.

Considering how he hadn't gotten in until almost three A.M., the presunrise wakeup call was the last thing Eli needed. He managed nevertheless to drag himself out of bed and fumble into clothes, hung over from the AFL's fund-raiser in Miami and the midnight flight back to Washington. April rewarded his efforts with a somnambulist's kiss and pulled the covers over her head. He stopped on his way out to look in on the kids, remembering how good it used to feel knowing the future was in Ted's able hands. And stopped again on the front lawn to watch the last stars yield to the light, thinking: All one could do was try to perfect a small part of the world . . .

The limo and follow cars were waiting for him, exhaust clouds rising into the cool air. The drive in from Chevy Chase rarely took longer than forty-five minutes, but owing to slick streets and a sunrise demonstration forming up along Pennsylvania Avenue, he didn't arrive at the White House until six o'clock. Members of the Jewish Defense League had taken to the streets to protest Ted's recent criticisms of Israeli President Shapir, banner-waving radical rabbis confronting riot police with stunguns and side-handed batons.

Teddy was in his room, a bathrobe-clad Alison told him as he stepped from the elevator. Eli's sense of misgiving blossomed into arrant concern when he let himself into the study.

The president, his back to the doorway, was seated at the controls of a video game—one of the new interactive models: an outgrowth of Air Force simulation modules, complete with display-packed command deck, virtual helmet interface, and waldolike gloves. The type either of Eli's sons would have killed for. The machine was presently emitting a frenetic chorus of modulating, digitalized sounds, and Eli stood spellbound, his hand welded to the brass knob of the partially closed door. Oblivious, Ted continued to finger-drum buttons and slam the deck's HOTAS side to side, until a simulated onscreen explosion put an end to his mad machinations and the soundtrack wound down to a kind of nefarious, mocking laugh. After lifting the helmet off, Ted cursed softly and lowered his head to the deck. The game disk's sleeve lay beside him on the floor.

XT: The Scourge From Space, Eli read, and called to Ted before he could reset the deck for another contest.

"What kept you?" the president said, looking over his shoulder.

Exasperated, Eli said, "I got here as fast—"

"Take a look at this."

Ted hit the reset button and the soundtrack recommenced, planets, moons, stars, distant galaxies, and nebulae resolving onscreen. As Eli watched, a column of blue drone-ships bristling with weapons pods took shape in the void and began to close on an Earthlike world, hammering away at the planet's defensive shield. Below were cities, ripe for devastation. The deck displayed target acquisition and discrimination readouts. Ted flipped to a secondary screen.

"They're after the president," he explained, indicating a small, worried figure pacing the floor of an underground bunker. "But I'm beginning to understand their strategy." Ted donned the helmet. "They outnumber us, of course, but they're victims of mechanized thinking. There's a pattern, you see, a repetitive mode of attack. Unrelenting but redundant. You let them through and they'll ladder down . . . But even at five to one, ten to one, they can be beaten. Look at these scores."

Ted entered a personal code and a list of numbers flashed onscreen, the latest figure several hundred-thousand digits higher than the earliest. Eli looked from the screen to his brother's flushed face.

"Is this what you got me over here to see?"

The president paused the game and stood up, pacing the room with the helmet on, his voice muffled.

"It's not in the right hand but the left. The right controls firepower, but manipulation is in the left. You take them out in waves before their third strike and—"

"Ted," Eli said, stepping in to take him by the shoulders.

"Ted, what's happening to you? You've got to come out of this, do you understand me? You're going to leave us no choice."

The president's eyes looked through him. "McVee should be apprised of this. We'll—"

"Ted!" Eli had to shake him roughly to bring him around.

"Oh, good Christ, Eli," the president said, taking a quick look around the room and collapsing against his brother's shoulder. "God, what's happening to me?" Eli let him cry, holding him, rubbing his back, easing him down onto the couch. Getting rid of the goddamned helmet.

"I miss her so much, Eli," the president said.

"I miss her, too, Ted. We all do. It's hard right now, this first year, but things'll get better. You've got to stop giving in to that . . . encounter. Don't you see how it connects? It was a bad dream, you've got to let it go."

Ted looked up at him, face contorted into a mask of grief, eyes brimming with tears. "Don't you think I'm trying to?" he said. "Don't you think I'd let it go if I could?"

Eli felt a wave of nauseating panic wash through him. "What can we do, Ted? Tell me what we can do for you."

"Help me," the president said, "help me."

The secretary of state looked defeated as he stepped into the quiet hallway, but his slack steps soon became a defiant stride that carried him in a rush to the Treaty Room phone. Loren Masters listened to his five-minute harangue without comment.

"I still don't see what more we can do, Eli," the physician said at last. "He refuses to talk to a therapist, he won't agree to medication . . . I've even tried to prescribe *herbs* and he won't touch them. We may have to face facts, son."

"I am facing facts, Loren. And I'm trying to make something clear to you: Any substitution at the Summit is going to be interpreted as an outright affront—even if we concoct some wild tale to back it up."

"Wild tale? How much wilder can we get?" Masters paused. "Miso-roshi maintains that Ouro's our best hope, that we shouldn't just sit around waiting for a crisis."

"Meaning?"

"Meaning we start taking Ouro seriously."

Eli yanked the receiver from his ear, stared sullenly at it for a moment, then hit the switchboard button and told the operator to ring Patrick O'Denvy's personal line. Exhausted, he lowered himself into one of the leather armchairs positioned around the Treaty Room table.

"Yes, Mr. Secretary," the FBI director said half a minute later.

"Pat, where's Gabriel Ouro now?"

"Just a minute, please . . . California. He left from BWI last night by private jet. There's been a kind of gathering of the clan in progress these past few days. It's all on tape if you need to hear it."

"I may want to. Where in California?"

"He's at Lakehaven, last report, presumably with the scientist, Woolley."

Eli gnawed at his lower lip. "Order your people to pick him up, Pat. Bring him back to Washington and hold him until you hear from me. Use any excuse you want: national security, immigration violations, income tax evasion for all I care. I'll see to all the necessary clearance and paperwork."

"Yes, sir."

"And, Pat. Give some thought to how we can sneak a shaman into the White House without arousing suspicion."

Ouro disliked flying—of the technological sort—but what he had to say to Woolley couldn't wait, and there was no profit in trusting that the Haven's phone lines hadn't been tapped. Face to face would be better in any case, he'd decided.

He was dressed in conservative slacks and tasseled loafers, hair pulled back in a neat pigtail when he came through the door to the physicist's quarters at LIAR. The outfit brought a smile to Woolley's face.

"You grow more acculturated every time I see you," Woolley said. "Should I be concerned about a growing conservatism?"

Ouro plucked the wool trousers away from his leg. "These pants and I are getting to know each other." He stroked the scientist's withered hand. Woolley looked wan but bright-eyed. The illness resided in him still, searching out weak spots, but Woolley wasn't affording it many opportunities. His lifeforce was strong, streaming out from his navel like plum-colored smoke.

"Is there some reason the two of you need to be friends?" Woolley asked.

Ouro grinned. "I'm an actor preparing for a part. Stepping into character. It's what's expected of me, and the least I can do."

Woolley motioned Ouro to a chair and sat opposite him across a glass-topped plotting table.

The two had met during Ouro's second visit to the States, when the team at Wiles ParaResearch were still wiring the shaman up to dermometers and plethysmographs, ECGs, PETs, and CATs; placing him in lead-shielded rooms and using superconducting quantum interference devices to detect changes in his body's magnetic field; covering his eyes with cotton-stuffed halves of Ping Pong balls, and piping the sound of ocean waves into his ears.

Woolley was working at the Stanford Linear Collider then, where weak force zero-zeros and Higgs particles were the grail of the day. But midlife had brought a weariness for the quest: It was the fiftieth anniversary of the Hiroshima bombing, of his time spent at Oak Ridge and Los Alamos; he was in the midst of a painful divorce; and several of his colleagues were succumbing to one illness or another. Woolley's personal demon arrived in the form of an ideopathic neuromuscular disease, which left him wasting away in a private clinic in Mountainview, with little more than a bed, a chair for visitors, and a laptop computer to fiddle with. It was there Ouro had first visited him, after hearing one of Woolley's papers delivered by proxy at an interdisciplinary conference sponsored by Wiles ParaResearch.

The shaman had asked him to take uncertainty to heart. There was, he opined, no such thing as a "classic case" in medicine, especially in illnesses that had yet to be named; so diagnosis and prognosis were oftentimes simply games played out between doctors and patients. In the absence of a *cause*, an observable etiology, there simply were no *vector particles* to hunt for. Rather, therefore, than look for a cure, Woolley should look to healing: to reintegration with self, planet, and personal cosmos.

The physical world was continually overcoming evolutionary restraints, Ouro had asserted; all Woolley had to make himself understand was that Nature not only made leaps but cabrioles and entrechats as well.

Initially unmoved by the shaman's claims, Woolley later relented and, under Ouro's guidance, had taken *mai'oni*, a hallucinogenic brew used by the Human Beings. Together they grappled with Woolley's insidious demon, the toxic evil in the cord and gray matter horns, and the physicist eventually found the songs and steps of power necessary to subdue it. Not a miracle cure, no Lord-of-Lourdes leap from the chair, but a slow and gradual remission that returned him closer to normalcy than he'd dreamed possible. Physicians cautioned him that the disease had merely reached a plateau phase and was likely to reappear with a vengeance; but that had ceased to be the point: Woolley had remembered what had been forgotten. He was healed.

And as he listened now to Ouro's revelations about the president's encounter, he asked himself what it was that Tedman Brady had lost, and whether the world would permit his finding a way back to it.

"And in spite of this he's still actively Head of State?" Woolley said.

"His followers know no greater loyalty."

"Apparently not. But then why don't they simply let you work with him?"

"They know what his enlistment could mean to the movement," Ouro said. "They suspect conspiracy. Not unlike our suspicions of them. It's up to me to convince them."

Woolley's eyes lit up in sudden realization. "Of course! This part you're playing—they'll only allow you to work with him if they have you under lock and key."

"We're under surveillance this very moment. I've tried to placate them, but words alone aren't enough."

Briefly Ouro's dark eyes emptied. He noted a surge in LIAR's electrical system; a disturbance in the dust motes that swirled in the air; a novel vibration in the floor—a telluric echo originating far to the south.

He looked hard at Woolley. "They'll try to infiltrate an agent into our midst."

"What, again?"

"But this one is to be allowed through. You must alert Flage and his security force. Perhaps the time for unity is at hand."

Woolley shot to his feet. "You can't trust them. They'll pervert our findings. The Star already has them worried. And just today we learned the Pentagon is about to issue new guidelines to observatories and research facilities. Rumor has it all observatory data is now going to be processed through the National Reconnaissance Agency. Research funds are being reallocated, shunted over to laser installations and the orbital stations. Isn't it clear what they're up to? They'll use the president's encounter as an excuse to bus nuclear warheads up there."

"It's up to me to reveal the tricks Brady's mind plays on itself," Ouro said after a moment.

"And if you can't? If he refuses to believe you?"

"Then he must be convinced that only we have the power to conquer his aliens."

Part Two

ESP-IONAGE

People are always on the watch for the "signs" which, according to prophetic tradition, were to herald and accompany the final "time of troubles;" and since the "signs" included bad rulers, civil discord, sudden deaths of prominent persons and an increase in general sinfulness (lawless chaos, robbery and rapine, torture and massacre), there was never any difficulty in finding them.

—Norman Cohen, *Pursuit of the Millennium*

Have You Hugged the Earth Today?

—WEM slogan

11 The Sanitorium of Overworked Coincidences

Reydak rode the rapidtrain to New York, in a second-class car packed with college kids wearing liquid sunglasses and audiowear jackets, leashed kinkajous and thonged climax inhalers. Third class was an even stranger mix of teenaged moms from Baltimore; Jamaican couriers running black-market drugs up from Florida; Indians sporting laminated pouches of Ganges water; and Arabs with Mecca-positioning wristbands. You could identify the few Wholists aboard by their tattoos, synth-crys brooches, and slightly bemused expressions and hushed conversation. There was something vaguely spine-tingling about the way they grouped together, embracing one another, making signs with their hands; and from a dozen seats away he tuned into their hushed conversations, catching repeated mentions of Ouro and the approach of the Blue Star. They were careful perhaps not to indicate direction, so the blur in Reydak's vision remained just that for the time being.

He downed a taco and Tecate in the club car, where two gangbangers in dog collars and white facepaint tried to figure a way to grab his Wise-Eyes wraparounds, the shades popularized by the Secret Service. One had given himself a wolfman look through mega-applications of Hair-Raiser to forehead, cheeks, and forearms; the other was rooster-combed, spiked and dyed. With their "Just Say So" shirts, foreign cigarettes, and portable game decks, it was easy enough to see what they were all about: a dark prayer for loveless, black leather dystopias; some post-apocalyptic nightmare world where they'd be free to drill holes in their heads and commune directly with their machines. The sad thing was that software warriors like Reydak were the ones most likely to bring that cynical vision about: doctored agents willing to implement the nation's fear tactics, killing sprees, and hidden agendas.

He had agreed to wear Cage's enhancements, with the promise that the AWED-man would undo the dirty work once the penetration op was completed. They had de-amped his ears some for citylife, and as a bonus speeded the healing of his leg with some sort of sea sponge derivative. When Reydak asked himself why he relented, he could only come up with the same answer he'd given himself after Sense Augmentation Center had enhanced his ears and hands, after SIG had gone to work on his limbic system: anything to fill up the hollow he'd carried around for forty-six years.

So it was a new and perhaps slightly improved Reydak who stepped out into Penn Station and transferred to the Hudson tube. A few environmental police patrolled the marble floor, routing indigents and urging pedestrians to remain indoors if possible. According to a warning from the surgeon general that flashed in LEDs at the heart of the underground terminal, an aberrant Indian summer blocking-high had stalled over the city.

The apartment SIG had procured was in a recently gentrified section of Jersey City, close to a CIA safehouse. A market area offering assembly-line hydroponic vegetables, Brazilian soybean meat, windbeans, or seaweed treats trucked in from Mitsubishi's Pacific Northwest aquaculture nori farms. The district had an occupied feel—Spanish, Japanese, and Indian subtexts on every sign and the streets filled with bikes and fuel-efficient imports—but the building was a secure one, with private sentries and half a dozen decent vending machines in the lobby. Reydak's tenth-floor rooms had a view of Staten Island's 300-foot-tall trash pyramid.

Technical Services Division had seen to a wardrobe—houndstooth tweeds, oxford shirts, flannel trousers, and tartan ties—and stocked the fridge with microwaveable food. There was an entertainment complex and a computer already jammed with electronic mail; an assortment of slick catalogues for the would-be spy; audio and video disks; a few expensive prints and repros; an overall single or Dual-Income-No-Children feel to the place. Technical Services had also sprinkled a good deal of WEM propaganda and paraphernalia about, including a game disk featuring a wounded animated character resembling Gabriel Ouro in search of a restorative elixir, and in the process forced to ford rivers, enter caverns, speak with plants and rocks, meet with hermits and spirits, gather sacred objects, and battle a host of demons and dragons—all to a drumming, shamanic soundtrack.

Reydak passed the evening perusing pamphlets and sharing New Eon insights with Wholists on WEM's 900 togetherness line, called "Entrainment Tonight." A woman named Maori wanted to meet him for lunch the following day, bent on showing him the shamanic path to multiple orgasms. If nothing else, the Wholists were ready to see the world out with a bang.

Surveillance International had the seventy-second floor of an Arab consortium–owned tower in lower Manhattan—the Ibn Saudi—two blocks north of the Holocaust Museum. The appointment was for two P.M., but Reydak showed up half an hour late just to jerk Wave around some. SIN's central office was more showcase than nerve center, and no sooner did he step from the stainless steel elevator than the advertising onslaught began.

He found himself sealed in a windowless antechamber, facing a single simulated hardwood slider flanked by an electronic bio-interrogator and a retinal scanning device. A polite, marginally feminine computerized voice asked him to address himself to each of these. His own experience told him that the tiled floor beneath the RSD concealed a body-weight indicator. A closed-circuit camera tracked his movements from one corner.

"Warning," a decidedly masculine voice intoned, "no weapons are permitted beyond this point. Please place the Ingram M-19 in the receptacle to the left of the door. Your weapon will be returned when you leave. You have thirty seconds to comply before anti-intrusion measures commence. Counting . . ."

Reydak grinned for the camera and showed it the ceramic handgun he ripped from a Velcro shoulder rig. When identifying the weapon, the voice had hesitated ever so briefly, allowing for a split-second search of the system's library. One day, Reydak promised, he'd return with something the computer wouldn't be able to match and identify. A panel large enough to accommodate a grenade launcher had opened in the door wall; Reydak inserted the gun and waited.

"Thank you," the voice returned. "You are now cleared for entry."

The slider pocketed itself and Reydak stepped into a carpeted reception room. The woman at the desk bid him good afternoon and flashed a flight attendant's smile. She oozed efficiency and predatory sexuality—Mata Hari with lacquered talons and lightpen. A holo-button Velcroed to her blouse strobed: *ORGONE DONOR.*

"Mr. Wave has been expecting you, Mr. Keane."

"Reich on," Reydak told her, smiling.

She buzzed him into a busy front office, where Wave had a sculpted bodyguard waiting. "This way," the escort grunted after a quick once-over. Reydak recognized him as a lineman recently sacked by the league board after failing a body scan.

"How 'bout those Hackers?" Reydak said to the back of the man's ill-fitting lime-green jacket.

"Fuck 'em," the guard spit over his shoulder, 'roid rage in his voice. "They put you on the bubble; so you boot their anabolics, wear their muscle, and they end up fucking you."

"Way of the world, man," Reydak said, sorry now that he'd asked.

"Valid."

The front room was crowded with desks and work stations, interspersed with product display holos and dioramas: intruders tripping time-based infrared beams or trapped in immobilizing foam: scaled-down minivans running up against tire-slashing teeth or spiked hedgerows of trifoliate orange trees. Jim Wave had a corner office of bulletproof window-walls and burgundy high-pile.

"Mr. Ground-truth himself," SIN's founder said, coming around the desk with a hand extended. "Late as usual. Seen any cigar-store saucers or flying Indians lately?"

Reydak took Wave's chair and put his feet up on the desk, smiling and nodding his head as he took in the view. The city was a forest of stone needles and obelisks under a tinted sky. "So this is what it feels like."

"You got that right, Karel," Wave enthused, keying instructions into the wet bar. "Nick, I should say. By the way, I don't approve the look—TSD has a thing for Ivy League. We'll fix you up with something more appropriate."

Reydak glanced around the room, noting Wave's electropulse exerciser, the on-off glass, the plastic interior smart-wall he could adjust for color. The desk was covered with brochures and specs for all manner of surveillance hard- and software.

Wave stood at the bar beaming. He was six four, late forties, and only slightly retouched; an electronics wiz packaged in the agile frame of a professional athlete. They'd met at the Sense Augmentation Center in Seattle, shortly before Peru and all that had gone down. It was still a subject of debate whether Wave knew more ways to maim and kill with hands and feet or with the sundry devices credited to his bizarre intellect. SIN employed a wide range of licensed investigators, exspooks, mercs, and cult deprogrammers for a wide range of operations, some private, some not.

Wave carried the drinks over and apparently undisturbed by the seating arrangement, pulled up a sim-leather and chrome affair for himself. Reydak lifted his glass, swirling colored cubes. "I trust you've done your homework, Mr. Keane."

Reydak sipped at aged scotch and set the drink aside. "I'm a successful salesman of cryogenic systems for a multinational firm. I've had a hallucinatory vision and been sick since. If my cover's blown, I'm working for SIN—tracking down the daughter of a wealthy client who got mixed up with WEM and hasn't been heard from since."

Wave nodded, tongue in cheek. "No one to my knowledge's ever lost a kid to WEM. But we can probably make it work if we have to. I'm your interface with SIG. Keyes wants everything back-channeled. Blind memoranda, the works." He narrowed his eyes. "I understand AWED went to work on you."

Reydak rubbed his nose, seemingly in the throes of some Pavlovian response. "Vat-grown pineal graft," he said, downplaying the disgust. "They figure my initial contact with a Listener's going to determine whether I move any closer to this inner circle or get sloughed off to the Centers."

"That's what we've been able to determine. Psychic triage. What did they program into you?"

"Damned if I know. Gland-man named Cage was in charge. Said he hinged it to 'subliminal compensatory psychic components.' All I get to do is trigger it."

"How so?"

"I won't know until I'm face to face with a Listener. I've got a smart-cap. I figure this Cage electron-etched the trigger-phrase on the backs of my eyeballs." Dirty tricks, Reydak thought.

"Christ, Karel, you ever think of resigning? You've got a spot here if you want it."

"Maybe after this one."

Wave fell silent for a moment, studying his drink. "You want to tell me what this is all about? I mean, it's natural for Keyes to place someone inside WEM—hell, I've been trying to do the same thing for two years now—but why the urgency all of a sudden?"

Reydak shrugged and brought his acting abilities to bear.

"Something to do with this Blue Star. Maybe the Defense Department's considering retargeting the lasers."

Wave assessed this. "Stories are reaching me, tales from the Hill. Important people involving themselves with the primitive and paranormal. Anything to it?"

"Rumors," Reydak said offhandedly. "A 'wilderness of mirrors.' "

"Uh-huh," Wave said, knowing enough to fold. He leaned across the desk, slid an orange appointment card from beneath one of the brochures, and sailed it over to Reydak. "Tomorrow morning, ten o'clock at the Rye Haven. Thirty minutes by train, then you'll have to jump a cab."

"I'll find it," Reydak said, staring at the card. "Pretty formal for a low-tech organization, aren't they?"

"Low-tech?" Wave snorted a laugh. "The Centers are chaff. WEM's testing for psychic power at Lakehaven Institute in California, and they're building god knows what on a piece of the Caribbean they bought. Colombian refueling stop in the old days. Major-league stuff. A lot stranger than your zombie warriors."

Reydak scowled. "What'd my afteraction make the eleven o'clock news?" He began to wonder if the entire op wasn't a cover; if maybe Brady himself hadn't agreed to fake an encounter, play the penetration targeted for WEM's inner circle . . .

"You realize we can't even wire you?" Wave was saying. "They've got their own exterminators. And I know they're thorough because a few of them used to work for me. A raider named Flage runs the low end. Hollywood money."

"Tell me."

"Venture capital on the legal side—cryogenics, movies, and animal patents. I know he had a hand in black market fetal, and California hung one on him for mainframe tampering." Wave threw back the rest of the drink. "More than meets the eye, pal, standard issue or upgraded. You going to have to keep your head low. A couple of spooks in there could dirty you."

"Does Keyes know this?"

"That's why you're working for SIN. Besides, you're the least known of the people Keyes considered."

"Feels good to be wanted, Jim."

Wave screwed up his face. "And one more thing, cowboy: Lose the Ingram. Salesmen given to close encounters don't visit Westchester armed to the teeth."

* * *

The Rye Haven, a turreted Tudor built in the thirties, was set in the print of a landscaped finger that jutted out into Long Island Sound. The entire peninsula had known better days before the Sound had been termed a disaster area, but there was still a stone-wall, iron-gate elegance to the place. The formal gardens, marble fountains, and sundials reminders of a bygone exclusivity.

A young woman wearing a Russian-made wristwatch greeted him with a smile, pushing back orange foam earphones and glancing up at him, the antithesis of SIN's receptionist. She poised her fingers over a terminal keyboard.

"Nicholas Keane," Reydak told her.

"That's K-E-A-N?"

"E," Reydak said, watching his name come up on the monitor screen.

"Nicholas Keane. A Listener will see you at ten," she said. There was something beatific about the way she delivered it, as if announcing an appointment with Saint Peter. A laminated computer-printed card emerged from a slotted device on the desk. She clipped it to a leather lanyard and handed it to him. "If you could just wear this around your neck. And please feel free to wander around. The grounds and first floor are open to everyone."

Reydak started with the house, tuning into conversations as he moved room to room. The place had a feel that was part clinic, part networking kibitz. People browsed in the paneled library, struck museum poses before pieces of primitive art, sat quietly in the den sipping juice or coffee. Quite a few were infirm—emaciated, stressed, wan without making it a fashion statement. The female-male ratio ran about four to one, which jibed with the stats he'd already seen. Lower and middle class, with a disproportionate number of second-generation Latin Americans and Asians. WEM didn't seem to be catching on with Aryans. There was also a kind of purposeful ambiguity to it all; people were sizing each other up out of the corners of eyes. A bit like attending a Company mixer, walking into a nest of officers and spooks.

"The FBI's been covering up for years," he overheard someone say. The speaker was a balding, ascetic type, talking to a fashionably dressed Hispanic woman in her early thirties. "You wouldn't believe what we've unearthed about their attempts to discredit the movement."

The woman wore a strained smile. Looking up, she locked

eyes with debonair Nicholas Keane for a moment. "There might be spies right here in this room," she said. Reydak glanced around the room furtively, drawing a laugh from her.

Shortly after ten, an effeminate silver-haired man approached him, blue eyes lingering on the namebadge for a moment. "The Listener will see you now, Mr. Keane," he said just loud enough to be heard. The clinic feel again.

Reydak's fingertips smoothed the patch he'd applied to his right carotid just before arriving; the trickle of glucose the derm supplied was supposed to ease absortion of the smart-cap drug. He palmed the capsule out of his pants pocket as the man led him upstairs, swallowing it before he reached the interview room. Franklin Cage would say only that the time-release capsule contained a synthesized neurotransmitter, which would both sicken the look of his skin and act as a prompt for the hypnotically implanted trigger phrase.

Reydak knew he had seven minutes, tops.

The man ushered him into a rotunda in the rear of the house, excused himself, and disappeared. The room was carpeted with Persian and Navaho rugs and adorned with textile wall hangings. Dozens of pillows and bolsters, but no furniture as such. Stark white light spilled in through tall leaded windows, Long Island's low profile visible through an unnatural mist. Reydak glimpsed speaker ports in the built-in bookshelves; a control panel of some sort low down on one wall. He was moving toward it when a raven-haired woman entered the room through a second door.

"Amber Swift, Mr. Keane," she said, offering her hand.

Score one for the good guys, Reydak told himself. Swift was a member of the inner circle, a sensitive SIG had tested years before. "Then I'm Nick."

"Okay, Nick." She smiled. "Please, sit down—anywhere you'd like," she added, seeing his confusion. "Search out your own place."

Natch, Reydak thought. He gave it about forty-five seconds, settling finally for a spot directly in front of the windows, one part of him still counting down the minutes. Amber Swift dropped gracefully into a cross-legged posture opposite him on the rug. "I like the view," he explained.

"You do?" She frowned. "I can't forget what we're looking at, Nick—which is dead air, more or less. A bleak future unless we do something about it soon."

"Yes, but the light," Reydak argued, covering. "It has a wonderful eerieness."

Amber inclined her head. "What sign are you, Nick?"

"Scorpio," he told her, reading from Cage's script. "But I've got Libra rising."

"Mutable air and fixed water. No wonder you enjoy the mist. That can be a troublesome combination, though." Her dark eyebrows arched, hazel eyes dancing over him. "I hope you're certain of your loyalties, Nick."

Reydak forced a smile. Amber was dressed in black slacks, a cashmere turtleneck, a necklace of pre-Columbian beads. She was barefoot, wore her hair in a French braid, and had obviously gone to some lengths to do what she'd done to her eyes and lips with liners, shadows, and colors. Sorry now that he hadn't taken Cage up on the pheromone cologne, Reydak wondered just where the tattoo might be. He could detect no scent from her, but something was stirring the air between them, invisibly reaching out for him. He tuned in to Amber's shallow but rapid breathing.

"Are you ill, Nick?" she said after a moment. "I mean, what brought you to us? I'm here to listen, and to help if I can. Is there anything you want to talk about?"

Reydak saw that the backs of his hands had lost color. Ye shall know the truth, he found himself thinking, and the truth shall set you free.

"Do you want to talk about it, Nick?"

Sonuvabitch, he thought, feeling the capsule kick in. The goddamned trigger phrase was right out of Langley's hallowed CIA halls. Keyes' hand in the choice was obvious; the SIG chief's way of reminding him not to treat the penetration lightly.

"It's . . . nothing physical," he began.

"I understand."

"Sushimi, my wife, my—"

"I'm going to put some music on, Nick," Swift said, activating a remote she wore on her wrist. "I want you to relax and listen." She reached for his hands as the sound of repetitive drumming issued from the speakers. "Listen to the drum, and let its beat soothe you, Nick. You can relax here. We've all been where you are, so there's nothing to fear, nothing you need hold back. Just open your mind, allow me to walk beside you for a while . . ."

Reydak experienced a touch of roller-coaster apprehension, a fleeting image of lava bubbling inside a volcanic cauldron. Could she sense that? he asked himself, as her hands caressed his.

Ye shall know the truth . . .

* * *

Amber felt a tide of energy drive into her, so intense and unfamiliar she wanted to let go of Nicholas Keane's hand. But a whirlpool of dark waters was already pulling at her, making disengagement impossible. *Deep, my god, so deep.* It was sexual the way it came to her, opening her up, washing warmth into secret places, taking her completely out of herself. The man's hands had broken out in sweat, each bead a point of tingling contact, amplifying the current, carrying her closer and closer . . .

Farm fields and rich earthy aromas, the interior of a house, a round-screened ancient television switched on. *That's My Boy:* a theme song from some imaginary life. She was seeing through the eyes of a young boy child, laughing as his father scolded the tv for misbehaving—the picture skipping, dancing to the drum, up, up, up . . . Mother's there dressed for an evening out in a long chiffon gown, by the door, waiting for the sitter.

And yet, she thought—Amber's own mind reasserting control—there was a *second* image: an older man, this Nicholas Keane whose hands she held in her own, mourning at a gravesite, mourning the loss of his Japanese wife.

The door flew open!

Amber felt herself stiffen, her legs begin to quiver, muscles spasming, out of control.

Something was landing in the fields, throwing blinding rotating light against the front of the house, creatures in zippered suits invading the front room, grabbing the father, grabbing the mother, dragging them off into that mad and dizzying light, under the loud wash of some unearthly engine, lifting, lifting . . .

"Killed them!" Amber screamed, while in the parallel vision a different set of creatures showed the man a vision of his lost wife . . .

Reydak heard a short scream and went on wide-eyed alert, his hands suddenly free of the Listener's hold. Swift lay on her side, sobbing, fetally curled, hands pressed to her face. She recoiled when he touched her, then came slowly around, turning to him, almost apologetic, her face streaked with tears.

"Are you all right?" Reydak asked, as much to himself.

"The entrainment," she said. "It sometimes affects—"

He watched her features distort.

"When!" she shouted at him. "When did this happen, Nick? What do you remember? Tell me, *please.*"

Reydak risked a look inside: AWED's implanted vision was clear as a good bar joke now, recently heard and well worth repeating. A close encounter, three months ago on the first-year anniversary of his wife's death. Japanese wife, he thought, concealing a sardonic smile, at her grave no less. The president's vision, retouched.

"Is your father alive?" she broke in as he began to explain.

Reydak stared at her. Was Nicholas Keane's father alive or not? Nothing in the phonied up 201 form in the Agency's Central Registry about that one; so he decided to answer for himself, as Karel Reydak.

"Yes, he's alive. Why?"

"Are you certain?"

"Of course I'm certain. I saw him a few days ago," he said, continuing to mix identities. Fuck, he wondered, had something happened at home?

Swift slumped to one side, supporting herself on her hands. She shook her head. "But I could hear him calling you, Nick. From . . . the other side. Do you understand me?"

"The other side, sure."

"But he was using a nickname—'Ray,' 'Raid' . . .'' The Listener exhaled heavily. "I'm sorry, Nick. I don't understand it myself."

Reydak backhanded sweat from his upper lip. If she was confused, that made two of them. But he couldn't let the opportunity pass.

"Maybe we could put our heads together and figure it out," he said leadingly.

She regarded him warily for a moment. "Of course, Nick, that's why we're here."

"I was thinking more like tonight," he said, locked in on her gaze.

12 For the President's Eyes Only

Ouro's sole possessions when he left the Human Beings were the gourd rattles and knife he had fashioned and the power crystal that hung around his neck on a thong. He had assumed the look of the forest's Indians, his dark hair long, his face slashed by initiation tattoos. While the mestizo homesteaders of the Brazilian interior seemed to regard him with suspicion, the police and soldiers rarely bothered with him. He carried a few nuggets of gold N'ntara had given him to buy his way out of possible trouble, and these had once been glimpsed by three down-and-out *garimpeiros* who followed him for a time with evil intent. But he had eluded them with little effort, first leading them through a teasing chase, then becoming invisible before their startled eyes.

In the Indian barrios of the burgeoning cities of the interior, he healed the sick of loss of soul, evil eye, and *pulsario*, and soon became known as a *brujo ayahuascero*—a white magician conversant with the powers of the vision vine. His patients were displaced *indigenos* and mestizos, in whom the blood of the disappearing forest continued to run deep. And as his reputation grew, the healing was easier to effect, and people began to seek him, or line the muddy banks where he set foot ashore.

Quimbanda, Macumba, and Batuque were typical of the fusion cults of the coast—heady brews of Christian dogma, the slave-imported chthonic worship rituals of West Africa, and the shamanic rites of the Amazonian red men, who were by extension linked to Siberian traditions. Brazil was a place of reunion, the cultural closure of humankind's migratory cycle. And in the candlelit verandas of barrio homes, mediums would summon their *encantados*—their familiars—and consult them for devotees in need of succor or healing, sometimes allowing the powers of the "enchanted ones" to possess them through the laying on of hands, the use of feathers and ritual scarves, or through chant and ecstatic dance.

It was among these cults that Ouro was to find eventual audience and acceptance. Stories spread about the one who was in touch with the spirits of light—the souls of those who had lived good lives and been awarded the privilege of journeying about the universe doing battle with evil on other worlds. Before long "upheaval" became the central focus of the shaman's session—the experience of rebirth from trauma—along with the distribution of quartz power crystals and acquisition of curative words and steps of power. But by encouraging spiritual independence, Ouro unwittingly roused the hostility of cult leaders who could not travel as deeply as he. And it was Dolores Sueño who had saved him from those out to swallow him.

She was four years old when her mother, a renowned Batuque medium living in Recife, made her swallow her first power beads; they had lodged in her right forefinger and given her dermal vision. At seven, when her *caboclo* father returned to the very wilderness in which Dolores had been born (lured there by a mischievous spirit, her mother would later claim), the young girl was contacted by an enchanted one, who told her that her mother would die. The force of the premonition rendered her mute, but upon the occasion of the ineluctable event, her mother's *encantados* had become her own to use and consult.

She was introduced to Ouro when she was seventeen and recognized in him a power far greater than any she had known; her own earth spirits dictated that she follow him and protect him from himself. She saw that he was impassioned but vulnerable, unwary of those who would oppose and thwart his ambitious drive for worldly power—a drive he himself was reluctant to acknowledge. So when she learned of the conspiracy against him, she acted without hesitation. Normally she would never have tampered with the spirits of the dead; but she knew that the cult leaders out to swallow Ouro were practitioners of sorcery, and quickly arranged for three exchanges of heads, substituting the sorcerers for three Batuque devotees who lay dying of wasting illnesses. The unexpected death of the first sorcerer brought puzzled reactions from the other two; but when the second took to his hammock one morning and died that same evening, the last one shut down his *terriero* and tried to lose himself in the interior. Magic, however, knows no bounds, and ultimately the unappeased *encantado* overtook him; Dolores learned that the man's canoe had capsized on the Río Negro, where he'd been killed by electric eels.

Ouro never learned of the exchanges she'd arranged.

Years later, aware of the importance of the president's close encounter to Ouro's own mission, she would once again undertake to do something normally out of the question: She would cut Ouro's hair . . .

Agent Kubark, on TDY in protective intelligence and shivering in a chill wind whipping through the narrow canyon between the White House west wing and the Executive Office Building, was unaware of these events, and so failed to recognize the shaman and his consort as they calmly approached the West Executive Avenue basement entrance, arm in arm like two off-course tourists. All he knew was that the detail chief was screaming something into his mastoid process about an unauthorized entry to the grounds. And by the time Kubark made sense of the command center's alert, Marine guards tugged along by snarling but still leashed canines were already closing on the couple from both sides and rooftop countersniper teams were moving into place. It was only then that Kubark's doctored eyes focused on Dolores Sueño's crowd-stopping face and shape, and he yelled for everyone to stand down.

Ouro had been the object of a nationwide manhunt for three days. He had simply vanished from sight when the FBI's directive ordering his apprehension had been issued, and various law enforcement details in the time since had reported seeing him at Lakehaven, at the Annapolis Haven, in New York City, sometimes in two places at once. And suddenly there he was on the South Lawn, shorn and handsomely attired, turning up out of nowhere.

But nothing short of a gorilla suit could have disguised Dolores Sueño. It was as if she hid spring under her clinging skirt, Kubark told himself. He had been fashioning a fantasy ever since that first day she and Ouro had been brought to Shangrila: *Kidnapped by a group of little green men who wished to observe the mechanics of Terran sexual coupling, he was forced to have repeated intercourse with an Earth woman who had already been taken captive and injected with a drug that prolonged and excited sexual heat—a long-legged Brazilian woman, floating naked now in the XTs' null-gee experiment chamber, nipples erect, legs spread wide, awaiting his hot-blooded swollen member—*

"What the hell is going on down there, Kubark?" the chief demanded. "Who are those two?"

The Secret Service agent winced and cupped a hand over the conduction-implant behind his ear. "It's Flying Bull," he said into his lapel, using the detail's codename, "and Ipanema."

"You're nuts, Kubark—follow-up, *nuts*."

"I'm telling you, it's them. Get Brother Rabbit down here on the double." Ouro and Sueño were no more than twenty feet from him now, the Marines' vicious Dobermans wriggling their rumps and panting like pups.

Eli Brady showed up five minutes later, asking "Where's Ouro? Where's Ouro?" with the newly outfitted shaman standing in front of him all the while. His hair had been neatly trimmed, and cosmetics of some sort had been applied to mask the blue cat's-paw lines on his cheeks. The suit and shoes would wear well anywhere in town. An inch or two taller, fifteen pounds heavier, Kubark thought, and Ouro could have passed for an agent himself.

News of Ouro's unexpected arrival reached the president in the Oval Sitting Room. Brady was pacing the worn carpet that had once decorated the Oval Office, finding unsought faces in the brocade designs of the window curtains—gray faces with scrolled eyes and fleur-de-lis helmets. A minute before the call came, they had been speaking to him, threatening him.

Fists pressed to his ears as the figure-ground heads broke into mocking, shrieking laughter, the president staggered to the pull cord and yanked the curtains open, pleating the alien faces. But their laughter was not so easily stifled.

Just then Alison entered from the bedroom, announcing herself with a few quick raps on the doorjamb. Her son's back was to her, fists still pressed against his head, bent arms forming matching triangles. Silhouetted in window light he presented a ghostly image, and Alison's left hand went to her mouth to quiet an anguished cry. She cleared her throat and called to him.

"They're here, Teddy."

Brady twisted around, his face so drained of color Alison could feel her own blood rush in response. "Get out!" he screamed at her, shuffling forward as if about to faint.

At the same time Eli, Kubark, Ouro, and Dolores Sueño came through the door to the Center Hall. The president was standing on—seemingly within—the carpet's presidential seal, and the shaman was immediately aware of Brady's distress. The mist that was Brady's aura was punctuated with coal-black masses flashing a kind of negative light. Fear and anger were consuming him, some miasmic presence permeating the room.

"Get out!" the president repeated, turning to face the window light.

Hearing the scream, Brady's in-close agents appeared at the door with machine pistols drawn. Eli and Kubark rushed forward, but were violently waved away.

"They're here!" Brady told Ouro, stricken. "In *here*! In this room!"

Alison moved to the window and began to fumble with the curtain pull, hoping to soften the intensity of the moment, darken the scene unfolding before her eyes.

"Don't touch those!" the president screamed at her.

Crimson flashes from the black holes in Brady's aura fixed her like bayonets, instantly crippling her. Alison slumped to the floor as Brady's fear began to synchronize itself with the room's malevolence. Eli threw his arms about his brother in a forward-facing bear hug.

"Get out!" the president screamed over Eli's shoulder. "I command you to leave!"

Ouro sidled up behind the president and pressed his hands to Brady's head, working his fingers firmly along his scalp, massaging away the fear, the aura's angry scarlet tones. The president collapsed in a heap, and was carried to the couch by Eli and Kubark. Dolores was kneeling at Alison's side, cradling the First Mother in her arms.

Ouro closed the drapes; then, when the president was asleep, began to run his dark hands over the raised design of the heavy fabric. There were messages here, more pronounced than he'd ever known.

Amber Swift slipped out of bed after Reydak dozed off, tying a loose knot in the kimono's salmon-colored sash as she tiptoed down the stairs. After switching on a ceiling spot in the kitchen alcove, she activated the phone and positioned herself before it, throwing a clandestine sideways glance at the stairway. This is just too weird, she told herself, aware of feeling like an intruder in her own house, of her nakedness beneath the silk. She cupped her right breast in her hands and recalled Nick's touch, the stubble of his beard against her neck and belly, the feel of his lips on her shoulders and thighs. It was just too weird: asking him home after dinner, warming things up with a fire and a dusty bottle of supermarket wine. But she had known from the first moment that she wanted him, and the depth of their rapport at the Haven had only lent inevitability to the evening. Still, this wasn't her style at all. She touched herself again, thinking how accustomed she had grown to her own hands this past year. Since Alan left; so used to her own techniques of ecstasy.

She regarded the phone-mate business card Nick had given her over dinner. CRYO-SYSTEMS, INC., she read, NEW YORK, SAN FRANCISCO, TOKYO. She glanced at the time, slotted the card, and punched for the San Francisco phone number, wondering if was too late there, as well . . .

"Cryo-Systems," a woman's voice answered. "May I help you?"

Amber said, "Nicholas Keane, please."

"May I ask who's calling?"

"Miss Smith*son*," Amber said. "Alex Smithson."

"Hold one moment, Ms. Smithson."

Amber waited, nibbling at a fingernail.

"I'm sorry, Ms. Smithson, but Mr. Keane is in New York just now. Could I have him return your call?"

"No, no, thanks, I'll phone back," she returned, somewhat relieved. She pressed the speaker and vid-tabs and keyed Amol Woolley's number at Lakehaven.

I mean, I hardly know the man, she thought, rolling her eyes toward the stairs again while the phone chirped a short song to itself. But a playfully wicked smile formed itself just the same. They hadn't gotten around to discussing Nick's encounter again, not with so much else to talk about: the accumulation of life's details that had led to her interest in astrology and blossomed into psychism; her failed and childless marriage; the profound changes the movement had brought to her life. Nick was interested in learning about Ouro, but she didn't tell him anything he couldn't have learned on his own, and nothing of course about the Concentricity, because that was what the nine had all agreed to at the beginning. It always made her feel like an espionage operative or something, but then that's what they were, to hear Terri or Leigh tell it: Earth's intel service.

Nick was shaken by the vision that had surfaced, but he was still in the denial stage and more puzzled than frightened. That would come later. He talked a bit about his wife's death, how he had tried to convince her to seek WEM's help. His Japanese wife, Amber reminded herself, wondering suddenly if the kimono had been a bad choice. He'd also mentioned how discontent he was with his career, a fact she filed away for later use, unhappiness and the *chimera*'s assault often walking hand in hand.

Her hands and lips had roamed his entire body in a futile search for additional clues; but what she'd found mostly was scars of all sorts, including a recent one on his thigh. That was probably what had compelled her to place the call, she decided now: a need for some objectivity after all this uncharacteristic involvement.

The phone's small viewscreen went from blue to silver on the third ring and Amol Woolley's shell-pink face resolved into focus. "Amber, hello. You're looking ravishing this evening," he said, smiling.

She arranged the robe to be less revealing. "I hope I'm not disturbing you," she told him quietly, leaning toward the audio pickup.

Woolley waved his good hand. "It's only eleven o'clock out here. I've still got two or three hours of life in me. Where are you?"

"At home. I, uh, want to send someone out to see you."

"And?"

She ran a hand through her hair, hooking strands behind her right ear. "I was thinking we could shortcut some of the usual channels."

Woolley's eyebrows went up. "Is it that important?"

"Yes, it is. He is, that is. His name's Nicholas Keane."

Woolley swung away from the screen to a keyboard. "Can you send his file through?"

"You can access it from the mainframe," she said. "But, Amol, there's a lot more to it than I entered."

"Here he comes now," Woolley said, gazing at his display screen. "Interesting," he added a moment later. "Cryogenic systems salesman . . . And yet another close encounter on the anniversary of a spouse's death."

"What do you mean, Amol?"

"Think for a moment, child."

And indeed it took a moment for her to make the connection between Nick's encounter and Ouro's recounting of the president's experience at Shangri-la. But instead of registering concern, Amber said: "Amol, do you know how many of these I hear every month?"

"Then what's so special about this one? What else do you know about him?"

"I've never felt anything this strong before. I'd appreciate it if you'd test him as soon as possible. We just might have gained a new member."

"Well, then, I'll be sure to get right on it. How soon will this Nicholas Keane be available?"

Amber checked an impulse to look at the stairs. "His business takes him all over."

"All right, tell him we'll work around his schedule, and I'll take care of everything on this end."

"Thanks, sweetie. And Amol," she added, "there's a good chance I'll be coming out with him."

The house was a mix of the homey and the high-tech, Reydak had discovered from his brief reconnoiter: cocooning room, tabletop room ionizers, a projection clock and cavitation sink, a radon-free indicator tacked to the front door post alongside an ornate brass mezuzah. Amber had taken his word that his blood was clean, even though he'd been more than willing to submit to what the street was calling "the prick test." But then, he'd taken her word, as well.

She found him awake when she returned to the bedroom, standing naked by a glass slider that opened onto the upstairs sunroom. "I missed you," he said, without turning around.

She stood behind him and wrapped her arms around his waist. "I had to make a call."

"Late call, huh?" Reydak encircled her with his arms before she could respond, then brought his hands across her hips to the flat of her stomach and deftly untied the kimono sash.

"Hey, you," Amber said in mock protest.

"I want to feel you against me," he said, parting the silk and hugging her once again, with a slight rhythmic motion of his arms, encouraging her to press herself to his back.

She'd gone through his pocket litter while he pretended to sleep; tiptoed downstairs to check him out. He'd heard most of the hushed conversation she had with the astrophysicist, Woolley.

Reydak had an image of Woolley's subatomic particles as cartoon characters emitting a host of Three Stooges sounds as they were pushed and pulled around the ring by LIAR's electromagnets. So, too, the rearranged protein molecules of Cage's enzymes and hormones, crying out for their displaced brethren . . .

Amber was flat against him now, up on toes nibbling at his

neck and ears, grinding her groin against his buttocks. He put a hand under her thigh and lifted her leg, fingers tracing a teasing line to her moist center.

"Oh, god," she said, shuddering, biting the back of his arm.

She wet her hands and reached between his legs, squeezed and stroked him, running her tongue down the small of his back as she kneeled behind him. Reydak leaned through the open doorway, supporting himself on outstretched arms; then pivoted around on his left foot to face her, roundhousing his right over her head.

Amber fell back on her butt, wide-eyed with surprise. "Is this going to be lovemaking or acrobatics?" she asked, looking up at him.

Reydak grinned and took a theatrically menacing step toward her, crouching as he approached. "Both," he said, pulling her foot to his mouth.

Laughing, she squirmed away, rolled, and snatched a pillow from the bed. He dove for her at the same moment and they collided into a nightstand, knocking out the tensor. They took things to the bed for a time, only to end up on the shag carpet once more, scrambling for position.

Fifteen minutes later they were on the floor of the sunroom, flat on their backs under a quilt they'd somehow dragged along with them, gazing up at curved panels of glass, flushed and breathless amid overturned wicker and potted plants. A cool breeze washed over them from a partially opened casement window, New York's inversion yielding to a Canadian high.

"Any chance of your being in California soon?" Amber said out of the blue. Reydak, hands under his head, looked at her askance.

"Possibly. Why?"

She propped herself up on an elbow to regard him, smoothing his hair into place. "I'd like you to take part in an experiment we're conducting."

"I was that good, huh?"

"Be serious, Nick. It has to do with your experience at Sushimi's grave." She took his face between her hands. "Listen to me for a moment. We believe that visions like the one you had signal the approach of a very critical period. I'm not trying to scare you—exactly—it's just that steps have to be taken."

"That's why I went to the Haven, Amber."

"I know that, and I'm encouraged you did. But there's something else. We've found that this transitional stage is also a time of heightened psychism, and we're trying to learn what we can about the actual physical processes involved.''

''And you figure I'm a good candidate?''

Amber took a breath. ''Yes, I think you are. But we're not error-tolerant. Sometimes the people we choose demonstrate remarkable abilities, sometimes they don't. But I do think you're right for it, Carl.''

Reydak's head snapped around; Amber had a hand to her mouth.

''I'm sorry, Nick, I don't know why I called you that.'' She shook her head. ''Ever since this morning . . . Shit, I don't know, I keep wanting to call you *Raydon*.'' A nervous laugh escaped her. ''Does that mean anything to you?''

Reydak worked his jaw. ''Earth body odor,'' he said.

''You're not angry, are you?'' she asked, trying to read him.

He favored her with a smile and took her into the crook of his arm. ''No, course not. Is Carl a lover?''

''I don't even *know* a Carl, Nick.'' She was quiet a moment. ''Is this as special as I think it is? Or is it one-sided?''

''It's real,'' he told her.

Amber squeezed his arm and whispered: ''You can see it, can't you, Nick? Tell me the truth.''

Reydak closed his eyes and wandered through the rules of the tradecraft. Then he raised a finger and pointed high in the northern sky, toward the constellation Pisces. ''There,'' he said resignedly, playing himself for the first time all day.

13 State of the Union

EXDIS/ TACNET NO COPY
TO: ENOCH KEYES
FROM: SIN-WAVE
O/RING SITREP 3
   ORANGE REPORTS CONDITIONAL LODGEMENT AFTER LIS-
TENING POST FLUTTERING. TECH INTERVIEW WITH BLACK-
MINDED LITTLE AUNTS SOP. BUT RETRIEVED AWED-BUILT CEIII
SPLITSCREENED   WITH   FEY   MINDSTUFF—FANTASIES?
DREAMS?—RE PARENTAL CAPTURE, DISAPPEARANCE, AND
MURDER VIA WHIRLYBIRD BOGIE. PLS. ADVISE.
   ORANGE FURTHER REPORTS NETTING O/RING SWALLOW
(FOLLOW-UP DOSSIER APPENDED) AND RECEIVING INVITE LIAR
FACILITY, CALIF. RSVP REQUIRED; PLS. ADVISE. NOTE: SWAL-
LOW TOP BLACK MIND AND COVER NOW SUSPECT. ORANGE
SUGGESTS DOWNFIELD BLOCKING IN EVENT OP HAS BEEN
DIRTIED.

Keyes contemplated the one-time computer-encrypted fax for
several minutes before placing it in an EYES ONLY envelope
marked for Milo Colton. He then asked his secretary to send for
Franklin Cage.

Colton would be pleased with Reydak's apparent success,
Keyes decided, especially now with Ouro sequestered in the
White House and, word had it, slated for inclusion among Tedman Brady's Jakarta Summit entourage. The president, the White
House physician, an Air Force intel officer carrying the launch
codes, and an Amazonian shaman . . . It made for quite a picture. Keyes was baffled by the committee's decision to continue
the charade; there were signs, however, of growing division
among the rank and file. Brady's own chief of staff was con-

vinced Ouro had somehow manipulated himself into place, offering up the recent South Lawn *materialization* as irrefutable evidence of his nefarious designs. Niles Obstat, Patrick O'Denvy, and Jose Darpa, while not entirely behind Base, were in agreement that Ouro's close proximity to the president constituted a major national security risk. Even Eli Brady and Loren Masters had begun to waffle some, at least to the point of expanding the bigot list to include Vice President Alfonse Capella, foreign affairs advisor Duke Cottel, and two or three members of the cabinet.

Keyes had already advised Jim Wave to give Reydak the go-to on LIAR. But if word of Reydak's initial success was encouraging, the bulk of the sitrep cable was troubling. It was possible, in fact, that the penetration had been compromised from the start, which suggested a leak somewhere along the line. Then there was the mention of the secondary stuff the Listener, this Amber Swift, had uncovered beneath Reydak's implanted encounter. Fantasies, indeed, Keyes thought, eager to hear AWED's evaluation.

The SIG director briefed the exoendocrinologist on the results of Reydak's visit to the Haven, but made no reference to the president's UFO or to Ouro's room in the House—although it wouldn't have come as much of a surprise to learn that Cage had found out for himself. The whole town was rife with rumors. Keyes also decided to hold back on mentioning Reydak's secondary encounter for a time.

"I am so pleased," Cage said, with a washing motion of his bone-white hands. "*So* pleased." None of Reydak's predecessors had made it to LIAR. "Now we need to devise some means of getting him through the next battery of tests."

"Do we know what WEM's up to out there?" Keyes asked.

"Not from direct sources. But it's easy to speculate, given Woolley's and Haguchi's backgrounds. We've been through all their writings, interviewed their colleagues, and assembled what I believe to be an accurate scenario. They're looking for *demonstrable* psychic ability—of a strong enough sort to influence collision reactions. However, tattooed or not, Amol Woolley is still a scientist, and as such he's searching for *objective* proofs."
Cage perched himself on the edge of the chair. "To be honest, Mr. Keyes, I think we should be more concerned with getting Reydak onto Inaccessible than infiltrating WEM's inner circle. The Listeners are nothing but functional paranoids; but this is-

land installation, Mr. Keyes, this island could be important to national defense.''

Keyes grunted. ''Inaccessible's National Recon's concern for the moment. Besides, Dr. Cage, either way Reydak's going to need straight A's to get in.''

''Yes, yes, we've been considering this.'' Cage showed a wry smile. ''Of course, if we could 'fake' this part of it, we'd have no need to fake it, would we? We know, however, that Haguchi has modified an MRI scanner to monitor brainwaves of an extraordinary sort, and we just might be able to razzle-dazzle LIAR's neural network by feeding it from a menu of atypical data.''

''More doctoring?''

''Some,'' the gland-man conceded. ''Not glands this time, but a Drexler biochip—a Molecular Electronic Device.''

Keyes had begun to sense a growing dislike for the man. ''Tell me something, Doctor,'' he said after a moment's reflection, ''what sort of encounter did your people program into Reydak?''

Cage looked offended. ''Why, merely the one you suggested, Mr. Keyes—a close encounter at a gravesite on the anniversary of the death of a spouse. With all the usual attendant material. I certainly wouldn't presume to countermand your authority.''

''But in order to make this work, you have to 'hinge' it on something—isn't that what you said?''

''Yes, of course. An extension of some of the dreamstate studies pioneered by Reydak's uncle—a 'differentiated amnesia,' if you will, or better yet a 'reduplicative paramnesia.' We first probe for repressed trauma, infantile fantasy, that sort of thing, then simply code in an overlay scenario. The vision is good for one time only. After that, the victim—er, subject— regains discriminatory control.''

''Anything out of the ordinary with Reydak?''

''On the contrary. Reydak's as near perfect a subject as one could hope for. We located some innocuous fantasy material and used it as a foundation for the implant.''

Keyes smoothed his tie. ''You didn't include anything about his parents . . . disappearing or being captured? Something like that?''

Cage stared at him blankly. ''Nothing of the sort.''

Keyes sat back in his chair to regard the AWED man over the tips of his steepled fingers. *Parental capture, disappearance, and murder via whirlybird bogie,* he recalled from Jim Wave's sitrep fax. Reydak was two years old at the time, he thought. And surely the memory was there. But *murder*: Was that Wave's word or the Listener's?

And how, in either case, had any of it leaked?

Goddamn Amber and her Lips-so-Slick neon gloss, Reydak told himself, with its pressure-activated polymeric moisturizing microsponges. And goddamn the feather tattoo on her rump and that beauty mark on her luscious vulva, a microplanet above her night-blossoming flower. Goddamn her mindreading talent, too; whatever it was that had elicited that discomforting parental scenario and had her only letters away from divining his name. Goddamn Cage and his AWED team, for that matter, with their deepsea-diver coveralls and biochip MEDs.

"Now this won't hurt a bit," Cage was saying, pneumatic hypogun in hand and eyes wrinkled up above the surgical rebreather mask. The safehouse room was part operating theater, part interrogation room. "There used to be trouble with tissue rejection, but we've since found ways to pacify the body's heat-response proteins."

Reydak bared his teeth. "I can't tell you how comforted I am."

"Now just relax, Colonel. It'll be over in a moment."

Reydak craned his neck to flash Keyes a daggered look; but the anger quickly subsided as his mind began to surrender to the liquid trank—pacified, just like those heat-response proteins Cage talked about.

He supposed there were a few things to be thankful for; topping the list the very fact that SIG was willing to continue the op even though it was likely he'd been dirtied. Reydak figured it was easier for everyone to suspect a leak than give credence to Amber's telepathic abilities. Anyway, the decision at least assured him of an expense-account trip to California, a shot at genuine sunshine. Amber had made plans to rendezvous with him at the Oberoi in San Francisco. From there, they'd pay a visit to the Golden Gate Center before driving up to Lakehaven.

The orders to report to AWED's hideaway D.C. lab for some glandular fine-tuning had put an end to two days of acrobatic lovemaking and intimate talk. Missing Amber, Reydak had passed the whole of the previous night hardwired into the Agency's Private Information Executive Database, reading through her electronic dossier and watching Staten Island's garbage recycling plants belch smoke over New York Harbor. PRIED drew its information from banks, credit card and telephone companies, computer communications systems, motor vehicle bureaus, post offices, supermarkets, and any number of consumer information datanets to collate and compile dossiers on individuals or businesses that aroused the Agency's interest or curiosity. With the touch of a few keys, Amber's dossier had filled in many of the details they hadn't gotten around to discussing in Connecticut: how much money she earned; how much she had and how much she owed; what kind of car she drove; what kind of videos she rented; where she liked to dine, shop, and have her hair done; and when and where she had traveled. But what the file couldn't tell him was just how high up she was placed in WEM's seemingly concentric hierarchy, or where she had gotten the idea that his parents were dead.

Reydak had checked to make sure, and Keyes had assured him that John and Anna were in fine health.

So maybe things weren't as bad as they seemed, he thought, well under the drug now. If only that blue fuzz in his peripheral vision would disappear and that new voice in his head would stop whispering his name . . .

"A remarkable subject," Cage told Keyes when the installation of the biochip was completed. "Capable of the most extraordinary regressions."

Keyes regarded Reydak's prone form on the table, unable to direct his eyes to less worrisome subjects. He sometimes yearned for a return to simpler times, when the idea of a perfect operative was someone who couldn't attract a headwaiter's attention, not some doctored cyborg. "You think he stands a chance at LIAR?"

"Who knows?" Cage said. "But he's sure to produce anomalous results. I've incorporated some posthypnotic suggestions of an infantile, oceanic sort. We'll trigger them with a computer-designed, molecularly remodeled harmaline derivative, acting in conjunction with a serotonin uptake-inhibitor." The gland-man chuckled. "Ironically enough, the drug is an enhanced version of the alkaloid in the hallucinogenic vine Ouro uses—*mai'oni*, or whatever they call it."

"He's coming around, Dr. Cage," a nurse reported.

"Good, good," Cage said, leaning over his subject. "Now remember, Reydak, you have access to all the secrets of time and space, of God and man and infinity. So when someone asks you to read their thoughts or influence a subatomic reaction, you can easily do so. It's all part of the cosmos you yourself contain; yours, therefore, to do with as you will."

Cage smiled approvingly at the precision of his surgical work on Reydak's skull. "Remember this as you surface from level six, through levels five and four . . . You will leave behind all memories of this procedure and our conversation. You will simply remember the signal and you will employ the signal when the proper time comes. Where are you now?"

"Three," Reydak replied, as if from far off.

"Very good. Now come up slowly, through level three to two and—" Cage suddenly broke off his count and said, "Stop, Reydak. I want you to go back down to four again."

Perplexed, Keyes took a step forward.

"Reydak, where are you?"

"Four."

Cage leaned in even closer. "Reydak, I want you to tell me what you told the Listener about your parents being kidnapped and killed."

"Hold on, Cage," Keyes started to say.

The AWED man whirled on him. "We have an opportunity to learn something important here, Mr. Keyes. The implant went wrong and it's critical that I learn why." He turned to Reydak again. "Now, tell me, Reydak, why did you lie about your mother and father?"

Reydak, sweating profusely, let out a small pained cry. "I didn't lie," he said in a childlike voice.

"Dr. Cage," the nurse broke in, "I'm showing a pulse of one fifty. Blood pressure is one sixty over one hundred and rising."

Cage checked the displays. "Answer me, Reydak," he said more sharply. "Do you believe your parents are dead, or was this an attempt to manipulate the Listener?"

"One seventy-five over one ten, Doctor—"

"Tell me!"

Reydak began to thrash about on the table, arms and legs fighting the restraining straps. His head shook back and forth.

"Break it off, Cage," Keyes demanded.

"Did you claim they were taken, Reydak? Taken by whom? By XTs? Did you tell the Listener they were taken by XTs?"

Monitors placed about the room were emitting unhealthy sounds, displays flashing warning signs. Reydak's body arched and spasmed.

"Doctor, he can't take much more of this!"

"Cage!" Keyes yelled.

"Tell me, goddamn you, tell me!"

Keyes sidestepped and gave Cage a short chop in the back of the neck, hitting the trapezius with just enough force and precision to bring the exoendocrinologist out of what appeared to be his own trance.

Cage showed everyone a confused look from the floor.

"You were overdoing things, *Doctor*," Keyes said, offering him a hand up. "Don't want to render the mechanism inoperable, do we?"

Cage refused the hand and struggled to his feet. "Surface," he said to Reydak, rubbing a shoulder all the while. "Come back up."

14 Red Sandwich

Air Force One was ordered to taxi to a nose-to-nose position with the Aeroflot Tupolev-200 that had brought the Soviet contingent to Jakarta, a bit of heavy-handed symbolism on the part of Suharto-Hatta's air controllers that was not lost on the photographers of the international press. The president and the State Department staff, umbrellas in hand, were ushered off to idling limos and delivered directly to the US embassy for a few hours rest before the Summit officially commenced. Since there was good reason to believe, as many did, that the Horn Crisis had been a prelude, a dress rehearsal for World War III, every nation that viewed itself a world power was represented in one way or another—if not in Jakarta's vast Pancasilia Pavilion, then in the teeming streets surrounding Merdeka Square and the gold-tipped monument that still served as the Indonesian capital's central landmark.

The roots of the Crisis could be traced back forty years, but most commentators chose to begin with the discovery of massive reserves of uranium in Ethiopia's southeastern deserts and the nation's subsequent border wars with Soviet-backed Somalia and Islamic Sudan. The outgrowth of these, known then as the Danakil Confrontation, had seen mules and camels side by side with Chobham-armored tanks and smart weapons. Eventually Saudi Arabia had become involved, then Egypt and the United Islamic Front, with each player claiming to have something at stake, and arms pouring in from every nation that didn't. But throughout it all the US and the USSR had remained spectators, the way mob bosses might. Until Premier Korzliev announced plans to move what he called a "peacekeeping flotilla" into the Red Sea. The Joint Chiefs urged a show of force in response, but the most Brady would agree to was a warship-for-warship match of the Soviet flotilla. Moreover, the president's statements at the time seemed to imply tacit approval of the premier's law-enforcement stance.

Both nations came under fire from the UN for what the secretary general termed ''a further contribution to global wariness engendered by the missile shields,'' and heads of state from all camps went on record to charge that the US and the Soviet Union, eager to put the latest of their annihilation toys to the test, were merely sniffing out a battleground suitably removed from their own spheres of interest.

General McVee concurred with the assessment in principle, but kept his thoughts private. For although the US had succeeded in nearly crippling the Soviets financially by forcing them to see the defensive raise, what good was a new weapons system if it couldn't be *used*—if the hand couldn't be called? Not that McVee was necessarily looking for a Hiroshima; it was simply a matter of combat curiosity. He was certain his Soviet counterparts were pursuing similar lines of thought. But no one, in any case, had bothered to pass any of this thinking on to the naval commanders of the opposing Red Sea fleets, who by this time had begun to taunt one another.

It was a nudge that finally prompted the ships to go to guns—an adolescent schoolyard ploy, only this time the boys involved had carrier battle groups at their disposal. And within hours of the first exchange the Soviets had airlifted a division into the Horn and begun to draw lines in the desert sands. Brady hemmed and hawed, postured some, but held firm to his word to keep all US troops out. Then, after a Labor Day weekend at Shangri-la, the president turned an about-face and ordered in the rapid deployment force. The Pentagon upped the nation to DefCon Three, and around the world intelligence communities, munitions manufacturers, scientists, and amateur astronomers began to watch the skies for signs of activity. But before a laser could be fired, a dozen world leaders who had been meeting in secret conclave demanded that the US and the Soviet Union take their squabble elsewhere or face the consequences. China announced that it was going to equip the Saudis with tactical nuclear weapons; South Africa, India, France, and Israel followed suit and revealed plans to hold what amounted to an open auction for warheads in an attempt to chastise Brady and Korzliev for their arrogance. Twelve hours later nuclear weapons were turning up everywhere one looked and the defensive umbrellas faced a new and unexpected challenge: For all at once the lasers and mirrors it had cost billions to raise in the name of peace seemed too remote to do any good.

Earth's problems remained on the surface, just where they'd always been.

All this time, however, Secretary of State Brady and the Soviet foreign minister had been searching for some way to avert a showdown. The way Eli read it, face-saving was more at stake than the issue of the Horn's vital but embattled resources. Both the president and the Soviet premier would have to agree on joint withdrawal, without evidence of either having acquiesced to the other. So what Eli drafted was a proposal for withdrawal that was to be hand-delivered to his brother and Korzliev at precisely the same moment. The accord was a model of diplomatic double-talk, phrased in such a way that neither man would appear to have initiated the appeal. The two were simply asked to respond affirmatively or negatively; and it had fallen upon Eli and Foreign Minister Tushenko to keep the awful vigil.

The Crisis was narrowly averted, and the war was now on hold. But rather than tackle the issues of territoriality that remained, the Jakarta Summit was meant to provide the US, the USSR, and the United Islamic Front with a forum for reestablishing dialogue. Somehow the rest of the world was supposed to feel indebted to the superpowers' enlightened leaders for having staved off WWIII; but the nonaligned and nonproliferation nations were more cynical than they were relieved.

For Agent Kubark, Jakarta was the same sense-assaulting mix of mosques, monuments, and squalor he remembered from his last tour, with all the same security nightmares. Despite its militaristic leanings, Indonesia's government placed severe restrictions on the toting of handguns even by authorized personnel, and was inclined to do everything it could to hamper riot-control precautionary procedures. But to Sukutomo's credit, the archipelago nation was a prosperous and unusually self-reliant one, and the president had somehow managed to keep the 300 million Muslims under his domain free from both the multitudinous entanglements faced by the United Islamic Front in Africa and the Middle East and the spreading Japanese power base in Southeast Asia. It was Sukutomo who had represented the nonaligned nations at the height of the Crisis, and in whose address to the UN Brady and Korzliev were referred to as "two rogue elephants charging across the planetary landscape."

Kubark's detail had been sent in five days earlier to confer with Protective Intelligence and to advance the stop. Foreign Intel hadn't reported the presence of any known lookouts, but the streets were crowded with saronged malcontent Islamic factions of all sorts, many of whom viewed the president and the defensive shield as history's most satanic terrorist partnership.

With Kubark, in a restricted tier of seats above the Pancasilia Pavilion's horseshoe-shaped conference table, was the newest member of the detail, one Agent Capezzi, according to the name-tag clipped to his jacket pocket, a short, dark-complexioned man with faint lines, perhaps scars, over pronounced cheekbones. At the table, the president and the secretary of state were separated from Premier Korzliev and the Soviet foreign minister by an arc of ninety degrees. Al-Fandi and the UIF contingent were seated opposite the Russians, with Nayland and Charcot, the European Community presidents, and delegates from various East African and Asian nations filling in the gaps. Jakarta's monsoon downpours had delayed the arrival of several lesser representatives and the hall was greenhouse hot, but introductory remarks were underway nevertheless.

Kubark gave "Agent Capezzi" a sideways glance and thought: Christ, I was only kidding.

The shaman had arrived with the president on *Air Force One*, acting as one of Brady's in-close protectors, but Potus had ordered Ouro transferred to Kubark's detail as soon as the president had departed the embassy for the Pavilion, the thought being that Ouro would only get in the way if anything went down along the motorcade route. But the whole thing was so cockeyed it made Kubark's head ache. What was the president going to do if flashbacks from the Aspen Lodge encounter persisted— make Ouro his permanent post-stander, his chief of staff, his secretary of the nonordinary? The way Kubark saw it, anyone with the power to awaken people from trances was likely to possess the power to inflict them. And suppose Ouro was KGB as Philbert Base feared, an awakened sleeper carrying out some insane Politburo scheme? Or maybe some freelance maniac straight out of Jules Verne with a master plan of his own?

The Sitting Room incident had left the Secret Service agent with some disconcerting thoughts about Tedman Brady, as well. But Randy Kubark wasn't going to do any talking about *delusions* or *possession*, no siree. Silence was the line of duty and he knew it. Besides, you started spouting unprofessional diagnoses and mentioning *paranoia* and you got drinks tossed in your face, just for starters.

Ouro turned a curious look Kubark's way. Without fail, the agent thought, looking elsewhere; every time he glanced at Ouro, there was the shaman glancing at him.

"Is there something we should talk about?" Ouro asked.

"What the hell could you and I possibly have to talk about?" Kubark snarled.

"You seem troubled."

"Damn right I'm troubled," Kubark said, folding his arms while Ouro gave him the once-over. "You give me the creeps, that's what, the heebie-jeebies."

Ouro grinned. "We all have our parts to play in this life."

"That's just the kind of shit I'm talking about." Kubark made a flustered gesture. "You stay where I can keep an eye on you, *comprende*?"

"And I'll try to keep an eye on you, too, Randy."

Kubark restrained himself. Ouro was too slight to be intimidating, but he was said to be a *capuerista*, a master of a kind of Brazilian foot-fighting. Certainly the man's eyes were as sharp as any doctored pair in the detail, and once or twice Kubark was sure he had seen and heard Ouro communicating with him through the implant *without moving his lips*.

He heaved his shoulders and began to sweep his eyes over the hall's front-row seats, tuning out of the tactical freq for a moment to hear what the spokesman for the UIF was gesticulating about. In his turban and robes, Al-Fandi was a wizard of a man, with a hawk's nose and dark flaring eyebrows; and he was taking full advantage of his crazed appearance to play the prophet of doom, charging both Brady and Korzliev with unprovoked aggression in the Horn and warning them that the shields would come back to haunt them in the minutes before Allah's sword put an end to the monstrous injustice done his heavens. Korzliev, the Russian bear personified, not only denied all charges but demanded that Brady acknowledge his complicity in manipulating the Horn Crisis, to justify, the premier remonstrated, *offensive* laser components secretly deployed in the US shield.

Brady countered with his telegenic aplomb—the Brady Flair: listening attentively to Al-Fandi's harangue and Korzliev's rebuttals, turning aside when the remarks began to drift from fact to effect, looking tolerant and eminently wise for the hall's cameras.

Then something changed.

Kubark heard the command post in his ear: "What's going on down front? We're getting nothing but snow on the monitors."

He stepped to the wooden railing at the edge of the tier and sharpened his vision. Camera operators on all sides of the conference loop were talking excitedly into their headset mikes, as techs scrambled around the floor checking circuit boards, feeds, and junction boxes. Kubark glanced at the overhead screens, where the president's ashen face was rolling.

"Where's Flying Bull off to?" he heard someone ask, and turned in time to see the shaman heading downstairs for the Pavilion floor. "Follow-up, where's Flying Bull off to?"

"Shit," Kubark muttered. Ouro was maneuvering his way toward the Soviet contingent.

"Don't draw undue attention," the detail chief cautioned. "Just keep your eye on him." Kubark took another look at the monitors before heading down; Brady, looking positively maniacal, was discernible behind intermittent flashes of lightning static.

"Kubark—" the chief started to update when the president slammed a fist down on the table, forcefully enough to send a deafening squeal of feedback through the hall.

"This is not your world!" Brady grated into the mike.

Korzliev and Tushenko exchanged startled looks as the translation reached them. Al-Fandi's side of the table was chattering up a storm.

"This is not your world," Brady repeated, more controlled this time, more threatening. The hall slowly quieted, anxious to hear history unfold.

The president launched a finger toward the lead camera. "For too long we've extended ourselves, reaching out to you time and time again only to have our signals fall on deaf ears. And now, when planetary peace is close at hand, you choose not to applaud our efforts but to conspire against us! But since you've felt compelled to single me out, I'll speak for all of us: Any attempts at aggression on a global scale will be met with the most severe countermeasures that can be mustered. Your advances *will be checked*. And I promise, there are many in this very room ready to rise up to the planet's needs when that moment arrives. Whatever your background, you have no rights to this world, no rights to occupy this hall with us!"

Mouths dropped open throughout the Pancasilia Pavilion. President Sukutomo, his black *peci* hat in place, tried to make an appeal in English from his seat at the table's midpoint. "Mr. President, speaking for all—"

"If the Day of Judgment is truly at hand," Brady continued, "then let the strong and faithful among us unite against evil's dark onslaught—that lecherous hand reaching out for us across the black seas."

"Shit, piss, and corruption," Kubark drawled, rooted to the carpeted steps. Korzliev, Tushenko, Al-Fandi . . . nearly everyone was standing—shouting, pointing fingers, hurling imprecations in a dozen languages. The audience was joining in, voices full of condemnation. But more than a few raised in cheer . . .

On the floor amid the growing chaos, Ouro sought to extend his senses, growing subtle and tenuous as he moved among the crowds. He sensed some powerful force at work in the hall, a force operating within arm's length, different from the miasmic stuff that had lingered in the Sitting Room, but of unsettling portent. He scanned the room with warrior's eyes, and located two, three, four members of the Soviet contingent whose minds were directed against Brady's. The Soviets had placed psychic agents in the hall!

Several of the warrior shamans spotted him at the same time. Ouro couldn't gauge whether their collective power was strong enough to affect Brady; but it suddenly occurred to him that he could make use of their presence regardless. Brady had to face the power circle—for his own sake, the Concentricity's sake, Earth's sake. For without the circle's support, there was little more the shaman could do. But the president's advisors would demand nothing less than a tangible threat before they permitted that. And now Ouro had one to offer them.

Kubark along with two dozen post-standers moved in to form a human fence around the president as the table emptied and a score of angry delegates stormed from the hall.

"We are moving the Monk out," Kubark reported. "We're outta here!"

Inside the cordon, Secretary Brady looked stunned. The president had turned to face his brother, composed now but obviously uncertain about all that had transpired. Kubark elbowed his way to the center of the melee, jerking his head from side to side, as much to spot potential trouble as shake clear a feeling of utter disorientation. Behind him, someone said, "Give 'em hell, Brady, give 'em hell."

Kubark swung around to catch sight of the man behind the voice, but lost him in the crowd. No matter though, because two others had picked up the refrain and spread it into the audience, many of whom were now on their feet, applauding wildly:

"Give 'em hell, Brady. Give 'em hell!"

15 Situational Ethics

Reydak got a quick look at first class as a flight attendant stepped long-legged through the sliding hatch. Screen stars and families of Japanese, he could see that much before the door hissed closed; who else could afford it? He switched off the seatback monitor and adjusted the tension of the headrest, leaning back into batik cushions and closing his eyes. The headache had been with him since the session with Cage, resistant to both the medicinal tofutti he'd hastily downed with a Lag-eze at Dulles and the somewhat stupefying telenet coverage of the president's arrival in Jakarta.

In his shirt pocket, sealed in its own bed of foam, was another of the gland-man's smart-caps, this one aimed at getting him past LIAR. It hadn't helped things any when Keyes showed some uncharacteristic concern after the session. *Concentrate on this Amber Swift*, the SIG chief had told him. *Forget about the cut-and-paste we've been putting you through, and just try to run her like you would any other agent.* If Reydak's head hadn't hurt so much, he would have laughed: run her, double her against WEM, when she had a way of looking right into the heart of him.

She was waiting at the arrival gate in California colors, eyes that matched her outfit, and jet-black hair in wild curls. "Do you like it?" she asked, stepping out of his embrace into a neat pirouette. "I did it myself."

Reydak confessed that he did, even if she was no longer the hazel-eyed priestess he'd first met. She slipped back into his arms and nuzzled against him. "I've missed you, Nick." Reydak held on to her, Keyes' advice running through his mind. *Run her, double her, do whatever you have to.* It wasn't proving all that difficult.

"Something wrong?" she said, gazing at him in that off-center way that usually spelled trouble.

Reydak felt his forehead. "Headache. I can't seem to shake it."

She dug two capsules from her purse as they rode a people-mover through the terminal concourse and handed them to him. "These'll help. They're Flitworm," she explained, catching sight of his dubious look. "You're so suspicious sometimes. It's just a chrysanthemum extract, dilates the blood vessels. Melva makes them up for us. She's one of the people I want you to meet—an herbalist."

Melva Chizedek, Reydak recalled from the O/RING file: ex-priest, homeopath, advocate of wicca and white magic.

"I rented a car for us," Amber said after a moment.

Reydak thought back to her dossier. "From Royobi."

"Hey, how'd you know that?"

"Just comes to me sometimes," he said, not half as comfortable with the lie as he should have been.

The rental was an RU-469, a Korean-designed sportscar manufactured in the States for export—a metalflake toy for the child resistant, with leatherette buckets, ultrasonic wipers, a cellular phone, and polyurethane spare. Reydak's headache wasn't entirely gone by the time they buckled in, but he was feeling a lot better than he had during the flight out. They drove with the top down, drinking in the sunshine like animals coming out of hibernation. Traffic was moving right along, and Reydak saw little evidence of the earthquake that had jumbled the roads less than a year before—Mother Nature's Ring of Fire warmup for the eruption of Kalau six months later.

They crossed the Golden Gate and kept to 101, tailing trucks with shapely aerodynamic rearends and following highway message chips for twenty minutes before heading west into arid coastal hills. Just under an hour later they were on the approach road that encircled the Golden Gate Center. One of seven located in the States, WEM's experimental prototype community-cum-theme park had been squeezed at astronomical cost into a tight basin of hillside grazing land and redwood-forested gorges. Intelligence had it that the Centers—said to be as different from one another as Mexico City subway stations—had been Percival Flage's contribution to the movement.

"I'm not sure I understand how all this links up with Lakehaven," Reydak said, as Amber steered the RU-469 into a parking space in the Center's expansive, color-coded lot. "Do the people who show up here have a crack at LIAR?"

"No," she said, talking over the car's comments on internal systemry, ambient temperature, and forecast. "I told you, only a few are sent to LIAR."

"So the Centers are a kind of exoteric church, then?"

"We're not a church." She looked at him over the RU's soft-top. "What are you asking me, Nick?"

"I mean, if LIAR's only for a few, where do *they* go for fun?"

Amber came around the car forcing a smile and reaching for his hand. "Let's save this talk for after Lakehaven, okay?"

"You're the boss," he told her, shrugging it off.

They rode a wheelchair-accessible maglev to the main gate, where several dozen people were awaiting clearance—broods of Mexican kids and Japanese women with parasols on excursion tickets from Hawaii. A white-haired Jesus issued him a name-badge similar to the one he'd received at the Rye Haven; Amber's bore a VIP overlay. Reydak noticed that many of the scanners and detectors concealed in the booth's structure and railings were products of Surveillance International. But there was otherwise little sense of the *spookery* he'd picked up on at the Haven. The Centers weren't for the visited, the possessed, or the walking wounded; they were designed to cater to garden-variety seekers—the same textbook mystics and restless spirits who did weekend designer drugs, patronized Aquarian clubs, and danced to House Music.

Reydak read shirts as Amber led him into the Center's live-in habitat area—a kind of solar-and-silicon version of a Mesa Verde cliff-dwelling community grafted onto a shopping mall. It looked as if a battalion of Soleri students and landscape architects had had their way with the place. Sections of terraced hillside were given over to soybean farming and genetically manipulated produce. Greenhouse domes and adobe houses equipped with solar gatherers and hydroponic growth vats rose above roads lined with photovoltaic lights and atmosphere-cleansing vegetation. Everything was degradable, recyclicable, hypoallergenic, energy efficient . . . WEM's dream for planet Earth. And everywhere Reydak turned were children, dozens and dozens of them with their transformable robots and find-your-fate software comic books, as carefree-seeming as Shangri-la's own. Some of the shirts pictured a pristine Earth, turned by a crowd of upraised hands. KEEP THE BALL ROLLING, they read, or MAKE IT A GOOD DAY AT THE POLES. Others advised: CONQUER INNER SPACE, CENTER YOURSELF and SIGN IF YOU'RE EXPERIENCED, and WEM: YOUR EARTH CARE SPECIALISTS.

At the center of the park—Reydak didn't know what else to call it—stood a stadium-size geodesic hemisphere, constructed as a series of concentric shells. An outgrowth of WEM's early nationwide workshops, the domes were where the actual alchemy took place: the acquisition of dream familiars, allies, personal songs, and steps of power. Gabriel Ouro serving as template for the grand design.

"We begin by helping an individual assess his or her state of well-being," Amber was saying as they approached the dome along a treelined street. Routing codes of the sort one might find in a hospital corridor angled off to level-specific entrances.

"You take a misery index reading."

"You could say that. It's important to know how happy you are in the world before you can make a new start. We look for signs of timesickness—some indication that an individual is too wrapped up in thoughts about 'saving time' or 'wasting time' or 'losing time.' We want to lead people back to what they've forgotten, what they've 'outgrown'—the eternal *now*."

"And where do you look for the now?"

"Well, you can start by asking yourself whether or not you're happy with your job, your work. Are you, Nick?"

Reydak could feel her probing around inside his head. "Yeah, I'm reasonably happy with my assignment."

"Your assignment."

"That's what work's all about, isn't it?"

Amber struck a thoughtful pose. "I'll have to think about that for a moment. But the question's an important one, because what we're looking for are factors that contribute to spiritual and physical well-being. Your periods of ill health this past year, the experience at Sushimi's grave . . . they're connected, Nick, do you understand? There's something deeper in you that we need to get at, but we at least have a place to begin."

Mention of the puzzle underlying Cage's implanted malaise brought a stab of pain. "So what goes on inside the dome?" he asked.

"Movement is inward," she said. "This isn't Mahesh Yogi's Heaven on Earth. Initiates must complete the training associated with an outer ring before they can progress to an inner one. Each ring has its own associated colors, sounds, bodily chakras, and planetary spheres."

"And price tag, I understand."

She gave him a firm look. "People have accused us of *selling* enlightenment, but that's not the case. Naturally it costs money to run the Centers, and naturally we urge people to move quickly. But with the governments of the world anxious to usher in Armageddon, do we have a choice? Remember, Nick, there's a world at stake.''

Reydak gestured to two women consulting a tactile map nearby, shirts adorned with crystal brooches. ''Suppose I'm only a crimson and you're a blue. Does that mean you have more power than I do?''

Amber frowned and urged him back into motion. ''It's not power in the way we've all been raised to understand it. The crystals are awarded for reinforcement, but power over one another is not what we strive for.''

''WEM doesn't want power?''

''We want to form a shield, Nick, that's all. We want to do right by the planet.''

Reydak kept hearing the same phrases from everyone connected with WEM; it was brainwashing of a sort. ''So what can I expect to find at the center of the dome?'' he asked, knowing full well that WEM hoped to place its drug experience there one day soon: contact with the spirits of the vine Ouro's Human Beings called *mai'oni.*

''Songs and steps of power. A singularity. That's where it all comes together.''

''And what's that cost?'' he continued in a teasing voice.

''Only your heart,'' Amber told him straight-faced.

In an air-conditioned cage set high in the Center's shining geodesics, a securityman turned a double take at a monitor screen as Reydak and his guide stepped out of the sunshine into the artificial light of the dome's outer ring.

''I'm seeing things,'' he muttered, just loud enough to activate his throat pickup.

''Say again, Raven,'' Control said in his ear.

Raven leaned forward on his stool, bringing his pointed features close to the display screen. ''Give me a boost on six, Control.''

''Name your target, amigo.''

''Dude standing near the door with the black-haired looker in curls.''

''The one with the arms.''

Raven's thin brows beetled. The guy's arms weren't anything to write home about, nowhere near as cut as his own. It was the tight-fitting shirt, was all, making them appear beefier than they were. "Target him," Raven told control. "Bring me in on the badge." He watched the screen as remotes tightened their shot. "Nicholas Keane," he read aloud. "Lemme see him again." Cameras centered Reydak's face in their field. "Gimme a pause and print on that, then run it through the library for a match."

"Roger your pause and print," Control responded. "Searching . . ."

A tone sounded and Raven reached down to tug a color closeup of Reydak from an output slot. "Christ on a crutch," he said, looking back and forth between the video photo and the monitor.

"Nothing on file in the bank," Control reported.

"Whatcha got, Raven?" a black security guard at the adjacent post asked, setting aside a comic-format textbook and castering over for a look-see.

Raven backhanded the photo. "I think I know this dude. Something faxed about the hair and mouth, but I swear . . ." After swiveling around to a keyboard, Raven entered the name.

"Nicholas Keane," Achmed read over his shoulder. "Came in from the Rye Haven." A flashing icon affixed to the name indicated that additional data was available to those with appropriate clearance. Achmed regarded the monitor a moment. "Hey, man, you know who that's with him? That's Swift, man."

Raven glanced up, then reached for the phone. "Good eyes, bro."

"You better contact the Wiz, man. He wants all irregulars reported. Word came down las week."

"Enabled," Raven started to say when LIAR picked up. "This is E-4 working security at GG," he told the operator. "Put me through to Woolley—on the pronto, sweetmeat." Raven covered the mouthpiece with his hand. "This Keane's no . . . Dr. Woolley, this is Raven over at GG. We got ourselves a double-A priority here. Badge reads 'Nicholas Keane'—K, E, A, N, E—but the name's Reydak, Karel Reydak. Data I'm displaying shows him working for something called Cryo-Systems. But I'll double-down he's a tech rep, Dr. Woolley—an undercover. Used to work paramilitary with the Agency's Latin American Division."

"Are you certain, Raven?" Woolley asked after a moment.

"I never forget a face, sir, even when they've been doctored." *And especially one that's fucked me over.* "Worked side by side with him in Peru a coupla three years back. Should we secure a midcourse correction?"

Woolley paused to consider it. "Uh, no, Raven, that won't be necessary. Just send through a thermal print picture of Mr. 'Keane.' "

Raven traded an over-the-shoulder look with Achmed. "But, Doc, he's down here at GG right now making goo-goo eyes with one of the Listeners. Plus, the screen shows this Keane's got a go-to for LIAR tomorrow. You're invitin' a virus in, Doc. I mean, this guy, Doc, you don't want to mess with this guy. He's souped up—psyops wetware straight from the Agency's cook-shops."

"I'll keep that in mind, Raven. And thank you for reporting it. But I don't want this man interfered with. You're not to do anything, do you understand?"

"Well, sure, Doc, sure," Raven said, trying to make it sound convincing. "We'll just let him through."

"Good. That's exactly what we want you to do," Woolley said.

"This is some floppy shit," Achmed said, after Raven had replaced the handset. "Wiz must have some particles loose. 'Less they're jus plannin' to run him, Raven. Feed him a lot a horseshit, send him back to Langley."

Raven nodded. "Could be," he said, mulling it over. "But this one ain't the man to run." Raven reached for the phone again and punched in Percival Flage's number.

"And Woolley ordered you to let him through?" Flage asked after he had listened to Raven's account.

"As queer as it sounds."

"The Agency penetrates the organization and Woolley doesn't punch help," Flage said more to himself. "At the same time he's hounding me to raise the roof on his pet project, and Ouro's off somewhere incommunicado . . ."

"It's so weird it's spooky."

"All right, Raven, listen to me," Flage said in a determined voice. "I want you to run a trace on this Reydak. Stealth him, keep me informed—just me, no one else."

"You and you only."

"Get on it right away."

Raven launched a grin at number six, where Reydak's face was centered onscreen. He formed his left hand into a pistol shape, forefinger pressed to the glass.

"*Pow!*" he said softly. "Got'cha, Colonel."

16 When a UFO Is Not an Angel

Brady entered his personal code, AVENGING ANGEL, and sat back to watch the field fill with squadrons of blue 3-D droneships. But reaching out for the HOTAS, he caught a glimpse of his refection in the monitor screen.

Elbows on the command deck, the president buried his face in his hands. *What have I done?* he screamed at himself. He deactivated the game and moved to the desk, where he lifted an antique wooden chest from the bottom drawer. Inside were mementos: a gold nugget said to have been grandfather Elijah's first find; battle ribbons and medals awarded to Jed Brady during the war; a rosary Brother Theodore had given him at Aguas Calientes; Catherine's wedding-day garter belt, her favorite ring, a small vial of the scent she wore . . .

"God help me," Brady said into his hands.

Twenty-four hours had passed since the aborted talks in Jakarta, and there was electricity in Washington's Thanksgiving air, a smell of ozone, a feeling of imminent storm. The UN Security Council had handed down their censure, Aeroflot liners waited at Dulles to evacuate Soviet embassy personnel . . . Although Washington had yet to hear an official reply from the Kremlin. All afternoon Brady had been listening to updates: mayors, governors, senators, all taking turns with the press. He had viewed and reviewed the video disks and still couldn't explain his actions. His media advisors were urging him to issue a statement—anything at all, lest continued silence take a greater toll.

Yes, Brady thought, he would have to say something soon:

My fellow Americans . . . *What have I done! In the name of God, what was I thinking of?*

The president heard a knock at the door, closed the chest, and replaced it in the desk drawer.

"You better get Capella over here," he said, as his brother entered the room.

Eli, in black tux for dinner, bit back his first reply. "I just spoke to the vice president. He's behind you one hundred and ten percent, Ted. He told me to tell you he won't make a move until he hears from you personally."

Brady took note of Eli's grim expression. "Capella's a good man; he'll make a decent president. A *sane* one, in any case."

"He backs your stance, Ted."

"*Stance?* Is that what he thinks I was doing?"

"That's what half the *world* thinks you were doing, Ted—putting the Soviets and UIF in their place."

"Jesus Christ."

Eli perched himself on the edge of the desk. "We're going to run with it for a while, Ted. But you've got to say something. No more procrastinating. I've been in touch with Tushenko. Moscow's waiting to hear what you have to say."

"And what the hell am I supposed to tell them, Eli? Do I tell them I wasn't talking to them—that I was talking to alien invaders? Do I go on prime time and tell every American man, woman, and child I've had a vision?" Brady raised a hand to the ceiling. "That something's coming for us?"

Eli's nostrils flared. "Ted, do you see what's happening here? Even after Jakarta, you can sit here and talk to me in a rational way." He gripped his brother's forearm. "You're not insane, Ted. Some . . . *thing* is working away at you."

The president gazed at Eli's hand, then up into his eyes, searchingly. "What is it, Eli?"

The secretary of state pushed himself off the desk and took several steps into the room. "Ted, it's Ouro . . . He claims that the Soviets had a team of *psychic agents* in the summit hall." A nervous laugh escaped him. "I don't know whether to go nuts from trusting him or *not* trusting him."

The president remained silent for a long moment, then shook his head. "I don't understand. What does all this have to do with us?"

Eli clenched his fists. "The vision, Ted, your goddamned vision and everything else that's been happening to you for the past two months." He put his hands down flat on the desk. "The Russians may have been manipulating this from the start. Ted, your mind's been *raped*."

* * *

"No!" Amber Swift said, showing Woolley her back. "I know Nick, I know him! There's some mistake, Amol, there has to be."

Woolley glanced at the door to the lab where the government operative was undergoing tests. "There's no mistake," he said quietly. "He was identified by a securityman at the Center. Apparently the two of them have worked together in some capacity." Raven's disclosures only confirmed what Woolley had suspected since Amber's late-night phone call, but he left this unstated.

She turned on him. "I still don't believe it—certainly not on the word of one of Flage's goons."

"But, Amber, that's what we hired them for. To protect WEM's interests, you know that. I don't understand your defiance."

The Listener ran a hand across her forehead. "It's just . . . Is he Nicolas Keane or not?"

"His name is Reydak," Woolley told her, "Carl or Carrol Reydak."

"*Reydak!*" Amber sobbed, raising her eyes to the corridor's acoustic tile ceiling—the name on the tip of her tongue for nearly a week. She looked at Woolley, then glared at the lab door. "That son of a bitch, that son of a bitch *used* me. And I've led him right into . . ."

Woolley laid a hand on her shoulder. "And that's precisely what we would have asked you to do had we known from the start. You see, Ouro divined they would attempt to infiltrate us."

"Because of the president."

"Yes. And his wish was that we allow their agent full access to LIAR, to the Concentricity, to everything."

Amber's contact-tinted eyes went wide. "We can't do that, Amol."

"But we must. Ouro believes the time has come to demonstrate our intent. If Brady and his advisors are willing to accept us . . . You know what it could mean for us. Everything we've worked for all these years, child."

Amber aimed a turquoise-tipped finger at the lab. "I don't trust them—especially now."

Woolley tried to read her face. "You and this man, this Reydak," he said slowly. "You're lovers."

"*Were*, Amol," she replied, reddening. "But I don't understand how he could trick me. I *listened* to him, Amol. I felt his vision, his suffering. How could they manage that?''

Woolley's eyes narrowed. ''Their methods are growing more sophisticated every day.''

If only they realized that the path they were following was the wrong one, he thought. That there was so much more to be gained along the one with heart. But, as it was, individuals like Reydak remained shadowy presences, as uncertain a thing as the nature of the particles unleashed by Godzilla itself. You could find out who they were or why they were, where they were or what they were doing, but never at the same time.

He showed Amber a tight smile. ''In many ways you're right not to trust them. But the world hurries us along. You know about the events in Jakarta?''

''We heard something on the news last night,'' she said absently.

Woolley nodded. ''Everyone believes that the president was admonishing Korzliev and the others for what happened in the Horn. But if you listen to the words you can hear Brady's encounter talking. His mind is at war, his conscious self firing warning shots at his unconscious.''

''I sensed it,'' Amber said, attentive now and thinking back to Nick's—*Reydak's*—reaction as they watched the news from the Oberoi king-size bed. His fingers tickling the small of her back, his breath at the hollow of her neck, the feel of him against her . . .

''I suspect that Ouro will have need for you,'' Woolley was saying. ''If, that is, he can convince Brady's advisors to listen to reason.''

''A healing circle.''

Woolley nodded. ''I should think. And it would be to our advantage to position one of their own agents in the circle. They have a phrase for it: We need to *run* Carl Reydak.''

Amber crossed the corridor and pressed her fingertips against the stainless steel door. ''So I should continue the partnership. For the good of the movement,'' she said, turning around.

''In a word, yes.''

Amber searched herself for the feelings of betrayal, degradation, hatred one would expect to find, but came up clean. Vanished, too, was the shock, the initial anger that had greeted Amol's revelations. Because on some deeper level she knew that Reydak had not only misrepresented himself to her but to his own people, as well; that the contact she had experienced beneath the tricksters' overlays was a powerful and valid one. Reydak had been keeping secrets long before he had come to her, long before he had joined whatever agency it was that employed and had tasked him. Reydak, for most of his life, had been keeping secrets from himself.

Eli's bigot list had more than doubled since its Labor Day inception; a few more names, he thought, and the committee might as well hold open meetings. But for the moment it remained an exclusive club: an interagency double-cross committee on the present threat . . .

"All right, who's next?" Philbert Base snarled from the head of the White House Cabinet Room's burled-ash conference table.

"Morgenstern," Dick Manning answered. The secretary of defense; muscular, happily married, a soft-spoken graduate of West Point.

"Show him in," Base said.

A security-status display above the door flashed red as the Treasury director entered the room. Morgenstern was tall, gray-haired, and impeccably tailored. His lined face showed up in prime time almost as often as Base's did. Base motioned him to the table's sole empty chair. "Please keep things brief and to the point," the chief of staff advised.

Morgenstern cleared his throat, snapped open the brass clips of his attaché case, and extracted a single page of printout. "As of three o'clock this afternoon, the market was still holding. We have no reason to anticipate dangerous fluctuations in Tokyo or Sydney, where things are just getting underway. The Arabs are pulling out, but their divestments aren't likely to prove critical in the overall trend. The Japanese and Germans are antsy, but they can't afford to move quickly. Real estate doesn't roll that way, in any case."

"What if they persist?" Manning asked.

"The secretary has drawn up contingency plans to threaten a response. If that fails, we have a tentative agreement from several central banks in Europe and South America to accept an increase in the short-term interest rate. The Federal Reserve is prepared to begin purchasing dollars, but I certainly don't think we have to worry about enacting a Section 23."

"That's Exchange Stabilization, isn't it?" Niles Obstat asked.

Morgenstern nodded. "The word on the street is that most of the major firms are advising their clients to hold. As we say, gentlemen: 'After emotion rules the day, the smart money buys.' " Morgenstern put the sheet aside. "We've weathered greater crises. I would add, however, that the president's address will be a strong factor in determining which way things swing from here."

"Next," Base said, when the Treasury man had exited.

"Roche and Rizing."

Base snorted. "Get those two spin doctors in here."

Eli sat back, tuning into the faint hum of the room's electronic noisemakers as the two media advisors were shown in. Roche, who was an inch or so shorter than his partner, took the chair. They were a handsome couple, identically so, brought up on power words and power meals. Eli had always had a devil of a time telling them apart.

"The numbers are surprisingly favorable," Rizing said, reading from a fact sheet. "Resistance ratios being what they were, it's hardly surprising. Sixty-three percent back the president's show of force, twenty-seven opposed, ten undecided."

"We're certain we can redress some of this negative assessment if the president goes proactive," Roche added, taking over. "The president's silence on the matter has thrown the sequencing off, but there's an open window to shoot for. We've pinpointed a number of hot buttons and passed our assessment along to the president's writing staff."

Rizing adjusted his tie. "We've also passed along our recommendations for presentation to the haberdashers. We feel the president needs to make a strong showing when he appears. The networks are of course awaiting word from the House."

Eli shut his eyes, trying to imagine Ted standing still for an image refitting.

"Did anyone understand what the hell those two were talking about?" Loren Masters said.

Base waved a hand. "It hardly matters, Doctor." He looked to Eli, to Jose Darpa and Duke Cottel. "Do we need to deal with the writers now?"

"That can wait," Eli told him in a fatigued voice. "We have more pressing matters to discuss."

The table fell silent as Milo Colton got to his feet. The DCI looked around the room for a moment. "There's no way to preface this without sounding like a complete jackass, so I'll come directly to the point: Ouro located a team of Soviet psychics working the Jakarta hall. It's his belief that this group was responsible for the president's, um, *diatribe*, and possibly for the Shangri-la close encounter itself."

No one spoke for ten seconds; then Base said, "Is this some kind of joke, Admiral? *Psychic* agents?"

"Call them 'agents of influence' if it makes you feel better, Mr. Base. Ouro made three of them from news coverage replays; two more from the Service's documentation videos." Colton nodded to Enoch Keyes.

"We've tentatively identified them as members of the KGB's 'Popov Group,' " the SIG director told the table. "An Eastern Bloc mystic, two White Russian magicians, a Pakistani dervish, and a Siberian shaman. They operate under the auspices of Department Fifteen."

"I'm hearing things," Base said in disbelief.

Herman Sachs of the Bureau's Cult Activities Division stood up to strengthen the pitch. "Long-distance hypnotic inducement had been *the* Soviet experiment for more than thirty years. Telepathy, behavior mod. Vasiliev, I think that was the name— *Experiments in Distant Influence*."

Keyes nodded in agreement.

"It makes a lot more sense to me than a close encounter," Niles Obstat commented.

Base glanced from face to face. "You're actually *buying* this? Over how much distance, Keyes? I mean, are we talking tactical or strategic?"

The implications were obvious: Assuming the Soviets had actually succeeded in perfecting psychic weaponry and had been using it against the president from the onset, they were operating either from afar, or from practically at hand—somewhere near Camp David, close to the White House, inside the Pancasilia Hall.

Patrick O'Denvy spoke to it. "If they had to position their people right in the hall, their range has to be limited. Why would they risk their cover otherwise?"

"Risk their cover?" Potus asked. "What, you think the Russians figure we'd sweep the hall for psychics before we let the president in?"

"*Depth* of influence could be related to distance," Sachs suggested. "The president was deeply . . . touched this time."

Base shook his head. "I can't accept your scenario, Colton, not at all. And frankly I find your willingness to embrace this repugnant. That fucking Indian's behind it. He tells you he's uncovered a nest of Red psychics . . . How does he expect us to verify this? What about it, Colton, can you prove this Popov Group was behind it?''

"The fact that such a group exists at all is reason enough to accept it, Phil,'' Obstat said. "All this time we've been operating on the assumption that weapons parity was being maintained, when all the while the Soviets have been readying a telepathic offensive.''

Base raised a threatening finger. "Don't one of you mention a *psi* gap, or I'm gonna shit.''

Loren Masters looked to Colton and Keyes. "But we do have a counterpart, don't we, gentlemen? Those demented types over at AWED?''

"They're not it,'' Eli said before either man could respond. "Ouro is our counterpart. He assures me that this form of 'distant influence' is well within his group's power to deal with. There are counterforce measures that can be taken.''

"*Ouro* assures you?'' Base said, the veins in his neck standing out above his shirt collar. "*His* group!''

Eli blew out his breath, steeling himself. "Ted is considering resignation. We've either got to take Ouro at his word and trust him, or allow Ted to step down temporarily. We can doctor up some excuse. But let's look at this thing another way for a moment: Suppose the Soviets are behind it, and by making Ted appear the aggressor they hope to enlist support of the Islamic Front and the nonaligned nations in a new push for Africa. Suppose they're figuring that a crippled presidency will box us back into the isolatory stance we had to adopt after Morrow. Do we just let this go, or do we give Ouro a shot?''

Base adopted a defensive posture. "Resignation is out of the question right now. But I think we should consider the possibility of assuming committee control of the presidency.''

"I'll push for Amendment 25 before I'll do that,'' Obstat said angrily.

"Ted won't stand for it,'' Eli said. "He'd rather see Capella take over.''

"*That* won't do at all,'' Manning interjected. "No one's going to listen to Capella. We'll have a coup on our hands.''

"You mentioned some 'countermeasures,' Mr. Secretary,'' Cottel said.

Eli voiced a quiet plea to the ceiling. "A countertrance. Ouro claims that his group can 'deflect' the Popov Group's inducement.'' He waited for everyone to simmer down, then added, "I may as well tell you that Ted has already agreed to it.''

Sachs said, "It's similar to radar jamming."

"Ouro needs six members to form his ring," Eli continued, "but he's willing to effect the countertrance under our supervision. His only condition is that it take place in a . . . power spot—someplace where Ted's personal and political power is maximized."

"You're talking about the House," Base said. "You're actually going to admit a bunch of starry-eyed cultists into the very sanctum of the nation's power."

"Ouro's already furnished us with the names and Mr. Colton's operation has run a thorough check on everyone." Eli met the look in the chief of staff's eyes. "It may interest you to know, Phil, that Colton's agent is one of the six."

Base fought down a laugh as he turned his attention to the DCI. "So your mysterious Agent Orange has made it over all the psychic hurdles and landed himself smack dab in WEM's inner circle, huh, Colton?"

"We received word early this afternoon that Orange has been asked to report to WEM's field office in Annapolis to rendezvous with the other five Ouro has tasked to take part in the countertrance."

"Come on, Keyes," Base said, "you know as well as I do your penetration's been dirtied. Ouro's just found a new way to feed us more of his lies."

"I say we let them try," Eli said, searching for support. "If the countertrance fails, we discuss options."

When it was put to a vote, Base was the only member to abstain. "I'm seeing the world come unglued before my very eyes," he was heard to mutter as the meeting broke up.

17 Agents of Influence

Compromised, Reydak told himself as the shorn shaman's black eyes found him. No two ways about it.

He was on the couch, squeezed between Amber and Terrine Contra, an Earth Mother in a billowing floor-length robe, who had embraced him like a long-lost relative at the Havens front door. In velvet-upholstered chairs on the sides of the couch sat Melva Chizedek—an infant nursing at her breast; Sue Vide, life-extension nutritionist; and UFO contactee and late-night tv star, Ray Mayana. Ouro and his stunning black accomplice were across the room by the hearth, silhouetted against the leaping flames of an afternoon fire like a tormented couple on the cover of a horror paperback.

"And our thanks to Mr. Keane for setting aside his personal business to join us at this late hour."

"Here, here," Contra said, showing him a smile and resting a pudgy ring-laden hand on his. Amber did the same from her side of the couch.

They had flown the red eye in from San Francisco after the visit to LIAR and the subsequent call from Woolley that announced Reydak's admission to the winner's circle—the Concentricity, as Amber and the others referred to themselves. Nine in all, excluding Ouro and Dolores Sueño, although he had yet to meet Florence States, Leigh Burmandy, Carmine Dover, and Hiawatha Fountain, all of whom were due to arrive shortly. But Reydak sensed that the five seated in the den comprised the core—an innermost circle—with Ouro the singularity around which they revolved.

"We don't expect miracles, Mr. Keane," the shaman was saying. "But trust me when I say that your talents will lend needed support to our efforts."

Reydak felt everyone's eyes turn on him: outer eyes, inner eyes, third eyes. *Compromised*, he reminded himself, *run*. What else could account for his inclusion? He was certain he hadn't been invited in on the strength of AWED's implanted vision, the depth of Amber's involvement—genuine or otherwise—the absurd particle-collision guesswork he'd employed at Lakehaven. Ouro hadn't gotten around to detailing the "talents" that had earned him a place in the circle, or just what "efforts" had brought the Concentricity members back to the D.C. area, but the shaman's presence alone suggested some critical decision had been arrived at in the wake of the president's actions in Jakarta. Jim Wave had had no word on what that might be when Reydak checked in with SIN; Reydak's orders were simply to follow through, dirtied or not.

FBI follow cars had shadowed them in from BWI Airport; Reydak had spotted their listening post parked near the Haven grounds. Disguised as an electrician's van, the vehicle's various sensors and antennae array had been incorporated into a jumble of extension ladders, pipe carriers, and a rather cumbersome roof rack.

"We have important work to do," Ouro said, stepping away from the fire, his eyes above the tattoos continuing to single Reydak out. "Two months ago your president experienced a terrifying close encounter at the mountain retreat he calls Shangri-la."

Reydak was alone in feigning a gentle recoil.

"But what I first assumed a vision is in truth a devious manipulation—a telepathic abuse carried out by a group of very clever but dangerous warriors assembled by a foreign power."

Amber and Terri looked at one another aghast, their sudden concern as real as Reydak's own. "My god, who are they?" Contra asked.

"A Soviet group," Ouro told her. "I detected their presence in Jakarta, and their united strength is not to be lightly dismissed. The ability to throw power is a thing grasped by only the most advanced sorcerers. Tomorrow morning we must attempt to deflect their influence and rid the president of this evil that torments him and endangers world peace. But it won't be enough simply to wrest control from them. We must work to fashion an envelope of power to surround Brady and insure his continued immunity. Our collective powers will sustain the shield. This could require several hours or several days—there is no way to divine the time needed."

"Where is the work to be done, Ouro?" Amber asked. "Here?"

Ouro shook his head. "On Brady's ground. We will be informed tomorrow."

Sue Vide said, "Is this group responsible for what he said in Jakarta?"

Ouro took a step toward the couch. "This is not our concern. There is something called national security we must address ourselves to."

Reydak was watching Vide when the shaman turned to him. "Do you still wish to take part in this, Mr. Keane?"

"Yes, of course," he said, perhaps too quickly. "I'd be glad to do whatever I can. I, uh, voted for him."

The two of them fell silent, searching one another.

"Then it's time we prepared ourselves."

Dolores Sueño stepped away from the stone hearth to take hold of Reydak's hand as he was getting up from the couch. A jolt entered her like the return of an *encantado*.

Raven had chosen ultrasuede and synthskin boots for the red-eye flight, but had changed over to fright wig, chrome-studded wristlets, and highheel-shaped inhaler for the early-morning drive into Washington—the off-hours image he favored. His one suitcase was crammed full of looks, apparel, and disguises to suit a dozen needs, with the few bugs he'd had time to pack stashed among them. The rest of it was in the back of his truck, parked in a long-term lot at SFO.

He had tailed Reydak and the stone fox up to LIAR, then back into the city, where they'd tucked themselves away in the hotel for a couple of hours while Raven prowled the carpeted hallway outside their sixteenth-floor room. He thought he'd heard Swift come at least three times. Major stud, that Colonel Reydak; or maybe just a doctored hard-on. He'd even found time for pussy in Peru—a sweet Indian-blooded tracker the nationalists had sent along to guide the team in. Reydak had probably been with her when the shit went down, shaking the sheets while the Senderos rained hell on them. He was going to pay extra for that one, Raven had decided.

Six seats behind the lovebirds on the skybus and not a hint of recognition. Raven had done more than test the waters; had actually borrowed an issue of *Time* from Swift. *Pardon me, ma'am. I don't mean to disturb you . . .* a regular cowboy gent, just dripping that sick Texas charm all over her. Jeez, how he'd like to, huh!

He could trace the masquerade habit to his teen years when his old lady's lingerie fit the bill, but who had time for looking back? He left that to the Listeners and the geeks and crips the movement attracted. He'd floated into his position as security officer after bumping into one of Flage's subsidiaries down Mejico way—running black market fetal and diamond back venom at the time. Before that it had been mostly freelance merc ops, making use of the crack training Uncle Sam had seen to. Small arms, demo, recon . . . there wasn't much he couldn't hack by the time they'd drummed his ass out on a psych section. Fuck 'em, if they couldn't take a joke. He'd made a bundle in South Africa—more from what he'd looted than from what he was paid—but squandered it just as quick. Returning Stateside like the prodigal son, he'd tried the high life in Vegas and Miami for all of six months, using the fingertips Sense Augmentation had given him to tease open a safe or two, the nose to sniff out cut-rate tunnel bunnies. But it wasn't long before banks started repossessing the new cars, hotels locking him out, and overnight he'd dropped from top-floor suites to scuzzy rooms in sleazebag motels. Right in there with the recombinants: the homeless and rump-wranglers, wetback dishwashers and fruitpickers, the dot-heads and their offal clans. He wasn't worried though: There were a dozen countries in Africa and SA in need of class mercs. And even if he did catch a round each tour, he'd live through it. The shrapnel scar that paralleled his hairline, for cases: It lent character to his face, intrigued a certain type of woman, and intimidated a certain type of man.

How could he have guessed that Peru would be his Waterloo? That the Agency would leave them without a pot to piss in. Virtual warfare it was meant to be, little of the hands-on wet work, death dished out by think-tanks and drone grunts. Until the Cubes had run a virus through the firebase mainframe, and the Senderos had come in like goddamned headhunters with their bloodstained machetes . . . It had sent him spiraling down into the misery, all right. But then along came Mexico, a follow-up stint at Flage's LA pussy parlor, an overseer's position at GG . . .

Stalking Reydak was like old times—a satisfying blend of tricky assignment and personal vendetta. "Nicholas Keane's" cover had checked out down the line, as Raven knew it would. But this "salesman" had called a SIN number from the hotel in

Frisco. Now maybe it was straight-up business and maybe not. Maybe Reydak had gone to ground and was now running a penetration for Jim Wave. But then who was paying SIN to infiltrate the movement, and why in fuck's name was the Wiz passing spooks to the hub?

In Crab Town things had taken an even more interesting turn. Raven had spent the day outside the Haven, slumped down in the front seat of the rental he'd parked a block away from someone or other's surveillance van. And goddamned if Ouro—sporting a new look—and Miz Brazil herself hadn't showed up in the middle of the afternoon, delivered right to the gate by a suspiciously federal-looking stretch limo. Raven had access to the Haven, was pretty close with the security chief, in fact. And it would have been easy enough to stroll in, but he kept to the car, unwilling to punch run just yet.

By six A.M. the following day, the shaman, Sueño, Reydak, and four of the Listeners were piled into that same limo and tearing down Route 50 to D.C. like important people. Raven had played it smart by staying ahead of the car for much of the drive, then falling back when they both hit New York Avenue's rush-hour traffic.

At just after seven, the limo had entered the White House grounds. Bypassing the Executive Avenue Gate for one of the less trafficked entrances off 15th Street.

Raven had cruised around the block a couple of times, past a demonstration in Lafayette Park by a group of health nazis— "Fuck the folk body!" he'd yelled out the window, flipping the bird and laughing at them.

He was parked along Constitution now, contemplating this latest twist. Invited guests? Did that explain Reydak's presence—had the secret agent man been tasked to play messenger boy and hand-deliver an invite to Ouro and his Ouija boards and quartz tuners? But why the Nicholas Keane charade, and the call to SIN? President Brady and Ouro, that made sense; Brady was recombinant. But why was Reydak under cover?

He left the car and walked to a corner phone booth, where he punched in Flage's vanity number. Leaning against the booth's plexicocoon, he let his eyes wander over to a row of sidewalk newspaper vending machines and their LCD headline displays.

BRADY BALKS, KORZLIEV WALKS!
BRADY SHOWS A STRONG HAND IN JAKARTA!
AMERICA'S GOT THE SPIRIT BACK!

Raven shifted his attention to the sandbagged and blast-shielded entrance to the White House, across a wide expanse of manicured lawn. He wore a wicked grin by the time Percival Flage picked up. "I got news," Raven said, "big news."

Eli's committee had listened to the Bureau's Haven tapes and decided that Ouro was sending them a clear message of intent. They further agreed on the solarium as their site of choice for the countertrance. It was thought that the large top-floor room, whose glass panels overlooked the South Lawn, would pose the least number of security problems. Some of the White House staff had been moved to Blair House temporarily, and Communication Agency techs had been up all night rigging the place for sight and sound and patching everything into the Cabinet Room.

Kubark was on sentry duty at the basement entrance when the limo discharged its seven visibly agitated passengers, but there was to be no official registration of names on this occasion, no passes issued. An all-too-brief frisk and the Secret Service agent was ordered to show Ouro, Sueño, and Reydak to one elevator, while Kubark's partner, Fusilli, escorted Terri Contra, Amber Swift, Sue Vide, and Melva Chizedek to a second.

Kubark stood with his hands crossed in front of his groin, left hand grasping his right wrist, Wise-Eyes staring into the gilded elevator's hardwood-framed mirror. Save for the hair, Ouro looked as he had first seen him, in white tunic and loose-fitting cotton trousers. The shaman was chanting, all but dancing in place. Wild and red-rimmed, his eyes seemed to glow in the car's dim light. Sueño had a look of barely restrained frenzy about her, black hair spiked, except where plastered by sweat to her forehead and temples. She wore a sacklike dress and a long scarf embroidered with symbols and a jumble of dyslexic letters. What Kubark had first taken for a bag was in fact a small drum fashioned from cured leather.

Kubark had heard a good deal about Karel Reydak lately; but regarding the singleton now, he could only wonder why Colton and Keyes put so much stock in him.

Awake for the past thirty hours—and having spent most of the previous night chanting, summoning power, and inhaling pipefuls of strong tobacco—Reydak had moved through the White House basement as if lost in a dream labyrinth. Down corridors of statuary and antique portraiture, the sad eyes of the past on him. Ouro and the Listeners had been trance dancing all night long, and Reydak was experiencing a contact high of such devastating rapport that his point of reference seemed in unrelenting motion. He might as well have been *absorbed* by some fourteen-eyed creature, whose sinuous movement was continually revealing new vistas of a brightly hued world. He was inside an antique elevator car even while ascending in a second one. And beyond that he was seated by a blazing fire in a tropical forest clearing. He was marginally aware of those around him: this catlike being that called itself Ouro and its satin-skinned drummer-queen . . .

The solarium's rattan and wicker furniture had been pushed to one side to accommodate a large circular table surrounded by eight wooden stools. Through tall windows poured oblique rays of morning light, bleached of color and warmth by an albescent sky. The president was seated with his back to the glass, sunlight outlining his still form but leaving his face in shadow. He, too, had been awake all night, cross-legged in prayer and meditation on the Lincoln Sitting Room floor. His mind was quiet now, the vision as distant and unreal a thing as the sight of these seven strangers positioning themselves around the table.

Dolores Sueño's initial whack on the drum brought everyone in the Cabinet Room to their feet.

"Adjust the volume on that goddamned thing!" Philbert Base shouted to one of communication techs. "Jesus H. Christ, it's painful enough to have to sit here and watch this without getting my eardrums ruptured in the process!"

Alison Brady reached out for Dr. Masters' arm as a closed-circuit monitor showed the members of Ouro's ad hoc power circle joining hands. The shaman himself was chanting, dancing around the table to the beat of Sueño's drum.

As Brady took hold of Terri and Melva's hands, he experienced a fleeting vision of himself returned to Aguas Calientes, a prisoner of the powerful auditory and visual hallucinations that would come after days of self-imposed fasting and sensory deprivation. It had often felt like a medieval drama then, and here was that familiar sense of dislocation, shifting his awareness into high gear, draining him of the will and power to direct his thoughts. That Ouro's chants were voiced in an unfamiliar tongue was suddenly less pressing than the dazzling geometries those vocal tones were eliciting; and Brady found himself slipping into a warm pool of protective fluid, abandoning the boundaries he'd been conditioned to maintain for something all-knowing in its pervasiveness . . .

The table was a spirit canoe Ouro circled with extraordinary steps of power, dancing to rhythms dictated by the drum—a syncopated pattern that jerked his mind about like a puppet. His breath came in shallow rapid bursts, battling the pressure that threatened his chest and heart. And the Old One was with him, ubiquitous cigar, floating left eye, crippled hand, and sly smile. *Keep yourself unflinching, monkey*, N'ntara's voice told him. *Whatever fearful things you encounter, recognize them to be of your own imaginings.*

Ouro regarded Brady peripherally, around the corner of his vision. As the egg-shaped luminous *waatum* revealed itself he was comforted by what he saw: great devotional swirls of crimson and white, uncoiling like snakes from Brady's center. Pulsating lines of scarlet light banded him horizontally, suffusing the aura with a rosy tint, a flush of purity, condensing into wispy forms like clouds.

But as the shaman watched, the cirrus shapes transformed to whirling gleaming coils of blue, indigo, and violet—an approaching storm front that began to obscure the president's form in a rush of leaden, memory-laden masses. Arrows of anger pierced this sooty haze like bolts of lightning, flashing outward at the power circle itself, threatening its integrity. Reydak felt himself acted upon by an overwhelming gravitational force that pinned him to his stool. Keeping hold of Amber and Sue Vide's hands took superhuman effort, their arms straining to maintain the circle but driven back from the table to the point of dislocation.

Search for a thrown crystal, monkey. Keep yourself unflinching . . .

The lines crisscrossing Brady's aura were vibrating with such violence that Ouro began to fear for the president's life; he seemed in danger of dispersing entirely. Sueño's drum beat had become frantic and wavering, and the shaman could sense the buffeting she was taking from clear across the room. Swarms of blood-red emanations had appeared in the air, birthed from the president's solar plexus, wiggling like crazed spermatozoa and massing at opposite ends of the solarium.

"Focus the goddamned picture," Base ordered, as a kind of electronic rash spread itself across the monitor screens.

"Trying, sir," the tech said, "but I don't think it's a system aberration."

Base glowered at the man. "What are you telling me—that we're all seeing spots before our eyes?"

The tech swallowed and found his voice. "Sir, it appears to be . . . *in the room*."

Eli, standing off to one side of the table with Masters, felt his mother's smoke-yellowed fingernails dig into the flesh of his arm.

The shaman caught sight of a power crystal lodged in Brady's heart. *Reach in for it, monkey*, N'ntara instructed him, *keep yourself tenuous and sly . . .*

But no sooner did he begin to move forward when the opposing swarms of airborne blood commenced their dangerous tug-of-war, charging the air with a shrill and unbearable tone. The room was like ice. Color drained from Brady's face and his breath came in puffs of steam. His arms jerked about, sending waves of frenetic undulations through the already-stressed circle. His head dropped to the tabletop, only to jerk up an instant later in a violent spasm, as some putrid-smelling presence seeped into the room.

Stationed just outside the solarium, Kubark, Fusilli, and half a dozen other agents were stomping their feet and trying desperately to massage warmth into their arms.

"It's ff-fffuuckkingg *freezing*," someone said.

Kubark heard the detail chief in his ear. "Get your men ready to go inside." Then: "Belay that. Maintain your position. Follow-up: Maintain your position."

The anteroom had begun to warm some. Kubark peered at Fusilli's hand-held monitor: Onscreen the solarium was back in focus once more, Ouro's circle of psychics relaxed, hands back on the tabletop.

"Is it over?" someone asked.

Reydak ran his eyes around the table, and for a moment glimpsed the scene through his own unaltered consciousness: President Brady looking as he'd seen him a hundred times on television and magazine covers; Amber, Melva, Sue Vide, and Terri eyeing one another in puzzlement; Sueño motionless at her drum. Only Ouro appeared unreal, poised opposite the president in a stance suggestive of martial arts, head lowered slightly and dark eyes wary beneath a pronounced brow ridge.

In the Cabinet Room the committee members pressed closer to the screens. Each of them was in the midst of forming a half-voiced prayer of thanks when a soprano voice issued through the speakers, a sweet-sounding feminine voice.

"*Wellll-commmeee.*"

It was the president speaking.

"Is this to be the summit then?" Brady's neck elongated, his face a mask of softened, rearranged features. *"Met before, haven't we? Do you think our power so slight your meddling can test the balance? What's done is done, the disease spread, the body infected beyond repair."*

"What the hell's going on?" Base yelled, out of his chair now, hands to his head. "Is that Ted talking or not?"

The president's lips curled back from his teeth, then arranged themselves into a hideous smile. The voice became disturbingly affected. *"You think this some petty struggle, life and death; but it is more. You intrude with your devices, hoping to forestall the end, enter our domain. But you must be stopped. So many imbalanced among you to use as we see fit. So many hands to fit for bombs. Pity. Just when you were becoming such useful idiots."* The president's right hand came up, wavering as it pointed across the table. *"Even that one among you who rightfully belongs with us."*

Alison Brady's pained cry broke the Cabinet Room silence.

"Get your people in there!" Eli screamed at Robert Potus.

Reydak felt the oak table begin to rise and tilt, levitating a foot before it slammed down against the floor. It rose again and came down harder this time; then again and again. The windows were rattling in their frames, hairline cracks running riot through the panes of glass. Across the South Lawn, the Monument itself seemed to be swaying.

The president went rigid and shot to his feet, shaking head to foot as if in the grip of palsy or grand-mal seizure, his contorted face a malevolent orange disguise. Dolores Sueño emitted a strangled sound as some unseen force central to the table propelled Reydak and the Listeners to all corners of the room. The windows imploded, launching a shower of wood and glass slivers. Reydak felt a whirlwind tearing at his clothes. He heard the table groan, saw it go up on one edge and split apart with a deafening crack. Pieces of wood impacted the walls with explosive force. One hand-turned leg caught Melva full in the face; a second all but impaled Sue Vide, and sent her careening backward toward the windows. Terri and Amber crashed into a hastily stacked arrangement of wicker chairs, which came tumbling down around them.

Reydak experienced a pain in his head that mirrored the anguished shrieks of the wood, his mind flooded with images of assault and pursuit; and from somewhere deep within him rose an almost familiar voice that tried to rally to his defense. A lump in his throat, regurgitated from the pit of his being, before the lights went out . . .

Brady was still standing, arms flailing wildly, torso locked in feverish twists. A howl was tearing itself from his throat, tendons and muscles bulging like cables under sunset flesh. Even Ouro seemed powerless against the intrusion, sprawled like some discarded toy amid the room's wreckage, face and arms bristling with blood-smeared glass needles and triangles. Carved wood and chunks of plaster loosed from the ceiling littered the floor around him.

. . . Reydak dug himself out from under a collapsed bookcase and the several dozen volumes it had once held to find Secret Service agents and techs attending to everyone. The president had apparently already been whisked out. Amber, her head bloodied, was glowering at him.

"His ff-finger pointed at you," she stuttered as a woman agent helped her to her feet. "You're the one who belongs with them. Spy!" she cried, collapsing into the agent's arms. *"Spy!"*

PART THREE

"HIATUS FROM NORMALCY . . ."

I would like to tell you, Senator, about my theories for harnessing the lifeforce. It would make nuclear power seem like child's play.

—Robert Walker as Bruno in Alfred
Hitchcock's *Strangers on a Train*

18 "Hello, Starshine"

In staunch defiance of Lake Michigan's chilling winds, the president stood motionless, hatless, and stern-faced behind the lectern's ballistic shield, while audio engineers waged war with sound system feedback. Outside the arena, water and gas cannons idling in the streets, a joint phalanx of FBI agents, Secret Service personnel, and local law-enforcement units were fighting to control feedback of a different sort. Protestors railed from behind wooden barricades, fueling Michigan's icy gusts with their waving placards, their angry contribution to wind-chill. It seemed like old times for those in the crowd pushing middle age—the surges and swells, the familiar chants and slogans. A GBS director ordered his cameraman to close on a sign that read: BRADY: DON'T PLAY CHICKEN WITH OUR NATION. And another done in scrawled, blood-red print: THE NEXT ONE WILL BE FOUGHT WITH STICKS AND STONES.

Kubark's eyes assessed the crowd from his in-close position on the rostrum. He could hear the demonstrators' chants above the rhythmical clapping of the audience, the sound of the wind, the high-pitched speaker screech. Why Chicago to deliver this much-awaited address? he asked himself. Why of all places had Eli's committee settled on Chicago?

The Secret Service agent watched techs begin a confused dance of ineffectual activity as the president, leather-gloved hands plunged deep into the pockets of his overcoat, delivered a firm look to the control booth. They knew better than to return a hopeless shrug, the media secretary having promised Brady's address to be nothing less than historic. But electronic snafus had become an intimate part of the president's life of late, both inside the House and out. It was remarkable enough that Brady was here at all, Kubark thought—that the secretary of state and his select committee had even allowed him to set foot outside the District, let alone address the nation. Word was that Niles Obstat and Jose Darpa had written most of the speech, and that Capella was being groomed to assume control of the presidency. But Kubark had also heard rumors to the effect that Brady had little memory of what had gone down in the solarium. The *gas explosion*, that was.

The feedback finally brought under control, the crowd began to quiet. The president placed his hands flat on the slanted top of the lectern and suffered through three false starts before his voice was resounding clearly through the arena and out over the plaza beyond. He was a few words along when he stopped, turning away from the teleprompter, to fix his gaze squarely on the crowd.

" 'In God We Trust,' " Brady said when the chanting had died down, " 'In God We Trust.' More than a national slogan, these four words represent a united affirmation of faith in our predestined course. And it is furthermore our *commitment* to that faith that God be given his due. For it is in *our* nation that He has placed *His* trust; and as long as the power of that trust lies in my hands, *this nation will not shrink from the obligations imposed by that holy alliance.*"

The crowd offered tentative applause, waiting.

Brady raised a clenched hand. "Any group with designs on the destiny of this planet had better take this into account!" His fist struck the lectern, sending a rumble through the arena's huge speakers and throwing the crowd into a frenzy. Brady let the applause continue for some time, then raised his arms over his head in a triumphant gesture.

At the same time, the sun, which all morning long had been playing peek-a-boo with fast-moving clouds, seemed to choose that moment to appear and bathe the arena in golden shafts of light.

Brady felt the warmth touch the back of his neck and infuse him with new energy. "We are in the presence of the Lord," he told the crowd.

And he said it so softly, so reverently, that the arena fell eerily silent. The words, the sussurant wind, the sunlight emanating from the stratified sky directly behind the president's back sent a wave of expectancy through the crowd.

"Coexistence has always been our stance. But we do not and will not tolerate aggression." The president swept his right arm back and gestured to the sun. "I see them marching out of the past to join us at the front: Minutemen, Davy Crocketts, and Pershings; Green Mountain Boys, rangers, and marauders; lonestars, lawmen, and rough-riders; doughboys, GIs, and Green Berets . . . All marching beside us, our forces growing in strength, converging, sure and confident of victory. A mighty river of men and women rushing victorious to the sea of blessed tranquility. A great spectral army in full battle array marching toward victory!"

"I see them!" a woman near the rostrum shouted.

"They're here!" someone else said, pointing to the sky.

"Look!"

"Oh, my God!"

"I see them!"

Against his conditioning, Kubark swung around to check the sky. People were rising to their feet, hands at their brows to stare into the sun. Media techs swung their cameras from body-watch positions to aim them at the clouds.

And the multitudes became of two camps: those who shared the president's vision of a ragtag army of celestial giants marching in unison across the eastern sky; and those in the crowd squinting perplexed into the diffuse light, seeing only wind-torn stratus moving rapidly across the face of the sun.

Andrey Nikolayevich Vasilov stepped into light snow from the black pool ZIL he had ridden out from Revolution Square. Winter had blown in with full force after the October Revolution weapons parades, and there was already a meter on the wooded grounds surrounding KGB Center. Vasilov secured his fur cap with a downward tug, raised the collar of his coat, and was just thanking the driver when he heard a man's voice call his name.

"Comrade Vasilov," the thin voice repeated.

Vasilov glanced over his shoulder. Popov was walking briskly toward him, moving like a penguin in his long woolen overcoat. Technically, the man was still with the S and T Directorate, but General Secretary Korzliev and Colonel Leshin, head of the Committee for State Security, had recently placed Popov and his small team of fakirs under the auspices of Department Fifteen, which dealt exclusively with biophysical weaponry.

"Comrade," Popov said, exhaling clouds like a little steam engine and embracing him. "You are here to see Leshin?"

Vasilov thought a moment, then nodded, forcing a smile.

"I, too." He took Vasilov's arm and began to steer him toward the curved front of the modern building. "This is most important, Andrey Nikolayevich, most important. But perhaps we can spend a few moments together afterward, just the two of us."

"I have shopping to attend to," Vasilov said, hoping that would do. But Dmitriy Popov only laughed.

"Nonsense. You will soon see that we have much to discuss."

Vasilov grunted noncommittally. He had known Popov for more than a decade, but no real friendship had been forged between them; and suddenly here was Popov full of good cheer and solicitous. Vasilov had to admit that he envied the man, the privileges Popov's successes had earned him—the sleek Lada sedan, the dacha on the sea, the spacious apartment on Mishkin Prospekt with shelf after shelf of Western texts and a complete run of Star Trek videodisks. Vasilov had never been there, but he was constantly hearing all about it. And he had to admit to feelings of guilt, as well, because not once had he known Popov to grow inflated with self-importance. The man some considered a *seer* continued to dress and behave as one of lesser station, often deferring amicably to his inferiors, many of whom would have taken pleasure in seeing him toppled.

"Just what is it that makes your shopping such essential business?" Popov pressed when they had been cleared through security.

"Personal items, Dmitriy Aleksandrovich. But essential ones."

"Then we can use my card," Popov said with a wink, leading the way into the elevator carriage. "I will take you to a place without waiting lines."

They had been recruited by the KGB the same year, albeit from divergent backgrounds—Popov as scientist, Vasilov as journalist—and in many ways their relationship defined the KGB and Politburo line on the issue of biophysical warfare, what the West called parapsychological weaponry. The Russian psyche had always been comfortable with mysticism and spiritualism—with shamanism, fly agaric mushrooms, ecstatic saints, Rasputin, and the Tunguskiy *divo*—but psychism hadn't become a true Komitet commodity until a French newspaper leaked a report that the American CIA was experimenting with telepathy as a possible means of communicating with nuclear submarines. As a result, Popov's team had begun to receive heavy funding, and, what with *glasnost* and *perestroika* then in vogue, Vasilov (with *Novosti* at that time) and a number of others had been instructed to encourage public acceptance of ESP.

Popov's group of Tungus shamans and dervishes was moved from Lubyanka to less obvious quarters in Kiev and tasked for the strangest of assignments—manipulation of weather, disruption at Olympic games and chess tournaments, interference at summit conferences—but Popov's golden opportunity had come when one of his team had divined and thereby prevented an assassination plot directed at the general secretary himself. Since then, Korzliev and Leshin had become obsessed with the idea of mind control.

The KGB chief was waiting for them in his third-floor office, pacing the mandala designs of his favorite Afghan carpet—one of the few permitted in the Center—a laboratory animal studying a complex maze. With him was General Borovitskiy of the GRU. The two men were sharing glass cups of steaming tea, and the room smelled of Belomorkanal 100s. It was the general who motioned Vasilov and Popov to be seated, while Leshin rapidly assumed his customary place behind the huge, brass-footed antique desk that had been passed down to him by a long list of predecessors.

The KGB chief motioned at the silver tea service and samovar on the desk and said, "Please, comrades," but they both declined.

Leshin shrugged and refilled his cup. "We must unravel this knot quickly," he said, addressing Popov. "Your information has received verification—the Secret Service agent was indeed Gabriel Ouro. Now, Comrade Popov, are you certain that he identified your agents?"

Well aware of Borovitskiy's skepticism regarding biophysics, Popov chose his words carefully. "While the rest of President Brady's in-close protectors were going through their usual pantomime, I myself watched Ouro single out five members of my group."

Borovitskiy shook his large head. Vasilov recognized the penetrating gaze that had become legendary. "Exactly what was your team there to accomplish?" the general asked.

"To concentrate on the American president," Popov said.

" 'To concentrate.' To concentrate in what way, comrade?"

Popov looked to Leshin for permission. "We were to direct ourselves to the president's colon, Comrade General."

Borovitskiy grimaced. "What manner of madness is this?"

"Diarrhea," Popov clarified. "To make it impossible for the president to think clearly. Perhaps succeed in sending him from the hall."

The GRU man thought for a moment, then laughed loudly, hands clasped over his belly.

"You may laugh, Comrade General," Leshin said, "but we know now that the opposition had its own agents of influence at work in Jakarta." He turned to Vasilov. "How long has this been going on, and how is it that word has not already reached this office?"

"I am sorry, Comrade Chairman," Vasilov began, "I—"

"Has there been any mention of Brady's affiliation with Ouro in the American press?"

Vasilov stammered, "N-nothing has come to light, Comrade Chairman."

Rising, the KGB chief began to pace in front of the bullet-proof windows that overlooked the Center's circular access road. "Nothing from our rezidents," he mused, "nothing from our illegals. Do either of you believe it possible that Ouro willingly allied himself with Central Intelligence?"

"It hardly seems in keeping with his profile," Popov proffered. "He is not only an extraordinarily gifted psychic, but a healer, as well. A man of God, some might say."

Borovitskiy took offense at the term. "The Politburo will require a plan for consideration."

Leshin whirled on Popov. "Understand me, comrade, this is no chess tournament. I will not stand before the Politburo with nothing but idle speculations in hand. Perhaps this Ouro has his own reasons for accompanying Brady. But my instincts tell me that all this is somehow connected to President Brady's maniacal posturing and empty threats."

Borovitskiy narrowed his eyes at Popov. "It wasn't your team that put those words in Brady's mouth, was it?"

Popov grew flushed. "Comrade Chairman—"

"I begin to wonder," Leshin interrupted. "Are the American *people* even aware that their leader is attending summit talks with an occultist on leash?"

The general waved his hand dismissively. "They know he associates with monks and poets. Why should Ouro bother them?"

"Exactly my point," Leshin said. "Why conceal the relationship unless there is something unnatural about it?"

Borovitskiy's bushy eyebrows danced. "An illness?"

"Perhaps a *psychological* illness."

Popov cleared his throat meaningfully. "My group actually did detect—"

"Vasilov, I want you to see to it that the international press is made aware of the situation. You have photographs, videotapes, some evidence of Ouro's presence?"

"I'm certain we do, Comrade Chairman."

"Then use them in whatever way your department sees fit. Perhaps leak them through the Institute for Policy Studies. I will clear things with the Central Committee and have the rezidents informed. In the meantime, Popov, I will need to know everything your section has on Ouro and this movement he heads. General Borovitskiy, your Information Directorate will want to review all our recent activities carefully—at least as far back as the East African War."

"Further active measures may be called for," Borovitskiy thought to add.

Vasilov watched the KGB chief at the windows. Snow was melting, running in rivulets down the glass. Vasilov couldn't help but see a wet affair in the making.

The oak table had been thoroughly examined, the voiceprint recordings checked and rechecked. Technical Service Division's problem was that all the real *experts* were over in WEM's camp. The Agency techs found no traces of evidence in the hardwood that could be considered analogous to the isotropic irregularities often observed in various metals following psychokinetic experiments. The two-and-three-quarter-inch-thick tabletop had simply snapped and splintered.

And the phenomenal event had fractured alliances, as well, Eli thought, as he ran his eyes around the White House Situation Room table. The meetings had been driven underground now, and there seemed little hope in rescuing Ted or the presidency. Philbert Base, Loren Masters, and the rest of the ever-expanding damage assessment committee were at each other's throats.

"*Countertrance,*" the chief of staff was correcting Herman Sachs. "I don't want to hear anyone else use the word 'exorcism.' Regardless, Professor, it was not a *gas* explosion, or a goddamned minitornado. Ouro planted a charge in the table. Your search detail just didn't do its job, Potus."

"The windows *imploded*, Mr. Base," the Service chief barked back. "There was no evidence of an explosive charge."

"It had nothing to do with Ouro," Loren Masters said.

"Then perhaps you'd care to comment on the voice we heard, Doctor," Base said. "A charlatan's trick if I ever heard one."

"You're familiar with the research that's been conducted on

cases of 'possession,' Phil—the inexplicable events that can accompany schizophrenia.'' The White House physician sought Eli out. ''Didn't *any* of you recognize something familiar about Ted's voice? Alison and I caught it right away—that was *Catherine*'s voice, Eli.''

Eli blanched. ''Catherine . . .''

''All that business about intruders and punishment . . . You remember the things Ted was saying when she was dying. He was ready to follow her into the afterlife and bring her home.''

''We could compare the voiceprints,'' Herman Sachs suggested meekly. ''I'm sure we have the First Lady on file somewhere.''

''You do that,'' Base said. ''And then you reread what Ouro's written about possession. He threw the vision and now he's damn near got control of the White House.'' The COS glared across the table at Niles Obstat and Jose Darpa. ''And a fine job you people did with that Chicago speech.''

''You know we didn't write in any of that 'In God We Trust' sermonizing,'' Obstat fired back. ''That was extemp on Ted's part.''

''The press is calling it 'inspired,' '' Duke Cottel pointed out. ''The *Times* compared Chicago to Fatima.''

Base threw the ceiling an imploring look. ''Splendid. And the *Post* is talking about 'a newfound Brotherhood of White House Magicians'—a goddamned *'pagan cabal.' *'' The COS glanced at Vice President Capella. ''And there'll be no handoffs, understand, Al?''

''Fine with me,'' Capella said, showing his palms.

Base snorted, then added, ''It's my guess we don't have to look farther than Ouro's mob to learn who leaked this thing.''

''I disagree,'' Milo Colton argued. ''I smell the hand of the KGB disinformation in this. It's possible they spotted Ouro in Jakarta.''

''What else *would* you smell?'' Patrick O'Denvy said. ''It's no secret where the Agency stands: You want Ouro in your back pocket.''

Colton looked the FBI director square in the eye. ''Stick to browbeating librarians, Pat. That's what you're best at.''

O'Denvy came halfway out of his chair, aiming a finger across the table. ''What about you and your goddamned stamp fiascos, Colton? Your 'art collection'?''

The DCI laughed. ''Just because you're stuck with Fort Hoover, Pat—''

"That'll be enough," Base said, loud enough to silence the table. "What's the blowback from the speech?" he asked Eli in a calmer tone.

Eli ran a hand through his hair. "Tushenko's gone home; the Soviets and the UIF are posturing, shuffling troops and artillery around. But as crazy as it sounds, the numbers are still reading favorable. The dissenters have grown louder but not necessarily stronger. The New York Market and the Chicago Merc say their circuit breakers are holding, and teladvisement's suggesting we control the spin on the Daley Arena incident."

"Control the spin how?" Base said.

"Bring in a team of ambiance directors from the coast for the president's next address. Holographic cloud projections, a suitable score, a handpicked audience of susceptible subjects . . ."

Duke Cottel stroked his chin and traded glances with Jose Darpa. "Could that work?"

Darpa played with the ends of his string tie. "Iss a lease wort a try."

"The climate's right," Milo Colton added, slipping a paper out of his briefcase and sending it around the table. "You talk about numbers, take a look at the Blue Star figures."

"Mass hysteria," Base said, impatient.

"It's the *Soviets* we should be worrying about," McVee said, seemingly filling the room as he stood up. Silent for most of the meeting, he'd reached the end of his rope. Ouro and the Whole Earth Movement didn't bother him at all—he'd had to deal with a Defense Department Meditation Club once, a "new aura" at the Pentagon—but the Reds were something else again. And McVee finally understood why the president had resurrected WANT-ADZE: It was Brady's way of applying XT attack scenarios to the Reds without riling his soft-sistered advisory staff. Sneak attacks from advanced deployment zones, broken codes, alien tongues . . . it was a stroke of genius.

"You're not taking this 'psi gap' seriously enough," he lectured the committee. "Why, we practically *gave* the shield to Korzliev, and all of you played deaf and dumb when I was warning you about their eximer installation at Krasnoyarsk—"

"General," Eli cut in, "we don't really need to go through that again, do we?"

McVee worked his jaw. "Mr. Secretary, I viewed the solarium recordings and I for one refuse to believe the Indian had anything to do with it. Now it's obvious to me that this Soviet team—this Popov Group—has a much stronger hold over the president than anyone realizes. In fact, I'm beginning to think this so-called Blue Star is nothing but a Red trick.''

"Ridiculous," Milo Colton said. "They don't have what it takes to pull off something like that.''

"What about the accusation, then, Colton?" McVee asked gruffly. "This someone who belonged to them . . . It looked to me like the president was pointing directly at your masking agent. He might even be the leak Mr. Base is looking for.''

"The recordings don't bear that out," the DCI said in defense, throwing Enoch Keyes a sideways glance. "The president could have been pointing to Ouro or one of his group." Colton folded his arms. "In any case, we're running a check on our operative," he added quietly.

McVee snorted arrogantly. "Wouldn't that be just like you boys over at Langley. Not only is your operation compromised right off the bat, but the agent you task to run the penetration turns out to be a KGB mole.''

The table fell silent for a moment.

"Just what does Ouro have to say about all this?" Masters thought to ask.

Eli studied his hands. "Actually, his thinking is close to General McVee's. He claims it's not, as you suggest, a case of self-inflicted illness. Maybe the anniversary of Catherine's death touched something off, or made Ted susceptible to outside influence, but it's not something Ted's *perpetuating*. In other words, it's not Ted speaking to Ted, but something speaking *through* him, using him, trying to disrupt the presidency . . .''

Eli looked up to find a dozen faces regarding him sadly and his voice began to trail off. "I think it's best we take a vote," he said at last.

Base, O'Denvy, Sachs, and Manning were still inclined to believe that Ouro was somehow behind things; while McVee, Cottel, Capella, and Robert Potus thought the Soviets involved. Masters, Darpa, and Obstat were convinced the president was ill. Colton, Keyes, and Eli declined to comment, but were still willing to accept Gabriel Ouro as an ally.

Enoch Keyes put a hand on the DCI's arm as everyone was filing out the Situation Room door headed for the steps. "Forty years ago I knew a man who was trying to warn everyone about a 'psi gap,' " the SIG director said in a confidential tone.

"Who was that?" Colton asked, just as quietly.

" 'Mr. ESP,' " Keyes said. "Pavel Reydak."

19 The Pucker Factor

"That's *Karel*," Reydak said to Amber's back, spelling it out for her.

"Carl, Carrol, Karel, what difference does it make? You lied to us, you used me."

Her face was tear-streaked when she turned from the window, but her ultratech eye makeup was intact. Her forehead wore a smaller version of the dressing Loren Masters had applied two days before, after the unsuccessful exorcism. It was the first time Amber had spoken to Reydak since.

The Bureau had returned him and the Listeners to the Annapolis Haven, where they'd been debriefed by the four members of the Concentricity who hadn't taken part in the power circle countertrance. Susan Vide and Melva Chizedek had been moved to a WEM-operated wellness clinic where they were recovering from their wounds; Mayana was driving the infant down to Melva's sister in Virginia Beach. Reydak assumed that Ouro and Dolores Sueño had remained with President Brady. No one was saying just who or what had been responsible for repulsing the shaman's efforts.

"And I don't care who hears us," Amber seethed in a low voice, gesturing to the tall hedge that hid the Haven from the street. "They're your people anyway."

"They're not my people," Reydak said. "They're FBI. Secret Service, maybe."

Amber stood akimbo. "That's splitting hairs, Karel. You're a government agent, so those are your people. Even the president identified you. You belong to them—he said it himself."

Reydak had thought it through a dozen different ways and still couldn't figure it. Keyes had assured him Brady was to have no knowledge of the penetration op the committee had designed;

so how was it the president had blown his cover? *If*, that was, Brady's finger had actually been pointing to him and not Ouro. In any event, Jim Wave had once again instructed him to carry on.

Reydak squared his shoulders, risking a step forward, and prized a SIN business card from his wallet. "Call them," he said, handing it to her. "This started out as a private operation. It has nothing to do with the feds. I wanted to tell you. You practically had my name anyway."

Amber glanced at the Auto-Dial card, tried to tear it in two, and ended up simply throwing it back at him. "What do you take me for, Karel? Of course they'll back you up. They'll tell me who you work for and what you make and all about the tragedy you experienced a year ago . . . They'll say anything to keep you on the job."

"It's not a job," Reydak insisted. "Not anymore."

She gave him a narrow-eyed smile, tears slick on her cheeks. "Time to turn on the charm, is that it, Agent Reydak? You've been found out, but maybe you can still seduce your way back in."

"Stop it, Amber. What we have has nothing to do with the rest of this."

She shook her head. "You're wrong, Karel, dead wrong. It has everything to do with this." She wiped her face and grew pensive. "I suppose I can't really blame you for trying. Maybe I can even forgive the suspicious, paranoid people who sent you." She regarded him for a long moment. "Ouro knew you were coming—someone like you at any rate. He told us to let you through, did you know that? We thought it would help."

Reydak held her vindictive gaze. "So who used who, Amber?"

Her mouth tightened. "Don't give me that crap. I didn't know who you were, and I certainly wouldn't have invited you into my bedroom if I did. I suppose it's too much to ask for anything *genuine* out of this world."

Reydak let it hang, inclined to agree. "Then what made you do it?"

"I've been asking myself every five minutes for the past three days, Karel."

Reydak took her by the shoulders, caressing her arms. "I want to know why. Was it on the strength of what I told you, or was it something you read between us—something stronger than all this bullshit about visions and mind control?"

She froze in his grip, glaring at him. "So you think it's all bullshit. You think we're just suckering people out of their hard-earned money, fattening ourselves up." She twisted out of his grip. "Tell me about the solarium, Reydak. Do you honestly believe we *arranged* that to happen? You think we'd poison the president's mind, then nearly kill ourselves in an attempt to set him free? Answer me—do you?"

"I think you're capable of it," Reydak said after a moment.

"But do you believe we *did* it, Karel?"

He shook his head.

"Say it," she demanded. "Say it so your goddamned friends can hear you."

"No," Reydak said. "I don't believe you arranged it."

Amber sighed wearily and slumped down onto the window-seat cushion. "I'm exhausted. And why does it seem so dark in here?"

Reydak saw that she was right: It was as if an immense shadow had fallen over the house; a darkness that wouldn't disperse no matter how many lights were switched on against it.

"There's something you need to do for yourself before you go," she said, looking up at him. "It has to do with our first contact—the one that almost gave me your name."

Reydak led her away from the window. "Listen to me," he said softly. "My parents are alive. I'm giving it to you straight, not as Nick Keane but Karel Reydak. I don't know anything about this UFO encounter. I've been looking for the damn things for twenty years and I'm still not sure I've ever seen one."

Amber puzzled over his statement for a moment, then said: "Let us help you—in our own way."

"The way you helped Brady."

"It's important, Karel."

Reydak pictured the solarium: the president howling like some banshee, the windows imploding, the table cracking . . . "I don't know," he started to say.

"In private," she told him, not much more than mouthing the words. "We have a special place."

Terri Contra was last to enter the Haven's windowless east-wing room, hobbling in on crutches and resting her bandaged ankle on an embroidered footstool. Amber was already seated at the low table, alongside Florence States, WEM's wild-haired psychic surgeon. Across from them sat Carmine Dover, fifty-something and founder of a corporation that manufactured sensory dep tanks and knockoff Power Pods; Leigh Burmandy, former debutante, call girl, tarot card reader, and life-extension author, who was said to be something of a shaman in her own right; and Hiawatha Fountain, the Concentricity's psychometrist. Fountain was black, close to sixty, his face crazed with burn scars he'd never had fixed. The power to *read* objects and exorcize virused computer mainframes had come to him in a hospital bed, shortly after a streetgang had dropped a Molotov into the St. Louis Goodwill box Fountain had called home for three years.

Reydak had to laugh. The room was the latest of WEM's surprises, all but concealed from the very mansion itself by false walls and doorways, and probably secure from all attempts at ELINT penetration. He recalled the briefing and all-night power session Ouro had held before the countertrance; how they had all gathered in the downstairs den, which was readily accessible to the Bureau's infinity mikes and laser windowpane vibration readers. Deliberately, he now realized. So there were secrets yet to be revealed, circles within circles within circles . . .

"I'm sorry I'm late," Terri said, coughing. "I was on the phone with Dr. Banjaree. Sue could be home tomorrow morning, but it looks like Mel will have to stay there for several days. They're having trouble controlling the bleeding."

"Poor dear," Florence said. "Is the child going to be all right with her sister?"

Terri nodded.

"I think we should go over there and see what we can do," Amber suggested.

Contra coughed again and cleared her throat. "I agree. We'll go tomorrow morning."

Reydak watched Leigh Burmandy's expression change from one of mild concern to apprehension. "Are you feeling all right?" she asked Contra. "You look pale, Terri."

"It's just this leg," Contra told her, reaching down to touch the soft cast. "Plus fatigue from all this worrying. I wish Ouro would call. This whole thing has me very upset."

"We can postpone this if you're not up to it," Amber suggested.

"No, no, I think it's important we go through with it." The Listener looked over at Reydak. "Are *you* feeling up to it, Mr. Keane? That's what matters."

Amber reached for Reydak's hand. "Um, listen to me, all of you. Karel and I have talked."

Contra mustered a broad smile for Reydak's benefit. "Welcome, Karel."

There was something about the way the rest of them echoed the welcome that spiked Reydak's hair.

"We should begin then," Florence said, taking Reydak's other hand and directing it toward a circular touch-screen centered on the tabletop.

Carmine had been setting up the rig when Reydak walked in.

The screen was an inch or so thick and some two feet in diameter. A series of concentric rings took shape as the screen was activated, quickly resolving into a haphazard arrangement of letters, numbers, symbols, and two-, three-, and four-letter words, at the center of which was the word ENTER. Responses were elicited by means of a transparent silicon sensor disk, and displayed on a video monitor Carmine had positioned to the left of the soundproof door. The disk was just large enough to accept the fingertips of five hands. Amber excluded herself to call the questions, while Dover fiddled with the monitor remote.

"We gather in good faith to seek the truth," she intoned rapidly, with eyes closed. "We voice our appeal to that which is without voice. That it may speak through us, we pray; that it may reveal unto us, we pray; that it may unburden us, we pray . . ."

Reydak felt a slight vibration commence in the disk a second before it began to whiz as if frictionless across the face of the screen, executing circles, loops, and figure-eights. He tried to raise his fingers some, but found them held fast to the disk's vibrating and faintly tingling surface. A moment later the disk came to an abrupt stop, shuddering in anticipation, seemingly floating.

"Is there a presence that wishes to commune with us?" Amber asked, glassy-eyed.

The disk shot across the screen to the word YES, then angled down to ENTER.

"Yes," a neutral sounding synth-voice said from the monitor speaker.

"Are you here to speak to someone in this room?"

"YES," again—from screen and speaker.

"Do you wish to identify that person?"

Reydak's heart raced as the disk found the letters of his name.

"Karel Reydak," Amber said, having trouble with the words. "Is it Karel Reydak you wish to speak to?"

"YES AND NO."

"You are reluctant to speak?"

"NOT RELUCTANT."

"There is someone else you wish to address, as well."

"ALL SOMEONES."

"You wish to speak to all of us, is that it?"

"YES."

"Speak to us then: What would you have us hear?"

The disk flew through a series of moves, tracing triangles, squares, and circles. The voice spoke as individual words took shape.

"SEEK-THE-STRENGTH-I-GAVE-YOU-HIDE-AWAY-THE-FEAR-THEY-LEFT-YOU-WITH-LOOK-TO-THE-PAST-FOR-MY-HAND-IN-YOURS-MY-UN-DYING-LOVE-AND-SUP-PORT-IN-ALL-THAT-YOU-MUST-BE-COME . . ."

Reydak wondered which of them was behind it. He stared into Hiawatha's inscrutable black face; at the sweat beading up on Flo States' broad forehead; the rings on Contra's thick fingers; the crysalis tattoo on Leigh's delicate forearm. One of them was propelling the disk, serving up nonsensical mutterings. Or maybe they'd agreed beforehand to use a couple of WEM's pat phrases?

"Who left the fear?" Amber said, clearing her throat. "Are you speaking to Reydak now?"

"YES."

Reydak was suddenly aware of how chilled the room had become. Fountain and Dover were coughing repeatedly.

"Can you tell him where this fear came from? Who left the fear?"

"THE NIGHT MACHINE . . ."

"What night machine? From where?"

"THE NIGHT MACHINE. THEIRS—"

Reydak sensed a subtle change in the disk's movements; it seemed rooted to the screen now, gravitationally bound the way his fingers had felt a moment before.

"Who speaks to Reydak?" Amber asked with some difficulty, rising from her chair. "Will you identify yourself?"

"FA—"

"Father? Father—is that it?" Her expression was schizted, her hands shaking.

"Let it finish," Reydak heard himself shout. "Don't put words in it's mouth."

Amber nodded. "Will you identify yourself?"

"FA-AM-ILY."

Reydak cursed under his breath.

"Your father's name," Amber rasped, turning to him.

"John," he bit out.

"John. Is it John who speaks?"

The disk whipped to NO and began to slam itself up and down on the screen as if to emphasize the reply.

"NO-NO-NO-NO-NO-NONONONONONONONONONONONONONONONONO . . ."

"We have to break contact!" Terri yelled.

Amber reached out a hand to help steady the disk. "Who speaks? Tell us who speaks!"

The disk hesitated, then raced through an unstoppable pattern of lightning-quick pentagrams.

"PAV-EL," the voice said. "PAV-EL-PAV-EL-PAV-EL-PAVEL-PAVEL-PAVELPAVELPAVELPAVELPAVEL . . ."

With all six hands still affixed to it, the disk rose straight up and plummeted with sufficient force to smash through the screen. Bright-red blood from lacerated fingers peppered everyone as hands and arms were withdrawn.

"Pavel," Amber said, clasping a bloodied hand on Reydak's forearm. "What does it mean, Karel—Pavel?"

Reydak leaned back from the table, checking himself for cuts while the Listeners picked glass splinters from each other's hands.

"It's Czech for 'trouble,' " Reydak grumbled.

"Paddle?" Raven whispered to himself in the dark. He tried it again, varying the inflection this time. "Paddle." Or 'pabble,' he thought and grinned, certain he had it. "Pabble, yeah."

Only what the hell did 'pabble' mean?

He yearned to scratch his head where the plastic loop that secured the earplug was tickling him, but there wasn't enough space between the one-by-twelve floor joists to manage it. As it was he was flat on his back, hands mummied across his chest, nose flattened against the subfloor of the Listener's sanctum sanctorum—a room that didn't show on the house plans and wasn't even wired in to the Haven's central security system. He'd had a bitch of a time just locating the chamber, secreted as it was among the east wing's funhouse maze of bedrooms, storage closets, stairways, and crawlspaces. But a bit of searching, measuring, tapping on walls, zeroing in on blind zones, and *bingo*, he was in.

And now he had the word: *Pabble*.

"Has to be a cipher," he decided, feeling his enthusiasm begin a slow backward slide.

Some sort of seance had been going on, with Reydak occupying the hot seat. The room's electronic noisemakers were doing a number on his hearing, but he'd heard enough to form a general idea of what was happening. A lot of the usual mumbo-jumbo, then *crash*! some asshole had dropped a glass or something on the floor right over where he was lying. The nigger with the Indian name, he guessed; or that Flo States who went around pulling sacs of sick shit out of people with her hands. Made him want to heave. *I got some sacs for you, Flo*, he thought, grabbing his testicles. But a glass—that was what it sounded like. A kind of big glass, though.

He had tailed the feds' eyes-only limo back to the Haven from the White House; watched Reydak's love canal climb from the exclusive comfort of the backseat with her thinking cap Johnson and Johnsoned. At first he figured: smacked her head on one of those goddamned antique sideboards, got sent home early. But that didn't run. Wasn't likely the feds would have sent Reydak along to escort her home. But if business at the House was a wrap, where the hell were Ouro, Sueno, the Bitchin' Witch, and the rest? Things weren't 'facing the way they should. Either The Man was using the Listeners, or the Listeners were using him. Had to be one or the other, because *using* was what the world was all about—Flage had taught him that much. If Brady had wanted to invite them to lunch he would have; but direct access to the House was something else altogether.

Then to add to the puzzle, who should show up a few hours later with a third leg but Miss Handout herself, Terri Contra.

By that time Raven had already decided to go inside for a closer look. Flage had notified the Haven security team he was sending an inspector in, so Raven was well received when he approached the gate—the feds photographing him from their black van. The chief had explained to him that most everyone had been sent away and certain rooms had been declared off-limits, even to internal security. But no one seemed to have the slightest idea what was going on—even the chief apparently wasn't aware that Ouro and some of the Listeners had been recent guests of the Prez. Or that they had a spy in the midst.

Raven heard rushed movements above him and adjusted the gain on the bug attached to the room's subfloor. Sobbing, too. Sounded like someone had taken some glass. Tough, he thought, chuckling to himself. These people didn't know what it meant

to be hard, rock hard to the point where you ate glass for breakfast and washed it down with motor oil—

Reydak said something. *Check trouble*, was that it?

Raven frowned. Were the Listeners putting the bite on him
for something, or vice versa? Who knew, maybe Reydak was
IRS now. Meant he'd probably be hitting the street, though.

Raven raised a hand, popped the bug away from the tongue-
and-groove, and began to inch himself back toward the rectan-
gular hole he'd cut through the plaster and lath of the first-floor
ceiling. Already concocting a new disguise.

"Don't bother with that," the president said, just as Ouro
was about to dump the contents of his amulet bag on the Sitting
Room floor. "I didn't ask you here to entertain me."

The shaman traded grim looks with his tall, dark apprentice.
"What is it you do want?" he asked, tightening the purse's
drawstring and slipping it back over his head.

Brady rose out of his lotus and took two menacing steps forward, regarding Ouro's suit and tie and short hair. The shaman
had been co-opted by them, made to do their bidding by fabri-
cating explanations for the vision, perverting its inherent truth.

"Why are you hanging around here instead of carrying out
the task He assigned you?"

Ouro extended a hand. "Let me see what you are feeling."

Brady took another step, slapped the shaman's hand aside,
and laughed. "Feel *that*," he said, and struck Ouro's hand again.
"Go ahead, tell me what *you're* feeling. You're in their power,
can't you see that?"

The Brazilian woman signed an observation, and Ouro began
to retreat, withering in Brady's laughing eyes.

"Yes, the vision speaks to me, I know you can see it. But I'm
free to embrace it now. There's no need to listen to your talk
about illness and healing. We're not in control here—we answer
to Him, and our mission is clear: to stop any who would interfere
with the grand design."

"What design is that?" Ouro asked calmly. "Can you de-
scribe it to me?"

The president threw his head back and roared. "Can I de-
scribe human history to you in a word? Can I explain the evolution of all thought to someone who looks for answers in tobacco
smoke and botanical stews?" Brady aimed a finger at the tall
windows. "They're coming. What else do we need to know?

You helped bring them here. Now it's up to me to undo your misguided handiwork.''

Ouro gazed into the light, then looked to Brady. "Who is it I've brought here?"

Brady heard the puzzlement in his voice. "Yes," he said, sniggering, "yes, you begin to understand. Now accept responsibility and act in accordance with your beliefs."

"Explain to me, then, tell me what you know."

Brady regarded the two of them in angry silence. "Leave me," he said. "Either carry out your task or I wash my hands of you."

"Tell—"

"Leave me!" Brady whirled, slamming his hand against a keypad set into the wall. His face was contorted when he turned around, his body beginning to stiffen and spasm.

Kubark, Fusilli, and a third Secret Service agent rushed into the room just as the president's feet were leaving the carpet.

"You can see which of us has become the more powerful," Brady ranted, casting an astonished look down the length of his levitated body.

He was three feet above the floor now, upright but wavering, and listing like an inflated parade balloon. "Get them out of here," he directed his agents. "I have washed my hands of them, do you hear me?"

The three men were paralyzed, too dumbfounded to move. Kubark managed a half-step in the president's direction.

"Don't touch him," Ouro warned the agent.

Kubark stared at him wide-eyed, then looked to Brady.

"Do it!" the president raged, settling back to the carpet. "Get them out of my sight."

With Brady back where he belonged, the agents rediscovered the will to move. Kubark cleared his head with a shake and threw open his jacket, revealing a holstered machine pistol. "I've been waiting for this for weeks," he said, just loud enough for Ouro to hear him.

The shaman relaxed his stance as the men moved in on him, braced for the blows to come.

20 Generation Loss

The Ganzfield Inn was a hole-in-the-wall bar on 175, within easy striking distance of NSA's offices in Fort Meade and SIG's College Park headquarters. It was favored by analysts and wiz kids from the inner circles of both agencies, the intel community's way of paying tribute to the real world by rubbing elbows with the cowboy truckers who normally stocked the place.

Reydak stood shivering by the front entrance, scanning the dimly lit front room for some sign of SIG's go-to man. Outside, the mercury was hovering just above freezing, but he felt chilled to the bone, a condition he'd taken with him from Annapolis, where some kind of respiratory virus was running rampant through the Haven.

Reydak spotted the go-to after a moment, a brooding figure perched guardedly over a drink at a corner table, and received the proceed sign. He nodded in return, directing a glance over his shoulder, unable to shake the conviction that someone other than the Bureau's lookout was shadowing him. But all he saw were truckers, suits, a smattering of NSA techs. A sad-eyed waitress passing a customer's fifty through a scanner. Somewhat relieved then, he helped himself to a mealy pretzel from the bar and headed for the Ganzfield's secure back room.

"I appreciate your meeting me, sir," Reydak said, shaking Keyes' hand. "It was a judgment call."

The SIG director gave him a quick once-over and waved him into a chair. "Wave said it was urgent. We're considering bringing you home anyway, now that Ouro's been shown the door."

"When?" Reydak asked.

"This morning. Things are getting more peculiar by the minute, but Brady's still calling the plays. Fourth down, goal to go."

"This mean they're letting Ouro off the hook?"

"Damned if I can figure it out, Colonel. Some of them are hanging on to the notion of a Red scare; the rest would just as soon see Ouro crucified. Me, I'm planning to sit here and drink myself stupid." He lifted his glass in a toast.

Reydak coughed into his hand. "I think his people are in over their heads, sir. They're a bunch of well-wishers out to change the world, but they've got no designs on Brady. If he comes their way, fine. If not, they go right on with their work. The thing is, Brady's called up something they haven't encountered before, and whatever that is, it's tearing them apart. A regular study, sir."

Keyes' eyes wandered over him for a moment. "You're not looking very well, Colonel."

Reydak rubbed his cheek. "Tell me something I don't know. We're all sick. They need an exorcist over there, maybe a team of shrinks, I don't know any more."

"Take it easy, Karel," Keyes said, buzzing for a waitress. "Have a drink—something to warm you up. And tell me what brought you here?"

Reydak took a deep breath, then laughed in a self-mocking way. "Uncle Pavel," he told Keyes.

Reydak had no real memories of his father's brother. He knew, however, that Pavel had been involved in psychic research in Prague prior to World War II and had later been forced to serve the Axis cause. When the Soviets invaded Czechoslovakia after the war, Pavel turned his talents to freedom fighting, and his escape from a labor camp and subsequent trek through Communist-occupied East Germany had for a time become the talk of Radio Free Europe. A group of concerned scientists secured him passage to South America; but eventually he had reached the States, married, and gone to work for the CIA, where, as a result of his contributions to Project MKUltra, he'd been christened "Mr. ESP."

"Died in fifty-five or so, didn't he?" Reydak asked, nursing a cup of mulled wine.

"February first," Keyes said flatly.

Reydak nodded. "Dad always told me you two were close friends."

"It's true, we were."

"So I thought you could tell something about him. I checked the files, but there isn't much there—except for background on mind-control experiments the Agency was running back then."

Keyes swirled his second, perhaps third drink. "What bearing does this have on anything?"

"What bearing," Reydak said, louder than he meant to. "I want to know why the hell Pavel's name came up while the circle was running me through one of their little games."

"Slow down—"

"And I want to know how Swift knew my name, and why she's telling me there's some kind of close encounter in my past."

Keyes waited a moment before he answered. "Wave accepts the scenario that one of WEM's security people ID'd you. From that point on it would have been easy enough to learn something about your past, even about Pavel, assuming they knew where to look. You put all that in the hands of some alleged mind-reader, and it's not hard to imagine her formulating a ploy to turn you, double you, who knows what they have in mind."

Reydak shook his head. "I've run it that way. But even if she cooked this up, how do we explain the table? How do we explain Brady fingering me?"

"There are explanations, Colonel," Keyes said calmly.

"How did he die?" Reydak asked suddenly. "Pavel, I mean."

Keyes looked away from the table. Reydak put a hand on the director's shoulder and forced him to turn around. "I'm sorry, sir, but I need to know."

Keyes tossed his drink back and set the glass on the table. "Talk to your father," he said, deciding something. "He'll have the answers you want."

"Not now," Percival Flage barked, shrugging Tawny's soapy hand from his shoulder.

Pouting, she straightened up to her full six feet, breasts, belly, thighs, and hips—all redesigned by Flage himself—a glistening bodyscape of scented bubbles and tantalizing swirls.

"But, baby, we're already soaped up," Ginger said from the tub, duplicating her sister's whine.

Flage rolled away from the phone screen and heaved himself up off the massage table, one hand curled around his surgically enlarged but presently flaccid penis. "Does this look ready?" he asked the twins.

"Want us to make the soldier come to attention?" Tawny asked, the tip of her tongue at the corner of her rouged mouth. Ginger was already sashaying toward him, leaving a slick on the bathroom's tile floor.

"Pause," he told them both. "Look, climb in the tub and rub yourselves together for a while. I need time to cogitate."

"But we could cogitate you, Percy," Ginger said. "You don't have to do it to yourself—"

"Think," Flage shouted, forefinger pressed to his temple. "Cogitate means 'think.' As in ruminate, cerebrate, or otherwise indulge in reflective activity."

"Zat mean you aren't even going to watch?" Ginger asked.

Flage muttered a curse and walked naked to the video system. "How 'bout I run you two through the house. Would that make you happy? Everyone'll be able to watch you."

"That would be great!" Ginger enthused, heading for the tub. "Come on, Tawny."

The more assertive of the doctored twins stopped to throw Flage a sullen look. "You know, Percy, you're not as much fun as you used to be. I think you're getting tired of us."

Flage shook his head, smiling as he approached her. "You know you're my favorites." He bent over to nibble at Tawny's right breast, making her giggle.

"Oh, Percy," she said in that hot, throaty voice her phone-sex video public couldn't get enough of.

Flage pinched her playfully on the rump. "Now go play with your sister and leave Percy to his musings." He watched her saunter off, marveling at the sight of his incredible redesign work, and exited for the bedroom.

Amol Woolley's call had put him in a grand if somewhat contemplative mood. The good doctor had asked for an update on the Inaccessible project, which, Flage had been happy to report, was rapidly nearing the operational stage. And in partial payment, Woolley had hinted he was in possession of information that might prove relevant to the mad fluctuations taking place in the market. By then, of course, Flage had already puzzled things out for himself, but the scientist's admission had reaffirmed his faith in the mighty power of the high-interest loan.

While Woolley had not said anything outright about Ouro's dealings with Tedman Brady, Flage knew all about the *Post*'s "newfound Brotherhood of White House magicians." His minion had served him well in that regard. And then there had been the calls from the president's media advisors to an ambiance firm Flage had a piece of. Questions—hypothetical, of course—about whether the studio had time to arrange a kind of F/X miracle for Brady's next speech. Something with a bit of biblical flavor, perhaps; a space-opera score full of trumpets and serious string swells. He was still piqued at not having been consulted beforehand—almost missing out on a piece of chief-executive action—but pleased to see that Woolley and Ouro were at last coming around to seeing things his way. After all, though it went by many guises there was only one true symbol: a $ by any name.

Flage snorted two hits of designer coke and stood by the bedroom window wall, lifting the brown vial to crowded hillsides and canyons, the city beyond, sprawled beneath an amber sky. We are only here for a while anyway, he thought. Until Earth warms and the poles melt. So why not just use it up and be done with it? What people failed to realize was that man was born to despoil, to pollute, adulterate, and destroy. The trick, however, was to do it in style.

And just let the IRS try to launch its investigations now. Let them try to shut down the Centers, accuse him of pyramiding, copyright infringement, patent violations, dealing in restricted metals. Why, he'd sing so loud about Brady and Ouro they'd hear him clear to Moscow.

Which was precisely the point.

Flage recalled the first time he met the shaman. During one of those WPF-sponsored workshops on healing techniques. Ouro and Dolores Sueño. Oh, to have furniture like that who couldn't talk, Flage had wished on countless occasions.

"You know, Gabe, you're not in Brazil anymore," he remembered telling Ouro at the time. "I mean, down there they fall for the spirit-possession thing, but you're in Tomorrowland now—the realm of the electronic bug popper and plastic ticker. And while you might not have a problem selling the shaman thing to nirvana noodlers and the rabbit food crowd, you've gotta keep the proles in mind if you want to be heard from large on the American charts—the housewives, the garbagemen, the road crews of the world. The ones who'll be coming to you to cure their cancers and cysts, their fatty tumors, jogger's knees and tennis elbows, their hemorrhoids, sexual dysfunctions, bad breath, and athlete's foot. The ones who'll be asking you to heal their marriages and bank accounts and overall malaise. You've got to convince them you can see them through their bad trips, poltergeist visitations, close encounters, deaths, and divorces. That you can speak to their skeletons, their ghosts, their departed loved ones, runaway kids, or household termites. Promise them shorter lines at the PO, Saturday morning parking spaces. You show them you're a *star*, Gabe, a crossover kind of guy, and we're talking the Coliseum here; the Garden, Gabe, the top of the hill . . .''

Flage felt a tug of nostalgia. And hadn't he been the one responsible for instituting the Centers, the saturation approach that had practically quadrupled WEM's membership overnight? He snorted two more hits—the spoon electron-etched by Woolley's people at LIAR. If Ouro had been smart he would have listened to him about the tektites as well. Quartz could be dug by the bucketful, but tektites—tektites were reminders of a collision between Earth and some godawful meteor that had tipped the planet on its ear.

Now *there* was power.

And here, too, Flage thought, positioning himself at the bedroom terminal and laying an affectionate hand on the monitor.

He understood now why Woolley had pushed him to bring Inaccessible in under the wire and kept quiet about Ouro's activities in the capital. In fact, it was all so obvious he wondered why he hadn't figured it out as soon as Raven had called from D.C. Alliances were being formed: Brady and Ouro, the CIA and the Listeners. And as for Inaccessible, there was only one possible explanation: The island installation was some sort of top-secret weapon.

Flage set his drink aside and called up a listing of his stocks and varied holdings. With advanced word of WEM's new partnership, there was major money to be made.

Apprised of the deteriorating situation in Washington, Amol Woolley ordered Dr. Haguchi's team off to Inaccessible and made plans to join the Concentricity at the Annapolis Haven. But instead of flying directly there, Woolley stopped over in Minneapolis to talk with Adam Hooct, the genial, articulate elder spokesperson for Wiles ParaResearch Foundation—the detour prompted by Amber's insistence that Pavel Reydak somehow figured into the perilous dilemma the Concentricity found itself in. It hadn't taken Woolley long to learn that Reydak had been employed by the CIA at about the same time Adam Hooct had served on the Robertson Panel, a mid-fifties government commission formed to investigate UFO phenomena. An astrophysicist himself, Hooct had then gone on to the Jet Propulsion Lab and CSICOPS—the Committee for the Scientific Investigation of Claims of the Paranormal—before ending up on the board of WPF.

"Pavel Reydak . . ." Hooct was saying. "I haven't thought of Paul in years. An extraordinary man. A Czech mind. His death was a great loss."

"Mr. ESP," Woolley said. The two men were sitting in the foundation's small cafeteria, which was much like LIAR's own.

"And later on Mr. UFO. Paul and his special-means group." Hooct laughed. "The Agency was little more than a collection of rundown buildings lining the reflecting pool then. Paul's group worked out of L, I think."

"What do you remember about him?"

Hooct sipped his coffee. "He was deeply influenced by Freud, Jung, Bretislav. Alchemy, hallucinogens, hypnosis, depatterning, differential amnesia . . . the Agency had them working on a strange assortment of things, all in the belief the Soviets and Chinese were doing the same."

"This was under MKUltra?"

"MKUltra, ARTICHOKE, there were a host of names. But I do remember Paul's urging operatives to think of themselves as members of a secret society—as Earth's benevolent programmers, altering reality with their bits of covert and clandestine work. But Paul took a hard line on UFO groups, especially some of the California cults."

"Why was that?"

"Connections between early contactees and fascist organizations—groups like the Silver Shirts and the *I Am* movement."

"Racist philosophy cloaked in mystical doubletalk."

Hooct nodded. "Paul told me the same sort of thing swept Germany before the war. The Luminous Lodge, the Vril Society, the Thule, the Ahnenerbe, that sort of thing. I've always believed you can trace the whole thing back to Blavatsky and the Theosophists. If economics was the war's conscious side, occult eugenics was its unconscious. And I sometimes wonder if all our New Age thinking isn't perpetuating it."

"Let's hope not," Woolley said. "We're trying to birth a new world, not destroy one."

Hooct snorted. "So was Hitler in his own satanic way. In any event, Paul dreamed up the men-in-black thing to deal with our homegrown variations of these cults. He knew most contactee types were involved with the occult, and he was certain he could play on their innate paranoia and sense of persecution by giving them mysterious men in dark clothing and black cars. He used Filipinos mostly. They were supposed to be 'shadows' or al-

chemical homunculi inadvertently brought to life by the groups'
occult workings.''

Woolley studied his withered hand. ''Did he ever mention
any specific groups?'' he asked after a moment.

Hooct thought about it. ''There was one: *Main Rouge*—no,
die Rothand, that was it.''

'' 'Red Hand,' '' Woolley translated. ''Who were they?''

''I'm not sure. An offshot of some Nazi cult, I think.''

''Operating in the States?''

''I was never really clear on that, either,'' Hooct said. ''I can
only tell you that Paul would blanch whenever anyone brought
up the name.''

''Did he ever mention any of the people connected with it?''
Woolley pressed.

Hooct showed his palms. ''Amol, you know what you're asking me? This goes back forty years.''

''I know, Adam. But just access that internal databank of
yours. I know you've got a file in there somewhere.''

Hooct put an elbow on the table and dropped his chin into
his hand. He shook his head for a moment, then looked up at
Woolley, grinning. ''Hupka,'' he announced. ''And someone
named Rossman.''

''Anyone else?''

''Rensler,'' Hooct said at last, ''Dr. Wilhelm Otto Rensler.''

A thick cloud mass blown in from the bay darkened the skies
above the Annapolis Haven. Ouro regarded it silently from the
French doors of the mansion's ground-floor den, preparing himself for battle. Two of the Listeners remained in guarded condition in the hospice; Terri, Amber, and Carmine were ill with
nausea, vomiting, and dehydration. Leigh Burmandy's wrists
had been opened wide by glass from the Ouija's shattered screen;
Hiawatha Fountain was blind in one eye; Florence States had
lost all feeling in her fingers and toes . . . They had sent everyone else away—husbands, children, assistants—save for a handful of security personnel.

A black diesellike film, resistant to water or solvents, had
begun to settle over the furniture, the carpets, the dishware and
foodstuffs. The Haven's electronics were plagued with problems, and small items were disappearing: the staples securing a
length of phone line to a baseboard; two refrigerator magnets;
ashtrays, books, pieces of jewelry.

Ouro recalled the president's admonitions, and in so doing heard N'ntara's voice deep in his thoughts.

You refuse to accept the power, the old shaman had berated him after one especially long and fruitless session with the vision vine. *Your mind has never let you forget that your mother abandoned you. All the power you were born with torn away by her leaving, and you have never been able to believe in yourself since.*

It had only meant increased dosages of *mai'oni* then; N'ntara's method for opening eyes to the Real World, his radical approach to psychotherapy.

And now Brady was lecturing him in the same fashion—accusing him of having brought evil into being, of refusing to accept responsibility for his actions. A punishment, perhaps, for lying to the president's advisors about the Soviet group. But what alternative had there been at the time? And if nothing else, he had at least glimpsed the power crystal embedded in Brady's heart; though he remained ignorant of just whose mark was upon it.

Ouro felt earthbound, hopelessly drained of light, perplexed by the very aspects of power that had kept him unflinching and impeccable. It was as if the cloud shadowing the Haven was sucking the life from him. The *chimera* stalking them all, materializing at will.

Lightning flashed in the cloud, illuminating the limbs of bare trees, an expanse of yellowed lawn. Ouro heard Dolores' drum begin to speak and moved outside, hands raised above his head as he danced steps of serpent power across the brick patio—a sinuous shuffle meant to evoke telluric power while allowing for evasive action. And summoned by these shamanic gyrations, white clouds began to roll in from the river to infiltrate the sky's dark and shapeless mass. He waited for an opening to appear, then reached out for Tedman Brady, feeling for colors, steering himself through currents of aquamarine and crimson, avoiding unbuoyed depths of red and blue black at the boundaries of thought, the suffocating presence of wrathful deities. The president, fetally curled and cocooned within a black- and red-veined sac, waited for him at the bottom of a deep circular shaft.

Light bled from Brady's etheric egg, discharging itself like bolts of electrical current, figure-ground like molten lava, like oozing arterial blood. There was a slow and loathsome spin to the egg, accompanied by the deafening sound of tortured steel.

Enabled now, the shaman's familiars unfolded their talons and attacked the net, desperate for purchase . . .

In response came a wave of focused force that left Ouro reeling, helplessly snagged between two worlds with the ground rushing up to meet him. Or so it seemed as the force threw him facedown against the abrasive surface of the bricks. He absorbed the fall in his left shoulder and cheek; heard the crack of cartilage and bone, felt stray fragments pierce the skin of his face.

But again he attempted to assault the net, on his knees now, fingers and claws rending at fibrous tissue, pulling and tugging aside the organic weave—a forest of tendonlike roots and branches, warm and pulsing beneath their taut sheaths, crunching and snapping at his grasp. And as his familiars continued to tear at the living lattice, Brady's tormented cry reached him in dungeon echo, the shrillness of his voice releasing a stain of sick color that suffused the world.

The next blow struck him in the chest, silencing his heart for an eternity, only to send the drumming of strained rhythms painfully into his ears. Ouro's back hunched like that of a frightened cat; his torso was hurled, lifted off the ground, and slammed down as if caught underfoot.

Spread-eagled, he was propelled from the shaft, his body heaved up, rolling involuntarily to one side, supine to an opaque sky.

21 Our Man in Lemuria

"Dis is close as I can bring you," the Romanian driver said over his shoulder as the cab was approaching the Haven. "Dey haf da street clost."

Reydak lowered the window and leaned out into the frigid air, catching sight of traffic cones, barricades, a backhoe in operation. The street and hedges fronting the house were covered in places by an inch-thick layer of black grit.

Nicu scratched his head and hit the meter's rate-stud. "Look like asphal truck overturn."

Reydak climbed out, handing Nicu a fifty and instructing him to wait. Up ahead, an EPA cop in an orange vest was waving vehicles away.

"You don't want to go in there, sir," the flagman said as Reydak walked by him. "FBI, Colonel," he added, in reaction to Reydak's puzzled look. "We had to fold the listening posts."

Reydak glanced around. "What the hell happened here?"

"We were hoping you could tell us, sir," the agent responded straight-faced. "Either this place is some kind of madhouse, or they decided to mindfuck us. Lights going on and off, glass breaking. You shoulda heard the stuff we were picking up: yelling, screaming, crying. Then this front blows in from the Chesapeake—a 'microclimate,' TDS called it. Our sensors were going nuts, electromagnetic readings off the graphs. Fucking tapes aren't worth a damn now; most of it's garbled. And something—God knows what, sir—something just streaked up out of that house like lightning and punched a hole in the sky. Next thing we knew, this shit was raining down on us."

Reydak stopped to gather a handful of the black pebbles from the street. They had a gummy, almost confectionlike consistency; and popping one between his SAC-hardened thumb and forefinger unleashed an eye-smarting, fetid odor. Reydak made a disgusted sound and brushed the things from his hand.

"Our people say its some kind of crystallized petroleum," the agent offered. "They figure it's been airborne since that Pacific eruption a few months back."

"And it just happened to fall here."

"It's what they're saying, sir."

Reydak eyed the sky warily, then gestured discreetly toward the house. "Is everyone still in there?"

"A few of them. People have been leaving all day long. Labcoat named Woolley showed up two hours ago. Chief said you'd know him."

Reydak grunted noncommittally and began to move off.

"Colonel?" the agent said to his back. Reydak swung around to face him, aware all at once that the man was trembling. "Do you believe in UFOs, sir?"

"I believe in nothing," Reydak told him.

The evil stuff was everywhere he looked, a coating of black hail clinging to limbs, lawn, and gardens. Every window in the Haven was open.

Amol Woolley answered the front door, wearing a polypro vest, a knit cap, and a painter's dust mask. "You better put this on," he said, handing one over.

The stench inside nearly knocked him over. Fires were roaring in the den and living room. "Where's Amber?" he asked, slipping the mask over his face.

Woolley directed him toward the den. Amber was curled in an armchair, a wool blanket wrapped around her shoulders. Her lips looked blue in the firelight. Contra looked as bad or worse. Ouro was cross-legged on the floor, his face bruised purple beneath the paper mask. Keyes had mentioned that Brady's polestanders had roughed him up some, but Reydak was surprised to see they hadn't restricted themselves to body shots. Sueño was with him, one arm draped over the shaman's shoulders.

Reydak exchanged uncomfortable looks with everyone, then walked over to where Amber was sitting. "I'm taking you out of here," he announced after a moment.

"Did you get the answers you wanted?" she said weakly.

"No. But I know who to see. I want you to come with me."

Amber looked past him to Woolley and Ouro. "You don't need their permission," Reydak said in a muffled, low rasp. "I want you to come with me. You're part of the answer."

Her sunken eyes regarded him. "All right. But you'll have to help me."

Reydak reached out to steady her as she pushed herself out of the chair. He put an arm around her waist and led her from the room.

The farther they got from the Haven, the faster Amber's condition improved; by the time Nicu had them across the Bay Bridge, she was strong enough to tell him about Woolley's conversation with Adam Hooct. Reydak was angered by their delvings into Pavel's past, although he had to admit they'd been a lot more successful than he had. Keyes knew plenty but wasn't talking. Mainly, though, it irked him to realize he'd lost complete control of the op, of his own place in the thing. *Die Rothand* was new ground, but the words sent a shiver through him that had little to do with the temperature.

His parents had retired to a converted farmhouse on the Eastern Shore after John had left the Defense Department several years back. Reydak tried to get out there at least once a month when he was in-country, and was good about letters and calls when he wasn't; but he hadn't seen either of them in almost six months now, well before Africa.

He was still trying to work out just what he planned to say, when Nicu swung the cab into the long driveway and he spotted the NOTAR medevac.

The tail-rudderless chopper was idling on the front lawn, rotorwash stirring dust and dead leaves, and the sight of it squatting there like some outsize alien insect sent yet another shiver through him.

Rene, who'd been both nurse and companion for the past five years, was waiting by the storm door. "Oh, Karel, thank God you've come," she said, hugging him. "It's your father—he's had another attack."

Amber followed him upstairs to the bedroom, where paramedics already had oxygen running. John had suffered from emphysema for a decade, but the frequency of attacks had been increasing lately. Anna was bedside, holding her husband's hand. "Karel's here, John," Reydak heard her say. "Everything's going to be all right, John, Karel's here."

Reydak put an arm around his mother's frail shoulders and kissed her forehead. Anna was sharp and strong-willed, still vibrant at eighty-three, with silver hair that reached her knees when it wasn't confined to its usual chignon. Anna saw him glance at the cigar in the nighttable ashtray. "Please, Karel, don't be angry with him. If it's what he wants, what can we say?"

John's rheumy eyes found him through the transpirator mask. The thing he'd hated most was losing his vision, the ability to pore through the history books that lined his office walls.

"Hey, soldier," Reydak said.

"Oh, John, don't," Anna said, as the old man began to pull the breathing device away from his face.

"Nonsense," John told the room in a wheezy voice. "I'm not about to lie here with my mouth shut while the rest of you discuss my funeral."

"Tough guy," Reydak said, forcing a smile.

"How are you, Colonel?" Reydak leaned over to embrace him, aware of the odor of death that clung to the bed. "Don't you worry, I'll be up and around in a week."

"Sure you will," Reydak said, maintaining the smile.

John coughed and kept coughing for several moments, while one of the paramedics stood by with a breather. "I know they didn't reach you, Karel," he said at last, weaker now. "So what brought you—one of your premonitions?"

Reydak exchanged a brief glance with Amber. "It can wait."

John focused on Amber for a long moment, then said, "No, I don't think it can." He looked up at his wife. "Leave us alone for a minute, Anna. You, too, Rene. We'll be fine."

"Keep it brief," a paramedic cautioned as he was leaving the room. Amber squeezed Reydak's hand and followed everyone out.

Reydak sat on the edge of the bed, regarding the cigar stub and shaking his head.

"I've had a long, full life," John said, "and tobacco's been a big part of it. Now, what is it, son?"

"It's about Pavel," Reydak began.

John stared at him.

"His name came up in connection with an op I'm running. I can't go into details."

"Go ahead," John said.

Reydak took a breath. "I know his MKUltra work had to do with UFOs, but did he ever talk to you about a saucer cult called *die Rothand*—the Red Hand?"

John shut his eyes and took a hit off the breather. "It wasn't a saucer cult."

"Okay."

"You know that Pavel was forced to work for the Nazis?"

Reydak nodded.

"*Die Rothand* was a special group formed by Hitler himself. One of his pet projects—an attempt to contact the Atlantean rulers of the last world age."

"Sounds like him."

"Seriously, Karel. Hitler believed the Reich a reemergence of Atlantis, so he assembled a team of European psychics to communicate with Atlantis across time. Pavel, much to his shame, took part in the occult workings of that group. Much of their work was done at Dachau, where they experimented with the same hallucinogenic drugs I. G. Farben was feeding to its slave laborers. They called themselves the Red Hand because . . . because they would commence their workings by dipping their hands into the bloody bodies of the recently slaughtered."

Reydak fed John the breather again and kept it close at hand. "We can talk about this—"

"No," John said, clutching his hand. "Listen to me: When Pavel arrived here in 1951, he told me the Red Hand had regrouped in South America. He claimed his former cultmates *were still carrying on with the work.*"

"Trying to contact Atlanteans?"

John nodded. "Pavel said it was the Red Hand who had helped him get out of Berlin after his escape from Czechoslavakia."

"But what did they want from him?" Reydak asked.

John sighed. "According to Pavel, they were somehow attempting to *destabilize* the world and render it safe for the return of the Reich."

"Destabilize it how?"

"He only joined the Agency as a means of crusading against occult and saucer groups he believed had aligned themselves with the Red Hand, Karel. He tried desperately to convince the Defense Department to take the threat seriously, but naturally no one would listen to him. He even turned to Israeli Nazi-hunters."

"And what happened?"

"No one was interested," John said flatly. "Oh, the Israelis would have liked to put their hands on Bormann or Mengele, perhaps; but you have to remember that many of the Nazis were working for us then—spying on the Soviets."

"Would've been easy enough to validate, wouldn't it? Some Nazi coven tucked away in South America."

"There was no need," John said, his eyes brimming with tears. "You see, we put them there."

Reydak frowned, then nodded in comprehension. "Paper, something—"

"Paperclip," John completed. "Operation Paperclip. There were people we needed—von Braun, Hugo Randolph, dozens of others. The Russians were helping themselves in Peenemunde and Thuringia, we had no choice."

"But who'd the Red Hand have?"

"I. G. Farben research scientists, mostly. Pacts were made with American oil and chemical companies. They received safe transit to South America, we got formulas for plastics and synthetic fuels."

Reydak snorted. "No wonder the Defense Department wouldn't listen to him."

John's hand tightened its hold on Reydak's. "I couldn't tell you, Karel," he said, crying. "I . . . I was one of the men responsible for the cover-up."

"Oh, Christ, Pop." Reydak stroked John's shoulder. "So Pavel died never learning the truth." He felt John's hand begin to spasm. "That's enough now," he started to say, but John still wouldn't let go of him.

"No, Karel, wait. Pavel and Frances . . . they died in a helicopter crash when you were two years old."

Reydak experienced a vivid flash of recollection: of stuttering sounds, a whirling wind, and flashing lights. A television set was turned on, a theme song—

"We've never been able to tell you." John was gasping. "Our love for you is so strong, we couldn't tell you—"

"What, Pop?" Reydak said, readying a call for the paramedics. John's breathing was dangerously labored.

"Pavel and Frances," he said between gasps, "were your *parents*."

"Medic!" Reydak screamed, shooting to his feet. John's back was arched, his right arm extended, fingers quivering. Anna, sheet-white and sandwiched between Amber and Rene, trailed the paramedics in.

"He told you," she said, wailing, "he told you!"

Amber threw him a questioning look from across the room, but before he could say a word, John's hand had seized his wrist. "Karel," he said, pulling him down to the bed. "The . . . the—"

The paramedics shoved Reydak aside and slipped the transparent transpirator mask over John's head. Anna collapsed crying against Reydak's chest.

"Don't you see?" Amber said, trailing Reydak as he slid open the pocket doors to John's office. "You were two years old. Your mind recorded the event but lacked the necessary vocabulary. That's what's been bottled up inside you all these years. But you've released it now and the healing can begin."

"Don't talk to me about healing!" Reydak stepped down into the room, wondering where to begin. John had tried to get something across to him before the paramedics had gurneyed him out, but his throat had closed up. He was on his way to the hospital now with Anna and Rene following in the family car. But Anna said that John may have been trying to refer him to the few things of Pavel's they had kept—his photographs, texts, and notebooks. Reydak had filled Amber in on most of it, but withheld mention of Operation Paperclip and the role John had played in the affair.

"It's natural for you to be confused and full of hate now," Amber continued. "But you've got to let it go. What they did to your parents is unforgivable, but it's long past."

It took a moment for her words to register. "What who did?" Reydak said, pivoting to face her.

"Why, the Red Hand, of course," Amber said, as if he were an idiot not to see it. "Your father was threatening to expose them, so they . . . stopped him."

Reydak stared at her, refusing to accept the explanation, let alone the alternative: that it was Operation Paperclip Pavel had threatened. That the Agency—

"What are we looking for, Karel?"

Reydak shook himself out of it, too overcome by events to sustain even his rage. "A book, a photograph, some mention of this Red Hand."

Amber inclined her head and began to read the titles along one shelf. "John's a history buff."

Reydak nodded. "World War Two."

"He's also something of a librarian," she commented. "Everything's alphabetized. Even the shelves are labeled according to topic. 'D-Day', 'Pacific Theater,' 'Post-War Berlin' . . . we could be in here for days."

Reydak spotted a glass-fronted oak chest and walked over to it. "Over here," he said.

Most of the titles were in German, but Amber was familiar with some of the authors: Thomas of Stitny, Chelcicky, Neruda, Capek, Kafka. There were scores of texts on physiology and microbiology; complete works of Freud and Jung; reproductions of alchemical texts and grimoires; books on psychism, psychotronics, and bionics. Amber pulled open the doors and began to run her fingers along the leather-bound spines.

Reydak pulled a book at random from the shelf, leafed through it briefly, and set it aside on the desk. Amber began to do the same, and in a short while they had emptied half the cabinet without result.

"This is hopeless," Reydak said in disgust. "I don't even know why the fuck we're bothering. My mystery's solved, isn't it? It's not like I'm doing some goddamned term paper on a Nazi cult. Fuck it," he shouted, hurling one of the books across the room.

Amber gave him a moment, then said: "Pavel was talking to all of us at the session, Karel."

Reydak glared at her. "Don't play me for a chump, Amber."

"The Red Hand connects with all that's been happening," she went on. "I know it, I can feel it."

"Then *you* deal with it," Reydak told her. "Knock yourself out."

"Will you help me box these books up?" she asked as he was on his way to the door.

"Why?"

"To take them back to the Haven. I want Hiawatha to feel them."

One-on-ones between the Oval Office and the Pentagon were as rare a thing as an honest commie, but General McVee wasn't about to question his good fortune.

"General, I've come by some advanced intelligence that will greatly benefit our cause," Brady was saying.

McVee stole a glance at the magazine on the president's desk. "Advanced intelligence. Yes, sir."

For the fourth time in as many months Tedman Brady's face had made the cover of a national magazine. The painting stopped short of caricature, but there was something impressionistic about it nonetheless: a suggestion of visionary fire in the eyes, a maniacal curl to the mouth. The legend read: FIRST PROPHET OF THE UNITED STATES, TEDMAN BRADY. Inside, heading the lead article, was a cartoon depicting the president in conclave with a loin-clothed shaman. *"I don't know, Ouro,"* Brady was saying, *"what do you want to do?"*

McVee had seen the issue and was anything but amused. And while there was perhaps some strategic value in allowing the public to believe that the president was convening with mystics when he was in fact battling the telepathic imperatives of Soviet psychics, that still didn't excuse the publishers' disrespectful and irresponsible approach. Yet another commie clique, McVee thought.

"Something too sensitive to be handled by phone or courier," Brady said. "Do I make myself clear?"

"Sensitive. Yes, sir." It was just like Base's committee to keep something from him, make the Pentagon the last to know.

The president's brow furrowed. "They've infiltrated our ranks, General."

McVee narrowed his eyes. "Those goddamned swine. Where—the CIA?"

"All around us." Brady pointed to the ceiling. "They're keeping a close watch."

McVee tracked the president's finger. "Holy Mother of God, some laser-optic system they've built into their shield sats. But don't worry, sir, we just can open up the garage, send out some KEVs. Won't even have to fire up the big guns."

The president was shaking his head. "Don't underestimate them, General. We haven't dealt with anything like this in a long time."

McVee's face mirrored his puzzlement. "Sir, I'm not sure I'm following you there. Nothing like we've dealt with in a long time . . . What does that mean, sir, precisely?"

Brady scowled. "You realize we must take care what we say."

McVee recalled the president's use of WANT-ADZE and nodded. "All frequencies open, Mr. President."

"That's good, General, because I want you to think back to the end of the last one."

"The last one . . ." McVee repeated to himself, then snapped his huge fingers. "You mean the Big One, is that it, sir? The end of the Big One?"

"Yes, we can call it the Big One, if you wish."

McVee thought for a moment, trying hard not to appear slow or dim-witted in the president's eyes. The war ended with Hiroshima, he told himself. Japs, island-hopping, Hiroshima . . . He looked at Brady aghast. "Don't tell me they've got salvage-fused missiles up there!"

"Pay careful attention, General," Brady went on. "Of course you're aware that our strength lies not in firepower but in defense."

"I've always maintained that, sir," McVee said, red-faced. "Despite the posture I've been forced to assume—"

"They're very quick, General."

McVee felt his jaw. "It's true they enjoy some boost-phase leverage, but—"

"And we'll have to be especially careful of motherships in the advanced deployment zones. They have enormous destructive potential."

Christ, McVee thought, what the hell did the Reds have up there—a directed energy weapon?

"But sometimes, General, the best defense is a good offense. So as soon as they enter our space, we take them out in columns—even though we're outnumbered five or ten to one."

McVee blew out his breath and ran a hand down his heavy-jowled face. "Jesus H. Christ, sir, are we ready for this? I mean, we're not even fully operational yet. Relying on two lasers and a couple of mirrors . . . Sir, if they've really got nukes or some DEW concealed in their architecture, I'd sure as hell feel better about it if we could ready some heavy orbiters of our own. Even if we don't use 'em straight off, sir, just to have a postexchange residual."

Brady was glowering at him. "Mutually assured destruction is hardly what I had in mind for this planet, General."

McVee blanched. "Does the president have some flexible response in mind?" he asked uncertainly.

Brady thrust a finger at him. "Understand me, I'll enter the code and the game will begin; but we can't let this go to three strikes, General. Otherwise we've lost it, they'll smash the ring, and the game will be finished."

McVee couldn't believe his ears. Brady wasn't talking preventive or retaliatory, but *preemptive*—an all-out preemptive first strike.

"General," the president said, "I want you to put the nation on alert."

22 Eso-Terrorists

Reydak watched Hiawatha Fountain's brown hands read through the four milk crates of books, journals, and notebooks Amber had insisted on lugging back to the Haven.

The street had been reopened, the black hail trucked off to who knew where. Little evidence of the pellets remained, except on the lawn and shrubs, where they had gone to sludge, giving the mansion grounds a funereal appearance. Reydak was relieved to find the place aired out; but no one looked the better for it, including Woolley, now as pale and tubercular-looking as Contra and the others gathered in the den: Leigh Burmandy, Flo States, Carmine Dover, Fountain, and Ray Mayana—the latter just returned from Virginia Beach. Vide and Chizedek were still hospitalized; Ouro and Sueño off somewhere in another part of the house.

The psychometrist was plucking items from the crate, sniffing them, holding them to his forehead above a gauze patch that covered an injured eye—one would have supposed he had spent time at Sense Augmentation Center, Reydak thought.

The process had been going on for well over an hour, but Fountain seemed to be onto something all of a sudden. "What is it, Hiawatha?" Terri asked, barely managing to suppress a cough. "What are you feeling?"

"Age," the old man said in a trembling voice. "Ancient things." He was holding what looked to be a dossier or precis of some sort, a word scribbled across the front cover Reydak couldn't make out. "Oh, man, I'm feeling strange things. Power stronger than any mainframe I've talked to."

"A device? A machine?" asked Mayana, WEM's androgynous-looking UFOlogist and high-strangeness contactee.

Hiawatha shook his head. "No, man, like assembled power, the power in old buildings and such."

"Stonehenge," Mayana encouraged, "the Great Pyramid, that sort of thing."

"I never been there, Ray," Hiawatha said. "But yeah, on that order. Only . . . God, it's some evil shit I'm feeling. And a thing like a . . . Oh, man, like a pair of rapist's jockey shorts. Some evil male fucking, you know what I mean?"

No one did; but Mayana gingerly asked if he could take a look at the file. As Hiawatha passed it over, several loose sheets drifted to the floor near Amber's feet. She began to scan them as Mayana opened the folder. Reydak heard her draw in a breath and snatched the yellowed sheets from her hand. They were handwritten in English, apparently torn from a journal or diary, with underlined and annotated sections in what Reydak guessed was either Czech or German. Pavel's name was at the bottom of one page, among a short list that included Rensler, Rossman, and Hupka—the names Adam Hooct had given Woolley in Minneapolis.

The name of the front cover of the dossier was "Plummer"— or Colonel Plummer, as Mayana referred to him.

"It's all beginning to coalesce," he directed to Woolley, unable to restrain his enthusiasm. "Rensler, Rossman, and Hupka were all members of the Vril—in Berlin, before the war." Mayana had been researching the names since Woolley's first mention of them. "Colonel Plummer was there at the same time."

"Yes, yes, it's all here," Dover said from the settee, where he was studying the file.

"Wait a minute," Reydak interrupted. "What's beginning to coalesce? And who the hell is Colonel Plummer?"

"A British explorer," Mayana said, then added, "of a sort. He spent twenty years in remote parts of the world trying to prove that Atlantis existed in fact, not legend."

"So Pavel had a file on him," Reydak said. "Get to the coalescing part, Mayana."

"The file may have been your father's," Dover said, "but not these handwritten pages. I think we have a piece of Plummer's journal here."

Reydak looked to Mayana again.

"Incredible. Berlin," he said, picking up the tale. "Before the war. Plummer fell in with a group of occultists who shared his beliefs. With one man in particular, a Dr. Schisler, who was close to Hitler and Haushofer, and a founding member of the Ahnenerbe—a secret society like the Vril or Thule. A group of Tibetans had settled in Berlin at about the same time, and Schisler is said to have learned from them of the existence of a cache of sacred tablets believed to date back to antediluvian Atlantis. When Hitler got wind of this, he ordered Schisler and Plummer—who was apparently already working for the Reich in some occult capacity—to travel to India and find the tablets. He already had others out searching for the Holy Grail, the Sacred Lance, the Spring of Eternal Life.''

"Plummer could have been a member of *die Rothand*," Amol Woolley ventured, "along with Hupka and the rest."

"It stands to reason," Mayana said. "The Red Hand must have represented the cream of the crop."

"John said they did their work at Dachau, didn't he?" Amber said, looking at Reydak, who nodded stiffly.

"We know that Schisler died of exposure in the Himalayas," Mayana continued. "But the story goes that Plummer, after a perilous two-year journey through Southeast Asia, finally located the tablets."

While Hiawatha shuffled over to stoke the fire, Reydak glanced around to see just who was buying into all this, and found nothing but attentive faces. He had come to expect as much from Amber, Terri, and Flo States; but even Woolley seemed entranced.

"Well," Mayana said, "with the aid of a sadhu from New Delhi, Plummer succeeded in translating a portion of the text that told of an instrument of terrible power—some sort of gnomon or stone monolith the ancients had used to control Earth's axis of orientation. The tablets called it Earthstopper or Earth Phallus, and it had apparently been the object of intense rivalry between the priesthoods of Atlantis, the so-called Right- and Left-Hand Paths."

The details got somewhat murky from that point on. Hitler may or may not have been privy to Plummer's discovery, but what was certain was that the search for the Earthstopper had eventually led Plummer to South America, where, in 1944, he disappeared without a trace.

"Unless these notes are not genuine," Carmine said from across the room. The man who had made sensory dep tanks a household word and as easily affordable as hot tubs walked over to the fireplace with the journal notes in hand.

" 'We are off the maps here,' " he read in a halting voice, between coughing fits. " 'Well beyond areas where others have set foot and seen fit to name. Our instruments and gear have proved unsuitable for the vagaries of this dark unyielding forest, but we tolerate the privation. Seldom, however, does the forest reply in kind; we are intruders, and Earth reacts to us like a living organism resisting infection.' ''

"Plummer began his journey in Manaus, Brazil," Mayana commented.

Carmine read from a second sheet. " 'This morning, while the bearers were hacking a portage for our rebuilt raft, I literally stumbled upon the first evidence: a small, tooled stone. And had I not at that fortuitous moment bent to repair a snapped bootlace, the find would have eluded me. By the light of our meager fires I have scrutinized it, and already I have identified glyphs that predate those on the tablets. The place is surely within our reach. My blood rushes when I contemplate what may await me there.' ''

Reydak got up to pace. The house was beginning to act its evil on him again and the cough was returning. But worse was the fact that the Listeners didn't seem to give a damn whether he was there or not. They were convinced they'd discovered something tied in to the president's breakdown, and weren't about to be talked out of it.

" 'My wanderings—if they can be termed this—have delivered me into the most incredible country,' " Carmine continued. " 'The land undulates like a sea of forest, water delivered from the nearby hills draining into this basin and forming hundreds of waterfalls and emerald lakes that glisten in the sunlight. Before sunrise there is an unearthly feel to the place; it becomes a very cauldron of mist, from the depths of which resound the wild and sometimes disturbing calls of birds and unseen life.'

" 'For a week now I've been investigating the site, too astonished by its majesty to set my hand to the task of recording its wonders. If the Incas knew of this place at all, it was obviously a mystery to them. There is evidence of the precision stonework the highlanders practiced, but by and large the stairways and trapezoidal portals are of monolithic construction on a scale that even they must have considered cyclopean. But the most important structure is the gnomon—a natural stone formation rising vertically from the cleft that secures it to a height of twenty feet. And I know that it is my destiny to reactivate it. For with the motherland destroyed, Earth knows no guiding or mediating hand. The remainder of my life will be devoted to contacting the high priests of the motherland and, by reorientating the world, clearing the path for their return.' ''

Reydak strode to the center of the room, holding his hands

up. "Didn't you say that Plummer disappeared in forty-four?" he asked Mayana.

Mayana nodded. "Nineteen forty-four, yes."

"So how could he have known the motherland was destroyed, when Germany didn't bow out until forty-five?"

Mayana and Dover traded looks. "It's not Germany he's referring to," Mayana said after a moment. "*Atlantis* was the motherland—the origin of humankind."

Reydak put his palms to his head in a theatrical gesture. "Stupid of me, huh? Forgetting Atlantis was the motherland."

"Karel, please," Amber said weakly.

Carmine cleared his throat. " 'But to activate the Phallus will require the assistance of my brothers in arms: Rensler, Martisse, Hupka, Sebastian, Ner, Rossman, Reydak . . . *Die Rothand* will reunite. We will assemble around the gnomon and we will contemplate this planet. And we will use the power to do what must be done.' "

Carmine lowered the pages. "Is there any doubt? Plummer somehow got his occult brotherhood safely out of Germany and into South America."

Reydak still hadn't mentioned Paperclip and wasn't about to now. Dover was motioning to him.

"Pavel returned to Czechoslovakia, and then he, too, was brought to South America after his escape from the communists."

"But instead of finding a group of fellow scientists waiting for him, he finds a reanimated bit of the Reich," Woolley thought to add.

"And this time they had real power at their command," Mayana said. "But he wouldn't have anything to do with them, so he fled, taking some of Plummer's notes with him, figuring he could get people to listen to him."

Amber said, "He enlists in the CIA to carry on the work, but there's only so much he can do. Meanwhile, the Red Hand is making plans to rid themselves of the nuisance they let get away, and eventually they kill him." She looked over at Reydak. "I'm sorry, Karel."

"It's the Red Hand who has President Brady's mind," Carmine concluded. "And it was their collective voice we heard speak through Brady." He pointed across the room. "Reydak *is* the one who rightfully belongs with them.

Ouro sat cross-legged in the heat of the Haven sauna, recalling a garden—the Amazonian garden of his apprenticeship. Rivulets of blood-tainted sweat trickled down his neck and torso, the disembodied voices of the Listeners reaching him through the house intercom.

The Old One had his thoughts, his true father.

It was shortly before he had left the Human Beings to begin his journey back. They had been chanting and dancing continuously, practicing cloud summoning and weather control, throwing live coals to the sky, biting the heads off live birds and waving the carcasses overhead. Bodies painted, covered with ash or clothed in frightening fanged costume, they had pressed themselves to the Earth in the hope of revitalizing the planet. Reverent to all things—the plants that provided food or poisons for their arrows, the trees that provided fruits or bark for their cloth, the Earth that furnished roots, and the rocks that held them up as they walked—the Human Beings had ceremoniously warned their universe of any coming disturbance, spit or urine, fire or the blade of a machete.

And that universe was repaying the kindness with warnings of its own.

Strange plants are revealing themselves, N'ntara had told him. *Plants not of this world age.* His ear to the ground at the time, face reflecting the great inner burden knowledge brought about.

Can't you hear the Earth's song, monkey—her pangs? She behaves like one injured and reeling with pain. The Old One had taken him by the shoulders. *You must speak to the ones who tap the Earth and sun to power their machines, who drain the soil and sky of their wealth. The Earth and sun give these things up to us, but there is no escaping the* doing *of the world, monkey. You must teach them how to repay what they borrow. You must help to put the world back on course . . .*

Reydak watched the transformed features of Terri Contra's face go slack in the den's lowered light. He had seen schizophrenics go the same waxy route; adopt the same resonant authoritative voice. But he wasn't about to rule out ventriloquism. Amber was asking the questions, just as she had during the electronic Ouija session.

"Can you tell us about site of the gnomon, OObe—this tumulus of power?"

Terri/OObe sighed. "There is much in the Akashic records about this place. But given the makeup of the beings who used the instrument nature had erected there, it was inevitable no

lasting good should come of it, that the place should become
the object of fearful rivalries.

"The instrument could tap powers peculiar to the sky's con-
figurations, but only by bringing about a change in the world's
axis of rotation. It was such the Left desired: a bold leap that
would catapult humankind into a realm of pure thought, hasten
its arrival at the turning point of time."

"Can you talk to us about the rivalries, OObe?"

Terri/OObe lolled her head and made a whistling nasal sound.
"Just before the end councils were convened to define the limits
of growth, the ends of power; to establish new boundaries and
designs for peace. Right and Left faced one another across the
gulf and there were discussions, disagreements, then argu-
ments. But how could the Left be made to understand that their
achievements were not amendments to humanmade order in a
world for the taking but denials of natural law, the Law of One?
Their disklike craft that defied Earth's efforts to keep them
rooted; their efforts to extend life, recombine its elements to suit
their sense of fashion; their belief in cures.

"There were animals with human heads at work in the cities
and power plants; humans with animal intellect in the corridors
of control. But this was not enough for some of them, and so
their efforts to usher in the new eon resulted instead in the Fall.

"The Right survived, albeit in remote places, obscure peaks
safe from the flood, the rising tide. But there was no feeling of
victory attached to this. For it was known that the Left's agents
were among them still, full of insidious intent and promising
to pave the way for a return—a way back from the heartless void
into which their own machinations had delivered them."

"And has some group been successful in bringing that
about?" Amber asked in a rush.

OObe's voice chuckled eerily through Terri's lips. "The little
paper hanger came closest to returning them to the throne. He'd
awaken to find their envoys standing over him in bed, hear them
call his name, whispering directives in an unknown, unholy tongue.
So he sent out ill-fated expeditions to locate their strongholds;
consulted with his high priests; embraced the march of historical
time in terms of hollow Earth and falling moons. At odds with
that dislocating relativistic universe coming into vogue, he made
his fears a national, then international concern, aiming at nothing
less than biological mutation and the apparition of a new race of
heroes, demigods, and god-men. Humankind freed from elemental control, Eternal Ice. And that primitive, beaten, unhappy, mys-

tically minded nation followed him, eager for protection, reenfoldment, enclosure, Eternal Spring.

"The Left tried to offer their assistance, but could not get through; the Right was still strong then. Riders on the storm returned empty-handed; his secret order failed to make contact. They had been searching among mistaken heights, false peaks. They lacked but that one instrument, that forgotten phallus of power."

Reydak wasn't sure how much more of it he could stand.

All eyes turned to Ouro and Sueño as they entered the room, and Woolley summarized what John Reydak, Plummer's journal, and OObe had told them.

Ouro could have told the Listeners in return of N'ntara's decade-old warnings; but it was Tedman Brady's solarium utterings he quoted when he stood up to address them—the Red Hand's warnings.

" 'You think this some petty struggle,' " the shaman recalled for them, " 'life and death; but it is more. You intrude with your devices, hoping to forestall the end, enter our domain. But you must be stopped. So many imbalanced among you to use as we see fit. So many hands to fit for bombs. Pity. Just when you were becoming such useful idiots.' "

Carmine broke the silence. "The words were directed at us."

Ouro nodded. "We have been the Red Hand's 'useful idiots'. Believing ourselves victorious in exteriorizing a symbol to forge our shield, when all we've done is summon them home."

Reydak looked around, bewildered.

"These instablilities we live with—these orbs of light and mysterious disappearances—have been bleeding in from the past. The manifestations of an archaic consciousness struggling to reassert itself. The Left has tried again and again to stage a return, appearing to us clothed in symbols that captured our imagination—the *chimera*'s garb. And now we have provided them with the one they sought."

Terri gasped as the weight of Ouro's pronouncement sank in: the star—still there in Pisces, still blue-shifted, still closing on Earth. The one the Concentricity had given the world was in itself the Atlantean return. The ruling priesthood of that transgressive state had once destroyed the world in their lust for power, and now their agents were beckoning them home. The Red Hand's reactivation of the Earth Phallus was effecting the planet's axis, tearing openings in the fabric of reality through which poured discontinuities—what were termed phenomena:

alien ships and powers, beasts and demons, the mutilated remains of their perverse workings, their efforts to mutate, combine and recombine . . .

"If we set it in motion, we can turn it around," Carmine said, with a coach's rallying voice.

Amber said, "If the Red Hand stands on the Left—"

"We're the Right," Terri finished for her. "Earth's counterforce."

Reydak made a valiant effort to keep up, feeling like a spectator at a doubles tennis match as his head swung from voice to voice.

"We must bring Susan and the others home," Flo States said. "It will require all of us."

"And Inaccessible," Woolley interjected, coming to his feet. "Our instrument against theirs."

"Pure thought against evil design."

Reydak—listening with measured amounts of amusement, fear, and paranoia—felt his testicles tighten as he suddenly sensed Ouro's eyes on him.

"What?" he asked defensively.

Ouro made a dismissive gesture. "I was only about to lament the fact the president turned me out. For certainly, if your father's claims are true, the nation's intelligence network could determine the location of the gnomon. Perhaps put an end to the Red Hand's activities."

Reydak began to wonder whether Amber had been eavesdropping on his conversation with John, or whether Ouro was trying to pick his brain. But either way, what were the chances the Red Hand had survived intact some forty years after Pavel's visit, that they would even be in the same place?

"What do you expect the president to do with a half-assed story like this?" Reydak asked all of them. "You figure he'd nuke the thing on your word? Take it out with lasers?"

Ouro continued to regard him. "I'm sure you're right. But I was thinking along different lines."

"Such as?"

"How beneficial it would be to have an agent in the field. A team, perhaps. One that could create a diversion while our counterforce was being readied."

In the dark and cobwebbed confines of the crawlspace beneath the Haven den, Raven smiled. He hadn't heard much of the early stuff, but he caught Ouro's suggestion about the formation of a team of agents in the field, and he knew straightaway he wanted in on the op. In fact, every nerve and muscle in his body was already crying out for it, as if some unseen hand was ready to push him up through the floorboards right into Reydak's arms. Payback time for the rear echelon motherfuckers who'd left him to die in the jungle, he thought. The Agency had fucked him over, and here was his chance to fuck back.

Something had always told him his turn would come to balance out past debts. And all at once he felt as if he had the strength of a whole goddamned army at his back.

"There's no logic to any of this," Reydak tried to tell them, the voice of reason now. "It's craziness. You're all looking for something to hang your paranoia on. First it was Soviets, now this Red Hand."

"Karel," Amber said, as if speaking for the room, "we don't have time to argue with you."

Reydak snatched Pavel's file from Carmine's hands and aimed a finger at Hiawatha Fountain. "You're going to take his word this thing's legitimate because as he tells you it *feels* legitimate? Pavel could have been working on a novel about Plummer, for Christ's sake."

Terri gave him a pitying look. "And the Red Hand, Karel? Is that also fiction?"

Reydak made an exasperated sound. "Look, I'm willing to concede there was a Red Hand operating under Hitler's direction. And maybe they did get back together after the war. But you're talking about a handful of octagenarian Nazis at the controls of some planetary . . . *pocket salami!* No power like that could go undetected. And to link these old men with Plummer and some battle that's waged through time . . ." Reydak laughed insanely. "You're asking for a quantum leap."

Amber reached out to take hold of his hand. "Karel, you're still battling yourself. Don't you realize most of what we have came from you? The memories I intuited under the scenario your Agency planted, the voice I heard calling your name, Pavel speaking to you at the session, John's revelations—"

Reydak threw her hand off. "Don't talk to me about that session. You could have run a make on me and learned about Pavel. You surprise me with all this shit Woolley's learned about him. You could have had some of that from day one." Reydak softened his voice. "Get out of here before it's too late, Amber. You're all infecting each other."

Everyone smiled thinly.

"I could no sooner take my own life than desert these people, Karel," Amber said. "You just refuse to see it. Even if you won't accept what happened at the session, think about who and what your father was. He specialized in the workings of the mind, Karel. He could have found some way to seed or indoctrinate your young mind with his concerns about the Red Hand. Trusting, maybe even *knowing*, that someday his efforts would bear fruit. All right, you can't believe Pavel could communicate with you through Ouija. But what about your own unconscious directing the disk around the screen? This is the way things are, Karel. SIN or whoever you work for didn't send you to us: *Pavel* sent you to us."

"To foil the Red Hand." Reydak snorted. "The same Red Hand that's manipulating the president, forcing him to start World War Three and clear the way for an Atlantean takeover." He shook his head in disbelief. "You're hopeless, all of you."

"You're one of us, Karel," Flo said.

"A card-carrying member of the Right, I suppose?"

"What about the Blue Star?" Terri asked after a moment. "Amber told us you can see it."

"So who's saying my head's screwed on any tighter than yours, Terri? But at least you don't hear me getting prophetic, do you?"

"Millions can see it, Karel. Or do you have some easy explanation for its appearance?"

Reydak's eyes found Woolley. "You're my best guess, Doc. You've got friends at observatories all over the world. Someone photographs the thing—a Wholist, probably—and you all decide to run a scam. You figure you need something everyone can line up behind, so you use the star. Suggestion takes over from there and pretty soon you've got a movement. Now you're doing the same thing with this Red Hand, hooking all the weirdness in the world on it—UFOs, paranormal disappearances, wars, disease, the president's episodes . . . But Brady's people aren't going to buy it, kids. You're putting yourselves out in the cold."

Amber lowered her head, something inexplicable in her eyes when she looked up. "You're wrong, Karel, we didn't 'hook' everything on the Blue Star, as you say."

"Then give me something to go on," Reydak said, searching the room for answers.

Ouro met his gaze. "There was no Blue Star," the shaman said flatly. "Not until we created it."

23 Conjecture Compromise

"The chopper was found a few days later in Pennsylvania," Keyes was explaining the following afternoon in the Ganzfield Inn's secure back-room booth. "The bodies of your parents were identified, but we had no information on the pilot. No prints on file with the Bureau or the Pentagon, no dental records, *nada*. TSD tried to run a trace on the machine itself, but turned up a dead end. Seems it was sold surplus to an interstate carrier that had gone belly up a year or two before. Pavel's past was so checkered, we ended up with a suspects list a yard long. It could have been the Czech STB, some disgruntled member of a saucer cult, a leftist Guatemalan who'd gotten wind of Pavel's hand in the Arbenz psy op . . ."

So many unbalanced to use as we see fit, Reydak recalled from the solarium countertrance session.

". . . Anna was sitting you, the night they were taken. She took you home the next morning."

All these years, Reydak thought angrily. He still couldn't come around to thinking of Pavel as his father. John and Anna had raised him from infancy, end of story. He figured he'd even be able to forgive them their duplicity one day, given the circumstances surrounding Paperclip and all. "How many people know about this?" he asked.

Keyes thought for a moment. "There were only a handful of people who knew at the time. Your parents kept to themselves, and John and Anna were second parents to you long before the crash. Now, outside of myself, I can't think of anyone in the family or on the Hill who knew about the adoption. Aren't many people my age left in the community." The SIG director made a weary sound. "I knew this op was going to turn circles, but I never thought it would lead to this, Karel."

Reydak looked away from the table. "Level with me, sir. It was an inside job, wasn't it?"

Keyes expelled his breath. "Over Paperclip, you mean. No, Colonel, I don't think so. There were rumors to that effect, of course, simply because your father had been getting so vocal about this Red Hand group. But it wasn't as if these people were war criminals, in spite of Pavel's making them out to be something even worse. Besides, we'd come out ahead in the deal. We made arrangements through the Vatican with La Esclusa to get them out of Europe, and the Spider took over once they hit South America. In exchange we learned of the whereabouts of some people we *were* interested in recruiting—research scientists for the most part, including a couple of geniuses from the Kaiser Wilhelm Institute."

"Do you know where the group ended up?"

"They tied up with some I. G. Farben concern in Peru. We were keeping tabs on them up until about ten years ago. They were into poppy cultivation then; maybe still are, for all we know."

"The name Plummer ever come up—a Colonel Plummer?"

"Not that I know of."

Reydak pinched the bridge of his nose. "Ouro and Woolley have themselves convinced these ex-Nazis are a bunch of reincarnated Atlanteans at the controls of some ancient weapon."

Keyes nodded. "I scanned your sitrep on the way over."

"The Bureau's listeners back me up?"

"It gets stranger," Keyes said. "About the only thing that wasn't garbled on the recordings the Bureau played for the committee was the talk centering around the Red Hand, which McVee and the chief of naval ops immediately interpreted as the *Soviet* hand. The way they figure it, the Popov Group might have numbered *Pavel* among their number if he hadn't fled Prague when the Russians moved in. They conclude that was the reason for your being singled out by the president during the exorcism." Keyes gave the back room an elaborate scan. "The SOS has forbidden us to use the term. Meanwhile, Base and most of the advisory staff continue to think Ouro somehow precipitated Brady's episode and are pushing to have the whole group picked up."

"That's a waste of time," Reydak said, annoyed. "They're their own worst enemies. Besides, they'll be on their way to Inaccessible in a day or so. Why not just let them go?"

"That was my recommendation to the committee, Colonel.

But not for the reasons you suggest.'' Keyes snapped open his briefcase and handed Reydak a NODIS-stamped manila envelope. ''Have a look inside.''

Reydak slid several aerial photographs and computer-generated enhancements out onto the table. He could read rivers, patches of forests, and cultivated land on some, where the rest showed little more than cloud cover, along with a concealed something or other that was emitting a substantial thermal signature.

Keyes said, ''The overhead imagery CPRs are courtesy of an Earth Resources sky-eye. We didn't want to tip our hand with the Pentagon by involving National Recon, so interpretations were carried out by imaging consultants at JPL.''

''So where am I looking at?'' Reydak asked.

''The last known location of our missing occultists. Just inside the Peruvian border from Bolivia, northeast of Lake Titicaca.''

''The place looks cloaked,'' Reydak commented.

Keyes nodded. ''Don't ask us how, but it is. Photo interpretation doesn't know what to make of the infrared paint, but the signature bears resemblance to a laser transmitter of some sort. It's too bad we couldn't arrange an air sample analysis flyby, but what with the political situation down there, we can't make too much noise about it.''

Reydak was silent for a moment, leaning back from the table, his gaze unfocused. ''The Sendero regime has strong ties with Moscow.''

''Exactly. So maybe there is something to this Red Hand business after all. Maybe they're even feeding power to the Popov Group by means of some orbital relay mirror.'' Keyes let out a shrill laugh. ''Listen to me, I'm sounding as scrambled as the rest of them.'' He gave Reydak a hard look. ''Karel, just between you and me, I'd rather be anywhere in the world but Washington right now. Brady's out of control, and this vision's become a walking Rorschach. Everyone's twisting it to suit his own needs.''

Reydak stared at the overhead-imagery photos. *An agent in the field*, he could hear Ouro saying. *A diversion.* He thought of Amber and forced her from his mind. ''You say you couldn't identify the pilot of that chopper.''

''We don't know who he was.''

''He could've been working for anybody.''

''Any number of suspects.''

"I don't suppose we could just airstrike this place."

"Not without provocation of some sort."

"And there isn't likely to be that."

Keyes linked his hands behind his head. "Course if this were the good ole days we could put together an executive action group. Say a team of highly skilled mercs who had no ties with any government agency, but who were willing to undertake a crash operation of their own. Say, ostensibly, to run a raid on a suspected poppy farm and processing plant. We could even provide transport, tactical weapons assistance, and a Global Positioning Unit to such a group. But of course these aren't old times, are they, Colonel?"

It didn't require a sharp ear for nondirectives to recognize what Keyes was after. "A friendly staging area down there would help."

Keyes grinned and sat up. "As it happens there is one. Place belongs to a coca grower who's on very good terms with the State Department. A former Bolivian general. He was one of the first to back our eradication efforts back in the eighties, so we rewarded him with an import license after legalization." The SIG director gave Reydak an appraising look. "You sure you're up to this? You look like you crashed and burned days ago."

Reydak showed him a nasty smile. "It's what I was built for, wasn't it?"

"Look, Karel—"

"I'll be all right," Reydak cut him off. "But I'd rather not just waltz in there if this place is within striking distance of the border."

"I agree you should go in undercover. What about a Low-altitude insertion?"

Reydak gnawed at his lip. "I'm thinking about mission essentials, sir. I'll need something more than off-the-shelf mercs for this one."

"I could provide you a list of Sense Augmented grads who've entered the private sector."

Reydak had lost track of most of his classmates, except for Jim Wave. He had heard three or four of them had found their way onto UN Ground-truth teams. "I'll see what I can put together," he said, getting up.

Keyes extended a hand, raising his drink to the other. "I wish you the best, Colonel. And here's hoping there's a world left for you to return to."

* * *

Raven slapped a Jackson on the bar and hurried out of the Ganzfield a few steps ahead of Reydak. He wasn't certain just who the captain had met with, but judging by the number of go-to spooks sprinkled around the front room, it had to have been someone placed close to the top. Once again Reydak had taken all the usual steps to shake a tail, but it had proved easy enough to infiltrate the parade of Agency cars that were following him all over town.

Raven had done his best to monitor the back room—crawling around on the floor of the Ganzfield's urinals with his pickup amplifiers, repeating the routines he used during Reydak's previous visit with Mr. Big—but nothing had panned out. Still, based on what had gone down at the Haven, it had to be the op that was under discussion, and Raven figured he was ready as he was ever going to be to spring the dangle operation he'd cooked up.

He hurried out to the rental and quickly rid himself of the wig, the brimmed staff cap, and plaid shirt. Fucking numbnuts redneck truckers, he thought to himself, their empty conversations, bloated bellies, and heartsick music. All the crap he'd had to endure sharing brews with them at the bar, feeding tokens into the boom box. *Marches* were what Raven preferred: loud, heavy on the drums, and martial. Music that gave a man a full-blooded erection; not drippy slide-guitar sentiment that made you want to stick a muzzle in your mouth.

He threw himself into the backseat and changed clothes, donning a strack outfit of creased trousers and epauletted shirt, spit-shined loafers, and a prosperous-looking overcoat. Then he arranged his hair just so and slipped out streetside, adjusting his course to intersect with the colonel's preoccupied strides.

" 'Scuse me," Reydak muttered absently as they bumped shoulders. They performed a short positioning dance on the sidewalk; but Raven decided to wait until Reydak was a few steps along.

"Colonel?" he said, just as Reydak was about to hail a cab. "Colonel Reydak?" Reydak turned toward him, drawing an obvious blank. "Raven, sir. I was with you in Peru."

The colonel's eyes brightened some in recognition. "Raven, sure, good to see you. How've you been?"

Raven pumped his hand. "Good as can be expected, sir. Peru sort of decommissioned me for a while, but I'm getting back on my feet."

Reydak regarded him up and down. "Well, you look good, Raven. I guess Peru left a bad taste for a lot of us."

"Roger that, sir. I only wish we coulda done more—kept those Red bastards from taking over."

"Things change, man," Reydak said in an understanding tone. "You get new people billeted on the Hill and you end up with a different view."

"Ain't it the fucking truth, sir—if you'll pardon my French."

"So what are you up to?" Reydak asked after a pause.

Raven shrugged. "Oh, this and that. I was in Africa for a few months on a private contract. You know, always looking for that special duty." He inclined his head to give Reydak a needy look. "You wouldn't happen to have a line on anything for one of your ex-grunts, would you, sir?"

Reydak looked uncomfortable, then let out his breath. "You were SAC-trained, weren't you?"

Raven grinned. "Almost a year of snoop and scoop, Colonel. Odorant binding protein enhancement."

"Point man, that was it."

"Always forward, sir."

Reydak mulled something over. "You know, I just might have something for you, Raven."

"Red, white, and blue work, I hope, sir. I don't go just anywhere."

Reydak nodded, impressed. "Strictly. But it's more in the nature of a privately funded recon."

"A bit of green attached to it, I assume," Raven said in a friendly, jocular manner. "The Eagle hasn't shit for me in a long time."

"You'll make out fine," Reydak assured him. "Where can I reach you?"

Raven scratched out the number of a local friend's phone on a Ganzfield Inn matchbook. "This dude'll know where I am."

"All right, then." Reydak reextended his hand.

"Look, Colonel, I've got wheels . . ." Raven announced leadingly.

Reydak followed him over to the rental and climbed into the front seat. Holding down a smile, Raven turned the key, and spent a moment gently revving the engine.

"Now, sir," he said, dropping the rental into gear, "tell me where I can drop you."

PART FOUR

THE INVISIBLE LANDSCAPE

Shelter days are here again
Freeze-drieds, canned food, and fear again
Let us sing MAD songs, launch codes again
Shelter days are here again

—from ''Waiting for the Warhead''
copyright The Sleeping Eunuchs

24 Mixed Messages

A wet snowfall had blanketed the capital, so weighing down the boughs of the White House Christmas tree that the stately fir resembled nothing so much as a gleaming missile, its warning lights flashing, white drifts like oxygen vapor at its base.

Tedman Brady was seated by the marble fireplace in the presidential office, a single television camera trained on him. A picture-perfect yule-log fire was blazing, a nostalgic air captured and about to be transmitted to millions of home screens, as if the footage had been shot years earlier, in another time and place.

It was to be Brady's third annual state-of-the-spirit address, and although his advisors had urged him to forgo it this year, he was determined to adhere to the tradition. The idea had been Catherine's, and he was certain she would be listening. Somewhere. As the director flashed him an on-air signal, Brady took a moment to gaze up at the painted stars that adorned the elliptical room's ceiling.

The camera tracked the president's upward glance and held the shot for what seemed like thirty seconds. Brady might almost have been praying. "My fellow Americans," he said at last. "My fellow planetary beings . . . There is a new light in the heavens tonight. And like that fabled star which summoned the innocent and faithful to witness the birth of a new eon, this heavenly sign sends out a call to the pure of heart. And like that desert's gleaming, this star's appearance signals the birth of a new spirit into the world, a divine eminence sent to do battle with the forces of the shadow."

Brady fell silent, staring intently into the lens while the director made frantic rolling motions with his hands.

"This time, however, the sacrifice will not be one man's alone, but will demand the support of *all* those who have followed the star's light across the dark wastes of the void.

"For tonight, my brothers and sisters—at a time when peace should reign supreme in every heart across the land—I must announce that a nefarious plot has been revealed to me. Our planetary agency has determined that an instrument of penultimate evil has fallen into the blood-red hands of our enemies."

Again Brady paused, the director and his support personnel agape.

"Therefore, in the president's status as chief executive, and in his inherent rights as commander-in-chief of the armed forces of the United States, it is my sworn duty and sacred obligation to inform you of the deployment of a new weapons system—a defensive ring that will bring a new world into being. Capable not only of *countering* the threats of our enemies, but of condemning them to that icy realm from which there is no escape!"

According to *Trendsetter*'s analysis of leading apocalyptic indicators, the chances for nuclear war and global holocaust increased from 30 to 45 percent following the president's short address—an assessment that prompted the *Bulletin of the Atomic Scientists* to advance the hands of their office Doomsday Clock to two minutes to midnight. The Office of Civil Preparedness and CIA's Board of National Estimates put the odds even higher, and in spite of the fact that the Pentagon had upped the alert to Condition Yellow, the mood of the nation was blue.

Save, perhaps, for several hundred acres of rolling countryside in eastern Oregon, where an atmosphere of festivity prevailed. Financed by a subsidiary of Percival Flage's own Cosmic Amusements consortium, the event had been advertised as a "Survivalists Weekend: A Pre-Doomsday Blowout." But the turnout had surpassed everyone's expectations: piggybacked Japanese pickups brought bearded hermits who had driven down from Canada; outlaw bikers on ordnance-carrying Hogs; families of freaks and dope growers in airbrushed vans and overhauled school buses; rugged-looking libertarians in offroad vehicles; gray-haired retirees in mobile homes; KKK members, white supremacists, Contra-Commies for Christ . . .

Months earlier, President Brady had made a television event of his filling in of the White House Citadel; but gathered in Oregon that sunny afternoon in December were the folks who'd taken the president's move as a sure sign to add additional rooms to their own bomb shelters. One could attend any number of lectures— "Nuclear War and You," for example, or "All You Need to Know about Decontamination, Defending Your Refuge, Food Storage,

Foraging, and Emergency Home Medical Treatment"—and hundreds of products and devices were for sale, everything from rad meters to solar-powered external perimeter sensor arrays.

A man's voice boomed out over the loudspeakers: "The deposition of large amounts of dust in the upper atmosphere could give us another year without summer, people. And that's going to mean crop failures and food riots, and when the cities on the coasts start emptying and everyone starts running for the hills, guess where they're going to end up? Right here, people, right *here*! And it's your land and your shelters they're going to be after, your food they're going to be hungry for. Because there won't *be* any land or food or potable water left anywhere else!"

Close to the podium a woman who had the same flannel, suspendered, waffle-soled backwoods look was hawking a pamphlet hot out of her desktop printer: *How to make people comfortable with the idea of catastrophe by throwing a shelter party.*

A few people, young urban types with Italian knits casually draped over their shoulders, were finding something humorous in that—or maybe it was something about the woman herself that was making them laugh. In any case, the woman let it go on for about two minutes, smiling away and shaking all the tension out of her long arms, before lunging across the table she'd set up at sunrise and grabbing one of the women by the yoke of her designer blouse. "I'm not gonna waste ya now," she snarled in the woman's face. "I'm gonna wait till you show up at my doorstep with your hair fallin' out and your mother's milk stinkin' of strontium 90. And even then I'm not gonna waste ya. I'm gonna wait till your flesh is fallin' off and you're barfin' your insides out and you're *beggin'* me to waste ya. And then"—she laughed,—"then I'm gonna let ya live."

Tempers were flaring in the White House subterranean Situation Room, as well.

"Don't try to bullshit a bullshitter, Colton!" Dick Manning bellowed. "I heard him with my own two ears—'revealed to me by our planetary agency.' So stop trying to cover your ass, and tell us what the hell the Reds have that's so REGAL your people won't even share it with this committee."

"That was *planetary* agency," the DCI said in a rankled voice.

"Semantics, Colton. I—"

"Dick," Philbert Base said sharply. "It's obvious the president's reference to 'a planetary agency' was directed at Ouro's group, not the CIA."

"He's talking about these goddamned *aliens* of his," Patrick O'Denvy chimed in, with Robert Potus backing him up.

Manning glared at the Bureau and Secret Service directors. "He said *red* hand, didn't he?"

"*Blood-red* hand," Colton corrected.

"Blood-red, red, it all means the same to me—*Russians*."

"Before you start throwing accusations around, Dick," the chief of staff interjected, "what's all this about a new weapons system?"

Herman Sachs spoke to that. "Mr. Base, the president has been apprised of the fact that Gabriel Ouro's group has sequestered itself on Inaccessible. They've constructed some sort of pyramidal installation there—"

Manning waved a fist. "The president and I have been discussing operational status of the shield and the possible deployment of pop-up defenses in the event of a Soviet sneak attack."

"There *is* no weapon," the White House physician said, flustered. "What's wrong with you people? You don't have to be a trained Jungian to see what's developing here—all this talk about 'shadows' and new stars in the heavens."

"Blue stars," Niles Obstat thought to point out. "*Blue* stars, Doctor."

Masters huffed. "The Freudians have a term that bears on this—'omnipotence of thought.' "

"A shitload of good *thought*'s going do against some Soviet spacebased emitter laser or a flock of salvage-fused MIRVs," Manning shouted.

Base leaned over the table to look at Eli. "Are you willing to discuss committee rule now, Mr. Secretary?"

Eli nodded, tight-lipped.

Base glanced at a sheet of printout and set it aside. "Both the Soviets and the Islamic Front have upped their readiness in response to our DefCon alert. As you know, the president has been meeting with McVee on a daily basis with the room turned off."

"Make your point, Base," the vice president barked.

"Just this: I don't know what to think about this 'nefarious plot' or this 'power ring,' but I for one am not comfortable with the thought of Ted having access to the Permissive Action Link 'football.' Frankly, I'm worried McVee will convince him to fall back and punt."

Eli cupped a hand over his mouth. "What are you proposing—we take it away from him?"

Base shook his head. "It's possible this whole thing could

blow over, and I don't want to give your brother reasons for turning against us later on.''

Sounds of mumbled agreement filled the room.

"Now, we can't change the Permissive Action Link System codes without involving the Pentagon. But what we can do is substitute a fake 'football' for the real one. After all, it's only a forged-aluminum carrycase with a terminal inside." Base cleared his throat. "I've already taken the liberty of approaching one of the linebackers."

"And?" Eli said.

"And the man's willing to deal. He's seen the changes in Ted. Says he doesn't want any part of starting World War Three. I promised him a trade up. No cash, just a position on my staff—Air Force intel liaison or some such nonsense. So what's it going to be, Mr. Secretary? That or invoke the twenty-fifth?''

Eli let himself sink back into the armchair, wishing he could just be home with April and the kids, wrapping presents, decorating the tree. They said FDR had been given to bursts of maniacal laughter toward the end, and god knew there was no want of even more recent examples of bizarre behavior in the Oval Office. But he hated to think of Ted's name entering the list. Lately Eli had found himself slipping into reveries about a reinstated submarine command; of *On the Beach* scenarios, featuring the whole family dining on New Zealand lamb and piles of succulent kiwi fruits while the rest of the world blew itself to kingdom come.

Make the world go away, he whistled to himself while everyone at the table turned to hear his response.

As had become their habit, Milo Colton and Enoch Keyes met at Langley to compare notes after the committee session. When they were done, the DCI listened to Keyes' update on Reydak's whereabouts.

"We've got a Courier B-11 ferrying the team in from a support site in southern Ecuador," the SIG director explained. "Once they're dropped, they'll have a mission-in time of seventy-two hours."

"Any luck with maps of the impact area?"

"Not much. Texaco did some survey work down there years ago, but there are more question marks on their charts than anything else. It's nothing but sheer canyons, white water, and some of the thickest jungle in the world—what the Peruvians call the 'eyebrow of the forest.'

"Why the hell would anyone choose a location like that for a transmitter?"

"We don't know that it's a transmitter, and we probably won't know until Reydak radios in. The cloud cover's still thick as shit, so whatever they're up against remains an unknown quantity." Keyes paused in a deliberate fashion. "We're still awaiting your word on contingencies for extraction."

Colton was nodding slowly. "We can't risk exposure at this point. You can have something standing by in the event they make it back across the border," he said flatly. "But as long as they remain over the fence, they're on their own."

"I can't understand it," General Secretary Korzliev told the Politburo members in a tired voice. "Six months ago, when Europe and the nations of the third world were condemning Brady for his overtures to us, he spoke of little else but his commitment to world unification. Now, a foolish incident in Africa and suddenly he's threatening us with war. It's bad enough our coffers have been near depleted in an effort to keep abreast of America's technological advances without having to consider a host of worst-case scenarios." Korzliev sighed mournfully. "Skirmishes along our eastern and western borders, ethnic rebellion in our provinces, *refuseniks* shouting their demands in our city squares. How much more of this can we take?"

While the dozen men at the long table fidgeted, exchanging uncomfortable glances with one another, Leshin directed knowing looks to Borovitskiy of the GRU and Nikolay Rudov, the commander of the Strategic Rocket Forces. *The old fool is signing his own death warrant*, Leshin thought. A minute more of these soft-bellied mutterings and the Politburo members themselves were going to drag Korzliev out of the Kremlin and hang him upside down in Red Square.

"Comrade Gen Sec," Defense Minister Grezenko said, "I appreciate the fact that certain, shall we say, *internal* pressures must be taken into account at these proceedings, but there is a sinister side to this . . . *reversal* on President Brady's part that is in danger of being overlooked." Grezenko's eyes communicated with Leshin and Rudovich.

"To begin with, Chairman Leshin assures me that American intelligence knows nothing about the present capabilities of our offensive weapons. Experiments with laser amplification and pulse-wave propagation have been undertaken far from the prying eyes of their reconnaissance satellites, and our recent advances in these and related fields remain most secret. As for this 'plot' and 'instrument of penultimate evil,' I can only assume that Brady is playing on America's obssessive concern with our fifth-generation intercontinental ballistic delivery systems. My *fear*, however, Comrade Gen Sec, is that the American Congress will play right into Brady's hands and equip him with the means to speed deployment of the orbital defense interceptor under construction in the state of New Mexico.''

''It's true the Americans have been dazzling our satellites,'' Borovitskiy said. ''And stealth bombers have on two occasions, now, reached their failsafe points.''

''But perhaps this was only in response to our troop deployments,'' Korzliev suggested.

''Perhaps, Comrade General Secretary,'' Grezenko said. ''But what other course was left open to us after Brady's words in Jakarta? I think the Americans are searching for soft spots in our shield.''

Korzliev blanched. ''But why is he doing this? Does he truly believe that America can emerge unscathed from even a limited exchange? Even if *half* the projected twenty percent of our Seahawks penetrate the shield, countless millions will die.''

''Acceptable loses,'' Grezenko responded, ''given the fact that America's submarine-based residuals would prevail. It is my belief the president is convinced that the deployment of an orbital weapon will narrow the escalation boundaries and justify a no-notice attack.''

''Incredible.'' Korzliev gasped. ''And I thought I knew the man. But what is this new star he mentions?''

''Why, the interceptor, of course.''

Korzliev's forehead wrinkled. ''But is this the thing so many of our own countrymen are pointing to lately? How can this . . . interceptor be *seen* when it has not even been deployed?''

The director of social programming stood up. ''That is something else, Comrade Gen Sec. Some sort of mystical trend that has infiltrated our borders and infected many of our misguided comrades. The 'Blue Star,' they call it.''

''Then perhaps President Brady has seen this thing,'' Korzliev suggested.

''It is nothing,'' Grezenko was quick to say. ''An anomaly of some sort. The ability to *see* it is apparently biophysically or even genetically based.''

''I can't see it,'' Korzliev lamented. ''Have any of you seen it?'' Heads shook around the table.

''Comrade Gen Sec,'' Strategic Rocket Forces commander

Rudov said in a carefully modulated tone. "With all due respect to Minister Grezenko's compelling but unfortunately *fanciful* evaluation, may I suggest that no such weapon exists. Our agents report that completion of this defense interceptor—even with unprecedented funding—is still years away." Rudov motioned to Leshin. "If you will permit Comrade Leshin to speak, I'm certain all this confusion can be laid to rest."

The KGB chairman rose from his place, inclining his head in salute and gratitude to Rudov. "Comrades," he began, "I wish to tell you about a man named Gabriel Ouro . . ."

Leshin spoke for close to forty-five minutes, during which time he summarized what was known of Ouro, the Blue Star, and the Whole Earth Movement; and how the shaman had recently allied himself with the president. The members of the Politburo listened in silence, despite their initial incredulity, and grew more accepting of Leshin's assessment with each minute, Grezenko and the Party theoretician included.

"So you see, Comrade Gen Sec," the KGB chief concluded, "that President Brady is simply—to put it as the Americans would—*not himself.* Brady, and perhaps his advisory staff, as well, has fallen under the influence of this millennial cabal, who obviously sees something to be gained from a nuclear exchange, limited or otherwise."

Korliev looked somewhat relieved. "Then no new weapons system is about to be deployed?"

Leshin snorted. "This raises a curious point, Comrade Gen Sec. As I explained, the cabal includes among its membership a number of former top-ranking physicists. Our intelligence indicates that they have long been at work on some secret project in the Caribbean— an installation, if you will, unlike anything we have seen before."

Korzliev threw General Mikail Antonskiy a questioning look. The head of PVO Strany, the National Air Defense Command, gulped and found his voice. "We have known about it for some time, Comrade Gen Sec, but there is no evidence to suggest that the installation has a military purpose. We thought it perhaps a house of worship."

"Perhaps it was, until recently," Rudov offered. "The Americans have been known to assume control of private research projects to serve their own purposes."

"What about it, Leshin?" Korzliev asked. "You have made the claim. Now do you have a proposal to offer this committee in the event we *are* suddenly confronted with some new weapon?"

"Yes," Leshin said flatly. "I propose that we destroy it."

25 Spread-Eaglists

"Billboards," Ramon Scadering said as the idea struck him. "Great goddamn free-floating billboards."

Merv Yclept glanced at him from the station's operations status display screen, the g-web belt cutting him very little slack. "What now, Ramon?"

Ramon gestured to the view through the narrow lookdown bay, the myriad components of the shield's architecture spread out below them, synth-crystal mirrors and alloy hulls glinting in the sun's light against Earth's resplendent blue, white, and brown backdrop. Bell shapes, spheres, cylinders, wafers, spools, and thickened disks, all bristling with antennae and latticework appendages like so many microscopic lifeforms suspended in a teardrop.

Ramon hit studs and twisted dials on his console, bringing up magnified images of a Peeping Tom and a five-year-old Keyhole on peripherals five and six. Close-ups of Israeli, Chinese, and Japanese sats occupied other secondary screens. "Look at this: McDonnell Douglas, Martin Marietta, General Dynamics, Northrup, Makita . . . Everybody's advertising their products. So what we do is get Coca Cola or somebody to lift a regular fucking billboard. Laser holo-optic flat plate-array of a hundred-foot can of the Classic."

Yclept raised his eyes to the padded ceiling of the cabin. "You know, it's no wonder there's all this padding around, Ramon, 'cause you're about two steps from space happy. I mean, first off, who'd see the thing except a couple of other black-yonderboys and Salyutniks?"

Ramon smiled tolerantly. "Merv, Merv, you lack vision, 'mano. Who's going to see it? How 'bout the hardsuits and chimps working the tugs? How 'bout the Japs and Frogs who'll be up here soon? How 'bout every backyard stargazer, every VIP they shuttle up here to gawk at us, every astronomer in every observatory around the world? It'd be like subliminal advertising, only legal.''

Yclept shook his head and swung back around to face his station. They'd been teammates on the Surveillance Control station for almost six months, but lately Ramon was beginning to exhibit signs of orbital decay. "Loosen your calcium feed, my man. Remember what that 'naut said when he was on-station—how there used to be a lot more green down below?''

"That old fossil,'' Ramon said. "What's he know? We log more time in a week than he logged his whole career. Fucking politicians, they have no vision.''

"Over eight thousand sats,'' Yclept continued, "dozens of mirrors, twenty thousand pieces of junk and debris, Russian RORSATS dropping like flies, and you want to start orbiting billboards. When's your rotation up, anyway?''

"Vision,'' Ramon said wistfully. "I can see it, Merv, a new society taking root up here. Not in these floating erector-set constructions, either, but in designer habitats. Domes, spindles, toruses, dual-keeled towers. Spin-gravity, giant Lepcon solar collectors . . . All these smart rocks and piezoelectric mirrors and hardened shells dismantled, mano; Earth orbit as a staging area for trips to—''

"We have contact!'' Yclept said, as a tone sounded at his console and klaxons blared elsewhere in the station.

"Shit, not again,'' Ramon said worriedly. It was the third time in twenty-four hours, the fifteenth in two Earth-relative days. Recon sats registering Soviet prelaunch emissions, then dazzled by some unidentifiable source. Twice communication protocols issued by the inboard Cray-4 paraprocessors had sent SAC and NORAD to State Scarlet. Word around the rim of the gravity well was that something similar had been happening to Russian ferrets; but if Strategic Air was behind any of it, no one was talking.

"Russians are spoofing us again,'' Yclept said, busy at input tasks. "Reading a series of high-dazzle events, sectors Charlie-Charlie, November-Zulu.''

Ramon enabled backup systems and checked his screens. "How, goddamnit? I don't see a fucking thing. Command center, this is Overlook,'' he shouted into the intercom. "You showing anything?''

"Negative, Overlook,'' a female voice answered from the

station's hub. "Threat Board's clear as day, but sat monitors are lit up like the Fourth down here."

"A nuke test? EMP propagation?"

"No hot plumes, no signatures, no fragment clouds. All EN-LOC lines are open."

"What about PNUTS? Check for emissions control measures, prelaunch ASA readings."

"Negative, Overlook."

"Is there confirmation from Bemuse?"

"Negative, again. Thule and Space Op Center White Sands are clear."

Ramon scanned his console's constellation of lights for any sign of system malfunctions. "It's gotta be lasers then; they're dazzling our sensors from Sary Shagan. Making us see things—"

"Encrypted uplink, amigo," Yclept announced. "I'm patching it through the externals."

"Ah, SURCON I, this is CINC-NORAD at Crystal Mountain, General Sheath on the horn."

"Go ahead, Cheyenne," Yclept responded.

"What's going on up there, boys? We have negative confirmation on your Cray downlink. Have you acquired signature or discrimination?"

"Negative, Cheyenne," Ramon said, "just a bunch of excited ferrets. We're tapping the area for chaff, sir."

"Can you approximate source of dazzle, SURCON I?"

"Trying, Cheyenne."

"Go to visual. Maybe they've got some sort of cloaked scrambler out there."

"Onscreen, sector by sector," Yclept told Ramon. They fell silent for a moment, eyes glued to video displays linked to the station's cassegrain-focus scopes.

"Probable dazzle source identified," Command reported.

Ramon read data as it scrolled onscreen. "Jesus, Mary, and Joseph, what the hell is this?" Yclept was staring open-mouthed at his console. "Open the overheads," Ramon told him.

"Awaiting your verification, SURCON I," a Cheyenne tech said. "Respond."

"On the way," Ramon said, reclining his seat some as the lookup hatch slid open.

Cheyenne was quiet for a long moment. "Is someone up there space happy?" Sheath asked at last. "Your readings locate the source outside the shield perimeter, repeat, outside the shield perimeter.''

"I realize that, sir," Ramon said, eyes up and disbelieving. "But we have visual confirmation." He tried swallowing to no avail. "I don't know what it is, sir, but it's big and blue and appears to be headed our way."

Amol Woolley, tie loosened against the island's tropical heat, worked his way along a stainless steel corridor, closing on the office Flage had promised him. He sidestepped pallets of space-age ceramics, ducked beneath anaconda-bundles of wire and cable feeds, wondering all the while just how crazy it was to believe the world could actually be *rethought*.

Inaccessible lay to the northeast of Grand Turk and Caicos, at the western edge of the Atlantic's expanse of gulfweed that had come to be called the Sargasso Sea. West and south rose the Blake Plateau and the oceanic ridges of the Greater Antilles; north stretched the Hatteras Abyssal Plain and the Bermuda Rise. The island was long thought to have been unoccupied before the European conquest of the New World, but privately funded ar-cheological digs had suggested otherwise: Submerged offshore were remnants of massive stone foundations, roadways, and cy-clopean blocks. Inaccessible and its closest and largest neigh-bor—the tip of an 18,000-foot Atlantic volcano—had known three flags before falling into the hands of a reclusive tobacco plantation owner in the mid-1800s. A replica of the man's At-lanta mansion still stood on the island's southern tip. WEM had acquired the island from a Colombian drug baron, who had used the place as a refueling stop for small planes laden with Florida-bound kilos of marijuana and crude cocaine.

What began as Woolley's Project Psicon had now become a kind of crisis relocation center for Ouro and his put-upon band of extrasensory warriors. Woolley, too, was at the receiving end of some of the Red Hand's intercontinental barbs, although he had not been nearly as badly affected as the Concentricity had. They were nevertheless reunited presently, Ouro, Sueño and the original nine. With broken bones and concussions, Susan Vide and Melva Chizedek were in the worst shape, the others having fallen prey to a wide assortment of respiratory and intestinal ills, none of which proved responsive to the healing techniques the Listeners had successfully employed in the past. Then there was the Concentricity's field operative, Karel Reydak, spun into their midst like an excited atom, now charging off on his own to loosen the Red Hand's hold. Woolley had come to think of the group itself as a kind of virus, an information disorder inhaled by the planetary body.

An excited state was precisely what Woolley had in mind for the Concentricity, the focusing of their power into a coherent light that would drive the Blue Star back into the dark void of its origin—

"Surprise!" Percival Flage shouted, popping the cork on a magnum of champagne as Woolley came through the office door.

Woolley's mouth dropped open. Flage, flanked by grinning, buxom blond twins in string bikinis, was outfitted in Hawaiian shirt, sunglasses, and straw hat.

"Shut the door, Doc, you're letting in the heat."

Woolley kicked it closed. "What are you doing here?" he managed.

"When do we ever get a chance to party, eh, Doc?" Flage asked, pouring champagne. One of Flage's retouched women put a glass in Woolley's hand. "To military contracts," Flage said, toasting.

"Military contracts?"

"Come on, Doc, don't play coy with Percy, I'm the king of coy. How long d'you think you could keep me in the dark about Ouro's White House connections?"

Woolley set the glass aside. "How did you find out?"

Flage grinned. "D.C.'s a town like any other. Ouro paying sunrise visits to Pennsylvania Avenue, the president's imageers looking to put together a sound-and-light extravaganza to top that bit of Chicago F/X, Brady on a mean streak . . . And your own eagerness to get this facility operational. Stands to reason it's all connected: Ouro's finally wised up and thrown in with the Knox brothers." Flage got to his feet. "To tell the truth, Doc, I'm glad to be gone. LA's not the place to be if the men with the codes are going to be calling each other names—even if it is all a bluff."

"Y-you can't stay here," Woolley stammered. "There's important work to be done."

Flage adopted a hurt expression and turned to the twin on his right. "Can you beat that, Ginger? Do I hear any thank yous? Does anybody say 'Hey, Percy, nice job on getting the climate control on-line.' No, it's been nothing but 'We need those gallium arsenide integrated circuit boards yesterday.' And 'Where's the glass-cloth insulation for these console columns?' And 'Why haven't the superconductor coolant lines been installed according to specs?' I mean, you people take too much for granted."

"You've been well paid."

Flage rolled his eyes theatrically. "You'd laugh if I told you my profit on this job. Hey, I'm doing charity work here. The least you owe me is a week or two of R and R." He motioned to the twins. "It's only me and a couple of close friends. We'll hang out on the beach, play with the hydrofoil, you go about your important work. Deal?"

Woolley's nostrils flared. "Just stay out of our way, Percy. The facility's off-limits to your group, it that understood?"

"When have I not stayed out of your way? I told you and Ouro from the start I'd hang in till the bitter end. So here I am, Doc. Now, work us some miracles, okay?"

The installation was a blinding pyramid of alloys, synthetic crystal, and degradable plastics, towering above the island's scrub as tall as a six-story building. Seamless and sealed, it was less like a research facility than an occultist's dream palace, complete with a spherical inner chamber that was to have served as a kind of anthanor for Woolley's alchemical work—a gathering place for particles of mindstuff, where the Concentricity would seek to *materialize* objects of its collective dreaming. Create by means of a sheer act of will—a truly platonic affair, the idea made real. They had already demonstrated the ability to influence subatomic interactions; the next step, therefore, would have involved doing away with the accelerator hardware that birthed the particles.

But refuge was now the primary concern; a place to hide from the Red Hand's reach. And right thinking was the focus. No parlor tricks or conjurings, but a determined effort by eleven individuals who hoped to alter the course of the future. Before the day ended, the eleven would be seated at their stations, neural helmets and dermatrodes in place, spaced at intervals around the circular base of the sphere like LIAR's particle-directing electromagnets. But presently they were assembled in the facility's unfinished conference room, while elsewhere Dr. Haguchi's teams worked frantically to ready consoles and monitors in the control booth.

Ouro had prepared a fresh batch of *mai'oni* for everyone to ingest, concocting it from the healthiest vines to be found in WEM's Florida greenhouses, and spicing it with helper leaves from plants gathered by moonlight and steeped together in ceremonial clay crocks.

"My father used to say to me: 'The world is nothing but potential,' " Ouro explained as he passed around cupfuls of *mai'oni*. " 'The world is something we are *doing*, monkey, and we have all been taught to agree on this *doing*.' There is power there, he told me, a power beyond knowledge."

Ouro reached under his poncho to grip the power amulet that had hung round his neck for close to twenty years. "This is *ruoimo*," he told the Concentricity, raising his cup like a holy chalice, "the power ring. It is the most important crossing a Human Being can undertake, for we seek nothing less than to reexperience the transgression and subsequent catastrophe that ended the last world age, and by doing so prevent its reoccurrence. Successful, we will gain the power to see everywhere. Should we fail, we will die, and the Earth will die with us."

He sipped and continued. "There is no escaping the doing of the world. We must believe in *human* being."

The shaman's permissive action codes.

Dolores Sueño and the nine drank.

Ouro showed his palms and motioned for everyone to rise. And one by one they filed from the room and assumed their high-tech stations around the base of the installation's spherical chamber.

Reydak steered clear of the trees and braced for impact. He could still hear the hum of the Courier's three-bladed prop, but the sound could have come from anywhere, the pilot's pop-up maneuver having returned the plane to low-hanging clouds. The cluster canopy was actually keeping him dry for the moment, but his feet went out from under as he hit, sending him down into a water-filmed patch of mud and clinging clay. He was disengaging himself from the chute harness when Jo Jo landed alongside him, an archaic Navstar backpack unit tipping him over on his back. With paperback-size devices available, Keyes' "gift" was a veritable stumbling block.

Rain was coming down in thick tepid sheets, but the surrounding jungle was quiet. From somewhere west of their position came the turbulent roar of a river.

"D'you see Raoul come down?" Reydak shouted.

Jo Jo motioned off to the left as he struggled to free himself of the Earth's suction. Reydak almost smiled at the sight and extended a hand. Standing six-three with shoulders three feet wide, Beads was the oldest member of the team. He favored a moth-eaten black beret, which he wore at a rakish tilt over thick salt-and-pepper hair. He was SAC trained in optical surveillance and had had his implants upgraded for merc work he'd done in Africa. Right now the big man was twisting left and right, letting loose a steady stream of choice invective. His primary weapon was an H&K, with telescoping buttstock, laser guidesight, and nightscope. The rest of the team carried similar weapons, except for Raven, their nose and point man, who'd insisted on a Japanese-manufactured quad-barrel autorifle.

After Reydak had helped Beads to relatively solid ground, they stashed the chutes and made for the treeline, where they found Raoul treating a forehead gash he'd sustained on the way down.

"Fuck this nap-of-the-earth shit," Potenchia spit.

"Hey, leg, we found a soft spot," Jo Jo told him, grinning.

Raoul eyed his teammates' chameleon suits, which were now as yellow as the rain-soaked earth. "Thanks, but I'll stick to the trees."

Potenchia was of Italian-Swiss descent, ex-Company and an expert climber with a doctored inner ear. He'd headed up a team that had humped a transmitter to the top of a four-mile-high peak in Nepal's Ganesh Himal. Potenchia was working high steel in Singapore when Reydak tracked him down for the op. Tall and trim with a full beard and moustache, he wore his ash-blond hair to his shoulders.

Manly Blades and Romeo Tango joined them a moment later, looking none the worse for wear. Both men had trained together at Camp Perry and taught in-close techniques to paramilitary units. SAC had laid in some permanent hand-hardware, and they'd done time as partners in Angola, Peru, and the Horn. A field med-tech, as well, Blades was swarthy and about as lethal as they came. Like Reydak, he was laden with high-velocity plastiques and an array of electronic sensors. Tango, in contrast, had the innocent look of a Mexican choirboy, but his reflexes were king-cobra quick and just as deadly.

"Anyone see Raven?" Reydak shouted above the downpour.

Raoul shook his head. Jo Jo Beads said, "We oughta consider letting that one go, Colonel." He twirled a finger at his temple. "Soldier of misfortune, man, loose Jesus nut. I've heard stories from guys who were in Angola with him—"

"What sort of stories, fuckface?" Raven asked, emerging from the thickets, weighed down with antipersonnel "contact breakers'' and the autorifle. His chameleon fit him like a well-tailored business suit.

Reydak threw Raoul a look as if to say *Where's your ears, hombre?*

Raven stepped boldly up to Jo Jo, thrusting his pointed face three inches from the larger man's. "What sort of stories, swinger?"

Beads smiled down at him. "Sorry, Raven. I must be confusing you with some other psycho merc."

Perhaps it was the assured control in Jo Jo's voice or the hurricane look in his eye that kept Raven from risking a groin or carotid shot. Instead he merely sniffed the air and said, "You're not regular, man. I can smell it on your breath. Either that or you ate shit for breakfast."

Reydak was beginning to wonder why he had brought Raven along, rhinoman or no. In retrospect it seemed an almost compulsive act on his part, as if he had somehow sensed it was Raven's destiny to ride with them from the moment they'd bumped shoulders outside the Ganzfield Inn. Perhaps that encounter had carried more premonition than omen of good fortune. "We're not being paid to engage each other," he said, placing himself between Raven and Bedds.

Beads shrugged. "Whatever you say, Colonel."

"And let's dispense with the honorifics—all of you."

"Just keep this dude away from me," Raven warned, squaring his shoulders and flourishing the frags cinched to his web gear.

Reydak shook his head, wondering what was going on; the op was less than a week old and they were already at each other's throats.

"Movement," Raoul announced suddenly.

"It's probably our contact, but let's play it by the numbers," Reydak said. The team fanned out to set up a kill zone.

A four-wheel-drive jeep with outsize tires bounded into the muck Reydak and Beads had called home for a time. Reydak watched it come to a halt, flashing its lights behind the rain.

"Carlos Tremoya," the driver shouted, stepping out into ankle-deep mud as Reydak, Blades, and Tango showed themselves. Two Indians in alpaca ponchos and brown fedoras climbed from the backseat.

Reydak made the introductions.

"These men will guide you into the area," the former Bolivian general added, wiping water away from his eyes. "Do you have someone who speaks Spanish?"

"*Hablo,*" Tango said, nodding to the Indians.

Reydak spoke the language some, but they'd agreed beforehand to let one man talk while the other listened. Judging by their highland look—leathery skin and high cheekbones—the Indians were Aymaras, Reydak ventured. Both had wads of coca stuffed into their cheeks. He thought of the smart-tabs everyone had downed in the Courier, wondering if it wasn't the time-release stimulants that were exacerbating whatever the team had brought with them from the MSS in Ecuador.

"Can you give us an idea of what we're up against, Tremoya?" he asked a moment later.

"Yes. The border is less than a day's journey, even in this rain. It is lightly patrolled in this area, but once you cross the Sinama you'll be entering Brother Cordoba's land."

"Brother Cordoba?"

"That's what he calls himself, yes. But don't be misled by the name. He's German, not Peruano. My father met him many years ago when he went by the name Bauer. Long before he turned his hand to the cultivation of poppies."

"Yeah, but *Brother* Cordoba?"

"There's an old monastery on the land," Tremoya said. "Didn't your people brief you?"

"A dope-growing monastery?" Tango said.

"You're surprised, but it is a common enough thing down here. The Church moves in mysterious ways, no? There's an airstrip, bodyguards, two dozen field workers perhaps, outside of the monks themselves."

"Monks," Manly Blades said, chuckling. "This oughta be some run."

Monks occupying a cloaked site, Reydak reminded himself. As Beads, Raven, and Potenchia emerged from the trees, he put some distance between himself and the Jeep and pulled a paperback-size satellite relay radio from his pack. After extending the antenna, he keyed in a coded initial burst that would eventually reach Rusty Keyes at SIG headquarters.

Later, when the gear was sorted out and the first guide had set off, Carlos Tremoya approached Reydak in confidence. "Tell me if you can, Colonel, what it is that this heroin grower has done to deliver the wrath of the United States military down on his head."

"Same thing that's called it down on every dope dealer Uncle

Sam does business with," Reydak said, readjusting the back-pack's Velcro straps. "Income tax evasion."

Six hours of steady uphill slogging, and eight pairs of eyes were peering from the undergrowth at a rope bridge spanning the cliffs above the white-water Sinama. The bridge—the first sign of habitation they had encountered since the drop zone—linked a narrow trail with an even narrower one notched in the cliff face opposite. Across the gorge, the pocked limestone rose straight up for close to forty meters. Unless they chose the notch, Reydak thought, the escarpment was going to require a technical assault.

One of the guides was chattering away, gesturing to something out of sight.

"What's with the indigs?" Raven asked.

"He says there's a tunnel half a klick along," Tango said, directing his response to Reydak. "We can save a day's walk if we take it."

"Probably hollowed out by runoff from the top of the ridge," Raoul speculated.

The guide rabbit-punched his midriff. "The water'll be up to our waists," Tango said.

"That's some translating, Romeo." Raven sniggered.

Raoul aimed his glasses at the cliff, plotting a course to the top. "It'll be slow going. Especially in this shit." They were soaked to the skin from perspiration as much as rain, the chameleon suits grasshopper green in the jungle's waning light.

Reydak looked at Raven. "You ran some tunnels the last time we were here, didn't you?"

Raven raised his eyebrows. "I'm flattered you remember, sir. At the time, if you recall, you weren't too pleased with my performance."

"I don't remember that, Raven."

"Well, all the better then."

Raven stowed most of his gear and crossed the bridge alone. "I agree with Jo Jo," Blades said when the pointman was out of earshot. "We should blow this guy off."

Half an hour later, Raven's all-clear came over the field radios; Reydak guessed it would be the last time they used them. Moving out, he turned to see the guides arguing with Tango.

"They won't go any farther," the hand-fighter explained.

"Why not?" Reydak asked them in Spanish.

"Some superstition or something," Tango said. "They keep

telling me this land belongs to the 'guards' or 'the guardians,'—
the ones who control the motion of the world.''

Shortly they were gathered around a stone wheel, regarding
it as if it were a prize piece in a museum garden. Heavy rain
was falling again, puddling on the stone's incised surface glyphs,
running in rivulets down grooves and symbols channeled into
its curved side.

"Looks fucking ancient," Manly Blades commented.

Raven laughed. "What are you, a goddamned archeologist?
'Looks fucking ancient,' " he mimicked. "If it was ancient,
you think it'd be just sitting out here in the open waiting for you
to trip over it? It'd be in some private collection by now."

"Smartass," Blades said coldly. "Just keep it up."

Reydak ran a hand over the lichen on the stone's surface,
recalling the extracts Carmine Dover had read from Plummer's
journal. Raven was right: There was something wrong with the
stone's just sitting there.

"Navstar shows us right on target, Karel," Jo Jo Beads said.

"Scanners showing anything?" Reydak asked Blades.

"A shitload of living IR, but nothing carrying a gun."

"Then we keep moving."

They had entered the southernmost pocket of a canyon,
steeply sloped east and west and cut by a river that fed the tunnel
itself. The altimeter put them at 1200 meters. The trail hugged
the bank, coursing in and out of thick vegetation—tall fern trees,
bamboo, and gnarled stunted oak.

Reydak found himself thinking about Ouro as they resumed
their pace. The last intel report put the Concentricity on the
Caribbean hideaway, and for some reason Reydak could not
explain, he seemed to have an uncanny sense of the place. True,
he'd been shown photos and overhead imagery of the pyramid,
but it was as if he could feel the heat of tropical sun, project
himself right into the heart of the facility, clearly visualize Ouro
and the Listeners grouped around some kind of containment
chamber. *They're sending to me*, he thought. And the realization
sent a cold jolt through his body.

The going was rough: They crossed and recrossed the river,
the rain continuing without letup, their gear snagging on vines
and creepers. But just as Reydak was beginning to sense an end
to the thick stuff, he heard someone up ahead shuck his load and
come barreling back down the trail.

Jo Jo yelled, "This is fucked, man! This is completely fucked!"

There was just enough light left for Reydak to see Blades putting out his arms to restrain Beads. "Relax, Jo, the only way out is up, so let's pick up your shit and get moving."

"You go up front and tell me that," Beads snapped.

Reydak and Blades regarded each other. "Move out," Reydak said uncertainly.

When they caught up with Raven, they found themselves staring at the tunnel all over again.

Tango said, "What the . . . How the hell did we get back here?" He turned to Jo Jo. "I thought you said we were on track."

"I did, man, I did," Beads shouted, jabbing a forefinger against the Navstar. "This op is fucked, I'm telling you."

Blades and Raoul came around hard on Reydak. "What's this shit about 'guardians,' Colonel?" Raoul demanded.

They tried it again.

The stone wheel was in better shape than it had been on the first pass, and sunset was long overdue.

"That's it, man, I'm gone," Beads announced, shrugging out of the Navstar. "This ain't worth shit, that's for sure."

He was half a dozen steps toward the tunnel when Blades blocked his path. "Listen, Jo Jo, we just took a wrong turn last time. The only way is up and out, so let's get humping."

Beads clenched his fists. "It's a fugue march, man. Now stand down."

Again Blades stretched out his arms. This time, however, Beads turned on him, hooking a powerful left toward Manly's face. But the Tae Kwon Do champion was long gone, and had returned a lightning curl to Beads' solar plexus before the radioman could launch a follow-up. Beads dropped and Blades went to his side, helping him regain breath control and offering water from his canteen.

"I don't know what's happening to me," Beads apologized. "My nerves are screaming at me." He looked up at Reydak. "I've never been too good with altitude, Colonel."

Raven had doubled back from the point and was regarding the scene, his nightfighter face-cosmetic etched by twigs and overhangs. "Altitude? We're at twelve hundred fucking meters." He laughed, shaking his head. "Some candy-ass outfit

I've signed on with. We can be up and outta this shit in another hour, but you rough-and-tumble types wanna go home.''

Blades shot to his feet, but Raven had already drawn his handgun. "How are you against explosive tips, Superman?"

Reydak raised his H&K. "Put it back, Raven."

Raven grinned at him. "Hey, Colonel, you an' I don't have a beef.'' He thumbed the safety on. "But this one's got steel fingertips. A guy's gotta protect himself.''

"Let's move," Reydak said, allowing Blades to take the point and falling in behind Raven. For the next half hour he struggled to keep himself from putting a burst into the merc's back.

Everyone kept expecting to see the tunnel show up around the next bend. Only when it was behind them for keeps did anyone speak. Reydak's jaw was sore from grinding his teeth.

The canyon opened into a broad expanse of waterlogged savannah, the rock shoulders of a double-humped mountain towering above them, twin summits lost in cloud. Angry that the team wasn't pushing on, Raven paced, chewing on smart-tabs while the rest of them ate gorp and blister-packed rations and discussed what they were going to do about him.

"We'll let him take the first watch," Reydak suggested.

"Yeah, but who's gonna be watching Raven?" four voices asked in unison.

Strained laughter; but it broke the somber mood of the day. The rain lightened and Blades and Tango fell out, the belated night too dark to be genuine.

It was just before sunrise when the rain recommenced and the ground began to heave.

Coming wide-eyed awake out of a wary half-sleep, Reydak gripped the bunch grass like a kid hanging on to an amusement park ride, the ground shuddering and buckling beneath him. Raven was watching him from several meters away, still on his feet somehow.

"It's starting, man, it's starting," the point man shouted, head thrown back in a gurgling laugh and mouth opened wide to blood-red rain.

26 Places of Conspiracy

"Obliterate a defenseless Caribbean island?" Korzliev said in shocked disbelief. "Are you mad, Leshin? The world has thought us butchers for nearly a century now, and you would have us legitimize their fears with an act of wanton destruction."

"Comrade General Secretary," Borovitskiy broke in, coming to Leshin's aid. "Surely Comrade Leshin wouldn't take up the committee's invaluable time unless his proposal had been clearly thought out."

Korzliev threw the KGB chief a hard-edged look. "What about this, Leshin? You have devised some way to achieve the objective without rendering it the first in a series of exchanges that would lead to global war?"

"I believe that I have, Comrade Gen Sec."

Leshin asked that two analysts from the GRU's Information Directorate be admitted. No sooner did the men enter than they set about readying the room's VDTs, VCRs, and still-frame projectors. A map of Inaccessible's corner of the world soon appeared on one of the screens. The older and taller of the two men used a lightpen to indicate a large island located northwest of the Concentricity's cay.

"Santilla," he began. "A somewhat barren, inhospitable, and presently uninhabited island with a long history of intense volcanism. Recent findings by drone craft launched from our biological research station in Cuba suggest that it is now entering a potentially violent phase."

As a cross-section of the volcano and surrounding seabed resolved on a larger screen, the second GRU man stepped forward.

"The seething magma at the core of the mountain is venting its gases through a series of suboceanic faults located along this line." The lightpen traced a path across the seafloor. "Seawater forced down into these vent shafts would become instantly vaporized if brought into contact with the molten rock. The resultant pressure would of course need to seek immediate outlet through the only shaft available to it—that is, through the cone itself."

Leshin and Borovitskiy traded glances across the table, wondering if Korzliev had swallowed it. The rest of the long table fell silent, waiting.

"You are telling me that you can *persuade* the volcano to erupt ahead of its natural schedule?" the general secretary asked at last. "Leshin," he added on an angry note, "what kind of lunacy is this?"

"Of course it might be necessary to employ several drone-launched low-yield nuclear devices to accomplish this, Comrade General Secretary," the GRU analyst rushed to point out.

Korzliev flushed. "Remove these idiots!" he shouted to the guards by the door. "And you, Leshin—"

"With the general secretary's permission," Borovitskiy said, rising to his feet. "We believe that general mobilization of our ground and sea forces, along with simultaneous realignment of our space-based technical means, will provide America's early warning systems with a suitable diversion and conceal our true intent."

Korzliev's plump hand slammed down on the table. "You call this a *diversion*—sending America to Defense Condition Scarlet and bringing flying-wing bombers to the edge of our airspace?"

"We are confident the Americans will not make the first move," Nikolay Rudov assured the table.

Defense Minister Grezenko thrust a finger at Rudov's beribboned chest. "They are *already* prepared to first-strike us, you fool!"

"Then what hope do we have in either case?" Leshin countered. "Comrade Gen Sec, would it not be advisable to put an end to this matter by destroying the island and *risk* an exchange, rather than commence a first strike ourselves or stand idly by while the Americans ready their own?" The KGB chief gave it a moment to sink in. "We can arrange for it to appear accidental. The worst we will have to endure is a censure from the United Nations and more of Brady's hollow threats and reprimands."

Korzliev marveled at Leshin's cold-bloodedness. The room

was deathly still when he said, "It will require very careful planning, comrades . . ."

Leshin fought down a self-satisfied smile. "I will alert our liaison with the DGI at Siete Millas to begin preparations."

"PVO Strany and the Strategic Rocket Forces will be likewise prepared," Defense Minister Grezenko muttered.

Korzliev sighed. "Comrades, I suggest we adjourn and reconvene at our Zhiguli citadel."

The men at the table voiced enthusiastic agreement.

"Shall the public be alerted?" Grezenko thought to ask.

Korzliev mulled it over. "Be circumspect. See that word is circulated quietly among the appropriate circles. We must avoid a panic."

"I will see to it, Comrade General Secretary."

"As our Chinese neighbors have recently suggested: Superwars are inevitable in a world that begets superpowers. Let us hope this is only a bit of Oriental rhetoric rather than a piece of inspired wisdom."

Every big board from Sparrevohn to Thule was lit up; something or someone had electronically convinced a group of recon satellites that a Soviet attack was imminent. And yet there were no confirmations of launch or release simulations. Just an uncorroborated report of a novel wave-maker sitting outside the fence, deep in interplanetary space.

"It must be in the system," NORAD commander-in-chief General Mylar Sheath said in a panicked voice.

"Begging the general's pardon, sir," a colonel seated at a VDT returned, "but we don't even have a clear fix on the object, let alone an optical. To assume that it's actually in our system—"

"The *computer* system, you idiot, not the solar system." Sheath banged the console like an angry consumer. "How can SURCON I be feeding us data on something that isn't even there? And if there *is* something there, what the hell's it doing outside the perimeter? You'd think the Russians were first-striking us from the moon."

"Apparently not everyone on SURCON I has a visual on the source, sir," a tech updated from her station. "SURCON II reports the same. There seems to be some confusion."

"We should never have put them up there to begin with," Sheath muttered. "Space *does* things to people."

"They did say it was *blue*, sir," the colonel suggested quietly.

Sheath shot him a look. "I won't have any of that Wholist talk inside my mountain, mister."

"May I remind the general, sir, of the protocols outlined in Project WANT-ADZE?"

Sheath returned his attention to the screen, recalling the president's recently televised address. Was WANT-ADZE actually a Soviet surveillance operation after all? And was this blue smudge a new weapon—some sort of chaff missile or laser-induced threat cloud? The general had visions of Korzliev laughing up his sleeve.

"Patch me through to General McVee," he barked.

The Big Board in the Pentagon's subterranean National Military Command Center showed North America under attack—by whom or what was anyone's guess.

"Sir, we've scanned the intruder six ways to Sunday," an enlisted ratings tech from Alabama drawled, "and the cloud remains an unknown quantity. Data from laser imaging radar and airborne optical adjuncts is onscreen."

"Let's see what these phased steerable beams are showing us, son," McVee said, leaning over the console. "Yep, just as I suspected . . ."

"Sir?"

McVee slapped the tech on the shoulder. "Dick, son. They're showing us *dick*." He walked briskly to the railing of the command balcony and ordered up a polar projection.

The Big Board rearranged itself, showing the real-time locations of SAC bombers and support craft, along with hot spots inside the USSR.

"Return to Robison projection," he commanded, and the board rearranged itself. "Give me Clear's perspective, then Flyingdale's."

And the board was again transformed.

They were the best part of the job—the god-views—he thought, as intelligence appraisals continued to pour into the room from all over the planet. From far outside its precious envelope and far beneath its despoiled seas; from recon sats and radar sites, Cobra Judy observation platforms and subconscious aircraft, acoustical sensors and lowly field spotters. All sniffing the air, probing the sky, listening with their ears to the ground for any hint of thermal blast or rocket exhaust, troop mobilizations or novel fleet deployments, silo openings or encrypted communiques. And all sent straight to him, to do with as he pleased. "I want all stations to go to DefCon Two," McVee announced.

Men and women on the floor below snapped to at their screens and consoles, executing new sequences of communication protocols as franked envelopes were conveyed to their stations by an elite unit of Pentagon support personnel.

The senior watch officer cleared his throat as he approached the command balcony railing. "Sir, intelligence reports unusually heavy traffic at all Moscow airports. Indications point to a select withdrawal of high-ranking officials. General Secretary Korzliev and the Politburo are believed to have settled into Zhiguli, sir, and the city's tunnels are rapidly filling up with Party officers and their families."

"Well, isn't that just like those Red bastards," McVee growled, arterial blood pounding hot and nasty in his temples. He could envision the long lines of ZILs and Chaikas; the Tupolevs stacked up over Vnukovo and Sheremetyevo. "Get me the president. Tacamo, Major—on the double!"

It wasn't enough for him that the armies of both NATO and the Islamic Front were fully mobilized, or that most of the nonaligned nations were looking for a rock to hide under until everything blew over. It wasn't enough that an acceptable percentage of the long-legged birds he hoped would soon go to launch were going to penetrate the Soviet shield and inflict untold damage on several major urban industrial centers, as well as the hardened silos they were targeted for. And it wasn't enough that most of the civilian population of North America and Europe were shivering in front of their tv screens wondering how they'd once believed Brady could make a difference.

No, what bothered McVee—what rendered all the rest of it appetizer without the main course—was the fact that Korzliev and his cadre of commie pundits were probably going to escape devastation: the luminous fireballs and radioactive clouds; the firestorms, Mach fronts, and conflagrations; the shock waves and thermal blasts; the gamma rays and neutrons; the flash-burn casualties, flame-burn statistics, and aftermath totals . . .

The watch officer had returned and stood gazing up at him.

"Speak, for god's sake!" McVee bellowed.

"Sir! SURCON stations report Soviet rocks leaving their garages and entering the traffic lanes."

"The president," a second officer reported, handing McVee a cellular phone.

McVee updated the situation report he had furnished the Situation Room only an hour before, emphasizing that the Soviets were realigning their shield satellites and relay mirrors.

"If I may speak freely, sir, those goddamned commie bastards are high-tailing it out of Moscow like rats leaving a sinking ship. I strongly advise that all White House Emergency Procedures be initiated immediately and that the president and all National Command Authority personnel transfer at once to the Airborne Command Post."

"I appreciate your concern, General McVee," Brady said after a long pause. "But we have to wait for the game to start. Now do you or do you not have a ready screen?"

"A ready screen, sir?" McVee stared at the Big Board. "Yes, sir, I can safely say that we do."

"Now, General, listen to me closely: Have any hostile moves been directed against our power ring?"

"No, not yet, Mr. President, but they're sending us static like you wouldn't believe."

"That's to be expected, General. Just be on the alert for rogues."

"Rogues, sir?"

"The small craft, the suicidal ones. They carry bonus points."

The line went dead. McVee went from staring at the phone to the board, which now detailed a downlink shot from orbital command. The attitude jets of three Russian kinetic kill vehicles flared briefly in the night.

Come on, sweethearts, McVee thought, just nudge us.

All eyes turned to Eli Brady as he stood unsteadily in the doorway to the EOB Electronic Situation Room. "What did he say?" Philbert Base demanded from the far end of the table.

Eli raised a hand to his forehead as if monitoring his temperature, then paced into the room, a stunned look about him. "He refuses to initiate any of the Emergency Procedures."

There was scarcely a man in the room, political or military, that didn't gasp. Moments before—from the same room—the president had spoken to McVee and been apprised of the latest Soviet actions. At the close of their brief exchange, Brady had simply gotten up and walked out, Secret Service agents and the Special Intel officer with the "football" hurrying behind.

"That's not all of it," Eli continued. "He won't under any circumstances board Kneecap."

"What's he planning to do—remain *here*?" Niles Obstat

asked in uncharacteristic falsetto. "With Citadel filled in? The House is hardened, but not *that* hardened."

"Does he want to go to Fort Ritchie?" Duke Cottel asked. "The Joint Chiefs are headed—"

"No," Eli cut him off. "He plans to stay in the Oval Office."

"And do what?" Base said, his voice cracking.

Eli shook his head and showed everyone a crazed smile. "He's making arrangements with network liaison now. He wants to bring the entire nation in on his decision making for the remainder of the crisis. To demonstrate his complete trust in the umbrella. He wants to prove that filling in the bomb shelter wasn't just some political act." Eli laughed in spite of himself. "If it warms up, he's going to arrange to have everything televised from the South Lawn."

"Good god," Loren Masters said.

"You mean *thank* god, Doctor," Base said to him. "Thank god we had sense enough to take the 'football' away from him. Does he suspect anything?"

"No," Eli told him.

Base glanced around the table. "All right," he asked, "who's going to be man enough to accept the handoff?"

Dick Manning, the secretary of defense, the rightful designate, studied his hands in silence.

"Don't look at me," Al Capella said, waving a hand. "You people got this one rolling long before I was called into it, so don't expect me to stick my neck out to save yours now."

"It's your goddamn neck, too!" the chief of staff snarled. "It could be every goddamned neck in the goddamned Western world. What about you, Eli?"

The secretary of state shook his head. "It's too monumental a decision for any one man to make—it always has been." Eli returned the stares he was receiving. "If it comes down to launch release, we'll all make the call. Maybe Ted's got the right idea: We should open up the phone lines and ask the country to decide. I mean, why not, it's their lives, their homes . . ."

"Bullshit," Base said. "They put us here to make those decisions, not to turn to them every time the shit hits the fan. But you're right about one thing: We're better off doing it by committee rule."

"Where?" Obstat wanted to know.

Base thought for a moment. "To be honest about it, gentlemen, I've never put much stock in any of the PES sites along the relocation arc. You think they'd have room for us over at Fort Ritchie, Manning?''

The secretary of defense jumped at the sound of his name. ''AMCC's the Pentagon's turf, but I don't see how they could refuse us, given the circumstances.''

''It'll mean setting up a roundabout communications relay,'' the DCI pointed out. ''McVee is still under the impression the president's calling the shots, so he'll look here or to the Airborne Command Post for release directives. That means someone's going to have to remain with the president. Either that or we bring the House comm-specialists in on this.''

''I'll stay,'' Eli said before anyone else could respond to Colton. ''I'm responsible for this whole thing anyway.''

''You're a brave man and a loyal brother,'' Base said, already sweeping documents into his briefcase.

''There's one more thing you should know,'' Eli said, as the meeting was breaking up. ''Ted means what he says about trusting the shield. When he goes on-air, his first remarks will be directed to the 'enemy high command'—his words. He's going to defy them to take the first shot.''

A world was taking shape inside Inaccessible's spherical psi-con collector: a pristine globe of blue, white, green, and brown, realigned on its axis, with its outer skies swept clear of weapons and debris and no Blue Star in its past or future. Woolley, Haguchi, and a handful of control-room technicians watched the monitors in awe.

Were Ouro and the Concentricity members aware of what they were fashioning? Woolley asked himself.

A ubiquitous buzzing sound rattled the room, and Woolley recalled the explanation Wiles ParaResearch had once offered for the audible tones *mai'oni* elicited: the metabolism of tryptamine-potent alkaloids within the cerebral matrix—the amplification to an audible level of the electron spin resonance of those very metabolizing molecules. Ouro had called them *vinesongs of the dream familiars*. Light sensitivity and space-time distortion resulted from the O-methylation of HIOMT, a pineal enzyme related to circadian function. *Clear sight*, Ouro said, *the opening of the inner eye*.

Power was bleeding out of the sphere into the facility itself, warping multihued free-floating geometric shapes throughout the structure, altering the molecular make-up of walls, doors, pylons, stanchions, and ceiling trusses; and Woolley began to fear that he had failed to take these surges into account when designing the place—that perhaps he had placed the stations too closely together and something analogous to neutron flux was occurring, a nonreversible build toward subcritical mass.

But something else was overshadowing his concerns. It was said that in the last two hours before planetary transformation humankind would experience twenty-eight extensions of consciousness, each comparable to life's passing from sea to land, or Earth to space; and in the final 135 minutes, eighteen barriers comparable to the appearance of life, the ascendency of language, and the achievement of immortality would be breached—thirteen of these crossings taking place in the last 75x10 to the minus 4 seconds.

And Woolley couldn't help but believe that the process was now underway.

He had come to view himself and Ouro as particle-paired, born of the universe's borrowed energy, poised now at the event-horizon of life's greatest mystery. And cross that horizon they would. The Concentricity was doing nothing less than taking advantage of the indeterminancy built into an information universe to birth an aneurism into a shadow domain—a geometry beyond geometry, a fractal highway to the other side of existence.

Woolley and the others were immobilized by what they saw onscreen. The world was collapsing in upon itself now, enfolding even the brilliance of its coherent light. And the pyramid was doing the same, transubstantiating as they watched, striving to scatter its trapped energy across the skies . . .

27 Illumination by Elimination

The world was coming apart. Reydak heard Beads scream, "It's blood I'm telling you, the fucking sky's *bleeding*," but could barely make him out in the downpour. Raven was on his knees nearby, baying like a dog.

Soft cap pulled low on his brow, the shuddering Earth throwing him into unexpected turns and corrections, Reydak moved toward the sound of Jo Jo's voice. The chameleon suit had gone red as the rain. Blades had a hunk of Jo Jo's sleeve in his hand and was holding the other one in front of the radioman's face.

"It's some kind of rust, Jo Jo," Blades said, letting the stuff pool oily and slick in his cupped hand. "Some kind of iron ore mixed into the rain."

Beads crippled him with an unexpected groin shot and ran, slogging through the soaked bunch grass like a broken field runner. Manly was lying on his side hugging his knees when Reydak finally reached him.

"I'll see to him," Romeo shouted, arriving a moment later.

The Earth was behaving itself once more but the red rain showed no sign of letting up. Promising himself it was just plain adulterated water, Reydak began to pursue Beads across the meadow, up into scree fields covering the lower slopes of the hump-backed ridge. Just plain rain, he thought, mixed with something Kalau had coughed up into the stratosphere eight months back. Hell, if the explanation was good enough for the Bureau, it was good enough for him.

He was a hundred yards short of a towering granite wall when the tremors recommenced. The sudden movement shifted the scree and sent him sliding, buried knee-deep in the jagged stones, back toward the flats. Beads was a good distance above him, teetering at the high side of the slope.

Romeo rushed by Reydak as he was trying to dig himself out, cursing but taking on the scree like a mountain goat. He was closing on Beads when the mountain gave one final spasm.

Rocks began to fall like meteors from the cloud-shrouded heights. The ones that buried Tango and Beads were enormous, and crushed the two men. Reydak was too busy spitting out the coppery taste of the rain to scream.

By the time he succeeded in scrambling up the slope, there was no sign of either of them. Raoul had to pull Manly away from the rocks and shale that had taken his friend's life. The ex-merc's maniacal efforts left exposed the alloy blades and hardeners SAC had implanted in his fingertips and elbows.

Manly wept while Raven howled in the meadow below.

Aftershocks continued for the rest of the morning, as the four of them worked their way across the savannah and over a low ridge of primevally forested hills. The deaths were on everyone's mind, but there wasn't much to say. Besides, Reydak thought, it would have been senseless to try and outshout the rain. It had gone blessedly colorless by sunrise. They'd held a ceremony of sorts, mumbled a prayer Reydak remembered from long ago.

Even without consulting Raoul—who was now lugging the Navstar—Reydak was certain they were gaining on the hot IR image that had shown up in the CPRs. The layout of the terrain matched the overhead opticals he carried. But movement was slow and numbing, almost as if a pressor field had been thrown about the place—some repulsing magnetic force.

By afternoon they were following a rock-strewn river down into a sun-dappled valley. Raven held point, with Reydak and Raoul a hundred yards behind, and Blades trailing. Raoul's enhanced auditory upgrades picked up the humming sound a few seconds before Reydak heard it. But by then Raven had a hand held up and was sniffing the breeze like a rabbit. Reydak caught sight of a dark cloud roiling up from the valley floor to meet them, and thought for a moment it might be smoke from slash-and-burn fires. But smoke didn't hum, he reminded himself.

At about the same instant he realized the cloud was alive.

The hornets, if they were indeed that, found the team almost immediately, and Reydak couldn't help think that someone was guiding the fucking things in on remote. A droning storm cloud one moment, a living tornado the next, funneling down on them in an elongated counterclockwise spiral. He was halfway to the riverbank when he heard Raoul stumble as the positioning unit straps snagged on the undergrowth. Potenchia cried for help and Reydak struggled around, batting a few black-bodied scouts away from his face. The swarm was at treetop level by then, crashing through the forest canopy like shotgun pellets. But hail was what came to mind—the black hail that had fallen on the Haven and surrounding streets. Transformed, somehow, to become the winged and bloodsucking venomous things that comprised the swarm. The air reeked of sulfur and worse.

Potenchia was screaming, semaphoring his arms as the things engulfed him in a kind of feeding frenzy, the chameleon suit broadcasting a different pattern every few seconds. His upper body was studded with dark, twitching bodies, battling one another for purchase. Reydak had taken more than half a dozen assaults himself, but the sucking-hornets were having trouble getting through to him. They would come in for a taste and dart off, visibly angered. At the same time, though, they were preventing him from reaching Raoul, and all the while forcing him back toward the steep riverbank. Fear and toxins coursing through him, the world was a white glare to his eyes, peppered with buzzing black forms. And suddenly he had a vision of Ouro in his jungle-cat guise: leaping at him from the center of that white light, heavy paws against his chest, pushing him over the edge . . .

He surfaced amid rocks in a welter of deafening white water and forced himself back under as the swarm had another go at him—an accomplishment made easy by the sensors and weapons still clipped, strapped, and belted to him. But in that instant he saw Blades had also made it in; which left only Raven, whose survival had ceased to be of pressing concern.

The swarm continued its attack the next couple of times he poked his head out, but the current carried him away from the thick of the cloud, and by the time the river had ironed itself out and Reydak had hauled himself up onto its muddy eastern bank, there were only a few drones buzzing listlessly about.

He lay unmoving for several minutes catching his breath, then commenced a worried inspection of limbs and torso. Palpating his abdomen touched off a deep-seated ache, but everything felt intact. His arms were swollen from sucker welts and one side of his face was painfully lacerated.

Raven was calling to him from the opposite bank.

Reydak felt cheated, although he had to confess the quad-barrel was a welcome sight. How Raven had managed to hold on to it was another matter, for his own H&K was gone, along with the flash radio.

"Where's Blades?" he yelled back, hands cupped to his mouth.

"He went by me," Raven said, motioning downstream.

Raven forded at a shallow point half a mile along and they began a search for Blades. Raven discovered him a few hundred yards farther on, one of Manly's metal-tipped hands thrust wrist-deep into his own gut.

Raven made a whistling sound. "The flip side of implants, huh, Colonel?" He sensed Reydak's eyes burning into him and took a comical backward step. "Down, boy, I didn't have anything to do with his exit. He musta hit a rock elbow-first or something. I sure as hell couldn't force him to tickle his spleen like that."

Overcome by a sudden wave of dizziness from venom and blood loss, Reydak crumbled and pitched forward into Raven's arms.

"Don't you worry, Colonel," the rhinoman murmured, setting him down and gazing intently into his eyes. "Raven's going to take good care of you."

An hour before sunset they got their first view of Brother Cordoba's redoubt. Clouds had the valley socked in, but shafts of late sun were hitting the hillside above their position. Below them, lining both sides of a narrow landing strip, were well-tended, terraced poppy fields. A vertical-takeoff aircraft was parked at one end of the strip near a small building with white stucco walls and a red-tile roof.

The principal structure was a dual-towered castle of ochre brick laid atop massive stone foundations. Tremoya's monastery. It was set on a hummock fifteen meters or so above the valley floor, and joined to it by two steep stairways and a switchback roadway. An arched entry gate led to an inner courtyard, where two jeeps and a sedan were haphazardly parked. On the slopes east of the monastery stood several large radio dish antennas.

"Now I can see why your people are so torqued about this place," Raven commented with elaborate concern. "They even got gardens down there."

"Raven, shut the fuck up," Reydak said, training audio field glasses on Cordoba's field workers. "The place threw off a thermal signature that sure as shit wasn't poppies."

"Hot springs," Raven suggested. "Just like up north, Colonel, where we got heads handed to us a couple-three years back. Remember?"

Reydak turned to him and nodded uncertainly, then focused the glasses on the VTOL. Several figures in long black habits and white bib aprons were off-loading clear plastic sacks of brown powder from an idling minivan.

"Uh, 'scuse me, sir, but those are *nuns*, aren't they?"

Reydak kept the glasses raised and said nothing.

Raven chuckled to himself. "Those glasses show what time mass starts, Colonel?"

"Let's go find out," Reydak said, struggling to his feet.

His body didn't want to admit just how badly it was hurting. He ventured the unplanned waterslide downstream had done it to him, torn something up inside or pulped a vital spot. Hardly mattered now, seeing that whatever caused it had put him in a very bad way: arrhythmic, fevered, disoriented. Shock had held him together for a while; probably gotten him from the river to the ridgeline, he decided, but the loan was being called in. He considered gobbling a couple of stimulant tabs but rejected the idea, guessing they would probably shut down his heart for good.

Which was probably going to happen in any case.

There wasn't as much uneasiness as he would have figured there to be; but then nothing was working out as he figured, least of all the place itself. He was aware he had come looking for answers to everything that had happened since Africa, and with the added weight Ouro, Amber, and the others had dumped on him before he left. He couldn't fault John or Keyes for his state, knowing full well no one had held a gun to his head when he'd signed on for the tour. But Pavel was a separate issue, the father some discorporate piece of his mind knew a lot better than the rest of him did. And it was the fear of having to leave that thread loose that was draining off the resolve. Or maybe it was the only thing keeping him on his feet.

It took them twenty minutes to descend the slope; on relatively level ground then, they began to close on the monastery, keeping to tall, yellow-flowered thickets that bordered the dirt road. From down here, the horror clouds piled up behind the brick towers and tile roofs looked both cinematically conjured and painfully familiar; it only took a moment to connect them to the skies over the Annapolis Haven that day the black rained down. Raven may have been wondering about it, as well, Reydak thought, because he looked as if he was about to say something. But just then the minivan cruised by their position and slid to a dusty halt not twenty meters away.

Four nuns stepped out from the side door, chattering in Spanish and eyeing the bushes where Reydak and Raven were crouched down, their suits glossy green with splashes of sun-yellow.

"Fuck! They made us," Raven whispered. "What good are we if we can't even hide from a bunch—holy *shit*!"

Reydak's mouth fell open as weapons appeared from under long skirts and the pocket folds of habits: handguns, machine pistols, and shortened automatic shotguns. The rear door of the van flew open and three more sisters leaped out, equally well armed.

After an instant of amazement, Raven let out a rodeo wail and crashed into the road behind the armed quad-barrel. "Nuns with guns, Colonel!" He yahooed. "Could you ask for a better fucking Christmas present!"

Reydak's ears shut down as the auto-rifle hammered several dozen rounds into the group, dropping half the nuns in a matter of seconds. But the rest were already hugging the road, finding cover and returning fire. Reydak hesitated—wondering why it should take more effort to scrap nuns than Ugandan zombies—but only for a moment. Then he did what any sane individual would do: answered the nuns with all the handgun allowed. Killing, after all, was a business like any other.

Raven continued to contaminate the area, traversing the unwieldy weapon with an accuracy that defied belief, even when the nuns began to shuffle forward holding babies in their outstretched hands. Even when they stepped out of the roadside foliage looking like tv moms and grandmothers; then models and centerfolds, all flourishing automatic weapons. Raven kept firing, the rifle's muzzle blast like a flamethrower; an evil wind mowing the women down. They fell like discarded ragdolls, limbs blown away; drawn and quartered by the overheated gun. Looking up to laugh as they landed—those that had faces left.

Reydak screamed through bared teeth, emptying clips with eyes closed, shrieks and the godawful sounds of death loud in his ears. Rounds stitched across the minivan's rear end blew the fuel tank, flattening what remained of the nuns and scorching the hair from Reydak's brow and forehead.

The world was silent for a moment.

"Hey, Colonel," Raven said as the smoke was beginning to clear. "What's black and white and red all over?"

He was down on his ass in the dirt, the gun muzzles popping and pinging as they cooled; he'd been hit three or four times in the legs and torso and was bleeding all over the road. Reydak dragged himself over to him, watching his own life leak out through a hole in his side.

"Guess we're committed now," Raven added, slamming a magazine into a 9-mm handgun. "Kinda reminds me of the time we crept into that Marañon village and those Sendera Marxists blew that ambush. Who woulda figured those black-haired beauties to be carrying?''

"I remember," Reydak said weakly, hearing vehicles begin to move out in the distance.

Raven regarded him. "You do? Then you must remember the time you left us to hold that bridge with those toy soldiers some asshole in DoD dreamed up—the ones the Cubes turned around on us with their virus—'member that? What a caution, huh?''

"You can't send a drone to do a man's business," Reydak said, quoting a line popular at the time.

"Val-*id*," Raven enthused. "Then a course there was that resupply we were promised . . ."

Reydak stiffened. "That wasn't the way it went down, Raven. We were ordered out. It was changes up top. Anyway, a lot of us stayed and got cut to pieces trying to get back to you."

"Yeah, that was the story I heard, too, Colonel, only I think you and the Agency already decided we were expendable. Maybe that you'd gotten your money's worth out of us anyway." Raven disarmed the safety and leveled the pistol at Reydak's groin. "Testicles," he said.

Reydak stared at him wide-eyed.

"Testicles," Raven repeated. "I want yours." He sighed and added: "Teamwork, enthusiasm, stamina, tenacity, initiative, courage, loyalty, excellence, sense of humor—all the shit you programmed into us then backed out of. Testicles. I want 'em, Colonel." He drew a knife from the sheath strapped to his ankle and dropped it in the dirt near Reydak's hand. "Either you cut 'em off and hand 'em to me or I'm going to kill you and take 'em myself. Which way's it going to be?''

Reydak held his gaze. "You're dying, man. Put a good face on it."

Raven laughed and poked a finger into one of his wounds. "What, these? These aren't real, Colonel. No more than those bitch nuns or babies were. We're just watchin' home movies, you and me. Red-letter days, Reydak: our lives flashin' before our eyes."

Reydak was too busy watching the wounded sister to hear him; she had bellycrawled her way from the smoldering van, a slick of blood on the road behind her. Thing was, she wasn't a nun any longer but a slight Oriental woman dressed in sarong and Malay blouse, a bit of gold gleaming in her grin. Raven's back was turned to her, so he didn't see the plastic sack until it was too late. A piece of sack, really; a meter section of shredded end. Reydak had the powdery contents pegged as heroin.

Raven's nose gave a slight twitch and he swung around, the automatic raised. But by then the woman was on her knees bending over him, the sack upraised in her nut-brown hands. She yanked it down over Raven's head and shoulders an instant before he fired. The three rounds were delivered at such close range they flipped her body several inches off the ground and set her blouse aflame.

Raven yanked the plastic off and whirled on Reydak, his face thickly dusted with the refined poppy powder, eyes swollen and tearing, nostrils plugged. Already in the throes of the drug, he fired once but missed; choked, spasmed, fired, and missed again. Going blue all over, as his olfactory enhancements sent the pure racing to his brain.

Raven clawed at his face, as if trying to dig out the implants. His eyes rolled up and he fell backward, dead, both cheeks marked by bloody parallel fingernail gouges.

Reydak rolled over and vomited, supporting himself on his hands. Vehicles were approaching from the direction of the monastery, dust clouds above the flowering bushes. He stripped Raven of minigrenades, det cord, and loaves of high-velocity plastique; then raised himself, crutched over the autorifle, and began to limp down the road.

They're chessplayers, McVee kept telling himself as the Command Center's Big Board flashed moment by moment updates. The Soviets were realigning their smart rocks, although they had yet to direct a move against a single American recon satellite. Something was dazzling an entire sector of ELINT and COMINT sky-eyes, without a hint of laser activity from Sary Shagan, Semipalatinsk, or any of the Soviets' ground-based facilities.

Had some new site gone undetected? McVee asked himself as he paced the curve of the command balcony railing. Or had the Reds really succeeded in lifting some sort of stealth directed-energy weapon or adaptive optic device into geosynch? The latter view had been espoused by General Sheath, CINCNORAD, who had since been relieved of duty after suffering a nervous breakdown at Crystal Palace.

McVee watched the board reconfigure, allowing his headset to dangle around his neck as he turned to study a host of secondary screens. The Soviets were deployed on all fronts—troops mobilized, bombers airborne, naval vessels arrayed, subs slipping through chokepoints—but there seemed no logic to it. Nearly every piece of hard- and software they possessed was shouting out electronic signals, pouring out signatures, jumping up and down for infrared scanners and moving target indicators . . . So why weren't their silos opening? Where was some hint of real muscle behind all the fancy footwork?

McVee almost laughed. Maybe the president's brazen dare had put the fear of God into them. Maybe they'd really bought all that nonsense about the shield's impenetrability, the power ring's survivability. McVee had to hand it to Brady: Going live with the apocalypse was a brilliant ploy. But it was unlike Korzliev to be so easily manipulated.

They're chessplayers.

McVee unsheathed a wireless mike from his belt and activated it; the pickup enabled him to communicate directly with central control and the neural network team—half of whom were Computer Emergency Response technopathologists employed to keep the AI virus-free.

"Talk to that computer of yours," the general ordered. "Tell DEITY there's too much goddamned extraneous information on the board. We can't see the forest for the trees. Tell it what we need to see are the anomalies, and see if the damn thing can't find a pattern to all this aimless roiling. Then have it isolate whatever's running counter to the current. Do I make myself understood?"

Several voices responded in unison.

Chessplayers, he thought. It would be just like them to open up half a dozen fronts simply to queen some pawn, checkmate a king.

McVee glanced at a tv monitor while he waited. There was Brady onscreen, big as life, radiating confidence, sipping coffee in the Oval Office while he showed the cameras some latest sheet of flash communication. It was absolutely crazed, the JCS chairman told himself, crazed and inspired.

"General McVee, we might have something," the senior watch officer said from behind the command balcony console. "Screens ten through twenty, sir."

Submarines, McVee realized, facing the displays and slipping his foam headphones back on. Ten through fifteen handled data from SOSUS—the Sound Surveillance System—while the rest collated input from PAVE PAWS on Cape Cod, Air Force Application Command, several ELF sites, and the SSIX subcom sats.

"Here's the glitch, sir," a tech informed him through the phones. "Screen seventeen at seven o'clock."

The mid-Atlantic. The screens encompassed everything from

the Azores to the Florida coast. "Enlarge three," he commanded, and the screen changed: Bermuda was at twelve o'clock, Puerto Rico at six. There were half a dozen Red boomers at the far right of the screen well within the fast lanes, their positions marked by red probability circles, their course headings northeast. McVee was surprised to see them so far from Europe; but already targeted, they didn't pose much of a threat. At seven o'clock, however, several dots were heading due west. "What do we have here—trawlers?"

"Negative, sir. DEITY had ID'd them as submarine drones—probably research ships out of Cuba."

"So what's the problem?" McVee demanded.

"The one at the lower left, sir. It just changed course and is now bearing west, southwest."

McVee stared at the flashing bezel that marked the ship's location. "Could be returning to their research station," he suggested. "Systems failure or something."

"Possibly, sir. But we have high confidence of a heading toward a flagged area."

McVee scowled and turned to the tech's station across the room. "We don't have anything in that neighborhood."

"The island's called Inaccessible, sir. Flagged by National Recon eleven months ago. Some sort of technical facility."

McVee cursed. The CIA hadn't informed the Pentagon of any secret installation. Goddamned Colton and his easy access to the president. It all ran on the DCI's friendship with Secretary Brady.

"Could those drones be armed?" McVee asked.

"They have that capacity, yes, sir."

Their pawn, McVee thought. The president's *rogue*!

"Have sensors air-dropped into that area immediately, and get me the latest overheads of that goddamned island. Send in your dolphins if you have to." He took two steps toward the railing, then whirled around. "And put me in touch with the president."

"My fellow Americans," Brady said, squarely facing the camera, "the time has come to inform General Secretary Korzliev of our dilemma."

Eli regarded him from the fireplace, tall drink in hand. Ted's tone made him think of kindergarten teachers and kids' video hosts.

"Any moment now the enemy will launch its first offensive, and we must be ready to meet them missile for missile."

The president gestured off to one side and the camera tracked the motion of his hand to fix on the harrowed face of the Air Force intel officer with the "football."

"As I've already explained to you, the portable control deck shackled to this officer's wrist will be my interface with NORAD command and countless sites we've implanted around the globe to ensure our defense. At the first notification of an attack, I will key a special code into the control deck, which in turn will permit the brave men and women manning our silos, aircraft, and ships to launch their missiles.

"But before we come to that, there's one more thing to be done." Brady pulled open a lower drawer and placed a gold telephone on the desk. "We refer to this as the Hot Line," he explained. "It had long been absent from this office, but I recently had it reinstalled for the express purpose of keeping lines of communication open between myself and General Secretary Korzliev—especially in times of global emergency."

Eli laughed to himself. He had already been on the phone to Tushenko, who'd informed him that Korzliev had knuckled under to a war-hungry faction of the Politburo.

Brady lifted the handset.

"Through a rather circuitous route, which includes the White House Situation Room—some fifteen meters below us—the Pentagon, New York City, and a host of communications satellites and relay stations, I will be able to speak directly with General Secretary Korzliev and the Party chiefs of the Soviet Union."

The camera closed on the phone with its simple keypad, then moved shakily back to Brady's faint smile. "Now," the president started to say, when a red phone on the desk buzzed. Brady recradled the Hot Line receiver, put the red handset to his ear, and listened for a long moment.

"Yes, General McVee," he said at last, "I understand . . ."

Philbert Base snatched up the phone almost before it rang. "It's Eli," he told the men gathered around him in the Alternate Military Command Center at Fort Ritchie.

"Put him on the annunciator," Cottel said in a rush. Base hit the phone's speaker button.

"I assume you're watching," Eli said.

Base made a face. "No, Eli, we're tuned into a goddamned game show. What the hell do you think we're doing!"

Everyone gave a quarter turn to the television monitor; on-screen, the president and the intel officer were inserting plastic keycards into twin slots in the forged alloy carrycase.

"Jesus Christ, Eli, he's actually ready to go through with it! What did McVee tell him?"

Eli sighed into the phone. "A remote-piloted Soviet drone sub is heading toward our territorial waters. It's carrying three one-megaton nuclear devices."

The color drained from the chief of staff's face as Secretary of Defense Manning placed the real "football" in front of him.

The collector sphere at the heart of the pyramid was dematerializing, the atomic chemistry of its structure fusing with the blinding energy that had been generated at its core. The facility was shaking itself, as if ready to burst. Ouro and the Concentricity were still at their stations remembering catastrophe. But surely dead, Woolley told himself with a speck of consciousness that remained his alone.

As they all were.

They were fast becoming one entity, one being, one *thought*, that had known no other moment in time but this one.

And yet Woolley had an instant to imagine what might happen if the pyramid's crystal apex was to open like an eye to the tropical sky, erupt and spew its contained creativity around the world where the millions who made up WEM's psychic shield would be there to deploy it.

Would everyone *remember*? Recall the original transgression and catastrophe? Follow the Concentricity across the threshold? A boundless universe in the making, given substance by single unified thought . . .

"Percy?" Tawny said in a questioning voice. "I think something's happening, honey."

Flage showed her a tolerant smile and removed the opaque plastic cups from his eyes. What a pleasure it was to bask naked in the sun, pick coconuts and grapefruits from the trees, breathe in the salt air. "What is it, sugar?" he asked, wiping sweat from his upper lip. Ginger was off splashing in the turquoise surf.

"I think maybe it's going to rain," she told him, indicating the sky inland.

Flage looked over his shoulder, a hand to his brow. He could see clear to the pointed top of the facility above the palms. An intense electrical storm seemed to be swirling like a hurricane around the peak.

"Fucking rocket scientists." Flage snorted, shaking his head back and forth.

28 The Heat of the Moment

Reydak stumbled under the weight of the quad-barrel, falling to one knee in the center of the dirt road that led to the monastery.

He used minigrenades to take out the first jeep, bowling them in as the vehicle was bearing down on him breathing its own fire. The explosions blew it off the road; it rolled over and played dead for a moment before bursting into flame. He trained the quad on the second, targeting more than two feet of bandolier into its front end, while soldiers in fancy black uniforms and jackboots came leaping out of the thing toting fifty-year-old submachine guns, running right into his reach, as if it hadn't occurred to them to do otherwise. The quad chattered away convulsively, dropping them by threes and fours. The ease of it surprised him, but not near as much as the arrow protruding from his thigh.

He reached a hand down to snap the wooden shaft, clenching it between his jaws when he moved out.

The enemy at the base of the rise were dressed in skirts of some sort and wielding machetes that looked for all hell like shortswords. But there were so many changes going on behind his eyes he couldn't be sure. In any case, the minigun made short work of them. He looked down the runway for the VTOL, but it was nowhere in sight. He knew he hadn't heard it lift off. In its place stood a catapult. Part of the tour.

Reydak was hallucinating something fierce by the time he reached the first stairway—the narrow steep run he'd seen from the top of the ridge now a wide flight of stone steps, worn smooth and slightly concave. Towering over him were archways and the lintels of trapezoidal portals constructed of monolithic boulders and precisely fitted stones. The air had a musty odor of ancient

252

things and was humming so loudly he could barely hear himself think. But that was okay, too, because he was weak and rattled enough to believe the ground was still shaking. At the periphery of his vision was a terminal darkness, especially where the sky should have been, that black and loathsome hurricane-ing mass overhead.

At the summit, he stopped once to moisten his mouth from a trickle of water leaking from the ceiling, and rid himself of the quad, if only to coax a few more meters out of his life; then necklaced himself with det cord and plastiques and headed into the monastery, a shuffling, bleeding timebomb.

Dying . . . But walking through his fear to confront them, because he knew there was reconcilation, answers, transformation at the end of it.

He found them in a sunken circular court roofed over by an arched stone ceiling—half a dozen small, gray-skinned, wrinkled little beings, clothed in metallic suits, robelike jackets, and pointed cowls that elongated their faces and gave their chins a tapered look. Their eyes were shades of blue, pupilless, and made to seem large and almond-shaped by sunken cheeks and sagging skin.

They reminded him of the aliens in his AWED-implanted vision.

From the center of the court rose an immense pillar that might have been pink-gray granite, either plunged into or thrust from a stone slab that hugged its base. The beings were cowering behind it, some in an attitude of prayer.

"Que desea aqui?" one of them stepped forward to ask. *"Quien le mandó?"* What do you want here? Who sent you? Reydak could hardly hear them above the buzzing noise in his ears.

"Reydak," he answered, as if that was all the explanation required—a response to both questions.

He could feel someone or something going to work on him again, just as when he'd had that glimpse of Ouro and his ring. He wondered if it wasn't maybe death itself, a premonition then and a sure bet now. But whatever was behind it was dividing him up inside, right and left pulling for their respective corners. Flashes of a concealed reality assaulted him—a coexistent experiential realm at variance with the one the octagenarian metallic monks were presenting, the Latin prayers and urgent pleas.

His eyes had lost vertical and horizontal control. It was as if he was seeing the order's spokesman through one eye then the other, the gaunt being shifting drunkenly in his vision. But the more Reydak stared at him, the more he came to see a twisted smile beneath the indignant gray-faced mask. And it helped to find that the others were running in tight circles to confuse him, muttering to one another, laughing up the wide sleeves of their jackets.

The leader placed his palms against the gnomon and smiled in a self-satisfied way. "You resemble your father," he said, turning around.

Reydak kept his reaction secret.

"Oh, yes, he was here. We brought him over from Europe to join us, we wanted his fellowship." He motioned to his brothers, who were stationing themselves at intervals around the stone phallus. "We formed a brilliant team once. But he thought our wish to complete the great work deranged. So we allowed him to leave—perhaps to prove we were even more potent than he dared imagine. And we let him continue with his little game of foiling us, working against our efforts to spread the fear, to open susceptible minds to the reality of Their return." The being took a step toward Reydak. "You see, to reactivate the power here is to reactivate Them."

He sighed. "It proved such a simple matter to place agents in the field to carry out our aims and report their findings. Our affiliates were more than happy to kidnap at random, drug and implant false memories of contact. All to further an acceptability, an enlarging of the paradigm. So many souls with the past this close to the surface . . . a small prick and all manner of things can be released.

"We didn't care about what you were doing with outer space— that void was for the taking. But your intrusions into inner space disturbed us. At the same time it was something we thought we could take advantage of. You've all become so susceptible now: so uncertain, so willing to believe in saviors or destroyers."

"You're Brady's aliens," Reydak managed.

The leader laughed. "Look at yourself and tell me which of us is the alien," he said, as the rest of them scurried around making beeping noises to themselves. "With your expanded senses, your devices of death, your mimetic suits and death rays. We're only a handful of men worshipping an ancient stone."

He regarded Reydak with a pitying look. "But if you've come to complete the work your father began, I suggest you've arrived too late."

"I'll make it," Reydak sneered, sickly aware of the puddle of blood thickening around his feet.

"That's not what I meant, you fool. Don't you realize we've *succeeded* in bringing Them back? We are the new current, Reydak, the pure of blood. We have moved child to child of this star to escort Their vengeance home."

Reydak swayed on his feet. "Bunch of sad old men with nothing to do but sit here dreaming about the past."

The monk lashed out a bony finger. "*Dreaming* the past, Reydak, not *about* it!"

Reydak regarded the phallus and grinned. "Yeah, maybe I can understand what you were after," he said, arming the charges cinched to his waist. "But not tonight, boys, Mother Earth's got a headache."

"You still don't understand, do you? We're not only the lens of Their power, but the filter, as well!" The desperateness in the old man's voice gave Reydak the first honest chuckle he'd had all day. "Destroy our work and Earth will have no guiding intelligence, Reydak. Destroy our work and you destroy the world!"

Reydak continued to set charges, hands running red with his own blood. He could feel the strength of their collective will urging him to back off, to walk himself outside and scatter himself to the four winds. But he centered himself on the quieter voice that was Amber's in eleven-part harmony, reminding him that a shield had been readied against the storm; that there'd be someone around to right the planet when it tipped . . .

The leader was standing in front of the gnomon, wide-eyed, with arms outstretched. "Let them return, Reydak. Why should you care?" he screamed. "What difference could it make to you? You've been one of fear's most adept agents, spreading terror, killing to promote your nation's faith. Fear is the transforming agent, Reydak, it always has been."

"I know," Reydak said, showing his bloodied hands. "I'm one of you." He lunged into the lead monk's open arms, propelling him backward against the stone shaft.

The others were making tracks for the door when the plastique blew.

Reydak's thoughts lingered a moment to watch the gnomon topple, then opted to die with the rest of him.

Ouro, and the organism the Concentricity had become, felt the power surge into them with the fury of a ravenous beast. The pyramid gleamed with its coming . . .

"We have a confirmed launch!" the senior watch officer told General McVee. "Three nuclear fish away!"

McVee reached for the red phone.

Brady answered, then typed AVENGING ANGEL into the "football" deck. His words and steps of power.

A party was in progress at the Alternative Command Center at Fort Ritchie. A group of enlisted rating techs had broken into the subterranean shelter's cache of recreational drugs and dispensed them to hundreds of eager hands: stimulants and depressants, narcotics, hynotics and hallucinogens, alkaloids, psychedelics and euphorics. Elsewhere, a rampaging band of Marines and IRS officials had discovered untapped tanks of ether, nitrous oxide, and amyl nitrite; thousands of cartons of carcinogen-laced cigarettes, and countless cases of chewing tobacco, whiskeys, champagnes, super-caffeinated coffees, and sugar-filled soft drinks.

Philbert Base pulled the "football" toward him and keyed in the day's permissive action link code:

!#&*!%*&$#!

In more than two hundred underground launch-control capsules buried across the nation, twice that number of men and women received the awesome directive:

YOU HAVE REPEAT HAVE LAWFUL COMMAND.

Missiles left their silos, while ground-based lasers in New Mexico and Texas fired excited light to relay mirrors in geosynchronous orbit. The mirrors in turn directed the light against Soviet satellites, which were already at the receiving end of repositioning commands.

Grezenko brought word of confirmed plumes to Korzliev in his tiny room inside the Zhiguli citadel. The Soviet general secretary sighed and gave the go-ahead for a massive retaliatory response.

The three warheads launched by the drone sub impacted on Inaccessible and detonated.

The Blue Star had arrived.

29 The Day the Earth Tripped

Woolley loosed a triumphant cry as his island creation was atomized; and in that final moment he saw the pyramid as a kind of cascade amplifier pouring forth a stepped-up current, a white source radiating new light from its center, where Ouro knelt weeping, delivering his release-hour message; high priest at this most critical mass but master of ceremonies, as well, his hand at the veil of the Unmanifest, WEM's widespread population of Experienced readying their right-thinking launch.

It was Zulu time, dreamtime, the moment of Aquarian conjunction arrived: Jupiter aligned with Mars, Earth and Blue Star mated. The bolt out of the blue we'd both feared and prayed for, a grand out-of-planetary-body experience that summoned us to engage the *chimera* and move beyond it to knowledge. Until then something had always prevented us from recalling the dark space in our past, but we'd taken the plunge and were now free to roam at will among the Akashic records, through that movement of light we called history. In exchange, though, we had to surrender ourselves to collapse, gravity's harsh demands; signposts along the way to the singularity read: IS THIS TOMORROW OR JUST THE END OF TIME?

The sun sighed and the stars disappeared, an immense ball of captured light appeared on every horizon. There was a nanosecond of absolute stillness without wind or sound, our blind let down, a moment of incredible stasis before the inward pull commenced, sending us spiraling toward the center of our collective close encounter. But the humming in our ears was real, the blinding lights and space-time distortions valid. And the shadowy figures were of our very own making: particle-etched into walls and sidewalks and parking lots. For we were not merely remembering catastrophe—the end of the past world age—but reexperiencing it; waking from a state of ontological amnesia, only to realize how often we'd been through this, and how often it would reoccur. Realizing, too, that it wasn't something we brought on by ourselves, but an event helped along by a conspiracy of Earth, planets, and stars; a synchronizing of micro- and macrocosmic rhythms and aspects. Because it was only through purification, the reexamination of initial trauma, that things could be swept clear; and only through destruction that we could come to see ourselves as we were: one family, masked in different faces throughout time. The original sin, the original transgression, was the misuse of power; and catastrophe, the world turned upside down, the catharsis—the one we'd helped to shape, the songs and steps of power we sought. The healing if not the cure.

Upheaval.

Once they used to come for us in the middle of the night—a fraternal group dressed in frightening costume—feeding us bitter-tasting leaves and hustling us off to dark forest clearings, dank and foul-smelling caves, or solitary huts roofed with animal skins or woven grasses. And later on they appeared in sylvan glens as radiant beings playing tricks or offering prophecy, dispensing warning or heavenly hosts. And finally they lifted us from vehicles along lonely stretches of highway, or snatched us from sleep in isolated cabins, light-driven spheres from the far side of space. But always their aim was the same: to open our eyes to the Real World, to afford us a face-to-face with nature's elemental force.

Our tribe, though, had expanded since those early times, our elders had much more to handle. And they couldn't wait for all of us to be called to power individually—not with our rituals nearly forgotten, our language fractured, our hunting grounds depleted, our territory threatened by outsiders—so we were all to be initiated together.

A fix of the corrective potion was required—a quick blast to shock the psychic system. And yet it couldn't be the botanical brew our ancestors used on us, but something more fitting: a dazzling display of sound and light, replete with the special effects we'd come to expect.

Do you remember where you were and how you felt that false dawn when the balloon went up; the cosmic tree bloomed, tall and straight, with roots exposed? What with the pillar toppled, something had to support the heavens. And if enlightenment was what you had come seeking in the shade of its brilliant canopy, you had certainly come to the right place.

Buddha sat there once, and Little Miss Muffet, and Sir Isaac himself, whose world view had us pinned down for so long.

But this was not a test; all stations of the Emergency Radio Network were playing the same mad songs.

Sitting zazen under California redwoods when the gong sounded and the lotus filled the heavens, Miso-roshi and his disciples understood. Sudden enlightenment was at hand, that grand passing away . . .

Although Percival Flage thought otherwise, while the hottest cosmic amusement of all mushroomed over him. He wished he could have been back home on house arrest in LA, if only to ride the coast to new lows.

Clair Senchant, whose booklet on the etiquette of shelter parties had done quite well at the rally, was entertaining two couples that day, her spacious shelter adorned with helium balloons and crêpe streamers for the occasion. They had lunched on flitches of salted deer meat from the one she herself brought down the month before with a 100-pound bow; preserves a friend had jarred months back; and one of the many bottles of domestic wine her husband had been storing away for the past several years. How could she have known then there was no safe shelter to be found?

Jim Wave, looking west from behind the bulletproof glass of his high-rise office, mistook the fireball for a New Jersey sunset. It was always the ones you didn't hear that got you, he thought.

Former CINC-NORAD General Mylar Sheath, decked out in straitjacket and radiation suit, was wondering what life underground would be like. If things went according to plan, the hollow mountain would receive only minor buffeting from the Soviets' retaliatory strike; but if estimates had been incorrect . . .

Thus far, the formula BM/C3I seemed to have worked—battle management, command, control, and communications. It was only the *intelligence* part that had him worried.

In the hills above the mountain, a small group of pronghorn antelope, saved from possible extinction by a concerned group of ecologically minded lobbyists, suddenly had to contend with a new threat.

General McVee, one of several thousand essential personnel locked away underground, had the privilege of seeing the Big Board go snow white with registered strikes. Dr. Wormwood, an Army chaplain at the war room lectern, had chosen a reading from Revelations for the occasion: " 'And to them it was given that they should not kill them, but that they should be tormented five months; and their torment was as the torment of a scorpion when he striketh a man. And in those days shall men seek death and shall not find it; and shall desire to die and death shall flee from them.' "

In a nearby underground room, Philbert Base and Loren Masters sat sharing a bottle of fine Napoleonic brandy the chief of staff had liberated from the White House stash before leaving for Fort Ritchie. Their eyes were glued to a monitor linked to camera remotes positioned around the District to record live shots of the flash disks. Base raised a glass to Constantine, who, like Tedman Brady, had lived to see his empire's capital relocated. Milo Colton and Enoch Keyes were even closer to the action in the main ring, sitting on the roof of the Agency's annex swapping the latest of ethnic jokes. The best of punchlines had yet to be delivered.

And there was the president himself—the man of the hour—stationed by the Oval Office French doors for half the world to watch, waiting for his new scores to light up the sky. He had contained them, all right, sealed the servants of God in their foreheads. *I await your coming,* he told himself.

Eli sat close at hand, racked on one of the stiff chairs that flanked the fireplace, wondering whether April and the boys were safely tucked inside some shelter along the relocation arc. Christmas would have to wait, he thought, until it was clear what the new year was bringing.

And in SURCON I Ramon Scadering watched the birth of countless small suns across the blue and white face of the planet, the time-lapse maturation of a thousand night-blossoming flowers. No touchdown this tour, he decided. But a big-money pool in the making: bets on who aboard might be the last Earthling in space . . .

We had awakened from a dream of reality into a nightmare; and for a moment it seemed that few of us would emerge whole from the experience—Earth's shadowy encounter, that reorientation in time and space. But Ouro and the Concentricity had pursued an oblique course across the event horizon in the hope of getting us through. And the path led through an antiuniverse straight back to Earth: for we were still young then and unprepared for space.

But we hadn't returned empty-handed, and our souvenir of the excursion was nothing less than a new model of the universe;

one with an option that allowed us to circumvent entropy when the need arose; to big bang an offshoot reality from the untapped potential of collective thought.

And as the drone sub's warheads turned Woolley's island to fire, psicons released from the facility's rare-metal womb began to propagate; to carry out WEM's quantum directive by interacting with alphas and betas, photons and neutrons birthed in nuclear furnaces man-made, reversing spin and number and charge, bending world-lines and carrying the fifth force to culmination, assimilating fire to spiritual energy, winter to Eternal Spring, and purifying the world.

Epilogue Atoms for Peace

Any prophecy that is fulfilled is a prophecy that failed.

—the Reverend Paul bar Solomon Source

The president threw open the Oval Office French doors and stepped out into bright sunlight and melting snow, a New Year's warm spell.

"They're gone, Eli," he said with his face upturned to blue sky. "The ring held. We've beaten them back."

Eli lifted his head from between his knees and gave the office a nervous glance. Had he slept? he wondered; it would have been just like him to sleep through the end of the world. But just what *had* happened?

The tv cameras were still positioned where the operators had left them after Ted had entered the code—Base and the rest activating the real link twenty miles away in Fort Ritchie. The phony football was still in place on the desk, pilot lights flashing small red beacons. The intel officer was nowhere to be found. And yet here was Ted, laughing, forming snowballs and pitching them in the direction of the Monument. Eli checked his watch and realized that more than an hour had gone by—more than enough time for Soviet retaliatory birds to reach their targets.

The red phone sounded and Eli nearly jumped out of his skin. Ted hurried in, grabbing it on the second tone and hitting the annunciator button. Eli heard McVee's voice at the other end of the line.

"—didn't get through, Mr. President. They were detonated in space by the Soviets' lasers." The words came slowly, deliberately; McVee's tone one of utter bewilderment. "But our umbrella appears to have done the trick, sir. Stopped the Reds dead in their tracks . . ." McVee's voice trailed off.

"It's all right, General," Ted told him calmly, in complete control of himself. "We did what we had to do."

"But, sir, I . . ." McVee swallowed and found his military voice. "I don't know whether I'm fit to run the show for a second strike, Mr. President. I swear, sir, I heard those long-legs raining down on us, the Big Board like a blizzard, sir, the heat, the death . . . The *death*, Mr. President. All around us, nowhere to turn—"

"Relax, General, it's over," Ted said. "There's no need for follow-up strikes. I want all our forces to stand down from alert status.

"But the enemy—"

"It's all right, General. We've beaten them, I assure you."

McVee was quiet for a moment. "We have, sir? You mean, they've *surrendered*? Have you heard from Korzliev?"

"I'm just about to call him, General."

"Uh, yes, Mr. President. We'll await your word."

Eli sat with his head sandwiched between his hands. *We're dead*, he told himself. That was the only explanation: The bombs had fallen, annihilating the world but condemning everyone to relive the last minutes of life over and over again. He and his brother were in *hell*. Like McVee, he had witnessed the fireballs, *experienced* the catastrophe, wept like a frightened child as it all passed away: his family, friends, and home . . . the horrible payback for abandoning responsibility, for not doing right by the world. The thought echoed in his mind, repeating itself in a dozen different voices . . .

Ted was just hanging up the red phone when the Hot Line flashed. "Yes, Mr. General Secretary," he said, motioning to the phone for Eli's sake.

"Mr. President," Korzliev said in the same shocked tone McVee had used. "Are we going to continue this?"

Ted grinned for the handset. "No, I don't think that will be necessary, Comrade Gen Sec. We're experienced now; we know what we have to do."

"Comrade?" Korzliev said. "Mr. President, I hardly know what to say. When I contemplate what happened . . . What could have happened, that is—"

"Yes, we're all very fortunate. But in prevailing, we've proved something to ourselves, haven't we? Sacrifices have been made, but we have prevailed."

Korzliev didn't respond immediately. "And will we be re-building our arsenals now, Mr. President?"

"I'd sooner talk about the joint projects we were discussing before the Horn Crisis. We owe the planet's seas and skies that much, don't we? Perhaps all our shield technology can be put to better use. What do you think?"

Korzliev cleared his throat. "Mr. President, I would like to believe you . . . but given our past—"

"Forget the past, Mr. General Secretary. I won't bring it up if you won't."

The general secretary laughed. "I do not think it can simply be forgotten. But perhaps we can keep the past in its place—in perspective, as you say."

Ted hung up the phone, yawned, and stretched.

"I'm going to lie down for a while," he announced.

Eli watched the president exit the office for the small study where he kept a futon daybed. He waited for the door to close, then rushed to the red phone and asked for McVee.

The general recapped the events of the past hour.

"And you mean to tell me *nothing* got through?" Eli asked.

"Appraisals are still coming in, Mr. Secretary, but it's sure starting to look that way."

"But what about—"

"Aside from the birds, we lost a herd of sats and relay mirrors—both sides—but the rest of the architecture's intact. We expected all kinds of electromagnetic pulse problems, but it just isn't happening."

"What about fallout, for God's sake?"

McVee exhaled audibly. "Nothing detonated, Mr. Secretary. And if any of them did, it's like something just vacuumed up the radiation. That's what air-sample readings are telling us anyway."

Eli shook his head wildly. "But, McVee, I saw . . ."

"Yes, Mr. Secretary, me, too. The whole Command Center did."

Both men fell silent for a moment.

"Only strange thing, sir, is that ELF monitoring in Wisconsin picked up two anomalous seismic events at about the same time we received the president's Permissive Action Link. A volcanic eruption in the Caribbean vaporized a couple of inconsequential islands, along with whatever it was National Recon had flagged down there. Funny thing, too. The Soviets report it took out the unmanned boomer we were watching on the board."

Inaccessible, Eli realized. "Were there any survivors, General?" he asked quietly a moment later.

"We've got a couple of rescue ships in the area now, sir. Latest word the Cubans picked up a man and two women who were apparently vacationing down there."

"And this second event?" Eli asked.

"An earthquake, Mr. Secretary, in southern Peru."

Eli replaced the handset and opened the French doors to the fresh air. A wind perfumed with early spring brushed his face, while sirens throughout the city sounded an all-clear.

ABOUT THE AUTHOR

James Luceno has made ends meet as rock musician, general contractor, astrologer, travel consultant, script writer, and pseudonymous co-author of a best selling mega-space opera series.

His first novel, *Headhunters*, was published in 1980; followed, after a long hiatus, by *Río Pasión* and *Rainchaser* (both published by Ivy Books.)

He resides, with his two children, in New York, where he has just finished ILLEGAL ALIEN, to be published by Del Rey Books in May, 1990.